"In this latest Mystery of Old San Francisco, justice is served in ways that will leave readers thoroughly satisfied and have them cheering at the end."
—Alyssa Maxwell, author of the Gilded Newport Mysteries

"Nancy Herriman has penned a clever, atmospheric mystery with interesting, diverse, and compelling characters that transported me right back to late-19th-century San Fransisco! I can't wait for the next book!"
—Colleen Cambridge, Agatha Award-nominated author of *Murder at Mallowan Hall*

"Clever and ever-capable nurse Celia Davies once again finds use for her considerable skills in this compelling series addition. *No Refuge from the Grave* is a tightly plotted, engrossing mystery that is rich in historical detail and vividly brings to life 1860s San Francisco."
—Ashley Weaver, Edgar Award-nominated author of the Amory Ames Mysteries

"Highly recommended!"
—Historical Novel Society, Editors' Choice on *Searcher of the Dead*

"You'll love the intrepid heroine, nurse Celia Davies."
—Victoria Thompson, bestselling author of the Gaslight Mysteries, on *No Pity for the Dead*

"A tremendously riveting read . . ."
—*Newport Plain Talk* on *Searcher of the Dead*

"Skillful storytelling . . . a standout historical mystery."
—*Publishers Weekly* starred review of *A Fall of Shadows*

BOOKS BY NANCY HERRIMAN

Mysteries of Old San Francisco

No Comfort for the Lost
No Pity for the Dead
No Quiet among the Shadows
No Darkness as like Death
No Refuge from the Grave
No Justice for the Deceived
No Rest for the Departed

Bess Ellyott Mysteries

Searcher of the Dead
A Fall of Shadows

Stand-Alone Novels

Josiah's Treasure
The Irish Healer

NO REST
for the
DEPARTED

NANCY HERRIMAN

BEYOND THE PAGE
PUBLISHING

No Rest for the Departed
Nancy Herriman
Copyright © 2024 by Nancy Herriman

Beyond the Page Books
are published by
Beyond the Page Publishing
www.beyondthepagepub.com

ISBN: 978-1-960511-65-2

To Vicki T.

✂ CHAPTER 1 ✂

March, 1868
San Francisco

Well, shoot, thought Owen Cassidy as a gust of wind coming off the cold bay sliced through a torn seam in his jacket. *I should've worn another undershirt.* Although wearing another undershirt would've required him to own a second one that was clean. Or, now that he considered the situation, required him to own a second one at all. Which he didn't.

He'd never had to worry about the number of shirts he did or didn't own when he'd worked at Roesler's Confectionery, where it was snug and comfortable. But he didn't work there anymore. Mr. Roesler had reached his limit with Owen getting involved in Mrs. Davies's and Mr. Greaves's murder cases and fired Owen. He couldn't really blame his old boss. But he did miss being around all those candies, the smell of chocolate lingering in the air, the gleam of sparkling clean glass display cases. The warmth. Nothing was sparkling clean or smelled half as good at the wharves. Maybe he should be thankful for the breeze, because he was sure it would smell a whole lot worse if it wasn't always windy.

"Cassidy!" the customs officer—Mr. Brodie, if Owen recollected properly—shouted. He was sorta fond of shouting. Or maybe he was only sorta fond of shouting at Owen. "Those cases have been weighed and recorded. You're free to load them onto your boss's wagon and get them delivered, you know. Rather than just stand there."

Owen tugged at his jacket collar, not that raising it did a lick of good against the wind piercing the jacket's seams, and conjured up thoughts more pleasant than how cold he was. Such as the fact a dead body probably wasn't going to turn up, like one did the last time he'd been hired to handle crates.

Shoot, Cassidy. Might be bad luck to think about that.

"Cassidy!" Mr. Brodie called again, scowling. It was a sad fact that plenty of folks both shouted and scowled at Owen and he was getting used to it. Seemed to happen all the time. Not Mrs. Davies, though. She never scowled at him. Well, not all that often, at least.

"Yes, sir!" Owen yelled back over the high-pitched screech of a ferry whistle signaling that the boat was departing from a nearby pier.

1

"And get out of the way. Passengers are trying to get to their conveyances." With a jerk of his head, Mr. Brodie indicated the handful of new arrivals making their way down the gangplank a steamer had lowered not thirty feet distant.

The longshoreman who'd hauled the crates off the steamer didn't bother to stifle his laughter. Thick with muscle, *he* probably never felt the chill off the bay. "If you're scared of hoisting cargo, kid, you might want to find another job." He added a few more words about how scrawny and worthless Owen was, but the sound of barrels rattling along a plank drowned most of them out. "And you are in the way."

Owen scuttled aside but not before sneaking a look at the passengers, jostling each other to be the first person to reach the carriage for the What Cheer House or maybe the one that would take them to the San Francisco and San Jose railroad depot. A mix of folks, their clothes creased and crumpled, coming in from Canada along with the cargo. Respectable but not made of money like the people who disembarked the big Pacific Mail steamships that made the two-week journey from Panama and let folks off at the Folsom Street wharf. Folks who'd come all the way from New York or maybe even Europe. Passage that far wasn't cheap. *Bet they all had more than one undershirt.*

"C'mon, Cassidy. Let's get this loaded." The driver for McCann and Company had climbed down from the wagon seat and proceeded to lower the tailboard.

Owen hefted the freight Mr. McCann had consigned onto the wagon bed. It wasn't too heavy, really. This time it was a shipment of stearine and adamantine candles along with several cases of boots and shoes. Considering the contents of the cases, he realized he could sure use a new pair of boots. Maybe a pair of French screwed-sole ones that might hold up better than his brogans. But how could he afford new boots when he couldn't afford a second undershirt? *Shoot.*

Owen was reaching for the final box when a woman shouting on the gangway distracted him.

"No, I do not need your help." She was the last one off the steamer and moving down the plank like she meant to get someplace in a hurry. Except she'd been last, so maybe Owen was misunderstanding the speed with which she walked, her hands clamped on her heavy brown skirts to keep them from recklessly swaying. "Please, get out of my way."

"Sorry, miss," said the unfortunate porter who'd been carrying her trunk, only to be scolded. He dropped it at the foot of the gangway with a thud. "Won't be bothering you any longer."

The porter marched over to a family struggling to load their luggage into a waiting carriage and offered his services. The woman frowned after him before turning her attention on the crowd of people on the wharf. Her gaze settled on Owen. She was really pretty in an almost strange way, with unusually high cheeks and large eyes, a fringe of black hair peeking around the edges of her silk bonnet. Had he seen her before? He couldn't recall, but he did realize he was gawping and looked away before she scolded him, too.

He did risk another look, though. The fellow she must've been searching for hurried up to her. After a hasty exchange of words, he hoisted her trunk and hauled it off. She followed at a steady pace. But before she disappeared into the throng, she turned and stared at Owen one last time, making him shiver.

• • •

"I'm worried about Mr. Greaves, Mrs. Davies." Mrs. Jewett finished buttoning the top of her checked rust-colored bodice, tidying her lace collar to fall demurely in place around her neck. "And I don't think he'd mind me telling you, as you two have become so close."

Celia, seated at the large walnut desk in her clinic's examining room, smiled to herself. There was a time not so long ago when Mrs. Jewett felt quite differently about her. Questioned the reason why a supposedly respectable English widow was visiting her tenant at his rented rooms. But Celia had only gone to Nicholas's rooms in hopes of persuading him to allow her to assist in a murder investigation. The first of several murders in the past year, as matters had transpired. *How gruesome, frankly.*

"You make it sound as though we are engaged to be wed, Mrs. Jewett." They had briefly kissed, shared words of affection, but she and Nicholas Greaves were most certainly not engaged to be married.

"He wants to marry you, Mrs. Davies. I know he does."

Did he?

Celia glanced out at the street, visible between the panels of the lace curtain fluttering at the window. Her view was of houses ranged up Vallejo, a glimpse of Telegraph Hill rising behind them, and the road that swirled dust after a lengthy dry spell. One of her neighbor's dark-haired children, too young to attend school, playing with a doll out at the curb. A view she would give up were she to marry Nicholas Greaves. Neighbors she would give up as well.

With a small sigh, she completed her notes about Mrs. Jewett's condition—she was undergoing the menopause, or the "change of life," as more polite folks preferred to call it—then closed her notebook, cleaned the nib of her pen, and got to her feet.

"A warm bath will help you immensely, I believe. But I expect you do not have the time to draw a warm bath and take care of yourself." Instead of constantly tending to Nicholas, whom Mrs. Jewett doted upon like a son.

"I don't, Mrs. Davies. I haven't ever had that sort of time, come to think of it."

"In lieu of some much-needed pampering, I recommend compound rhubarb pills. They might help ease some of your discomfort. The apothecary on Montgomery should be able to provide those for you. Tell him I sent you." She handed her a note with instructions for the man.

"Thank you." Mrs. Jewett tucked the folded paper inside her embroidered bag. "I would have gone to my regular physician, but this is a delicate matter and I don't always like speaking with him about womanly concerns."

"I am flattered that you trust me with your care." She'd never come to Celia before today, though. Maybe the reason for this morning's visit had more to do with Mrs. Jewett's worry about Nicholas than her discomfort around her physician. "Now, tell me why you are concerned about Mr. Greaves."

"Why, those letters, of course." The other woman's forehead creased. "Hasn't he told you about them?"

Secrets, Nicholas? Too many secrets between them, even still. Patrick Davies had been fond of keeping secrets, and those secrets had destroyed their marriage.

"What letters, Mrs. Jewett?" Celia asked, attempting to sound dispassionate and likely failing.

"He hasn't told you." She shook her head. "I shouldn't have said anything."

"Well you have, so you may as well explain what these letters were about."

She drew her fringed shawl around her shoulders. "Some fellow, some awful-looking fellow who scared the life out of me, dropped them off," she said. "Along with a photograph of Mr. Greaves with his two sisters, taken a while back."

"I do not comprehend why anyone would send him another print of a photograph he already owns." Celia was familiar with the daguerreotype Mrs. Jewett referred to; she'd seen it herself on the occasion of her boldly visiting Nicholas's rented rooms.

"I don't think he does either, Mrs. Davies. Not so far as I can tell," said Mrs. Jewett, keen to tell all, now that there was no turning back. "The letters were from his sister Meg. Addressed to a friend with the initial *S*. She'd written them in the months before she died."

"He showed them to you?" Celia asked, certain she no longer sounded dispassionate but rather a trifle jealous.

"Oh, no, Mrs. Davies. I snuck a look." She paused as she comprehended what she had just admitted. "Only because I care about him so greatly, you understand. He was terribly upset when those parcels arrived. He thought I couldn't tell, but of course I could. He's not as difficult to read as he likes to think he is."

In the beginning of their acquaintance, Celia had found Nicholas frustratingly difficult to read. Closed. Reserved when around her. He had less to fear from his landlady, she supposed.

"Isn't it possible that the person who gave Mr. Greaves those letters merely wished for him to have items that had once belonged to his sister?" she asked. "A sentimental souvenir, albeit a few years late."

Mrs. Jewett frowned. "And send some smelly thug to deliver them to my door? Menace me?"

"I concede that the choice of courier challenges my idea, Mrs. Jewett."

"Just so," she replied. Perhaps Nicholas should employ Mrs. Jewett to help with his cases. She appeared to have caught the detecting bug. "More significantly, the letters came with a note, which said it was time he learned the truth about his sister before it was 'too late.' Too late, Mrs. Davies!" she exclaimed. "And no signature to give a clue as to who they were. They want to scare him. That's what I think."

"But why?" Celia mused aloud. And why now? Years after his sister had taken her own life.

"That's what I was hoping *you* might be able to work out."

"Not easily accomplished when he has not even informed me of those letters or the warning, Mrs. Jewett," she said. "Has he received anything else from this mysterious sender?"

"Nothing since the final parcel two weeks ago," she said. "It's been keeping him awake at night, though. Rustling about. I hear him pacing in his room at all hours."

"Nothing at all for two weeks?" The length of time explained the inattentiveness she'd noticed in him recently. He'd been distracted by those letters. "There may no longer be anything to worry about, Mrs. Jewett. Perhaps the threat is past."

"You don't really believe that, do you, Mrs. Davies?"

Not only had Mrs. Jewett caught the detecting bug, but she was beginning to sound like Owen Cassidy.

"I fail to see what I can do to help," Celia replied crisply. "Mr. Greaves has not confided in me, so he does not want me to know about the letters, nor does he want my assistance in the matter. I assume he is attempting to discover the identity of the person who sent him those parcels and what they meant by doing so, and will resolve the affair without my interference." As Nicholas might term her involvement.

"Now, Mrs. Davies, I am very disappointed. I thought you'd want to get to the bottom of this situation and sort it out," she said, just as crisply. "Because I'm not sure that Mr. Greaves actually wants to find that person, or understand what they meant by sending him those letters and that photograph. He claims he's tried to track down the fellow who made the delivery, ask him what he wants, but he hasn't had any luck."

"Then that is all it is, Mrs. Jewett," she said. "He is not avoiding finding this individual. He has merely not been successful."

"If Mr. Greaves really wanted to find them, Mrs. Davies, he would've," she insisted. "No, I think he's scared to learn more about his sister. Truly scared."

• • •

"Do you want me to keep looking for the fellow who delivered those letters, sir?" asked Nick Greaves's assistant. Taylor sucked on his cigar, the tip flaring orange, then released the smoke, tendrils drifting off on the breeze.

Nick paused at the edge of the sidewalk, the North Beach and Mission railroad car rattling by, the horse's hooves clattering over the street cobbles. It was a gray day, heavy with clouds, suiting his mood. "We've done all we can, Taylor."

"You're sure you don't want me to keep asking about him?"

"I'm sure," Nick said, crossing the street after a crate-laden wagon, come up from the wharf, had lumbered past behind the horsecar.

"Doesn't seem right to leave a dangerous fellow like him wandering about on the streets, though," Taylor said, unwilling to let the topic go. "If you don't mind me saying so, sir."

"We don't know that he's actually dangerous, Taylor."

However, the fellow had scared Nick's landlady so badly that for days Mrs. Jewett would startle every time somebody knocked on the front door. One time, her nerves getting the better of her, she'd taken a cleaver with her to answer the bell. The sight of a woman hoisting a massive knife had terrified the butcher's delivery boy, who dropped the wrapped chops he'd been delivering and run for his life.

Two weeks had passed, though, and there'd been no more visits, no more parcels. No more old photographs of Nick with Meg and his twin sister, Ellie. No more warning words about needing to learn the truth about Meg before it was too late. What truth was there to learn about her? He already knew everything there was to know about his younger sister. The worst and most important truth being that, after Nick had left for the war, the once carefree girl she'd been had turned melancholy. Fallen in with the wrong sort of people, according to Uncle Asa, who'd taken Meg in when Nick had gone off to fight in a bloody and horrific war thousands of miles away. She'd ended her life while he'd been away battling Confederates and his own personal demons. If some person thought he didn't know *that* truth about Meg, well, he regretted to inform the individual that he very much did. Except he couldn't inform them, because they'd ceased communicating as abruptly as they'd started.

Taylor paused to drop the stub of his spent cigar on the curb, crushing it with the heel of his boot. A tan mongrel trotted over to sniff at the stub, hoping it was food, before loping off disappointed. "Maybe the parcels and all were just a prank, sir, and the person realized it wasn't so amusing after all."

"A very cruel prank, Taylor, that wasn't amusing in the least. But you might be right."

They arrived at City Hall, situated across from Portsmouth Square and its scraggly trees, and the location of the basement police station. Also situated near the Bella Union Melodeon and a number of taverns. Convenient, if a police officer was in the mood to arrest somebody. Wouldn't have far to go to find a plentiful supply of miscreants on any given night.

Nick turned into the alley alongside the building.

Taylor hurried after him. "What do you want me to do now, though? Sir. Mr. Greaves, sir."

Nothing? Leave it be? Nick badly wanted to leave it all be.

"It seems like there's nothing left to do, Taylor," he replied. "Maybe the individual left town and that's the reason I haven't heard more from them. Even though the fellow who made those deliveries told me I would hear from them." Or maybe they were dead.

Nick threw open the alley door that led to the station and stomped down the stairs.

"But to have wanted to warn you before 'it was too late.' That was what the last message had said, wasn't it?" his assistant asked.

"That was what the message said," Nick replied, weaving his way through the scattering of desk and chairs in the main station house. A thick blue haze of smoke, which masked the stink from the adjacent jail, drifted close to the ceiling. Its source was the tip of a cigarillo one of the cops was puffing as he examined police records at his desk.

"Doubt they would've left town without telling you more, in that case," Taylor continued. "If they were hoping to warn you that you might be in danger."

"We don't know exactly what those words mean, Taylor."

"But still, they wanted to get information to you before something bad happened and they never did," he said. "Just downright odd."

Dead, then. "You've done enough. We have other cases to work on." *Leave it be.* Let it rest along with Meg's memory.

The booking sergeant guarding the door to the cells glanced over at Nick and Taylor. "Mullahey's been looking for you, Greaves. In fact, I think he might be in your office right now."

Nick nodded his thanks and entered the detectives' office. Detective

Briggs was absent, as was common, and so was the new guy, Detective O'Neal. That was not as common. He had been in that morning, though, because a half-consumed mug of coffee sat on the corner desk he used. O'Neal never finished his coffee, probably because he'd figured out that the sludge cooking away atop the heating stove in the station was barely worth drinking.

Officer Mullahey stood up from the chair he'd taken. "Thought you'd be in soon, Mr. Greaves."

"Not like you to hang about the station waiting for me."

Mullahey frowned, the expression twisting his already crooked nose, broken in a long-ago brawl with a criminal. Or so he'd always claimed. "It was important I see you," he said. "A body's been found, Mr. Greaves. In the bay. First light this morning."

Nick tossed his hat onto his desk, fluttering the papers that were always stacked there. An increasing number lately. He'd been too distracted by Meg's letters to attend to them. To care about a burglary at a dry goods store. To investigate a knife fight at a tavern located at the edge of the Barbary. Uncle Asa, the man he'd followed into this job, the best detective Nick had ever met, would be angry with his negligence. If he were still alive to witness it.

"A murder, I assume." Almost every month a man's dead body was being fished out of the bay or one of the lakes. Most of the deaths were accidents, but some were suicides. However, Mullahey wouldn't be telling Nick about the death of another wretched failure who'd come to San Francisco seeking their fortune, only to discover that fortunes had been gobbled up by the lucky few, men who didn't like to share. Which left murder.

"Yes, Mr. Greaves. He was killed," the officer said. "Fellow had been shot, it seems, before somebody went and tossed him into the water off Washington Street wharf."

"What do we know about the man?" Nick asked, dropping onto his desk chair. Which squeaked, because that's what it always did, no matter how often Taylor tried to fix the source of the noise.

"He looks to have worked on a ship, based on his clothes," Mullahey answered. "A sailor, maybe. He was wearing a sack coat of water-resistant duck and pants handsewn from an old sail."

"You know what to do. Get to work talking to the ship and ferry captains about any missing seamen."

"I've already started, Mr. Greaves." Mullahey reached into his coat pocket and pulled out a thick leather cord. "He had this around his neck. Thought you might want to have a look at it. Might help us discover who he is."

The cord was strung through the loop of a gold locket. Nick's pulse skipped. *It can't be. It can't be.*

Mullahey dropped the cord and locket onto Nick's desk. "There's a painted miniature inside. Of a young woman. Pretty. Along with a few strands of hair. Hers, I'd be guessing."

Hair that would be the mellow brown of a chestnut and softly curling.

Taylor shifted on his chair and leaned forward. "What is it, sir? What's wrong?"

Nick reached for the locket and sprung the latch holding shut the lid, a wisp of hair drifting free and onto the desk. A face, one that had taken to haunting him at night, stared back from the glass surface it had been painted upon. He'd almost forgotten how lovely she'd been. Almost.

"It's my sister, Taylor," he answered, his hand shaking. "My sister."

Meg.

✂ CHAPTER 2 ☙

"I'll only lift a corner of the sheet so you can take a quick peek at his face, Mrs. Jewett," Nick said. "It won't be pretty, but I need to know if this is the fellow who brought those parcels."

The section of Massey's Coffin Wareroom set aside for the coroner to use had a stuffy, rank odor to it. A stink that mingled with the tang of embalming fluid seeping in from another part of the building. The smell was making Nick nauseated. It was sickening his housekeeper too, based on the greenish hue of her face. Or maybe it was the prospect of having to look at the bloated face of a dead man.

"I understand, Mr. Greaves," she replied.

Mrs. Jewett clutched a cotton handkerchief to her nose. Was it helping with the smell? Nick doubted a scrap of cloth could put a dent in the stink. She'd pulled it out the moment they'd entered the undertaker's and shuffled past the coffins for sale, some with their lids open to display fancy padded linings. Past a collection of black hearse plumes and other funeral trimmings. Past Massey himself, who'd rushed over to them the moment the bell had rung, only to realize it was Nick and a witness, not someone interested in purchasing a casket. One day the coroner—these days it was Dr. Letterman instead of Nick's old friend Harris—might warrant his own morgue, instead of having to find space in an undertaker's business. There were rumblings that the state legislature might finally pay for a dedicated mortuary. Massey would be disappointed. He likely made money off the folks who came to the makeshift morgue to identify people. Why look for another undertaker when you were already inside the coffin wareroom of Atkins Massey?

"Are you ready, then, Mrs. Jewett?" Nick hated putting her through this, but it was necessary.

She gave a brisk nod, brave as ever. "May as well get it over with," she said, her voice muffled by the handkerchief.

He peeled back the cloth, revealing just enough of the man's face for her to get a glimpse. According to Taylor, who'd spoken with Dr. Letterman, the fellow had been shot twice before being dumped in the bay. At least the killing hadn't been a bullet to the head. That really would've been a gruesome sight.

Mrs. Jewett pulled in a breath, leaned over for a better view, and

11

shook her head. "That's not him, Mr. Greaves. I'm pretty sure. He's awfully . . ."

Blue and a little bloated, thought Nick. "I know."

"But I'm pretty sure it's not him, Mr. Greaves," she said. "I should have a look at his hand to be certain. The right one. There was something wrong with it, I remember."

Nick located the corpse's hand beneath the sheet and pulled it into view. Perfectly normal, aside from the color and the swelling.

"Not him."

He replaced the covering. Who was he, then? Somebody who'd known Meg well enough to have been gifted a locket with her picture and a bit of her hair inside. Maybe he'd even been the person, the *S*, that she'd addressed her letters to.

Mrs. Jewett had retreated, putting space between her and the cloth-covered corpse stretched out atop an oak table. "Do you have any idea who he is, Mr. Greaves?"

"All we can tell, based on his clothing, is that he worked aboard a ship." Aside from the locket, there hadn't been any sort of identification on him. Nick took her elbow and led her out of the building and onto Sacramento Street. The day's clouds had lifted and the sunshine made him squint. "Mullahey and Taylor are asking questions down at the docks right now, enquiring about missing seamen. If they don't turn up any answers, we'll put a notice in the papers."

She raised her hand to shade her eyes, her bonnet brim inadequate to the job. She was still clutching her handkerchief, and it flapped against her cheek. "He wasn't the fellow who delivered those parcels to you, but he must've had something to do with them."

"We can't conclude that, Mrs. Jewett."

"I can't see how a fellow gets killed right after your sister's letters were delivered—"

"The deliveries stopped two weeks ago," Nick interrupted. "The man on that morgue table wasn't murdered and tossed into the bay two weeks ago, Mrs. Jewett. His body was in the water only a couple of days, according to the coroner."

"I can't explain the timing, it's true," she conceded. "But I can't see how the murder of a fellow who owned a locket containing a portrait of your sister—God rest her—is not connected to those parcels."

Did she want to become a detective, too? Owen Cassidy and Celia were enough to contend with; he didn't need his landlady joining the group.

"Thank you, Mrs. Jewett. You can head back home now. I'll be sure to let you know what we find out about the man," he said. "And who killed him. Don't worry."

"I always worry about you, Mr. Greaves, as you well know," she said. "Mrs. Davies is worried, too. Now that she's aware of the letters. Which you should have told her about, by the way," she chastised.

Nick's jaw tensed. "You've been talking to Celia Davies?"

"Of course I have. Somebody needs to get answers, if you're not going to."

Great.

• • •

"Hello, Mrs. Davies."

"Hello, Sergeant," she said, greeting the officer who registered the latest residents of the jail cells. For some reason, the main police station did not smell as bad as it usually did. The windows were open, which would help. "Is Detective Greaves in his office?"

"No, he's gone to look at the body that was brought to the coroner this morning, ma'am. Fished out of the bay near the Washington Street wharf."

"A body?" Another murder, no doubt. How sad. She wondered who it was and quickly reminded herself that she was not actually in the business of solving crimes. Even if crimes and criminals seemed to find their way to her with alarming frequency.

"I'm afraid I can't say anything about it, ma'am."

"That's quite all right. Do you expect him to return soon?"

He grinned; he had long ago given up attempting to force her to leave rather than wait in the detectives' office, and her persistence amused him. "I expect he will, ma'am. He's been gone . . ." He shot a look at the clock on the wall. "Been gone about an hour."

She thanked him and opened the door to the office. It was not empty. A fellow she'd never seen before was seated at the desk in the corner. "Forgive me. I did not mean to interrupt you."

He got to his feet. He was young, not unattractive, clean-shaven with a close-cut crop of dark curly hair and light green eyes. "Might I help you, miss?"

His voice flowed with the lilting rhythm of an Irish accent. It was much like Patrick's voice, if Patrick had ever sought to even out the cadences of his homeland. He even resembled her deceased husband, aside from the color of his eyes. The detective's question had been asked with a hint of suspicion, debating, no doubt, if she was a victim or a witness or maybe even a suspect, although the latter never willingly wandered into the police station.

He scanned her from tip to toe and noted her black dress. Skimmed over the wedding band she continued to wear on her left hand. "Might I help you, *ma'am?*" he asked, modifying both his words and his tone.

She'd promised Addie she would cease wearing both the ring and mourning for Patrick, but there were times the attire came in handy. Especially when it adjusted people's attitudes.

"I am looking for Detective Greaves, Detective . . ."

"Detective O'Neal, ma'am."

Irish, indeed. Nicholas had not mentioned that there was a recent addition to the number of detectives, though. Mr. Taylor must be upset; he had been hoping for the promotion for a long time. Instead he had been bypassed by a fellow who appeared to be no older than he was and therefore unlikely to possess much more experience.

"My apologies, Detective O'Neal," Celia said. "You must be new." New yet unabashedly confident, based on the set of his shoulders and disconcertingly probing gaze.

"Do you come to the police station often, ma'am?"

More than Nicholas liked. "I am acquainted with Detective Greaves." It was all the answer she was willing to supply.

He cocked an eyebrow. "Are you."

Her cheeks heated. *Blast.* "I can wait out in the station for him to return from the coroner's."

"No need, ma'am." Detective O'Neal flapped aside his coat lapel, the movement revealing the gun holstered at his side, retrieved a key from an inner pocket, and locked the top drawer of his desk. "I was just about to leave."

Not the way the situation had appeared to Celia upon entering the room. Perhaps he sought to rush off and collect intelligence about the blond-haired woman in widow's weeds who frequented the detectives' office and was acquainted with Detective Greaves. The booking sergeant could no doubt provide a satisfying quantity of gossip.

"Then I shall wait here for Detective Greaves to return."

The detective wished her a good day, collected his hat from a hook by the door, and strode off. Out in the main station, Nicholas greeted him before marching into the room.

"Why am I not surprised to find you here, Celia?" he asked, trying to act annoyed. Or perhaps he truly was annoyed. Mrs. Jewett might be able to read him, but Celia still found comprehending his current sentiment to be a challenge.

"I do find the police station to be the best place to locate you, Nicholas."

A muscle along his jaw ticked. "I'm sorry you haven't seen much of me lately, Celia."

I am growing used to the situation, unfortunately. "You have a new detective, I see," she said, pulling over one of the room's chairs to take a seat. "Detective O'Neal?"

"He's not *my* new detective." Nicholas dropped onto his desk chair, which let out its usual squeal of protest. "And O'Neal's not that new, from what he tells me. He worked here as a regular police officer while the war was going on. Been told he was with the Chicago police force in the years between then and now. Not sure why he returned to San Francisco. He knew my uncle Asa when he was a detective, though. He used this same desk, you know."

He meant his uncle, not Detective O'Neal. Nicholas paused to scan the surface of his desk as if he might unearth mementos from when his uncle had sat there. He only occasionally mentioned the man whose skills as a detective he'd so admired, but when he did, his expression invariably turned sad. As it did right then.

"Detective O'Neal appears to be very competent."

A statement that distracted Nicholas from his ruminations. "He seems all right. He's only been back a few weeks, so I haven't had enough time to form a judgment."

"I see." She drew in a breath. What she had to say might upset him. "Nicholas, I'm here because—"

"I know why you're here, Celia." He frowned. "Mrs. Jewett gave me a good idea."

"Why didn't you tell me about receiving your sister's letters, Nicholas? Along with the photograph?"

His frown became a scowl. He was most definitely annoyed now.

"Mrs. Jewett shouldn't have said anything about them, Celia. They're not important."

"What do you mean, they are not important? Of course they are." She stretched out her hand, but he made no effort to respond in kind. She should not have allowed him to put the width of his oak desk, stacked high with papers, between them. She sat back. "Someone had a reason to send you her old letters, Nicholas. To warn you. They *must* be important."

"I've explained to my landlady and I am going to explain to you, Celia, that they're just letters filled with bits and pieces about what she was doing," he said. "The typical contents of a woman's letters to a friend."

"That is all?"

He exhaled. "All right, Celia. Meg was worried about something she'd found out, but I have no idea what that was," he said. "Maybe she'd heard some unkind gossip about her."

"Unkind gossip." Mrs. Jewett was correct; he did not want to learn more. Or he was working hard to appear unconcerned about the matter. Why? "And the warning?"

"It's most likely just a cruel joke."

"Honestly, Nicholas, you can be so frustrating," she said. "Did you locate any of her former friends to discover if they might know who she'd sent those letters to? Who may have therefore been the person who'd sent them to you."

"After four years? It's been four years, Celia. Almost to the day," he said. "And I couldn't find any of her friends. She didn't appear to have that many, and the folks where she'd lived before she'd died weren't much help."

"I thought she had lived with your uncle prior to her death."

His expression hardened. "She moved. More than once in the last few weeks of her life," he replied. "I'm sorry, but this really is none of your business, Celia."

It is, Nicholas. It is because I love you and am desperately worried about you. She'd not speak those words aloud, however, with the office door open and at least one officer lurking nearby to overhear. Actually, several were out in the station at the moment, based on the three or four different voices she could hear talking.

Celia tilted her head to the side and considered him. "When did you speak with Mrs. Jewett today? It had to have been after she came to visit me this morning, as I believe you do not normally go home to eat your midday meal."

He narrowed his eyes and refused to answer. He could be infuriatingly stubborn.

"I must presume, then, that Mrs. Jewett accompanied you to the morgue sometime after I'd spoken with her," she guessed. His gaze flickered. *Correct, Celia.* "And who might it be that you needed her to identify? My conjecture is that the man who delivered those parcels is the man found dead off Washington Street wharf, and you wanted her to have a look at the corpse, as you'd not seen this individual yourself. You may as well admit that I have guessed correctly, since I am positive that Mrs. Jewett would be happy to speak with me about the matter."

"Damn it, Celia, must you always get involved?" he asked.

Yes. "Who was he, Nicholas? The man who was fished out of the bay."

"*Not* the man who delivered the parcels."

"That is all you are going to tell me? Nicholas, why are you being so secretive? I only wish to help. I do not 'get involved' because I am a busybody with nothing better to do with my time. You know that," she spat. The handful of officers out in the station halted their conversations to eavesdrop. *Blast.*

"Somebody who'd worked aboard a ship, based on his clothing. That's all we know so far."

A mariner. "Nothing more than that?"

His brown eyes, which could be so warm but were far from warm right then, focused on her face. His expression was cold and guarded. Were they suddenly adversaries?

"He had a locket with Meg's portrait inside," he said flatly. "I recognized the locket immediately. The second Mullahey took it out of his coat pocket." He reached inside the top drawer of his desk and retrieved a brown leather cord. A simply decorated gold locket dangled from it. He gently set down the item. "My father gave it to Meg when she turned sixteen. Intended for her to give to the man she loved when the time was right."

"So this man had been her beau?"

"In the few letters of hers that reached me on the battlefield, she'd never mentioned a sweetheart."

What other explanation could there be, though? "What was the cause of the man's death? Drowning?"

"He was shot twice in the back and thrown into the bay," he said tersely. "A couple of days ago is Dr. Letterman's assessment."

I should be patient with him. Her probing questions were not the cause of his cold aloofness. Rather, he was constructing walls, guarding himself because he was being forced to relive the pain of losing his sister.

Which, if I am being honest with myself, my probing questions are only aggravating.

She glanced at the door and got up to close it. She leaned back against the wood. "Nicholas, you could be in danger. Who ever sought to murder a friend of your sister's may intend to harm you, as well."

"If somebody wanted to kill *me* because I'm Meg's brother, Celia, they would've done so years ago. I'm not exactly hard to find, and it's no secret Meg and I were related."

"Which, despite your intentions, does not fully reassure me, Nicholas." She pushed away from the door. "I am very concerned for you. Those letters, the warning, and now this man's murder . . . I cannot help believing that you are in danger."

His gaze held hers. "I'll be careful, Celia."

"But will you be careful enough?"

• • •

Harris strolled into Nick's office, taking a look back over his shoulder before appropriating the chair Celia had been using. "I just passed Mrs. Davies on my way in here. Another investigation for the two of you?"

Nick leaned back in his chair and scrubbed his hands through his hair, his fingers tangling in the strands. It needed cutting. What else had he been neglecting while he'd been preoccupied with those damned letters? He'd been ignoring cases, the paperwork atop his desk piles of guilty reminders. Ignoring Celia. "Stop grinning, Harris."

"Sorry, Greaves. I didn't realize that I was."

Ignoring Harris, too. Now that his friend was no longer the coroner and had lost an excuse to come into the police station to discuss suspicious deaths, they rarely saw each other. Nick didn't circulate among the crowds that a well-off doctor and his wife tended to socialize with.

"Don't mind me," Nick said. "Are you here because of the body that was found in the bay?" Harris might not be the coroner anymore, but that didn't mean he'd stopped being interested in police business. His medical practice clearly wasn't keeping him busy enough.

"I ran into Dr. Letterman just an hour ago," he answered. "He said you were planning to stop at the undertaker's to inspect a corpse stored there. A shooting death is my understanding."

"I've been."

"Dare I ask if that was why Mrs. Davies was visiting you?" Harris asked.

"She knows about the dead man now." That and Meg's letters. "Letterman told Taylor that the fellow had been shot twice before being tipped into the water. Not a suicide."

"Definitely not, since he was shot in the back." Harris lifted his eyebrows. "You look surprised. Didn't Dr. Letterman give Mr. Taylor the details about his wounds?"

Nick folded his arms. "No, he didn't."

The former coroner shook his head. "I can't understand what it is with you two."

"He's taken as much a dislike to me as I have to him, I suppose."

"If he dislikes you, Greaves, it's because you're being a stubborn ass and refusing to accept that *he* has been elected as the coroner now."

There probably was some truth in that statement. "What other details did our newly elected coroner not share with Taylor?"

"There was a small quantity of water in the man's lungs."

Nick sat forward. "He wasn't dead when he was tossed into the bay."

"Close to death, I would guess, but not dead. You should go to the inquest, Greaves. It's being held . . ." Harris retrieved his watch and flipped open the lid. "In an hour. You could get all the details then."

"Why should I bother, when he gave all those details to you and you're here to share them with me?"

Harris chuckled. "You *are* a stubborn ass."

"Back to our murder . . . our likely murder victim. Given that there was water in his lungs, he was probably killed somewhere nearby, in order for him to still have been alive after being plugged with bullets." Alive and gasping for breath. Sucking in only salty water.

"However, the amount he inhaled didn't drown him. He was pretty near death already. He could've been brought to that wharf from a mile or more away."

The structure extended off the end of Washington Street, beyond a large grain warehouse and into the bay. One of a dozen or more wharves and docks—Nick had lost count—that jutted into the bay in this part of town. Sailing vessels and steamers and ferries jostling for slips. Businessmen fighting for scraps of land to set up warehouses along the shore.

"Or he could have been pushed off a boat," Nick said. "He was wearing clothes that suggest he was a sailor."

"However, it's not likely somebody wouldn't report a shipmate being shot on board and then getting tossed into the water, Greaves," Harris countered.

"Mullahey and Taylor have been questioning ships' captains and ferry owners. No reports of a missing deckhand yet," he said. "Maybe he worked on a steamer heading out to Honolulu or China, and the captain hasn't been close enough to land to relay a message."

"If that's the case, it will be a while before you learn who he is."

Nick drew in a breath. The locket was still on his desk, and he ran his fingertip over its surface. The metal was cold, its decoration too shallow to feel. "He knew Meg, Harris."

"Your younger sister."

How much had Nick ever told his friend about Meg? Harris wasn't the coroner when she had died, so he hadn't handled her body. Hadn't had to determine along with a jury that she'd killed herself because life had grown too terrible for her. That had been left to Harris's predecessor, a man who'd struggled to find somebody to take responsibility for Meg's corpse, even though Asa was in the city and looking for her. After leaving his house, she'd moved to the edge of the city, out near the Mission Woolen Mills and the Deaf and Dumb Asylum east of Mission Dolores. Then into a cheap hotel near the brothels, her hair dyed red and living under an assumed name. She hadn't lived there long before she'd stumbled upon the ultimate way out.

"Somebody sent me a packet of her letters a few weeks ago," Nick said. "Along with a photograph of us."

"Do you know who?"

"No indication," he replied. "The sender included a message that it was time I learned the truth about her before it was 'too late,' but they didn't sign it."

"And now a friend of hers has been shot dead and thrown into the bay." Harris narrowed his gaze. "You could be in danger, Greaves."

Nick grabbed the locket and shoved it inside his desk drawer. "Celia has already shared her concerns about that possibility, Harris."

"And maybe you should listen to her. To me. For once."

Maybe.

❦ CHAPTER 3 ❧

"Has Mr. Taylor ever mentioned parcels that Nicholas has recently received, Addie?" Celia asked her housekeeper. Addie and Mr. Taylor had been stepping out for several months now, and no doubt regularly discussed Celia and Nicholas when they were together. The sort of confidences shared by two people in love. "A packet of his sister's letters delivered by a strange, possibly dangerous, fellow?"

"No, ma'am." Addie stacked the clean linen towels she'd brought into Celia's examining room, fresh from the racks where they'd been hanging in the warm kitchen to dry, on the corner table. "Is this dangerous fellow delivering letters the reason Mrs. Jewett came to visit you?"

Celia finished her notes on the patient she'd just seen, a young girl afflicted by epilepsy. She'd had to inform the child's mother that there was nothing she could do to help. Which caused the woman to stomp off, her daughter in tow, in search of another medical practitioner who could provide a remedy for the girl's fits. Perhaps they would recommend bromide of potassium, a popular "cure." Or a round of cupping and a quantity of leeches to be applied daily. There was a fellow in San Francisco who provided such services. Any number of charlatans existed to take the woman's precious money and leave her child no better off.

Celia tucked her pencil inside her leather-bound notebook and closed it. "You guess correctly, Addie."

"What did Mr. Greaves have to say?" she asked, giving the tidily stacked towels a satisfied pat. "'Tis why you went to the police station, was it not?"

Celia was rarely able to conceal her movements from her housekeeper's watchful gaze. She only snuck about to protect Addie from unnecessary anxiety. Although too often her anxiety *was* necessary.

"Yes, it was." She shifted in her chair to better face Addie. "He was reluctant to discuss the letters with me and wanted me to believe they were unimportant, when I suspect they very much *are* important. Why else send them to him now, all these years after his sister died?"

"They've upset him. Poor wee lass, gone so young," Addie said and added a murmured prayer.

"A friend of hers was pulled from the bay this morning. Shot before he ended up in the water," she replied. "I cannot be positive the murder is related to the delivery of her letters, but the timing of the murder seems too coincidental to not suspect they are linked."

Addie narrowed her eyes. Celia could anticipate what was coming next—a scolding. "So, you've another investigation to get caught up in."

"Mrs. Jewett is worried about Nicholas, and now I am too," Celia said. "How can I not offer help?"

Addie opened her mouth to carry on with her reprimand, but she was—mercifully, thought Celia—interrupted by a knock on the front door.

The person who'd knocked called out from the entryway before Addie could rush off to answer, "Mrs. Davies?"

Celia got to her feet. "In here, Owen."

He trotted into the clinic with a grin.

"Why bother to knock if you've nae intention of waiting for someone to respond, Owen Cassidy?" Addie chided.

"I didn't think I needed to wait, Addie," he said, his cheeks pinking. "Ain't I . . . aren't I welcome to come in?"

"You are always welcome, Owen," Celia said.

"That's what I thought. I finished up with my deliveries today and, um, thought I'd stop by and see how everybody was doing. Since I was in the area and all." He glanced down at his trousers, noticed they were covered in grime from hauling freight, and took to swiping at them. "If you don't mind, that is."

"Addie has been busy with laundry today, so I do not know if there are any treats in the kitchen at the moment."

Addie smiled lovingly at the boy. Who'd ceased being a boy some time ago, but who they both would likely forever think of as the ragged and starving lad they'd taken under their wing.

"Perhaps you'd prefer to stay for supper?" Addie asked him. Although he was no longer as ragged as he used to be, Owen's relentless appetite left him nearly as hungry. "I've a beef soup stewing on the cooking range. But there are biscuits in the jar, if you can't wait to eat."

"Thanks, Addie!"

"Come along, then," Addie said, resting a hand on his back to guide him over to the door linking Celia's clinic to the kitchen at the rear of the house.

"Wait, Owen," Celia said. "Have you spoken with Mr. Greaves lately, by any chance?" Perhaps Nicholas had asked for Owen's assistance in locating the person who'd delivered his sister's letters, rather than utilize police resources like Mr. Taylor or Officer Mullahey. Owen had proven useful before.

Addie scowled. "Now, ma'am, don't be getting the boy involved in one of your schemes—"

"Thank you, Addie."

Owen's green eyes brightened. "What is it? A case?"

"What do you know about Mr. Greaves's sister, Meg?" Celia asked. Nicholas might be reluctant to revisit his sister's final days, to possibly uncover unwelcome details about her, but Celia had no qualms. Someone had sent him Meg's letters to remind him about her. To warn him. And now a man had been murdered who once had been her friend, or something more. The sender's motives were unclear, but the more Celia learned about Meg Greaves, the closer she might get to exposing those motives. To understanding what, if anything, those letters had to do with the death of a sailor. "Has he ever mentioned her to you?"

"Ma'am," Addie grumbled. "Mr. Greaves will have this all in hand. You've nae need to involve wee Owen."

"I don't mind getting involved, Addie," he said brightly. "I don't know much, but I can show you one of the last places she lived. Would that help?"

"Yes," Celia answered, evading Addie's reproachful gaze. "I believe it would. Shall we say, early tomorrow morning?"

• • •

"The notice in yesterday's afternoon newspapers looking for information on the dead fellow got results already, sir," said Taylor, trailing Nick through the main room of the station house. Since Nick wasn't walking particularly quickly, Taylor kept running into him.

Nick had spent the night reading Meg's letters—for the fifth or sixth time, maybe more. Probably more—and was exhausted. He'd given his face a rough scrub with a cloth that morning and had paid even less attention to his hair. Mrs. Jewett had frowned at him when she'd set out coffee and toast in the dining room, but had refrained from commenting on his bloodshot eyes or rumpled clothing. He wasn't happy that she'd told Celia about those letters, and she was mindful that the less said to him when he was in a sour mood, the better.

"Oh?" Nick asked his assistant. That *was* fast.

"One of the man's friends read the notice and went to the coroner's to look at the body first thing this morning," Taylor said, slowing to avoid clipping the heel of Nick's boot. "He's waiting in the detectives' office right now. A Mr. Loomis."

The man was waiting in the chair Nick used for both witnesses and suspects, his back to the door. He'd pulled his black wool derby from his head—revealing a bald patch—and was anxiously tapping his fingers on the hat's crown.

"Mr. Loomis," Nick boomed, startling the man.

He glanced up at Nick. "You scared me."

That was the point—to knock him off-balance. Mr. Loomis might've come into the station as a concerned friend of the deceased, but he could just as easily be a killer hoping to deflect attention from his guilt or to figure out what the police knew about the case.

"Sorry about that." Nick took his chair and rested his elbows on his desk, tenting his fingers and staring at the man over their tips. Loomis had a round face made more round by a pair of massive muttonchop whiskers. Excess hair trying to make up for the balding. Nick should tell him the attempt never worked. "I hear you're a friend of the man fished out of the bay yesterday."

"Neighbors is more like it, Officer."

"Detective Greaves."

Taylor had collected his pencil and notebook and slipped into the office, shutting the door behind him.

"Mr. Loomis here was just starting to tell me about his neighbor, Taylor," Nick said. "Please continue, Mr. Loomis."

Loomis cleared his throat, sending his protuberant Adam's apple diving beneath the knot in his necktie. "Friendly neighbors, mind you. Would share dinner now and again. Maybe go to the saloon a time or two. Not that I'm a drinker, of course," he added, shooting a look at Taylor, note-taking as usual and making folks anxious.

"What is your friendly neighbor's name, Mr. Loomis? I haven't been told."

"Sy. Sylvanus Eckart."

Nick lowered his hands to the desk. Sy. Meg had addressed her letters to an *S*. He and the dead man with her locket might be one and the same person. "Did he ever mention a woman named Meg or Margaret to you?"

Loomis's brow creased for a moment. "Nope. Not that I can recall."

"Do you recall him owning a gold locket with a woman's picture inside?"

He shook his head. "Nope. But I haven't seen Sy much lately, Detective. He'd been away from San Francisco for a while before taking one of the rooms in the building where I live. The apartment right below mine, in fact."

"You're positive the body you saw was his, though."

"I am, Detective. Even though he was a bit . . . puffy," he said, pulling a face. "We go back a ways. That's why I'm sure. Never expected he might drown himself, though. Didn't seem the type. But then, I suppose you can't right tell about folks. One day acting happy, the next, dead."

The notice requesting information had been vague about the man's actual cause of death and apparently the coroner had been vague with Mr. Loomis as well.

"He was wearing what resembled sailors' clothing, Mr. Loomis. Did Mr. Eckart work aboard a ship?"

"He did. Back when I first met him, he had a job with North American Steamship. The ships that carry the mail to New York City. Employed as a carpenter, I think. Not quite sure, though," Loomis said. "After that, he started working on the packets to Oregon. Didn't care for them so much, although he moved up there, I'm pretty sure."

"Oregon?"

He nodded. "And one time he told me he'd been a deckhand on a clipper brig sailing to Kanagawa. Japan! Can you imagine? A whole 'nother world." His round face took on a dreamy expression. "I woulda liked to work on a ship sailing across the oceans, but I don't have good sea legs, you know? Plus it's mighty hard work. I'll stick to keeping books at the flour mill. Not likely to drown there. Dang. Guess that wasn't a proper thing to say, given what happened to poor old Sy."

"You said he moved into the apartment below you. When was this?"

"Three weeks ago. Or maybe four."

Three or four weeks. Interesting.

"Sy didn't seem to be working at the moment, though," Loomis went on. "Not sure if he was planning on moving back to San Francisco permanently. Not sure what he was up to, exactly, and he didn't want to tell me. Keeping to himself, mostly."

"When you last saw him, was he acting like he was afraid?"

"Jumpy, maybe. But afraid?" Loomis shrugged.

"Did he have any enemies that you were aware of? Folks he complained about, or who he owed money to, or who might've caused him trouble?"

Loomis's glance took in Taylor and Nick. "Why are you asking me about him having any enemies, Detective?"

"Sy Eckart didn't drown himself, Mr. Loomis. He was shot—twice—before somebody threw him into the bay." Nick wouldn't mention that Eckart had been shot in the back, a detail that was worth keeping quiet. Had Eckart been fleeing his assailant? Or had the killer snuck up on him and shot him from behind, without warning or confrontation, like a coward?

"Shot?" Loomis sat up straight, his fingers tightening around the brim of his derby hat. "Somebody killed Sy?"

He sounded surprised. Maybe he was.

"When was the last time you saw Mr. Eckart?" Nick asked. "Alive, that is."

"Um . . ." He swallowed again, sending his Adam's apple lurching. "Friday, I think it was. Yes. That's it. Friday."

"Three days before his body was found, sir," said Taylor, looking up from his notebook.

"Yes, Taylor." Based on the coroner's assessment of the condition of Eckart's body, he might have been killed Friday evening. Loomis may have been one of the last people to see him alive. "What was he doing Friday when you saw him, Mr. Loomis?"

"He'd asked me to meet him at one of the taverns he'd taken to drinking at. One of those nice German *lagerbier* taverns," he said. "That was the last time I saw him, Detective."

"How did Mr. Eckart seem to you that day?"

"Skittish as a starty horse, Detective. Not himself."

"Did he explain what or who had upset him?"

He swallowed again; his throat must be parched. "Could I get some water?"

"I can help you with that, Mr. Loomis, when Detective Greaves is finished," Taylor said, sounding less sympathetic than usual. Maybe he only had a soft spot for the women who occasionally occupied Loomis's chair.

"So, Mr. Eckart was upset . . ."

"He was. I got the feeling it was because of a fellow I seen him talking with right when I came in." He nodded over his recollection. "I'm sure that's the reason, Detective. That fellow upset him."

Eckart's killer? "Can you describe him?"

"Just a usual fellow, Detective," he said. "An ugly mug, sorry to say. Dark hair? Not too tall or short, neither."

Could describe half the males in San Francisco, and was not enough to go on. "That's all?"

"Well . . ." He grimaced. Admitting to being a witness had a way of twisting a person's stomach, sometimes. "I saw the fellow reach for his glass of beer and it looked like he was missing a couple of his fingers. On his right hand. Not so bad that he couldn't pick up his glass, though."

Nick sucked in a breath, loudly enough for Taylor to hear and look up from his notes. What had Mrs. Jewett said about the man who'd delivered those parcels? That there was something wrong with his right hand.

The old wound in his arm began to ache. He'd massage it, but then Taylor would notice that, too, and get to worrying. "Eckart didn't tell you who this man was."

"Nope. He didn't say much at all Friday night, Detective. Like I've been saying," he replied, squinting at Nick like he was wondering if he'd been paying attention. "Just wanted to drink."

"Did you leave the tavern with Eckart? Or did he head off separately?" With a man missing a few fingers who might've shot him in the back, say.

"He headed off on his own," he said. "That fellow's got to be Sy's killer. Don't you think, Detective?"

"Which tavern was this?" Maybe one of the waiters knew the man and could help Nick find him.

"Bauman's."

Nick glanced over at Taylor, whose eyebrows had danced up his forehead. Damn, thought Nick. Of all places. He'd been avoiding a return visit to the tavern—avoiding a particular woman who worked there, actually—but he couldn't avoid it or her any longer.

He rubbed the ache in his arm, Taylor's worry be damned. "Where were you Friday evening, Mr. Loomis, after you and Mr. Eckart parted?"

"Played cards with some mates in my apartment for a while. Went to bed. That's it."

"And your mates will vouch for you?"

He nodded vigorously. "But that fellow killed Sy. Not me."

Nick stood. "Thank you, Mr. Loomis. Tell my assistant where we can find you, if I need to ask you more questions."

"Why might you need to do that?" he asked and scrambled to his feet. "I already told you who it was that killed Sy."

"Taylor, show him out."

• • •

"Owen, did Mr. Greaves ask you to accompany him out to where his sister used to live?" Celia asked, shifting her weight in hopes she might find a more comfortable position on the hard wood bench of the Mission Railroad line. Sadly, resting on her left hip proved no more comfortable than on her right. "Or did you follow him?"

"Nothing so sneaky as that, ma'am!" he protested. "It was that I saw him outside the station last week, looking to be in a hurry. Which meant he was on a case. So I insisted that I come along to wherever he was headed." He grinned. "He couldn't shake me, though he did try. I was stuck to him like a burr."

"Luckily for us," she said. "What did he say to you?"

"Not too much. Just got to talking a bit about Meg and that she was his younger sister," he said, looking pensive. "That she'd had a hard life, at the end. Made me feel sorry for her."

Owen understood all the miseries entailed by a "hard life."

The horse drawing the car clopped along as they traveled south and away from the heart of the city. Leaving Addie to get in a fluster over Celia's decision to visit one of the last known lodgings of Meg Greaves in the company of an overexcited Irish lad, eager to prove his usefulness. Addie did not fuss too loudly, for Barbara was upstairs in her bedchamber and would certainly overhear, upsetting her. One woman in the household becoming upset was enough.

"Meg Greaves took her own life, Owen," she said quietly, squinting against a cloud of dust swirling through the open window.

"Shoot. That's durned awful," he said. "Sorry, ma'am. That's awful."

"That it is," she replied, the wheels bumping over an uneven section of the rails, jostling her. Bloody awful.

"No wonder Mr. Greaves is so upset," Owen said, scooting back to the end of the bench because the rough ride kept sliding him into her broad black skirts and he was uncomfortable with the overfamiliar proximity. When they had first become acquainted, he'd clung to her like the mother he missed, the woman who'd abandoned him along with his father. Celia missed those days. "He's got to blame himself for her having had such a rough go."

Oh, how he does. "One might think it is not so terrible to live out here, along the edge of the city."

"I'd like it, ma'am," he said. "But then I'm not a young lady on her own."

"Possibly lost and afraid."

Owen lapsed into a mournful silence and peered out the window. The scenery beyond flowed in sandy swells toward the western hills, where houses, some grand and others not so much, became fewer and farther apart. Space to breathe, Nicholas might say. Air that smelled of pasture, sagebrush, and sometimes of the sea. Not of manure or sewers after a long dry spell or of a nearby tannery. This was not the first occasion that Celia had traveled to this area. Once was to a racetrack with Nicholas, not far from the fresh breezes of the ocean, to investigate a different murder only a few months ago. Years earlier, she'd visited Willows Gardens with Patrick, when he'd still been feverish with the thrill of recently moving to San Francisco and keen to see all the sights. Still happy. Still in love with her. He'd wanted an evening's pleasant entertainment. To take a ride on the merry-go-round or have a cooked meal in the shade of the trees. Or have a drink at the liquor saloon. His primary goal, as it turned out. All of which had cost dear and had provoked an argument. One of many they increasingly had.

"As nice as it is, something had to have gone wrong that made her want to keep moving around, Mrs. Davies," Owen said. "So bad that she ended up . . . you know . . ."

"Yes, Owen," she said. "I do wonder how she was earning her way." The possible answers were unsettling.

"Mr. Greaves said that the housekeeper who oversees the place out here told him that she'd had a job as a saleswoman," he replied. "In a mantilla maker's place. No, wait. I think Mr. Greaves said it was a dry goods place. Or maybe an auction house."

"Ah." Not as bad as she'd feared.

"Apparently she'd lived in several other places, but she didn't stay long at any of them," he added. "She must've been keen to get away from whatever was bothering her."

Or whoever.

"I might've learned more from the housekeeper if Mr. Greaves had let me talk to her, but he didn't let me get anywhere near the house. Wait." Owen leaned over to point out the window. "Is that the Mission Woolen Mills?"

The mills' sprawling hulk lay ahead, its multistory wood and brick buildings occupying several acres and manufacturing the finest—or so they declared—blankets and flannels. Items produced by the Chinese laborers who occupied the ramshackle lodgings clustered on one side of the grounds. "Yes, it is."

"We're close, then. We need to stop at the next street."

Was there a risk, making enquiries out here? Nosing about, as some might describe her actions. "Was this the place where she died, Owen? Do you know?"

"I got the impression she was found in a ratty hotel close by the cribs near the docks, ma'am. Shortly after moving from here."

"I'll not inquire how it is you are familiar with the location of the town brothels, Owen," she said, making him blush. "Why did Mr. Greaves not go to the hotel to ask questions?"

"I take it he did, but she wasn't there long enough for anybody to get to know her."

"I see."

"What are we looking to ask about, Mrs. Davies?" he asked, getting to his feet.

"Excellent question," she said. "We need to find anyone who knew Meg when she lived here. Hopefully we shall succeed where Mr.

Greaves failed."

"We can do it, ma'am."

"I pray you are correct, Owen," she replied. "Our goal, then, is to discover the reason why someone held on to four-year old letters until recently, when they were sent to Mr. Greaves. With a mysterious warning attached."

"A warning?"

"Which is why we must help Mr. Greaves with this investigation. That warning." Smiling up at him, she shook off any misgivings and stood. "So, if you are ready, lead the way."

CHAPTER 4

"I need you and Mullahey to go back to the docks to ask about the man with the missing fingers," Nick said, striding along the sidewalk. "We need a name for him."

Taylor, who'd paused to light a cigar, scurried to catch up. "They're probably tired of seeing us, sir. Mr. Greaves."

"Maybe in their irritation they'll actually tell you something, just to get rid of you."

Nick paused at the intersection. Taylor would be heading east to the shorefront. Nick had a *lagerbier* saloon to visit. A saloon that was not too far from the police station, just beyond the Barbary, and not a typical one for Mr. Loomis to visit, according to him. Except on Friday, at Eckart's request.

"Are you planning on going to Bauman's, sir?" Taylor asked.

"That is where I'm heading."

"Oh."

His assistant sounded disappointed. Nick understood why. Mina worked at Bauman's. At one time, he'd almost believed himself in love with her. Mina was beautiful—dark-haired, lush-lipped, smooth-skinned—and good company. Caring, when he'd most needed compassion, after he'd returned from the war and his convalescence in an Army hospital. When he'd discovered Meg was dead. When he'd needed more healing than any one person could provide. She'd been rash to have ever fallen for him, and it wasn't like her to be rash. He'd been avoiding Mina, but he should have figured that that situation would not last.

"Listen, Taylor, I simply need to find out if Mina or Bauman or even Mrs. Bauman has ever encountered the man with the missing fingers. Learn what they know about either him or Eckart. That's the only reason I'm going," Nick said, annoyed that he had to explain, to defend himself. He deserved the look in Taylor's eyes, though. He hadn't always been the most decent of men. The war had nearly robbed him of honor. "Not because I've got a hankering to see Mina Cascarino again."

"That makes sense, sir."

"I'll see you later at the station."

Nick turned down the street he'd strolled dozens of times before.

The door to the basement saloon, accessed down a short flight of stone steps, stood open. It was nearly midday, and he expected Mrs. Bauman was already at work frying wurst in the tiny kitchen beyond the main room.

Nick crossed the threshold, his eyes taking a few seconds to adjust to the dimness inside; the gas lamps suspended from the tin ceiling hadn't been lit yet, leaving a lone lantern to do the work.

Bauman, a barrel-chested German with a booming voice, was cleaning tables. This was a nicer saloon than most of the ones Nick had ever been inside, its reputation a result of the saloonkeeper's high standards. The cleanliness extended to the floor, which Nick's boot soles didn't stick to.

Bauman heard Nick's footsteps and looked over. "Detective Greaves," he stated without his usual broad smile. "It is a long time since we have seen you here."

He hadn't been in since last fall, when Nick had suspected Mina and another of Bauman's female employees, a singer, in the murder of an aspiring politician. The newspapers hadn't been kind to Adolph Bauman and his *lagerbier* saloon, and his business had been affected by the unfriendly reports by the press. All of which explained Bauman's scowl.

"It has been," he said. "Didn't think you'd welcome me."

Bauman didn't refute Nick's comment.

"Mina does not work here any longer," he said, taking his damp rag over to the bucket sitting on top of the walnut bar.

"I didn't know." Why should he, though? It's not like Mina stopped in the station to chat with him on a regular basis. Or ever.

Bauman grunted a response. "I only hire men to work for me now. The police were always in here, asking if the women were serving beer or dancing instead of just singing. Questioning if I was breaking the law." He glanced over at the corner of the saloon. The piano that had once stood there was gone.

"I didn't anticipate that officers would start harassing you after that case, Bauman."

He tossed the dripping rag into the bucket, soapy water splashing over the edge. "Maybe not, but they did anyway."

And Bauman blamed him.

"I should visit her parents. See how she is doing." They lived next door to Celia, ironically. He hoped Mina had landed on her feet. Losing this job would've been devastating.

"She will not want you to."

"No. She won't."

Bauman eyed him. "So you can leave now, Detective Greaves."

"I didn't come here just to speak with Mina." But he *had* wanted to see her. Damn, but he had. And not simply because Mina, who seemed to be friends with most of the people who worked in the saloons and taverns in this neighborhood, might have a name for the man with the damaged right hand. Maybe his feelings were more complex when it came to Mina Cascarino than he cared to admit to himself. "You might be able to help me with an investigation."

"Why might I help you?" he asked angrily.

Mrs. Bauman had left the kitchen to stand in its doorway. She spoke to her husband in German, "Adolph" and "Herr Greaves" the only words Nick could understand. He didn't have to understand her words, though, to recognize that she was scolding her husband. Whatever she'd said worked, because Bauman stopped scowling and she went back to her stove.

The saloonkeeper sighed. "What do you want?"

"Thank you, Herr Bauman." Nick crossed the room to lean against the bar. "Have you ever heard of a man named Sylvanus Eckart? His friends call him Sy. He came in here on Friday night, I've been told. With a man named Loomis."

"Sy Eckart?" he asked. "The name is not one I remember hearing. He might have been here on Friday. I do not know."

Not as regular a customer as Loomis believed, then.

"What about a fellow, average size, who's missing some fingers on his right hand?" Nick held up his hand to demonstrate, making a stab at which were the correct fingers to fold under as if they'd been chopped off. "I was told he was also here on Friday, along with Eckart and Loomis. Do you remember him coming in?"

Maybe a meeting with this fellow was the reason Eckart had come here, Loomis acting as an unwitting form of protection or a witness. Having somebody with him that night hadn't stopped Eckart from getting killed, though.

"He drinks here now and then. He is not the sort of fellow I want in my saloon. Dirty. Rough. I do not like how he looks," he answered.

"He may have been here on Friday, but I do not remember."

"Do you happen to know his name?" Nick hunted through his pockets for a scrap of paper that he never had on him, relying on Taylor to be prepared. He did find a pencil, which wasn't going to do much good by itself.

"I do not," said Bauman. "He usually has no friends with him, so no one calls out to him for me to hear a name."

"No friends?" So, he didn't come here to meet up with his compadres, since it sounded like the fellow didn't have any. Which made Nick wonder why he chose to drink at Bauman's. The pleasantness of the surroundings? The wurst Mrs. Bauman cooked up? Or did he come in here looking for Nick, who very much used to be a regular customer? Hoping to deliver a warning in person. Instead of scribbled on a piece of paper.

"Does this fellow ever speak with any of your waiters?" Nick asked. "Somebody who might know his name?"

Bauman's frown deepened. "He liked Mina. When she was still with me."

Damn. He was going to have to talk to her, after all.

• • •

"*This* is the house that Mr. Greaves visited, Owen?"

Celia eyed the home from the dirt road. It was an attractive building—white, two stories, a portico that stretched the length of the front and offered shade to anyone seated beneath it, somewhat Spanish in appearance—with a picket fence and an expanse of sandy grass between her and it. The house was not quite what she'd envisioned when she'd thought of where a wretched, despairing Meg might live during what would turn out to be the final months of her life. Instead, it was not grand but not hardscrabble, either, and situated across from a vegetable farm, which offered an agreeable vista of tidy green rows of plants. A scattering of conveyances traveled the dirt roads in the vicinity, their wheels spinning up dust. Smoke gently billowed from the distant stacks protruding from the Mission Woolen Mills. And the three-story classical façade of the stately Deaf and Blind Asylum rose from the landscaped grounds of a nearby lot. A pleasant location, actually.

"Yes, Mrs. Davies. It's the house."

"It confounds me how Meg Greaves managed to find herself out here. Four years ago there would have been far less activity than we now see, Owen, and few houses." The noise, the smells, the commotion of the city encroaching ever nearer. "Distant from the work situation she had in town. Inconvenient."

"Maybe she found the place based on a rental advertisement in the newspaper, ma'am," he said.

"Perhaps."

"It's a fine-looking place, ain't . . . isn't it, Mrs. Davies?" Owen admired the structure from beneath the brim of his cap, which cast a shadow across his freckled cheeks. "Don't think she lived in the main house, though, but in a small building off to the side along with other folks. Not sure exactly, because Mr. Greaves was pretty angry when he was finished talking to the woman who'd answered the door and didn't have much to say on the way back into town."

"As you have expressed confidence in our ability to get answers, Owen, let us discover what we can learn." Celia headed toward the fence gate. Fortune favored the bold, as the saying went. Even if she was not feeling bold, at the moment. But the sun had driven off the morning's clouds, and the air smelled fresh and clean, and she was taking courage from it all.

Reckless courage, perhaps.

"Have you figured out how you're going to explain why you're asking questions?" Owen asked, trotting after her.

"I shall inform them that I am her cousin, visiting San Francisco from Pennsylvania to search for the young relative I'd lost touch with and have been so worried about." Pretending to be a distant relation had worked before. Sometimes not always fully successfully, she had to admit. "I cannot give my real name, as I unfortunately have become rather well known through the various articles about me in the newspapers."

"But if you've been so worried about Miss Greaves, ma'am, you took an awful long time getting to San Francisco to visit her," Owen pointed out. Wisely.

"I shall explain my delay by claiming that I have been in mourning for my husband. Which is not precisely a lie." Celia indicated her black dress with the sweep of her hand. "Prior to that, I had to remain at his bedside to tend to him in his lengthy illness, which is why so many years have passed before I could make the journey west."

"You sure that story's gonna do the trick?"

No. "What is the worst that can happen if I am not believed?"

Owen's expression shifted as his brain sorted through a variety of outcomes, some of which might be unpleasant, or downright perilous.

"Should I go with you?" he asked.

"Did anyone at the house observe you with Mr. Greaves?" The twitch of a ground-floor window curtain indicated that they had been spotted, so it was likely too late for her to suggest that Owen keep out of sight.

"Since I didn't go to the door with him, they might not have."

Good. "Perhaps while I am asking questions at the house, you can speak with that young man over there." She indicated a teenaged boy who'd wandered out into the field of lettuces and cabbages with a hoe. "Learn if he had ever met Meg Greaves or knew of her. Knew of any friends who may have been trusted enough to be given a packet of her letters for safekeeping."

"I'll get right on that, Mrs. Davies."

He dashed off and Celia pushed open the gate. She strode up the graveled path, climbed the short flight of wood steps, and paused in front of the door, painted to imitate black walnut.

Courage, Celia. Courage.

She knocked and a slim woman with severely parted hair, streaks of gray among the brown, answered. She wore a simple gown of green check, tailored well. A servant or the mistress of the house?

"Might I help you, ma'am?"

"Yes. Perhaps you can do." Celia tried to see past her, into the passageway beyond, but the woman's body blocked most of the view. "I am searching for Margaret Greaves or anyone who knows anything about her. When last I received a correspondence from her, she gave me this address."

She perked an eyebrow. "She did, did she?"

"Well, yes, she did," Celia replied. "Although it has been many years—"

"Four, by my reckoning."

A woman familiar enough with Meg Greaves to know that.

"Oh, dear. Has it been that long? I suppose it has been," she said. "Perhaps I have already failed in my mission, then. I've come a great distance, you see, in search of my cousin. All the way from Pennsylvania, where I had been living with my husband, who passed away a few months ago after a lengthy illness."

She folded her arms. "Did you, now."

"Do you know where I might find Meg?"

"I'm sorry to break bad news to you, Mrs. . . . ."

"Mrs. Walford." Celia's maiden name. She'd made use of that ruse before, too.

"Sorry to tell you, Mrs. Walford, but your cousin died four years ago."

Celia gasped and pressed a palm to her open mouth. "I had no idea. She never indicated in her letters that she was unwell."

"From my understanding, her death was sudden."

"Illness? An accident?"

"Sudden," the woman said and pursed her lips, unwilling to gossip about the real reason for Miss Greaves's death.

Celia lowered her hand. "Now I comprehend why I did not hear from her in all this time," she said. "Poor girl. Poor, poor Meg. So young."

"I'm surprised her brother didn't inform you of her passing. He'd be your cousin too, right?" the woman asked, her gaze scanning Celia again.

"Her brother and I are . . . estranged," Celia claimed, retrieving a handkerchief from her reticule. She daubed the corner of her eye to clear away nonexistent tears. She used to feel guilty over the ease with which she could play-act while interrogating witnesses or suspects. It was a trifle unnerving that she no longer did. "And I have so little family left. I should be gracious with him, but the circumstances are difficult."

The woman appeared to accept her explanation. "He came by here last week," she said. "Asking questions about Miss Greaves just like you are. Looking for friends of hers who may have been trying to contact him recently."

"Oh? How very odd of him to do that."

"I couldn't help him out."

"Is there anyone here I can speak with who might have known Meg or been with her in her final days?" Celia asked. "I may be able to draw comfort in my grief by learning she was happy in her life."

The woman's expression tightened. At least she did not lie and pretend that Meg had been happy. "None of the staff who were with us at that time are with us any longer, Mrs. Walford."

"But you were here, Miss . . . might I ask your name?"

The woman hesitated before answering. "Mrs. Victor."

"Thank you, Mrs. Victor, for taking the time to answer all my questions," Celia said, offering an apologetic smile. "You were here when Meg was."

"Yes, but I didn't know her more than is polite between staff and our renters."

"Ah. Of course. I would like to locate and speak with her beau, at least," she said, tucking away her handkerchief. Total conjecture, albeit a reasonable guess, that the relationship between Meg and the dead man found with her locket was a romantic one. "They had been so in love, and I'd imagined the reason why I could not find Meg's name in the city directory when I arrived was that they had moved away. How wrong I was."

"I am surprised her brother didn't also ask about her having a fellow. He wanted to find everybody and anybody else."

At the time, Nicholas had not known to. But Mrs. Victor's response had proven Celia's guess to be a correct one.

"Had you ever met her sweetheart?" she asked. "Wait. How foolish of me to ask. Of course you'd not have done. You only had a passing relationship with my cousin."

"I've seen him once or twice. Recently, too. Not two weeks ago," she answered. "I was helping prepare for a luncheon Mrs. Chase was hosting and he showed up at their house on California Street. Wanting to speak with Mr. Chase. Urgently."

Well, then. This is news. Her pulse ticked upward and her skin tingled with the excitement she often felt during an investigation.

"Who are the Chases?" she asked.

Mrs. Victor's gaze narrowed. *I should know who they are, apparently, if I am Meg's cousin.*

"Your cousin used to work for Mr. Chase, Mrs. Walford," she replied, her tone as wary as her gaze. "At his auction house. The Chases own this house and used to live here, until a couple of months ago. Mrs. Chase got tired of living out in the wilderness, as she refers to this area, and wanted a place nearer the city. They have a new home up on California near Larkin."

A desirable location on the southwest flank of the California Street hill. The prosperous of the city were eyeing the area to raise their grand homes, once access to the hilltop was improved. If Celia were offered the choice, however, she would prefer this spot. Where one could breathe.

"How silly of me to have forgotten, Mrs. Victor. But then, this has all been such a shock," she said. "I confess I am curious why Meg's beau came looking for Mr. Chase recently. So long after my cousin's death. Did he and Mr. Chase have business together?"

The woman barked a laugh. "Business? Mr. Chase and some seaman off a ship?"

He *had* to have been the man fished out of the bay yesterday. "Then what could he have possibly wanted?"

"No idea, Mrs. Walford. I didn't hear more than a few words of the conversation he had with Mrs. Chase. I was busy and had to get back to the kitchen," she said. "Furthermore, Mrs. Chase got rid of him quickly. He was loud and agitated. A bother to the household."

Agitated. "Do you know his name, by any chance? I would like to contact him."

"A Mr. Eckart. That's what I recall."

An interesting recollection for a woman who was barely acquainted with Meg Greaves. "And there is no one else here who could speak with me about Meg?"

From the depths of the house came a shout. The voice of an irate woman, whose summons made Mrs. Victor flinch. "Afraid not, Mrs. Walford. Nobody."

"Perhaps I might gain more information from an employee of Mr. Chase's. Someone who worked alongside Meg," Celia said, sensing that her welcome, meager as it had been, was reaching its end. "Might I have more luck at his new home? Or perhaps at his auction house? As I've mentioned, I would like to better understand Meg's last days, even though it is far too late to help her."

"I'd recommend you not bother Mr. Chase at either of those places, Mrs. Walford." She clasped the edge of the door, readying to close it.

"Why? I merely mean to enquire after my poor deceased cousin. Why might Mr. Chase take issue with questions about Meg?"

Mrs. Victor scoffed. "If you try to talk to him, you'll find out.

Good day," she stated. And slammed the door.

A dismissal that was all too typical.

• • •

"C'mon, you can talk to me," Owen pleaded with the kid. He'd been trudging after him, crisscrossing the plot of lettuce without learning hardly nothing. Anything. "Honest you can."

The kid, whose name was Joe, grunted. He seemed to prefer to do that over speaking actual words. Although Owen had managed to learn his name, which was something. He did hope Mrs. Davies was having more success at the house, though.

"All I want to know is if you remember a girl named Meg who used to live over there." Owen pointed the general direction of the house. "Four years ago or so."

Joe, who had a flat-nosed face beneath his big straw hat, stopped scratching at weeds with his hoe and straightened. "Why might I recollect a girl from four years ago who used to live at the Chases' old place?"

They'd gone over this a few times already, and Owen was starting to feel like a horse being ringed, going around and around while Joe was the fellow holding the long lead in the middle of the corral. A good investigator wouldn't allow the questioning to happen this way. He would've gotten answers already.

"Because you've admitted you lived here then." Owen had said that a few times, too.

"I don't talk to folks about stuff like that." He scratched his nose with the rounded end of the hoe's handle. "And I shouldn't be talking to you, neither."

"Stuff like what?"

"I gotta get back to work before my pa gets mad I'm not finished yet." Joe started hacking at the dirt between the rows of lettuce.

"Listen, Joe, a friend of mine . . ." He wouldn't mention that his friend was a cop. Or that Mr. Greaves was Meg's sister. "A friend of mine who used to be a friend of hers got some of her old letters recently, and he's just trying to figure out who it was who sent them. To thank them, you see?" He also wouldn't mention that the message that had accompanied the letters had sounded sorta threatening, according to Mrs. Davies. Then Joe would button up for sure.

"I don't know anybody at that house. Why would I? I'm just a farmer's kid."

"But what about the servants? You must've talked with them at some point. You live across the road." Shoot, Owen had had a word or two with just about everybody who lived in his lodging house as well as a lot of the fellows who passed on the sidewalk outside it. It was downright unfriendly not to talk to folks you saw all the time.

"Nope," Joe said but he didn't look at Owen while he said it.

Owen hopped across the row of lettuce and marched to where he could face Joe directly, instead of talking to his bent back. "Joe. My friend really wants to find this friend of Meg's who's trying to contact him but stopped for some reason. It's really important and I'd like to help him out." Owen leaned down to stare Joe in the face, his eyes hidden by the brim of his hat. "So can you help me? What 'stuff' aren't you supposed to talk about?"

Joe looked up. "It ain't smart to be askin' questions about the Chases."

"Why's that? Are they criminals or something?"

"Did you hear what I said?"

Barely. Joe mumbled when he wasn't grunting. "Of course I did. But all I'm doing is trying to find friends of Meg's and that doesn't seem to be a question about the Chases. Not exactly."

Joe—who had crossed eyes, Owen realized—was staring at him. "He's dangerous and somebody died because of him."

Owen's pulse skipped a beat. Or a bunch of beats. "Who died, Joe? Who?"

"Somebody. And it's better not to ask any questions about it, according to my pa," he said. "So you just need to go away. That's the only smart thing to do when it comes to the Chases. Just go away and leave them alone."

✄ CHAPTER 5 ✗

"She is not here, Mr. Greaves." Behind the screen of his thick mustache, Mr. Cascarino's mouth was set in a deep scowl. His dark eyes were scowling too, if that were possible. "You can go."

Mina's father stood on his porch with Nick, the front door firmly closed at his back, his arms crossed. Bauman wasn't the only one unhappy with Nick. But if Mr. Cascarino refused to tell him where Mina was, Nick was confident he could get one of the younger Cascarino children to confess. He'd have to find a way to get to them, though, with Mr. Cascarino guarding the door like a mastiff.

"Not here?" he asked, studying the street-facing windows. A black-haired girl looking to be four or five years old peered from inside the parlor to his right. Her mother's firm command, issued in Italian, jerked her back from the window. "She does still live here, doesn't she?"

"*Sì*. But not here now."

"Where can I find her then, Mr. Cascarino? It's important," Nick said impatiently. "She might be able to help us locate a fellow I'm searching for. A man who I believe has information on a murder."

"She is not to be involved with you anymore."

The statement referred to more than Nick's police investigations. "I need to speak with her, Mr. Cascarino. Please. We're trying to locate a fellow who used to chat with her when she worked at Bauman's. An acquaintance of his was pulled out of the bay yesterday with bullet holes in his back. Do you understand?"

"I speak English, Mr. Greaves," he snapped.

"This same fellow delivered a package of my deceased sister's letters to my landlady recently, along with a warning for me," Nick explained. "You have to realize how serious this all is, Mr. Cascarino. How much it means to me to figure out what's going on."

He didn't respond, but his scowl softened. Maybe Nick was getting somewhere with him. Maybe.

"I need Mina's help. I need *your* help. Please," Nick repeated, not usually one to beg.

"I will tell her you were here. That is all I can promise." He spun about and charged inside with an agility Nick didn't realize the man possessed.

Damn.

Reseating his hat, he descended the steps and glanced over at the house next door. Celia's house. Fate always had liked to play games with him, but to put the two of them side by side like this was almost cruel. He should go over and apologize, though, for having been curt with her at the station yesterday. For letting the obvious concern on her face frighten him. It scared him, having her care so much.

Addie Ferguson, carrying a long-handled corn broom, stepped out onto the porch. She noticed Nick staring at the house from the sidewalk.

"Mr. Greaves," she called out.

Too late to walk away now, Greaves.

He walked over and climbed the steps. "Is Celia in her clinic, Miss Ferguson?"

She cleared her throat and took to swiping the broom across the porch. "No."

"All right, you can tell me where she is."

"She isna home," she said, the rhythm of the broom increasing speed, bristles breaking off and creating more for her to sweep. "'Tis all I know."

"Are you sure? Because you're acting guilty, which means you know exactly where she's gone and it's someplace I won't be happy about."

She shot him a hasty glance. "She didna tell me exactly where, Mr. Greaves."

"Did she take her black portmanteau with her?" The bag she carried her medical supplies in when she visited her patients.

"Um . . ."

"She didn't, did she? No, she did not." Nick exhaled. "Do I need to send Taylor after her to make sure she's not getting herself into trouble?"

"Oh, no, Mr. Greaves. You dinna have to send him. She took Owen with her," she said, as if a skinny teenaged boy was adequate protection. Cassidy meant well, but he wasn't Taylor. "You've nae need to frown at me, Mr. Greaves. I'm nae more content about matters than you are, but you canna stop her when she gets an idea in her head."

"Don't I know it," he said. "But since you're being secretive, I'm forced to conclude she's off investigating."

Addie resumed sweeping.

Great. "And you're not going to tell me where she is."

"If Mrs. Davies wanted you to know where she'd gone, she'd have left a message for you."

That was true.

She straightened, her fist tightly gripping the broom handle. "Now I've a wee question for *you*, Mr. Greaves," she said. "Why were you next door at the Cascarinos'?"

"I'm looking for Mina. Not for personal reasons," he added hastily.

"Weel, 'tis glad I am to hear that," she said. "Because Jer—Mr. Taylor and I do get to fretting over you. And that poor lass."

"Wait, what did you almost say?" Nick didn't know his assistant's first name, only ever seeing 'J. E. Taylor' on official documents. "Taylor's first name. What is it?"

She perked her chin, copying a habit of Celia's. "If he hasna told you, 'tis because he doesna want you to know, Mr. Greaves. Any more than Mrs. Davies wants you to know where she's gone."

"Obviously." He liked to believe that he and Taylor were on friendlier terms, but his assistant had yet to break the habit of calling Nick "sir." "I'm looking for Mina because she might know the name of a suspect in the murder I'm investigating. The one Celia is also prying into."

"She isna 'prying,' Mr. Greaves. She is helping you."

Which he might welcome if "helping" didn't put her in harm's way so often. "Tell Celia I came by and that I'd like to hear whatever it is she and Cassidy have learned while they're out helping me."

"Should I also tell her you were looking for Miss Cascarino?"

"I'm looking for anybody who can give me the name of a scruffy fellow missing several fingers on his right hand who used to be a customer at Bauman's. Who also was a friend of Sylvanus Eckart's, the dead man found in the bay yesterday," he replied. "That's what you can tell her."

"Weel. I shall do that, then."

"Good day, Miss Ferguson." He descended the stairs and charged up the road. Without Mina's assistance, who knew how long it would take to find the damned fellow with the missing fingers. Time he didn't want to spend.

"Signor Greaves!" A young boy, his cap pulled tight over his thick dark hair, was chasing after him. He nimbly dodged a break in the sidewalk planks, avoiding tripping. "Signor Greaves!"

Nick stopped to wait for him to catch up. He was fairly certain the kid was one of the Cascarino children. He couldn't remember his name, though.

"Yes?" he asked when the boy, breathless, reached him.

"You look for my sister."

"If you mean Mina, I am."

"I can tell you where she works." He glanced over his shoulder in the direction of his house. None of the other Cascarinos appeared to have realized he'd sprinted after Nick, and he relaxed. "She sells . . ." He gestured at his head, then tugged on a strand of his hair.

"She sells hair? Oh, you mean she sells wigs." Quite a change from singing in Bauman's. Undoubtedly safer, though. Her parents must be relieved; they never had liked her job at the saloon, where she met all types of men. Some missing fingers. Others like Nick. "Where at?"

"I show you."

Nick extended a hand. "After you."

Won't Mina be surprised to see me. He only hoped she didn't scream.

• • •

"Joe told you that somebody died because of Mr. Chase?" Celia asked Owen. She kept her voice low, as they appeared to have garnered a substantial amount of curiosity from a fellow seated across the way. He must have excellent hearing, able to catch her words over the rumbling of the horsecar. Or she had exclaimed too loudly when Owen had initially relayed what Joe had said. Likely the latter.

Owen cast a glance at the fellow, who was pretending to be reading a newspaper, before answering. "He did, Mrs. Davies. He made it sound like Mr. Chase is a dangerous criminal."

"Joe was likely exaggerating, Owen, in order to encourage you to leave."

"He didn't act like he was exaggerating, ma'am," Owen said. "He's genuinely afraid of them, I think, and piped down pretty quickly after telling me, like he was gonna get whipped for having let the cat out of the bag."

He clutched the edge of the seat to stop from sliding into Celia as they rattled along Howard. Soon, they'd make the turn that would take them to Sansome. The bench was no more comfortable on the return trip than it had been on the way out, tempting Celia to recommend they disembark once they crossed Market at the heart of the city. But then she'd have a long walk uphill to reach home.

"And if Mrs. Victor also told you to not bother the Chases, doesn't that mean Joe was telling the truth?" he asked.

"Perhaps. But I wonder who he meant, and when this supposed death occurred," she said. "*If*—and I mean *if*—what Joe claimed is true and not merely malicious hearsay."

"He must've meant the fellow found dead in the bay, ma'am. Don't you think?"

That had been her first thought, too. But she must not jump to conclusions. "*If*, Owen. Who or what Joe meant is complete conjecture at this point."

"Oh," he replied, dejected.

"I do need to inform Mr. Greaves of Joe's comment," she said. "But I believe I shall also speak with Mrs. Hutchinson about the Chases. Discover what she knows about them. If they are considered to be dangerous criminals or merely the unfortunate subjects of jealous gossip."

Jane Hutchinson could unearth the most deeply buried nut of information when she set her mind to it.

"Could you . . ." Color rose in Owen's cheeks, obscuring his freckles. "Could you, um, maybe ask Mrs. Hutchinson if Miss Grace ever asks about me? I mean, I know she's busy at that ladies' academy she goes to, and all. So I guess I shouldn't expect much."

Celia smiled softly at him, remembering the aches and longings of her own first infatuation. She'd been around the same age as Owen and no more wise.

"I am confident Grace thinks of you often, Owen," she said, though Grace Hutchinson, beloved daughter of a well-off real estate developer, possibly did not. Why add to his aches?

"Ask anyway, okay?"

"I shall." She glanced at the man reading the newspaper, who'd folded it closed and appeared to be dozing, his heavy chin drooping over his shirt collar. "Aside from Mrs. Victor's warning to not ask the Chases questions, she told me that Meg's former beau—his name is Mr. Eckart, by the way—showed up at their new, and likely more impressive, residence on California Street. Recently. Wanting to speak with Mr. Chase."

"Recently, huh?" he asked, excited again like a bloodhound locating a fresh scent.

"Curious, do you not agree?" she asked. "More curious is the timing, so close to when Mr. Greaves received those packets of his sister's letters." So close to his own death, as well. Perhaps Joe had been referring to Mr. Eckart's murder.

No jumping to conclusions, Celia.

The horsecar slowed to collect a handful of passengers, who climbed aboard and made their way down the center aisle past Celia and Owen. One of the men took in her black widow's weeds and tipped his hat. A far more polite reaction than the smirks she occasionally received when she traveled with her medical bag.

Owen scratched the back of his neck as Mr. Taylor tended to do when he was perplexed. "But what does this all mean, Mrs. Davies?"

"That I need to collect more information, Owen. Not only about the Chases, but about Meg's final days, as well."

• • •

"Here it is, Signor Greaves." The Cascarino boy stopped in front of a store on Washington, located a few blocks south of where he and his family lived, and waved at the sign painted on the door.

Atwood Bros. Wig and Toupee Makers. A selection of their wares—wiglets in black and brown and red and even gray, cascades of curls a lady could attach to her own hair to supplement what she had, and toupees of various sizes to cover unsightly bald spots—was on display in the window. Maybe he should tell Loomis about the goods available for sale.

Nick squinted through the glass. He didn't spot Mina inside. "You sure?"

"I am sure. She works here." The kid looked expectantly at Nick.

"I suppose you want some money for your assistance." He hunted around in his pockets for his coin purse and pulled out a nickel. "Here. I'd thank you properly, but you haven't reminded me what your name is."

"Angelo."

"Thank you, Angelo. You going to be okay making your way back home alone?"

He stuck out his thin chest, straining the buttons of his wool vest, which looked to have been bought or made for him when he was younger and smaller. "I am seven years old."

"In that case, why aren't you in school?"

Angelo snatched the nickel from Nick's hand and sprinted off.

Drawing in a breath, he squared his shoulders and eased open the door. The shop bell let out a weak ding, not loud enough to alert the woman assisting a customer examining a collection of wigs. The place smelled pungent from hair salves—sold to those who hadn't given up on trying to regrow their own and weren't interested in a wig yet—and the medicinal tang of Bully's Toilet Vinegar, bottles of which were arrayed on a nearby counter. He'd always thought Bully's stank like it was meant to chase off bugs rather than be used as a perfume.

"This particular wig is made of German hair, ma'am, which is the best available," the saleswoman, her back to Nick, was explaining. Her thick, dark hair—not artificially enhanced by any of the products on offer in this place—was neatly arranged in elaborate braids that coiled at the nape of her neck. Elaborate for her, when she never used to make time for such fussiness. "You can see how fine the hair is, and it is purchased at great expense. Thirty dollars a pound."

"Which explains the cost of the wig," the customer sniffed, rubbing the strands between her fingers. The woman's bonnet was pulled tightly about her head and hid any of her own hair. Maybe she'd had a fever and lost a lot of it. "But another person's hair . . ." She shuddered.

"I can assure you that the hair was thoroughly washed and is completely free of any insects or the like."

The woman frowned. "But how can I afford twenty dollars?"

"Perhaps Mr. Atwood will be willing to offer you a discount, ma'am. As a special customer," she said. "Would you like me to fetch him?"

"If you would." The customer glanced over at Nick with a confused smile. He'd removed his hat, which showed he wasn't in the store because he was in search of a toupee. "And then you can help your other customer there."

"Customer?" Mina turned to face the door. And glared. At least she didn't scream. He'd apologized several times for how he'd treated her when they were still together. Maybe she'd finally forgiven him. "Let me fetch Mr. Atwood," she said to her customer and marched off into a back room.

"Oh. My," said the woman with the head-hugging bonnet. "That was rude."

"Not to worry, ma'am. Miss Cascarino and I are old acquaintances."

She eyed him speculatively. "I see."

Mina returned with Mr. Atwood. A short fellow with a heavy thatch of blond hair—real or an advertisement for the products he sold?— and a drooping mustache, he hurried over to the woman. Mina gave Nick a black look and made for the back room again. Nope. She hadn't forgiven him.

"Miss Cascarino," he called out, striding across the store after her. The scent of her tuberose perfume floated in the air. Some things would never change about her—her ready temper when it came to him and that intoxicating aroma.

"Excuse me, sir." Mr. Atwood intercepted Nick before he reached the doorway she'd exited through. "You're not allowed back there."

"It's urgent I speak to Miss Cascarino, sir." He would pull out his badge, but he didn't want Mina's new boss thinking she was in trouble with the police. "A family matter."

"Oh?"

Nick fixed a worried look on his face. "It's her brother Angelo."

"Oh. Something bad? Well, then. I'll let her know." He disappeared behind the curtain and returned with Mina.

"Thank you, Mr. Atwood," she said, dismissing him. "What's happened to Angelo, Nick? Is it bad?"

She rested a hand on his arm, anxiety darkening her already deep brown eyes. He braced himself for the thrill that used to surge through his body when she touched him, even when that touch was only her slim fingers on his coat sleeve, and felt relief when it didn't occur.

"Is there someplace more private we can talk, Mina?"

She dropped her hand. "You haven't shown up because of Angelo, have you? I don't know why I thought you might have. My parents would never send *you* with news." She glanced past him toward Mr. Atwood and the customer. Likely trying to gauge how loud she could get without her employer hearing and getting upset. "What the hell do you want?" she hissed between her teeth. "And what do you mean, coming here? I have a new job, no thanks to you, and I'd like to keep it."

"No, no, Miss Cascarino. Your brother will be all right, I'm sure,"

Nick said at full volume, then lowered his voice. "A man has been murdered, Mina, and you might know the name of one of the last people to see him alive."

"I am not getting involved in another case of yours, Nick. The last one nearly ruined me."

"It's not *my* fault you were a suspect in that one," he said under his breath. "Please. Let's go outside and talk for a couple of minutes. That's all I'm asking."

"That's all?"

"That's all."

"You'd better not be lying to me, Nick. Any more than you've already lied about Angelo," she hissed and stepped around him. "Will you excuse me for a second, Mr. Atwood? I need to speak to Mr. Greaves about my brother. He has gotten in trouble at school again, it seems."

"I despair for the boy," Nick said, shaking his head.

He took Mina's elbow and guided her through the store and outside before Atwood thought to ask why he'd come to the store to discuss Angelo's supposed bad behavior at school rather than go to the Cascarinos' house to inform his parents.

"Make it fast, Nick. I really don't have time for you," she said once the front door had closed behind them.

"I'm looking for the name of a fellow who used to come into Bauman's. A man missing several fingers on his right hand," he said. "Herr Bauman told me the man used to try to strike up a conversation with you when you were still singing there."

She paused, possibly debating how giving him the information might benefit her, because he could tell she had information.

"Just tell me his name, Mina. The sooner you do, the sooner I'll be able to leave you alone."

She exhaled and scanned the street, busy with the usual traffic of a Tuesday afternoon. Men on horseback, wagons, pedestrians, a peddler hawking jewelry that he claimed was made of gold but was likely pinchbeck. Was Mina hunting for somebody to rescue her from having to talk to Nick, or simply trying to collect her thoughts?

"Raymond. His name is Raymond," she finally said. "I don't know if that's his first name or his last name, but that's how he introduced himself to me."

Raymond. Blast, he could really use Taylor right then. "What do you know about him?"

"Not much, except that he enjoyed pinching me."

"That's it?"

"All right. I think he works at a sawmill somewhere. He often had sawdust in his hair and on his clothes when he came in. And he was a bit deaf," she said. "But that's just my opinion. It's not like he ever told me what his occupation was."

"Did you ever see him with a man named Sylvanus Eckart? Sometimes called Sy?" he asked. "He was murdered late Friday, according to the coroner's best estimate. Raymond was in Bauman's that evening and so was Eckart."

"I don't remember if he ever came into the saloon with anybody, Nick," she said. "Raymond usually drank alone. No surprise. He wasn't the most pleasant person."

Bauman had said as much, too.

"If you're still friends with any of the waiters at Bauman's, could you find out if Raymond ever also talked to any of them? See what they might know about him? Him or Eckart?"

"I do not want to get involved, Nick. I'm sorry."

"It's important, Mina."

"Aren't all your cases important, Nick?" she asked, her eyes searching his face. "Isn't your work more important than anything else? Sure always seemed like it to me."

"You know how I am, Mina. I'm not going to pretend I could've ever acted differently." He could apologize—again—but why bother? "This case is personal, though. The man who was killed, Eckart, knew my sister Meg. And this Raymond fellow delivered a pile of her letters to my lodgings a couple weeks back. The two events are possibly connected, and I need to figure out what's going on. Before somebody else dies."

❧ CHAPTER 6 ❧

"I'm always flattered that you seek out my assistance when you have a case, Celia." Jane Hutchinson took the cup of tea—oolong, of course—which Celia offered and lowered herself onto the settee. "Thank you for the invitation."

Jane had chosen to wear a tawny-colored day dress that beautifully set off her coloring. She looked well, seemingly as recovered as she could be from the miscarriage she'd suffered in January. At least as far as external appearances were concerned, and perhaps an explanation for the choice of gown, expertly tailored and new. Fresh armor worn to fend off any probing questions about her health. However, as Celia was well aware from personal experience, the pain of the loss would never fully depart.

"You are welcome, but we both know Frank's opinion about my seeking out your help," Celia said. *I must be careful with Jane and not overtax her.* An investigation into murder was not a relaxing stroll in the park or an afternoon spent shop gazing. "He hates it—for good reason, since I have exposed you to danger in the past—and would be downright irate to learn that you find my requests 'flattering.'"

"Surprisingly, he's given up protesting, Celia. He didn't complain at all when I said I was coming here to visit you. Probably because he knows I need to escape the house," she said. "He's decided that all of our bedrooms must be refurbished, and the house is an uproar of paper hangers and painters. I welcome any excuse to get away from the noise. I've been so desperate, I even convinced Hetty to accompany me to see the whale on display at Long Bridge. Twenty-five cents to gaze on the poor dead creature captured out in the bay. It made Hetty ill and she begged off her work for the rest of the day because of her queasy stomach."

"Barbara's tutor took her to see the animal. They were equally unimpressed. And queasy," Celia said, pouring herself tea and settling onto the chair opposite Jane. "I expect that Frank did not complain because he is distracted by the paper hangers and painters. The instant the ruckus dies down and he has a moment of quiet in which to think, he'll resume protesting."

"Based on the pace of their work, that moment will be days and days in the future," Jane replied. "Who is it you want me to collect gossip about this time?"

"The Chases," Celia said, sipping from her tea. "As incredible as this will sound, Mr. Chase may be connected to a recent death. The murder of a man who was once in love, I believe, with Nicholas's sister Meg."

"Frank told me she took her own life. He heard the news when he returned from the war," Jane said quietly. "Not from Mr. Greaves, of course. He and Frank weren't speaking by that point."

They retained a *froideur* to this day, their relationship forever made frigid by the death of Frank's brother on the battlefield, which he blamed on Nicholas.

"Now it appears someone wishes to remind him of her and that terrible event," Celia said. "Two weeks ago he received a package of Meg's letters from an unknown individual. Mrs. Jewett came to see me yesterday to tell me about them. I am grateful to her, because Nicholas never did. She is worried about him."

"Letters? All these years later?"

She nodded. "Around the same time as the delivery of those letters, a man identified as her beau visited the Chases' house on California Street looking to speak with Mr. Chase," Celia continued. "Agitated was how his behavior was described to me. He was tossed out. And on Monday he was found shot and floating, dead, in the bay. A fellow named Mr. Sylvanus Eckart, according to what Mr. Greaves told Addie earlier today."

"But a visit by the fellow, even if he was agitated, doesn't seem to be enough proof that Mr. Chase is in any way responsible for his death," she observed.

"Perhaps not, but a neighbor's son informed Owen—he sends his best to Grace, by the way."

Jane gave a sad shake of her head. "Poor Owen," she said. "I will let her know."

"As I was saying, a neighbor's son informed Owen that his father believes that Mr. Chase is responsible for someone's death."

"That could be anybody, Celia. Or complete hearsay."

"Which is what I told Owen."

"Do you understand the connection between Mr. Chase and Mr. Eckart?"

"The only possible connection I have so far discovered comes through Meg Greaves herself," she answered. "She used to work for Mr. Chase at his auction house. Not that her work there links Mr. Eckart to Mr. Chase, I realize."

"Unless . . ." Jane frowned and set down her cup of tea. She'd not been drinking it, as it was. "Ah."

"You are wondering what I am wondering, I presume," Celia said. "If Mr. Chase had pursued an unwanted relationship with her." Forced himself on her, a vulnerable young woman in his employ.

"A sickening thought, but, yes," she replied. "And enough cause for animosity between Mr. Eckart and Mr. Chase. Except that it's not Mr. Chase who's dead, and many years have passed since any untoward behavior might have occurred."

"Mr. Eckart was a mariner of some sort." Celia speculatively tapped her fingernail against the teacup resting in her lap. "Perhaps he's been at sea and not had the opportunity until now to seek revenge. And perhaps Mr. Chase was able to defend himself before Mr. Eckart exacted that revenge."

"What does Mr. Greaves think?" Jane asked.

"I've not yet informed him about what Owen and I learned this morning." Celia had been too busy with the unplanned arrival of a patient to make a trip to the police station. "However, the person who'd sent him Meg's letters included a warning. This case could be dangerous for him." *And for me.*

"Then we shall be extremely cautious."

"Jane, all I want from you is whatever you know about the Chases," Celia said, regretting her impulse to involve Jane again. One day her friend would be seriously harmed.

"Not much, actually." Brow furrowed, she sipped her tea and collected her thoughts. "Mr. Chase, Archibald Chase, runs an auction house on Montgomery, as you've already learned. He and Mrs. Chase have a new house built on the southwestern edge of the California Street hill, which you also have learned. I gather it's sumptuously furnished and decorated."

"Filled with prime pickings from the contents of his auction house, no doubt." Other people's misfortunes his gain, and at a discounted price.

"I hear they own not one but two pianos!" Jane said. "They have four daughters, but the oldest three are married, so I don't understand why they need a house with a dozen rooms. In addition to a carriage house and stable on their large lot."

"You do know the wealthiest people, Jane. And I mean no insult by that observation."

She smiled in response. "Frank would like to move closer to where the Chases are. He claims that the hill their house abuts—presuming the hill isn't leveled as some folks have been clamoring to do—will become the most sought after real estate in San Francisco," she said. "However, I love our house and have no interest in moving. So he has resorted to refurbishing instead."

"This is all you know about the Chases?"

"No rumors that Mr. Chase may have caused somebody's death, if that's what you're asking, Celia."

"His former neighbor is not the only one sharing salacious tales and warnings about the Chases, Jane," Celia said. "A woman at their prior residence out by the Mission Woolen Mills strongly advised me to not ask them any questions."

"I haven't heard a peep that implies that either of them are murderous individuals," she replied. "And you'd think I would've heard something as sensational as a tale involving somebody mysteriously dying. Although I haven't attended many social events lately."

Celia set down her tea and leaned across the table toward Jane. "I am sorry. It is thoughtless of me to ask for your help. You are still recovering." She looked so well that Celia had momentarily forgotten about the baby Jane had lost.

"I do not mind. Honestly, Celia," she said, holding Celia's gaze and smiling to ease her concern. Celia sat back. "Your request does come at the perfect time, however."

"How so?"

"I've received an invitation to an entertainment that Mrs. Chase is hosting to raise money for one of her causes. She frequently hosts these sorts of entertainments, now that they've moved into their new house near town. This one is in support of the Society for the Prevention of Cruelty to Animals."

"The what?"

"It's an up-and-coming cause." Jane reached for one of the biscuits Addie had provided along with the oolong. "The benefit is scheduled for tomorrow night. I hadn't been planning on attending, but it's a perfect opportunity for you to meet her. I'd be happy to take you," she said and bit into the biscuit, careful to capture the crumbs with her plate.

"Are you certain?"

"Yes, I definitely am," she replied, once she'd finished her nibble. "I'll tell Frank I've changed my mind about attending. He won't question me about it."

"But you'll *not* tell him I am going with you."

Jane grinned, nearly as wickedly as Owen when he was feeling particularly devilish. "Now, Celia, there are some secrets worth keeping from my husband. And *that* would be one of them."

• • •

Nick sifted through the jumble of Meg's letters spread across his desk. He'd stopped at Mrs. Jewett's on the way back from Atwood's wig and toupee store to collect them, but bringing them to the station felt wrong. Worse than wrong. Downright sacrilegious to allow something so precious inside the detectives' room.

"Evidence in a case, Greaves?" O'Neal, the new officer, stacked some papers he'd been reviewing and tapped their edges on his desk to straighten the collection. He indicated the letters with a nod of his head. "What you're looking at there."

Nick had almost forgotten O'Neal was in the room with him, he'd been so absorbed in examining Meg's handwriting. Hoping that a clue might be found in the way she'd formed a particular *g* or had abbreviated a word. But there weren't any clues. And he was clutching at straws.

"Maybe," he said, sitting up straight. His back hurt from hunching over his desk too long. "Not sure."

"Might I help?" O'Neal offered.

Nick hastily swept Meg's letters into a pile. "Thanks, but that's all right. What case are you working on?"

"Looking into some smuggling." He finished tapping the stack of papers and set them down in a neat pile.

"Opium?" Nearly every week customs officers seized a supply of opium that folks had attempted to sneak into the city without paying the tariffs, jars and boxes hidden inside false-bottom crates or concealed beneath piles of imported rugs. "Or whiskey?"

"Fancy goods," he said. "Trying to figure out who's been receiving them in the city. The person's been elusive so far."

"Hope you catch them."

"I plan to," he said, full of confidence. Nick had been the same, in the beginning. "Would be quite a feather in my cap."

"Well, good luck."

"Thank you." O'Neal got to his feet. "No luck on your murder victim, though?"

"We're following some leads. We have a name for him and for a fellow seen with him the day he died."

"Heard he was a friend of your sister's."

Nick stiffened. Who in the station was talking with O'Neal about Meg? Mullahey? One of the other men? Not Taylor. He wouldn't. He knew how much pain having Meg's name bandied about would cause.

"Yes," he replied brusquely.

"It was awful, what happened. I met her once, and she seemed sweet," O'Neal said, ignoring the warning in Nick's voice. "Asa was broken up. Destroyed by her death. I'm sorry. I really am."

Not as much as I am. "Thank you."

"Your uncle once told me that her sweetheart hung around a rotten crowd. He worried about that."

Nick considered O'Neal. "Why are you telling me this?"

"Thought you'd want to know, Greaves," he replied. "Didn't Asa ever tell you?"

No. "Any names for the members of that rotten crowd?" He was being prickly with O'Neal for no sensible reason. "A fellow named Raymond, maybe? Or Loomis? Anybody else?"

"Loomis. That name sounds familiar."

"Thanks."

O'Neal nodded, grabbed his hat, and strode out of the office just as Taylor walked in. Out in the main station room, the booking sergeant called out to O'Neal in Irish. The two enjoyed a hearty laugh together.

Nick frowned. "I don't understand why O'Neal bothers me so much, Taylor." Or why all the cops appeared to like him so much. Even the ones who hadn't known O'Neal when he'd first worked at the station four years ago before leaving for a job in Chicago.

"Can't say, sir. He seems all right to me," Taylor said, taking the chair in front of Nick's desk.

"Nobody annoys you, Taylor," Nick said, making a tidy stack out of Meg's letters.

"Did you find anything in your sister's letters, Mr. Greaves?" he asked, hunting for a cigar in his coat pockets.

"I've been rereading them so often I think I have them memorized, but not learning much of use," he said. "Other than she used to visit Swain's Bakery, when she had spare change, to buy fruit jellies."

She'd always been fond of anything made from apples in particular. They'd had a small orchard on their farm in Ohio. When fall arrived and the crop ripened, she used to beg their mother to make pies or apple butter with them. Nick used to laugh over her antics. Used to laugh a lot, back then.

He refocused on Taylor. "You like to take Miss Ferguson to Swain's, don't you?"

His assistant blushed. "Um . . . yes, sir. It's nice."

"That's good."

Taylor peered at him, a worried furrow in his brow. He was always worried. Just like Addie Ferguson and Celia. "Yes, sir."

"Were you or Mullahey able to confirm what Loomis told us about Eckart?" he asked.

"We did." Taylor set down the half-smoked cigar he'd located in one of his pockets and retrieved his notebook. He flipped through the pages until he got to the one he was looking for. "He was employed by the North American Steamship company at one time, just like Mr. Loomis said. As a carpenter aboard ship. Doing repairs or fashioning crates and whatnot. Was out at sea a lot, as a result."

"And the story about him moving to Oregon?"

"Others down at the wharves who knew Mr. Eckart confirm that," his assistant said. "Worked the packets for a while before moving up thataway. Nobody's sure why he did, though."

"Because my sister was dead and he had no reason to stay in San Francisco?"

"Maybe so, sir." Taylor collected his cigar. "He came back here a few times over the years since moving to Oregon. None of the men I spoke with about him realized that Mr. Eckart had been in the city the past few weeks until I told them."

"Trying to keep a low profile."

Taylor shrugged and put away his notebook. "Seems like it, sir."

But why? Because he suspected he might get killed? "O'Neal informed me that my uncle Asa disliked the men Eckart was friends with, because he was my sister's beau," Nick said. "Loomis was supposedly one of them."

Taylor lifted his eyebrows. "Mr. Loomis? Should we be suspecting him of killing Mr. Eckart?"

"Worth considering."

Taylor contemplated the stack of Meg's letters. "Still don't understand why you got those letters, Mr. Greaves," he said. "If the *S* your sister addressed them to is Sylvanus Eckart—which seems likely, right?—why would he have sent them to you? Why not keep them himself?"

"I would have kept them, if I were him."

There'd been a woman, a pleasant young lady Nick had met before volunteering to serve during the war, who'd sent him letters while he'd been away. He'd held on to those for a while, even though he'd never pretended he was serious about her. Doubted she thought he was, either, but she'd faithfully sent messages anyway. Her patriotic duty, maybe. Her letters to him had represented the normality of home, though. Someplace far from gunfire and blood and death, and for that reason alone had been precious. Sad that he couldn't recall her name.

"Unless Mr. Eckart wanted you to keep them safe," Taylor said. "Because he was afraid something bad was about to happen to him. You were her brother, after all, and might want them."

To do what with them? "Meg mentions a woman named Judith in her letters to him. There's one time in particular . . ." Nick hunted through the letters to find it. "Here's what it says—'Judith reminds me that you'll be back soon.' A friend of Meg's, obviously. Why not send the package of letters and that photograph to her?"

"What if he did, sir?" Taylor struck a match and lit his stub of a cigar, puffing until the tip flared orange. "Maybe this Judith woman had been given the letters for safekeeping and *she's* the one who sent them to you."

"Why not return them to Eckart? Since he was back in San Francisco and looked to be staying for a while."

Taylor sucked thoughtfully on his cigar. "We need to find her too, don't we?"

"Nobody I've spoken with so far remembers any of Meg's friends,

Taylor, and certainly not some woman named Judith," he said. "It's as if anybody who ever mattered to her has vanished or gone to ground."

"Or been killed," Taylor added.

Nick tucked the letter back into its spot in the stack. "I did get a name for the man with the missing fingers. Part of a name, that is. Raymond. Don't know if that's a first name or last name," Nick said, avoiding mentioning Mina. Stupid, when Taylor would assume that's where the information had come from. "I was told he worked in a sawmill. And that he did often frequent Bauman's."

"Want me to ask one of the officers to keep an eye on the saloon and see if Mr. Raymond returns?"

"I doubt we'll be seeing Raymond at Bauman's anytime soon, Taylor," Nick said. "If he didn't kill Eckart himself, then he probably knows who did and will lay low as a result."

Nick exhaled and turned his chair to face the window, look out at its partly below-grade view of passing legs. The sun was out, promising a nice day while he was stuck in this gloomy, smelly office. He needed to get outside. Stretch his legs. Walk and think.

"So here's a key question—how did Raymond ever get ahold of Meg's letters to Eckart?" he asked. "Who gave him her letters and that photograph? Judith? Eckart? Somebody else entirely? And what do they want me to do?" *Time to learn the truth about Meg. About everything. Before it's too late.*

"Hm," Taylor mumbled.

Nick turned back to his assistant, who'd smoked his cigar down to a nub. "I'm back to where I started, Taylor, with no more idea what the truth about Meg is that I'm supposed to learn than when I first got those letters."

"You'll figure it out, sir. I know you will."

Glad somebody had faith in him. "Do you know if Mullahey is finished looking around at Eckart's place?" They needed more clues. Anything to go on.

Taylor used the ashtray on Briggs's desk to stub out what was left of his cigar. "I'll get over there and find out, sir."

"While you're there, see what you can discover about Loomis. He lived in the same building," Nick said. "Maybe we are ignoring an obvious suspect in Mr. Eckart's death."

☙ CHAPTER 7 ❧

"Where were you this morning, Cassidy?" Mr. McCann, the commission merchant who Owen worked for, glared at him. Glaring was worse than scowling, and Owen sort of missed a simple frown. Mr. McCann fisted his hips to add heft to the ferocity of his expression, delivered from beneath the thickest, darkest brows Owen had ever seen on a person. His boss didn't need to add any heft, though; the bark of his voice was alarming enough. "We had ten packages of furniture to offload this morning. Goods I was commissioned to procure by three different store owners. I had to hire one of the dirty kids that hang around the pier to load the wagon, Cassidy. Maybe I should give him your job, if you don't want it."

Shoot. He was gonna . . . going to lose another job. Mrs. Davies would be really disappointed in him.

"Um . . ." *Quick! Think of something!* "I was helping the police identify a smuggler, Mr. McCann."

The improbability of the explanation startled the glare clean off his boss's face. Claiming he was helping the police—which he was, in a way—had worked with Mr. Roesler as an excuse for missing work. Only one time, though, Owen reminded himself. The second time he'd tried it hadn't gone as well.

"A smuggler?"

"Yes, sir." Owen cleared his throat and stood straight. As straight as his body would agree to, given that he wanted to hunch against that durned cold breeze whistling between the ships docked at the wharf. The wind was bothering Mr. McCann, too, because he kept having to clap his hat on his head to keep it from blowing off. "You see, there was this suspicious fellow the other day down by the warehouse—not the one you use, sir, the one next to it—talking with this other suspicious fellow. And you know there've been a lot of reports about opium being smuggled on the Hong Kong packets. Not that the Hong Kong packets come in around here, but, umm . . . so when a police officer came by asking folks if they knew anything about those fellows, I told him I thought I did, and he took me off to see if I recognized the guy over at the Clay Street wharf. Unfortunately, he'd run off." He concluded his made-up story with a sigh.

"What did this suspicious fellow look like?"

"Oh, a regular sort. Hard to describe, actually."

"But you'd recognize him if you saw him again."

"Um . . . yes, sir. Because he reminded me of my brother."

Mr. McCann's eyes narrowed. "I thought you were an orphan."

That stung. Owen hated being reminded that his parents had abandoned him and were likely dead someplace. Had to be dead someplace to explain why they'd broken their promise to fetch him in San Francisco once they'd found a new life and settled down. Two years had passed since they'd made that promise. Two years was an awfully long time, but he did keep hoping they'd either turn up or he'd find out where they'd gone to.

He stared Mr. McCann in the face. "Doesn't mean I don't have a brother, Mr. McCann." Even though he didn't.

"Well . . . Don't offer to help the police or the customs officers and miss work again, you hear, Cassidy? There are plenty of other kids who'd willingly take your job as porter and likely be better at it."

Owen couldn't decide what was more insulting in Mr. McCann's comment—being referred to as a kid or being told he wasn't good at his job. "You mean you don't want me helping the law, sir?"

His boss stepped so close that the gold pocket watch chain draped across his chest came near to brushing against Owen. He stank like he'd bathed in Farina's cologne. Owen held his breath. "Not if it keeps you from doing your job, Cassidy. Am I clear?"

"Yes, sir."

Mr. McCann strode off, but not before barking an order to the wagon driver, who'd been listening with rapt attention.

Shoot. I shouldn't have gotten sassy with Mr. McCann. Too late to apologize. Not that he really felt like apologizing. Because shouldn't Mr. McCann *want* Owen to help the customs officers find smugglers, if they actually ever did ask for his help? Unless he . . .

"Best not to consider that Mr. McCann might be a criminal, Cassidy," Owen muttered to himself. Because once he started thinking that of his boss, he'd have to start thinking that just about anybody down at the wharf could be.

"Cassidy, are you talkin' to yourself again?" shouted the wagon driver.

"Reminding myself I need to do a better job."

"Heck, I coulda told you that," he replied, guffawing.

Frowning, Owen scuttled over to where a stack of crates consigned by several of Mr. McCann's customers stood waiting. The wharf area was crowded that afternoon, a large steamship having arrived from Shanghai not a half hour ago, and folks jostled Owen in their rush to reach their destinations. Voices speaking foreign languages swirled around him like eddy currents in a stream, their clothing a bright whirl of colors. He'd hate to lose this job, even if he was cold half the time. Being down at the docks was kind of thrilling. If you didn't mind the gruff longshoreman, or the stench of fish, or the piercing ferry whistles, that was.

One voice out of the many caught his attention, and he looked up from the crate he was moving in order to search for its owner. He spotted the woman, weaving her way through the pack of disembarking passengers, her eyes fixed on the man she was approaching. What was she doing at the wharf again? He'd noticed her getting off a boat only yesterday.

Strange, thought Owen. Mighty strange.

"Her again." The wagon driver, who'd climbed down from the seat to rearrange crates on the bed, was staring after the woman too.

"It's sorta odd, isn't it? I'm sure I saw her down here yesterday."

"Oh, I've seen her lots of times at the wharf." He chuckled. "Bet the mariners she's visiting aboard the ships enjoy her company."

"What? She does what? Oh." Owen blushed over how naive he could be sometimes. She didn't look like that sort of woman to him, though. When he'd first arrived in San Francisco and had sheltered in alleyways and behind warehouses, he'd met plenty of street girls. None of them had looked like her. For one thing, this woman, in her cinnamon-colored dress, her bonnet trimmed with ribbons, appeared to be too well-fed. "I dunno about that."

"Cassidy," the driver said with a grunt as he hoisted a crate onto the wagon bed, "you've got a lot to learn."

• • •

Her two afternoon patient appointments dispensed with, both of them thankfully uncomplicated and quick, Celia collected her hat and cloak. Before Barbara noticed she was heading out again, she departed the house, quietly shutting the door behind her. Her cousin's tutor was keeping Barbara so busy with studies that they'd converted the rear upstairs bedchamber into a schoolroom, affording Barbara more room to work than the dining room table provided. An additional benefit, at least so far as Celia was concerned, was that its more distant location made it harder for Barbara to overhear Celia's conversations. Such as the brief one she'd had with Addie, telling her she was headed to the police station to report what she and Owen had discovered that morning.

Celia splurged and took the Omnibus railroad to City Hall rather than walk from Vallejo. She turned up Clay just as Nicholas charged through the police station door and out onto the street.

"Nich—Mr. Greaves!" she called, switching from his Christian name when she noticed another policemen departing the station at the same time. The fellow shot Nicholas a knowing glance and chuckled as he strode off.

"Miss Ferguson finally told you that I'd come by your house," he said once she reached him.

"Have you been waiting for me?" She consulted her Ellery watch, pinned at her waist. "How did it get to be half past three in the afternoon already? I am sorry I did not come by earlier, if you have been."

"Are you going to explain where you and Cassidy were poking around this morning?"

"Should we conduct your interview out here on the street?" She gestured toward the people walking by on the pavement. As they were in the vicinity of City Hall, the men and women—mostly men— comprised a motley assortment of city officials and folks attending court proceedings. "Or might we find a more pleasant location?"

"A new coffeehouse has opened on the corner two blocks north of here. We can talk there. The place is never very busy." He took her elbow and tugged her up the road.

"You need not drag me to there, Nicholas. I will accompany you without complaint."

He released his grip. "I can never be sure, frankly."

"No need to be touchy, either."

He charged ahead of her, his pace forcing her to scurry to keep up. He'd not walk so rapidly if *he* had to struggle with a crinoline and heavy skirts.

"So, where *were* you and Cassidy this morning?" he asked. "Don't bother denying having gone someplace with him. Addie told me you had."

"We went to the Chases' former residence out near the Mission Woolen Mills."

His steps slowed. "What were you doing out there?"

"Precisely what you suspect we were doing—asking after your sister. Just like you had done last week," she said. "And before you chastise me, I only went in response to Mrs. Jewett's concerns about you and those letters you received."

"She really shouldn't have bothered you." He resumed striding along. "And this is none of your business, as I've already told you."

Celia caught hold of his arm, bringing him to a complete halt. "You should have immediately told me about the letters, Nicholas. Why did you not?"

"Because I didn't want you doing this, Celia."

"What?"

"This." He motioned at her with a wave of his hand. "Investigating. Asking questions."

"Nosing about?"

He stared down at her, the shade offered by his hat brim deepening the brown of his eyes. "Let me deal with those letters and Eckart's murder, Celia," he said. "I don't want you involved, and I don't want Cassidy involved, either. I've got a lead on the man who delivered those letters, name of Raymond, and who might've been with Eckart the day he was shot. Might be our killer."

"Don't you want to learn the interesting piece of information I discovered about Meg's beau, Nicholas?" she asked, forging ahead. "Of course you do."

He rolled his eyes. "Go ahead, Celia."

"I discovered that her beau visited the Chases' California Street house two weeks ago, agitated and urgently requesting to speak with Mr. Chase."

"They told *you* about his visit."

"When you went to their house to enquire about Meg and her letters, Nicholas, you were unaware that she might have had a beau. I was aware, after guessing that the deceased man wearing your sister's locket was more than a mere friend," she said. "Mrs. Victor told me that her beau's name was Mr. Eckart. Your murder victim."

"What specifically did he want from the Chases?"

"Mrs. Victor did not provide details. He wished to speak with Mr. Chase and was so agitated that Mrs. Chase had him removed from the property," she answered. "Nothing more."

"Hm." He turned on his heel and continued up the road, more slowly this time. "Did you get the names of any of Meg's friends? While you were out at the Chases' former residence collecting information I wasn't given."

"I was told that anyone who may have befriended her no longer worked for the Chases."

"Same thing they said to me. Even when I asked about a friend of hers named Judith," he said. "Meg mentioned the woman in one of her letters."

Celia fell into step alongside him. She wished that she could entwine her arm through his, enjoy the warmth and strength of it, and stroll as though they were merely taking the air, with no concerns and certainly no murder to investigate. However, they had far too many concerns to casually stroll anywhere, so she did not entwine her arm through his.

"Owen learned an interesting tidbit from a neighbor of the Chases'," she said. "A former neighbor, that is."

"He would."

"There is gossip that Mr. Chase is responsible for someone's death, and that it is very unwise to bother them," she said. "Could the gossip be referring to Mr. Eckart, do you think?" Or to Meg, she did not add.

He reached up to massage the pain in his old wound. "I don't remember any police reports about Chase. As innocent as a newborn kitten, as far as I'm aware," he said, his voice as taut as the fingers he'd wrapped around his arm.

"I would dismiss the comment as well, Nicholas, were it not for the fact that the woman who answered the front door at the Chases' former house also advised me to not question them. A hazardous occupation, apparently."

"Chase is dangerous, is he?" He scowled, his thoughts possibly spinning the same direction as Jane's had gone.

"I have been mulling over the reason why Mr. Eckart recently sought to confront Mr. Chase—"

"He's been away for a while. Oregon."

"Ah," she said. "Anyway, I was assured that his motivation had nothing to do with a business relationship with Mr. Chase. So his urgent need to speak with the man must be somehow due to Meg. That is all we can conclude."

He stopped at the intersection. The coffeehouse stood across the way, its door thrown open in welcome, customers at tables visible through its large plate-glass windows. Signs advertised that they served Chartres Coffee and drink brewed from freshly ground J. A. Folger beans. With a pang of regret, she realized they'd likely not be enjoying any of the beverages on offer; Nicholas appeared ready to complete their discussion outside on the street.

"'We,' Celia?"

"Would you prefer that I'd said '*I* can only conclude'?"

"I don't know what I'd prefer you to say, other than a remark along the lines of wishing me good luck and that you're heading back home right now."

"Honestly, Nicholas," she replied. "Anyway, as I was saying, Meg must be the link. She used to work at Mr. Chase's auction house. Mr. Eckart was her beau. He may have met the man through her, or had learned something about him through her. But what I cannot fathom is what precisely was Mr. Eckart's reason for his visit and why now? Why return from Oregon now?"

After a final squeeze, Nicholas dropped the grip on his arm and stared down at her. "You're planning on paying the Chases a visit yourself, aren't you? To gather more information on what Mr. Eckart wanted."

Her cheeks heated. Why she was blushing at being caught out, she'd no idea; his question was not unforeseen. "I have learned of a fundraising event Mrs. Chase is hosting tomorrow evening."

"And you plan to attend, even though you've been directly warned that questioning them is unwise," he said, his expression thunderous. "They don't want to discuss Eckart and they really don't want to discuss my sister, Celia. Don't you get it? A girl who worked for them killed herself. Drank enough laudanum to end her life in a hotel room she'd rented for the night. They were fortunate to avoid any associated scandal when it happened. They don't want me or you digging up the past and putting the dirt on fresh display."

"You do not want me taking advantage of this opportunity, even if I could discover that Mr. Chase is potentially culpable for Mr. Eckart's death, Nicholas?" she asked. "Or potentially your sister's death? Is Mr. Chase somehow responsible for it?"

"If the gossip is correct and not just gossip, Celia, that's all the *more* reason for you to wish me good luck on this case and go home," he said. "And not come back out."

"I cannot stay locked in my house, Nicholas. No matter how much you'd prefer that I do," she retorted. "I have patients to attend."

"You do know it's *my* job to conduct investigations, not yours, Celia," he said. "Despite what they write about you in the newspapers."

"I am well aware of your occupation and mine, Mr. Greaves."

He groaned. "And I suppose you've talked Mrs. Hutchinson into going along with your scheme, since she's probably acquainted with them."

She smiled and refused to answer. He'd only shout at her if she confirmed Jane's involvement.

"I'll take that as a yes," he said. "You know you're putting her in danger, Mrs. Davies. Again. How much longer do you think Frank is going to put up with your antics?"

Antics, now. "We shall be careful, Nicholas. Completely discreet and careful."

"I'm not even going to bother to respond to that."

Which he did not, at least not verbally. He let the glower on his face speak for him.

• • •

Surprisingly, Celia agreed to return home. Well, at least she'd acted agreeable about it. She'd do what she wanted whether or not Nick approved. They weren't married; he couldn't stop her. He probably couldn't stop her even if they were wed.

"Damn it, Celia," he muttered under his breath as he descended from the horsecar, catching the disapproving eye of a young woman waiting to climb aboard after him. "Sorry, miss," he said, but not waiting to see if she accepted the apology for his language.

He hadn't known what to make of what she and Cassidy had learned. Chase responsible for somebody's death? Was the reason Nick hadn't heard any rumor to that effect because the death had been too recent? Or because the death had occurred four years ago, but nobody dared speak up against the man because it would've been too dangerous?

Damn it, Celia.

Nick turned up Market Street. Their best, maybe only, source of answers to at least some of their questions was a man missing fingers on his right hand. Mina had described Raymond as having sawdust in his hair and on his clothes. She'd thought he worked at a sawmill, and Nick agreed.

Most of the city's sawmills were situated on Market or adjacent streets between the terminus of the railroad and the wharves. Their proximity to each other made the task of asking about a man named Raymond a whole lot simpler. All Nick had to do was take a stroll from one to the next, showing his badge if the fellow unloading logs or the foreman was reluctant to respond.

He had no success at the first few sawing and planing mills he stopped at. By the sixth one, he was starting to question his strategy. Plus, he was starting to get hungry, which didn't help his mood.

A large sign spanned the roof of the next mill he visited. It advertised that the place manufactured doors, sashes, blinds, and moldings. Along with other custom items. All Nick needed, though, was information on Raymond and where he might find him.

He stepped through the door to the office.

A fellow, noting orders in a ledger book opened on the counter in front of him, looked up. "How might I help you with your project, sir?" he asked with a broad smile, more obsequious than welcoming.

"No project. I'm looking for a man named Raymond who might work here." Nick shortened the conversational give-and-take by flapping aside his coat lapel to show his badge.

The man blanched.

"Um . . . yes, Officer. You should, um, speak with the foreman. I'm new and don't know all the men, you see." He twisted toward the door that linked the office to the mill. It barely muffled the thunderous noise of the equipment. "I'll fetch him, if you'd like." He took a few jerky steps towards it.

"No, I'll go find the foreman myself. Thank you."

Nick swung open the connecting door and was met by the rhythmic thunk of the steam engine's pistons booming through the building, the hiss and squeal of escaping steam, the high-pitched buzz of saw teeth slicing through wood. Heavy leather belts hung down from the spinning central camshaft that was powered by the engine. The belts turned the shafts that ran the saws and planers and lathes, clacking as they rotated. Raymond had fared better, losing only a few fingers, than a five-year-old boy who'd been killed at a planing mill—maybe even this one, but Nick couldn't recall the details from the article he'd read—when he got caught in the machinery a year or so ago.

Lumber was stacked everywhere, propped against walls, tucked into corners and onto large wheeled carts. The building smelled of tarry machine oil and sweet sawdust, which shot off the blades and into the air to land on every surface. The equipment, the floor, the men. And their hair, where it wasn't covered. Mina had been under the impression that Raymond was deaf. Nick would be too and in no time, if he had to work here. He shouldn't complain about the noise from the street outside his office window any longer.

Not far from the door Nick had come through, a boy was counting and bundling cut boards. A job that might not cost him his fingers. Or his life.

"I'm looking for a fellow named Raymond," he said to him.

The kid looked up from what he'd been doing and squinted at Nick. "What?"

"Raymond," Nick said louder. "A man named Raymond. I've been told he's missing some fingers on his right hand. Does he work here? Do you know?"

"Who are you?"

Nick showed his badge. He could pin it on the outside of his coat like Taylor and the other officers wore theirs, but he valued keeping his identity as a detective private. Although it seemed that every criminal in San Francisco could spot a detective, no matter what he was wearing, from a mile away.

"What did he do?" the boy asked, his eyes wide.

"So there *is* a fellow named Raymond working here at the mill."

"Sure. Raymond Fuller. But I ain't seen him for a couple of weeks," he shouted over the piercing shriek of a saw.

"A couple of weeks." Gone around the same time he'd delivered that final parcel of Meg's letters to Mrs. Jewett's.

"Yep," the kid said. "Don't right know what happened to him. Maybe the foreman fired him. He did like to fight with the other fellows."

Just like Mina had described him. Unpleasant. "What about Sy Eckart. Ever heard of him?"

The kid shook his head. "Nope."

"Hey! What are you doing in here, bothering my worker?" a tall man, his self-importance swelling his chest, bellowed. The foreman.

The kid hustled back to his stacks of boards as the fellow stomped over. "If you're a customer, you need to talk to—"

"Not a customer. I'm looking for Raymond Fuller. Do you know where I might find him?"

"I don't, but if you ever find him, tell him he's not welcome back here."

"If you fired him for fighting, I presume Fuller already knows he's not welcome back."

"I didn't fire him. He just stopped showing up one day," the foreman replied. "And a good riddance to bad rubbish, I say."

☙ CHAPTER 8 ❧

Mr. Chase's business, that of auctioneer and commission merchant, occupied three consecutive addresses along Sansome Street, so large was the enterprise. When she and Nicholas had parted, Celia had agreed to head directly home. However, the police station was so near to Mr. Chase's auction house that she found she could not pass up the opportunity to ask a few questions.

O what a tangled web we weave, when first we practice to deceive . . .

A bit of guilt-inducing wisdom from Sir Walter Scott.

Celia hurried across the road, her skirts lifted high to avoid a steaming gift a horse had recently deposited upon the cobbles, and paused in front of the window of the central-most address. A sign announced specific sale days—Mondays and Wednesday for the catalog sales of clothing and shoes and fancy goods; Thursdays for the sale of American and imported dry goods, silks, embroideries, etcetera. Etcetera comprising a large and enticing list of possibilities. Once she concluded her mourning period, she could use a new dress. Perhaps Mr. Chase's auction house would have a lovely taffeta fabric in blue at a reasonable price. Presuming he hadn't been jailed for the murder of Mr. Eckart by that time.

"Celia, you are getting ahead of yourself," she murmured. Simply because the son of their former neighbor believed Mr. Chase was responsible for a person's death did not mean he actually was.

The auction house might be closed, since it was Tuesday and therefore not a sale day, but she reached for the door handle anyway. Just then, the door itself opened and a man stepped through. Tall and rather dashing-looking, he acknowledged her with a doff of his black top hat before strolling off down the road. Not closed, then.

She entered the salesroom, the overhead bell clanging with unexpected volume. The window shades were only a third of the way up, leaving the capacious room dimly lit, and it took a moment for her eyes to adjust to the gloom. Trunks and crates stood in soldierly lines around the perimeter, waiting to be opened and inventoried. A selection of the contents of others had been set out for the auctioneer to display to the bidders tomorrow, people who would occupy the stacked chairs waiting to be arranged in front of the auction stand. A cassimere overshirt was folded alongside a linen duster and a pair of trousers and vest appropriate for summer wear.

A side door opened, allowing Celia a glimpse of a large warehouse, before a stout man with wire-rimmed spectacles hurried through and closed it.

"I'm sorry, ma'am, was the front door unlocked? It shouldn't have been. Today is not an auction day so you need to come back tomorrow," he said breathlessly, as though he'd sprinted from the deepest depths of the building upon hearing the shop bell.

"But I passed a gentleman on my way inside," she said in her most polished British accent, which, she realized, was becoming diluted from years of living in America.

"Ah, well, that was Mr. Hunter. He's not a customer," he said. "In the meantime, you can peruse one of our catalogs, if you'd like."

"Pardon me for intruding, sir."

He gave a tight-lipped smile. "It's not a problem, ma'am, so long as you weren't expecting to be able to purchase any of our goods today."

"Oh, no, I was merely strolling down the street—I often take solo strolls, much to the chagrin of my housekeeper, but I find them so consoling—and noticed your establishment. Upon reading the name above the door I realized that a friend of mine had once been employed to assist with the auctions here. She is no longer . . . forgive me." Celia retrieved a handkerchief from her reticule, readying it should the need arise to appear to be crying. *Honestly, I should attempt a career on the stage.* Scandalizing everyone she knew. Including herself.

He extended a hand to console her and thought better of his forwardness before he touched her sleeve. "A friend of yours? A female?"

"Yes," she sniffled. "She has passed away, you see. It has been many years but I continue to often think of her. Such a bright spirit. So lovely."

The clerk furrowed his brow. "It's been a while since we've had a female assistant. Mr. Chase has decided it's better to strictly employ men, even when we have women's and children's clothing on offer. He finds them more . . . competent with our customers."

How charming. "You knew her? Margaret Greaves?" she asked. "That was her name, although most people called her Meg."

His expression shifted, turned wary. "Interesting that her brother came here asking about friends of hers last week, but he was told to leave," he said. "I might've been able to help him but I wasn't here that day, and nobody else—except for Mr. Chase—knew Miss Greaves. And like I said, he was turned away. Politely, of course, because he's a policeman and we don't want to annoy the police."

Nicholas hadn't mentioned that he had come here. No matter, since it appeared he'd not learned anything of use.

"However you *were* acquainted with her," she said. "Dearest Meg."

"She quit not long after I joined the company, so I can't say that I was all that acquainted with her, ma'am." He removed his spectacles and wiped them with a scrap of yellow cotton cloth he retrieved from his waistcoat pocket. "A shame she quit, though. Enjoyed having her around. Made the day pass more quickly."

Oh, Nicholas. To have lost her . . .

"I only hope that the cause of Miss Greaves's departure had nothing to do with your employer," Celia said. "That he was not—how shall I put it?—forward with her."

"We've had other women working here before Miss Greaves who didn't seem to have any trouble with Mr. Chase," he stated candidly. "But I could tell Miss Greaves didn't like working here anymore. Became upset and jumpy. Missed her last scheduled auction to assist with, in fact. It was after that event that Mr. Chase implemented his rule about only men getting hired to work here."

"And she never explained what had been bothering her?"

"She didn't talk to me about it," he replied. "I did try to get her to tell me. It's been a long time though, ma'am. Hard to recollect exactly."

"Was there any indication her upset was due to a problem with her beau?" she asked. "A Mr. Eckart, I believe his name was."

"He was Miss Greaves's beau? Huh. Funny that he came here recently, too."

"How very intriguing. When was this?"

"A couple of weeks back. Wanted to speak with Mr. Chase," he said, blinking blindly at her. "Two folks—and now you—who knew Miss Greaves coming here to ask questions lately. Sorta strange, don't you think?"

"I do." Clearly, Mr. Eckart had been keen to speak with Mr. Chase and Mr. Chase appeared to have been equally keen to avoid him. "I wonder what he could have wanted with Mr. Chase."

"No idea, ma'am." He restored his spectacles to the bridge of his nose. "But I will tell you that he wasn't as easy to get rid of as that police officer."

"And now he is dead. Such a tragedy. Murdered."

"Murdered?" he asked, choking a little.

"Indeed so. Very tragic." She stared down at the handkerchief crushed in her gloved fist and shook her head. "And for me to have recently heard the most horrid rumor about Mr. Chase. It is unfathomable."

She peeked at the clerk, judging his reaction. Had his eyes enlarged behind the distortion of his spectacles' lenses? It was difficult to tell.

"Oh?"

Celia glanced around before leaning in to whisper. "That he is responsible for someone's death! How frightful to consider!"

"Mr. Chase? Responsible for . . . Certainly not! Never!" he insisted. "He's a very trustworthy businessman. Very trustworthy."

Thou doth protest too much, methinks. To twist Mr. Shakespeare's prose a trifle, but another quote worth bringing to mind.

"I would expect nothing less from a man I have heard so much about," she said. "Ah, well. I suppose it is for the police to discover who killed her beau. And for me to accept that I shall never learn what was troubling Meg so greatly."

He tucked away his square of yellow cloth. "I reckon the only person she might've talked to about her worries was her friend Judith. Judith Whelan."

For a man who claimed to have been barely acquainted with Meg Greaves, he knew quite a bit about her.

"Judith Whelan." A full name for the woman mentioned in one of Meg's letters, and a crumb that might lead Celia along a trail. With hopefully a less perilous outcome than had befallen Hansel and Gretel.

"That's the name. She worked someplace nearby and they used to walk home together after they were done for the day," he said. "Miss Greaves introduced me to her friend one time. She was very polite and a right pretty young thing."

A reason to have not forgotten her. Even though it had been a long time. "Have you seen Miss Whelan since then?" Perhaps she was still employed nearby.

"A few times, but not for a long while now," he said. "Which is a shame, because she was right pretty."

•••

"I haven't seen hide nor hair of Raymond Fuller since Thursday, Detective." The proprietor of the men's hotel stood in the center of the hallway, his arms folded across his thick waist.

The day before Loomis reported seeing Fuller with Eckart. The day before Eckart was murdered.

"Thursday," Nick said.

"Yep. Left without paying his bill," he replied. "If you see him before I do, remind him he owes me ten bucks, will ya? Or maybe just arrest him, since you're a cop and all."

Ten dollars was a considerable bill to run up, when this place only charged—according to the sign affixed to the wall outside the front entrance—twenty five cents a night for a furnished single room. Less per night when paying by the week.

"He delivered a package to me a couple of weeks ago and I've been trying to contact him about the contents," Nick said.

Trying to understand the intent behind the message that had accompanied Meg's letters. *Learn the truth . . . before it's too late.* Mrs. Jewett thought it was a warning meant for Nick, but with Raymond Fuller having seemingly disappeared, he was starting to wonder if they'd both read that wrong. Maybe Fuller had been afraid it was going to be too late for him.

The hotel owner peered at Nick. "A package? Fuller delivered a package to you?" he asked. "Doesn't sound like something he'd do. Unless he's lost his job at the sawmill and has taken to being a delivery boy now. Amazed they kept him on there, after he chopped off half his hand. More amazed he wanted to stay. The job did pay well, though. Although the money never managed to regularly pass from him to me."

"He isn't at the mill any longer," Nick said. "Heard he quit a few weeks back. Just stopped showing up."

"Guess I won't be seeing any of the money he owes me, then." He added a curse word under his breath.

"Do you know an acquaintance of his, a man named Sylvanus Eckart?"

"Sy? Sure do." He tutted. "I heard he was found dead in the water off a dock yesterday. Such a shame. Shot, wasn't he?"

Were the details in the newspapers already? Nick had been too busy hunting down Raymond Fuller to grab one off a newsboy and read what had been reported. "What can you tell me about Mr. Eckart?"

"He used to live here. A few years back," he said. "Which is how he got to know Fuller."

"What about him as a man? A bad sort?"

"Sy?" The landlord shook his head. "Not my experience of him."

Then why had Asa been worried about him courting Meg?

"He came by looking for a place about, oh, three weeks ago? Or maybe four," the landlord was saying. "Looked like he might be staying for a while this time, but I didn't have any rooms available."

"'This time'?"

"He's been in San Francisco off and on for the past several years, Officer. Never more than a couple of days," the man replied. "Claimed he couldn't stand to stick around, with all the bad memories. His sweetheart dying, you know."

Nick's stomach tensed and his old wound burned. "Yes, I do know," he said. "Did Eckart explain what had brought him back to the city this time?"

"Somebody had given him a reason to think he could fix an old problem. That's what he told me. Fix an old problem," he said. "He didn't want to tell me more. Thought it wouldn't be wise for me to know."

Interesting.

"I didn't have any rooms available, though, so he said he'd go find a place with Loomis," the landlord continued. "Wish I could've helped him out. Maybe he'd still be alive, if I had."

"Why do you say that?"

"Because then he wouldn't have gotten mixed up with Loomis again. Always asking Sy for money, I heard." He shook his head. "From what I understand of him, Detective, he's nothing but trouble."

• • •

"What are you doing at the dining room table at this hour, Cousin? It's after seven and dark outside," Barbara said from the doorway at Celia's back.

Nicholas hated to sit with his back to doorways or open spaces where people might sneak up on him and take him unawares. Perhaps she should copy his habit and utilize one of the chairs on the opposite side of the table. Then she would have noticed Barbara's approach through the parlor.

"I am reviewing my patient notes," Celia replied.

"Don't you usually write notes at your desk in your clinic?"

Exhaling, Celia set down her pencil and shifted to look at her. Barbara, her arms folded atop the floral-printed plum wrapper she wore over her nightclothes, frowned back.

"Come and sit, Barbara, and tell me what is on your mind."

Barbara flounced into the room and dropped onto the chair at the far end of the table. She hid in the shadows beyond the reach of the light emitted by the overhead gas chandelier. However, Celia had no need for more illumination to read her cousin's unhappiness. The sentiment radiated off of her like heat from a stove.

"Mrs. Reynolds wants to host an exhibition of her students' skills, like all the schools do at the end of the term, even if it's not the end of the term yet," she said. "More like a halfway point exhibition of our talents. Minus all the singing and piano playing that goes on at ladies' colleges exercises. Thankfully. But still . . ."

"An exhibition sounds like an excellent idea." The woman must be feeling the need to prove she was worth the money families were spending for her services.

"I suppose, except she suggested I compose an essay on the value of women and their right to suffrage," she said. "I told her I didn't want to write on that topic because it would be pointless."

"I see." Women might one day gain the right to vote, but would a half-Chinese female like her cousin ever enjoy the privilege as well? "I suspect she was not pleased by your response."

"No, she wasn't. After she lectured me for a good fifteen minutes on the need for an unrelenting fight in order to ever gain justice and fair treatment for women, she relented," she said. "I told her I'd much rather demonstrate my ability to solve algebra problems, like the boys do when they're subjected to public examination at term ends. You know, Cousin, I think my proposal alarmed her. Apparently the value of women doesn't actually extend to showing off their mathematical intelligence."

"I trust you two came to a compromise."

"Mrs. Reynolds agreed to let me translate passages of French, instead."

"You've been studying French?" How was she not aware?

"Yes," she replied tersely.

Gad, Celia. You will blink and one day find Barbara a full-grown woman if you do not pay her more attention.

"I apologize for not staying abreast of what Mrs. Reynolds has been having you study, Barbara. I do care about what you're learning," she said. "And I am very pleased that she is teaching you French. I look forward to the exhibition. I honestly do."

"Thank you."

"You are most welcome."

Smiling, Celia picked up her pencil and collected her notebook, ready to resume her work, but Barbara did not get up from the table.

She laid down her pencil again. "You did not come in here simply to lament your tutor's plans for an exhibition, did you?"

Barbara set her jaw. "Mr. Greaves came by earlier today, which means you've gotten caught up in one of his cases again, haven't you?"

"He does not want me 'caught up' in any of his cases any more than you do," she replied. "He was looking for Mina and wondered if Addie had seen her lately."

"That's what I thought. Addie can be awfully loud."

Apparently no room in this house was far enough away to keep Barbara from overhearing conversations Celia would prefer she not be privy to.

"What's Mina done now?" her cousin asked. "Is she a suspect in another murder?"

"No, she is not, Barbara, and that comment was unkind," Celia replied. "I thought you liked her."

"I do." She dropped her chin and began to pick at the narrow band of purple ribbon cuffing her sleeves. "Why was he looking for her?"

To renew their relationship? That had been Celia's first thought, immediately followed by a sharp pang of jealousy.

"Miss Cascarino is acquainted with a man who used to frequent Bauman's. A man who delivered a packet of letters to Mr. Greaves that had been written by his sister shortly before she died," she answered. "He is trying to find him."

"Letters from his sister? That's awful," she said, looking up from her cuffs. "I mean, he probably doesn't want to be reminded that she died so terribly."

Celia couldn't remember ever mentioning to her cousin that Meg had taken her own life. Addie had likely been the source of the information. "The letters have indeed upset him. I wonder if the sender realized how deeply they would distress him."

"Hasn't it been a long time since she died, though? Why deliver them now?"

"We have all been wondering that, Barbara."

"So you *are* helping him," her cousin said, accusingly. "That's why you went off with Owen this morning and why you were gone this afternoon. Investigating again."

"I know you worry for me, but Mr. Greaves's landlady asked me to help," she said. "A warning note accompanied the letters, Barbara. Mrs. Jewett and I are both very concerned that Nicholas could be in danger."

"Which means you'll be in danger, too."

"I could never live with myself, Barbara, if something terrible happened to Mr. Greaves and I may have been able to prevent it."

Barbara studied Celia's face. "You really care about him, don't you?"

The question surprised Celia; her cousin had never directly and sincerely asked about Celia's feelings for Nicholas before. "Yes, I do. It has taken me a while to realize just how much," she answered softly. "But so much stands in the way."

"Your husband is dead, Cousin."

"I was not thinking of Patrick, Barbara. But rather Mr. Greaves's memories of the war, of the pain of losing people he loved, the pain of losing his sister . . . Those memories are not dead for *him*," she said. "And now these letters have resurrected feelings, ghosts, that he had imagined he'd put to rest. All of these hurts stand in the way."

Her cousin leaned forward, into the glow of the gaslight. "If you care for him, truly care for him, don't let those barriers stop you, Cousin," she said, her voice deeply serious and thick with emotion. "Or you might regret it. For always."

Celia stretched her hand across the table, and Barbara reached out, intertwining her fingers with Celia's.

"I know I would, Barbara," she said and gripped her cousin's hand, drawing on her unanticipated strength and compassion. "I know."

• • •

Nick tugged his coat collar up, guarding his neck against the evening chill creeping along the streets. The smell of approaching rain hung in the air. He'd stopped at the station hoping that Taylor or Mullahey had left a message about what they may have found in Eckart's apartment, but there weren't any messages. The fruitless side trip had meant he'd taken longer to get home and now might get rained on. At least he had a suspect to pursue in earnest, starting tomorrow. A man he'd had in his office and had let go. Loomis. Nothing but trouble.

His upturned collar only marginally helped keep out the cold. He sped along the road. The butcher where Mrs. Jewett purchased her meat was closing up for the evening and nodded at Nick through the store's window, a brisk acknowledgment before resuming lowering the blinds. Lamps in the rented rooms above the place flared to life, pinpricks of yellow light showing the holes in the curtain drawn against the night. Along the road ahead of Nick, a man in a calf-length duster hurried along, his body briefly illuminated by the streetlamp pooling light on the sidewalk. He moved on, plunging into the darkness again. Aside from him, the street was quiet. Not unusual, but for some reason the silence made Nick's skin prickle. He used to savor quiet, but lately it too often signaled that a fresh disaster was just around the corner.

Mrs. Jewett had left the dining room curtains open, the gasolier's glow brightening the path to the porch steps. Riley heard his approach and began barking, his nose pressed against the window of Nick's street-facing upstairs room, probably leaving a smudge.

"Hold on there, boy. I'll be right up," Nick called just as his stomach rumbled. He hadn't eaten since . . . he couldn't remember if he'd had lunch. He probably hadn't.

He took the front steps two at a time, slowing to check if his boots were muddy and he needed to make use of the iron scraper on the porch. It wasn't until he reached for the front door handle that he noticed the note, folded in half and tacked to the doorframe.

He ripped it free and opened it. Only three words were written in a sloppy hand on the paper, but they adequately conveyed the author's message.

You're next, Greaves.

❧ CHAPTER 9 ❧

"Did you or Mullahey find anything interesting in Eckart's room yesterday?" Nick asked Taylor, who was collecting his notebook from his desk.

His assistant squinted at him. "You all right, sir? You look tired."

Nick rasped his knuckles against his jaw. "Need a shave, that's all."

"You sure?"

Sometimes Taylor was too damned observant. And persistent. "Received a message last night. Somebody's not happy that I'm investigating Eckart's murder, it seems," he replied. How else could he interpret that note? "Don't worry, Taylor. I'll have the men who work my neighborhood beat keep an eye out. What about Eckart's place?"

"We didn't finish. It was a mess, sir," he said, collecting a fresh pencil, too

"Eckart's apartment?"

"Yep. Somebody had turned it over. Looks like the door lock didn't work well," he answered. "It took a while to sort through it all, and then Mr. Mullahey got pulled away by Captain Eagan."

Blast. "I'd like to know who got there before we did."

"Nobody noticed anybody, Mr. Greaves. I asked," he said. "Mr. Mullahey is back there this morning. Oh, and I got this from Miss Cascarino this morning. Found it on my desk."

Mina had always been an early riser. Nick read the note quickly then stashed it in a coat pocket. "Thank you, Taylor."

"And Mr. Loomis is in your office."

"Did you look into the alibi he gave us for Friday evening?"

"Haven't been able to confirm that he played cards with anybody that night, sir."

"No surprise." Nick pushed open the door, Taylor following him inside. "Thank you for coming into the station again, Mr. Loomis."

Loomis looked a whole lot less comfortable than he had yesterday morning. A typical reaction from folks who'd been summoned to the station after thinking they were finished answering police questions. Nick had warned him, though.

"I need to get to work, Detective," he said. "Will this take long?"

"That's up to you," Nick answered, taking his chair.

"Did you . . . ahem, did you find the fellow with the hand that's missing fingers, Detective?" Loomis asked, clenching the brim of his black derby, which sat on his lap. "The man who killed my friend Sy?"

"Now here I thought Sylvanus Eckart was just a friendly neighbor, Mr. Loomis."

Loomis cleared his throat again, which rattled with phlegm. Nick hoped that whatever was wrong with him wasn't contagious. "Um . . . well . . ."

"Right." Nick leaned back in his chair, which squeaked, and folded his arms. "To answer your question, we haven't found the fellow, although I have learned his name."

"That's good."

"It would be if he hadn't skipped out on his bill at the men's hotel he'd been staying at and not left a forwarding address."

He considered Loomis. Did he look like a murderer? Some of the officers, Briggs especially, believed that criminals had distinctive features. Angular foreheads frequently came into question, as did a skull that protruded at the back. Briggs mistrusted thick necks, too, even though his own wasn't all that slim. Nick, however, had interviewed too many guilty people in this office who didn't fit Briggs's idea of what a criminal looked like. Beautiful women. Handsome, well-dressed men. Loomis simply looked scared.

"While I was searching for this fellow, Mr. Loomis, I was told something interesting about you," he said.

"Oh?" the man asked, a sheen of sweat springing up on the rounded dome of his forehead. Was it a shape Briggs would be suspicious of? Nick hadn't a clue, and he wasn't going to consult Briggs to get his opinion. "What was that?"

"That you are 'nothing but trouble,'" Nick replied. "What do you have to say to that?"

"That's an outright lie, Detective. An outright, insulting lie!" He jumped to his feet. "I demand to know the name of the fellow who slandered me like that."

"Please sit down, Mr. Loomis," Taylor requested in his calm voice, the one suspects and witnesses tended to listen to. Which Loomis did, retaking his chair.

"The individual who told me didn't have any reason to lie, as far as I could tell, Mr. Loomis," Nick said. "So I'm going with the assumption that he was being honest."

He dug out a handkerchief from his coat pocket and mopped his forehead. "Well, he wasn't."

"He suggested that *you* could be the reason Mr. Eckart is dead. He'd also heard that you owed Eckart money," he said. "I asked around the station this morning and discovered that you've been in trouble with the law before. Isn't that right, Mr. Loomis?"

Taylor looked surprised; Nick hadn't had the chance to share the information with him yet.

"I was found innocent, Detective. I'd only just arrived in California and fell in with the wrong group of men. I didn't know they were forging bank bills," Loomis said, his handkerchief not keeping up with the torrent of sweat collecting. "Besides, counterfeiting isn't the same as cold-blooded murder."

"Your good friend Sy Eckart was shot in the back, Mr. Loomis. Chicken-hearted murder is how I would describe it."

He blanched. "I didn't do it, Detective. I didn't kill him."

"But you did make sure to rush into the station in order to accuse a man missing some fingers of the crime." Nick leaned forward and propped his elbows on his desk. "You know what I find interesting about your story that he'd been at Bauman's on Friday with Eckart, Mr. Loomis? None of the waiters at the saloon remember the fellow being there on Friday." Amazingly, Mina had done as he'd requested and spoken with Bauman's staff. That was what she'd written in the note she'd left on Taylor's desk. "They make a point of keeping a lookout for him, since he annoyed the women who used to sing there."

"They, um, they don't remember?" he asked, squinting at Nick. He probably needed glasses after spending his days bent over account ledgers. Or counterfeiting greenbacks.

"No, they don't," Nick said. "Did you see him with Eckart at all on Friday, Mr. Loomis?"

"I . . ." He crushed his damp handkerchief in his fist. "I . . ."

Taylor rolled his eyes and flipped to a new page of his notebook. What notes could he have made to fill up the prior page? It wasn't as if Loomis had said much.

"Well, Mr. Loomis? Did you see Eckart with that fellow this past Friday or not?"

He opened his mouth, readying a reply, shut it again as he further considered his response. He spluttered some more and finally spoke.

"I've realized that I misspoke, Detective. It wasn't this past Friday that I saw him at Bauman's. It was the Friday before."

"An odd mistake to have made. Confusing this past Friday for the one a week earlier."

"I've been under a lot of pressure lately, and I get confused easily. I apologize."

"In fact, Mr. Loomis, the waiters don't recall him coming into Bauman's for several weeks now."

Loomis studied his hat and didn't respond.

"Who are you protecting, Mr. Loomis?" Nick asked. "Yourself?"

"I did not kill Sy."

"We can't confirm your alibi, by the way," Nick said.

"I'm innocent!" He shot a glance at Taylor but did not find any sympathy there, either. "I didn't kill him!"

"Then maybe you came into the station with some story about a suspicious fellow because you're protecting the actual killer."

"Why would I be protecting somebody? I'm just trying to help the police."

"Is that so?" Nick stared at Loomis, long enough to make the fellow squirm. "Who is it, Mr. Loomis? Must be somebody you either care a lot about or somebody you're scared of, is my guess."

Loomis stuffed his handkerchief into his pocket. "I don't intend to say any more, Detective. I'm not going to say any more."

"Give us a name, Mr. Loomis. Somebody shot your friend and you have a good guess who it is."

"Sy had plenty of enemies, Detective. Plenty," he said. "He was always nosing about, noticing things he shouldn't."

"Such as?"

"You've never worked at the docks if you have to ask that question, Detective."

The docks. An interesting tidbit. "Did Sy Eckart ever mention Archibald Chase to you?"

The name caused Loomis to blink. If folks wanted to lie better, they needed lessons on how to control their eyes. And their sweating, which Loomis continued to do in profusion, forcing him to reclaim his handkerchief.

He patted it across his high forehead again. "I don't recall Sy ever mentioning Mr. Chase or his business."

"That's odd, Mr. Loomis, because Mr. Eckart went to visit the Chases not long before he died. Had a heated exchange with Mrs. Chase and was thrown out of the house," Nick said. "Funny he never told you about that."

"Well, he didn't. Like I said, we weren't close friends."

"Mr. Loomis, if you're scared of the person you think killed Sy, it would be best for you to tell us his name," Nick said. "Before they decide to kill somebody else."

"I'm not going to say any more," he repeated.

"That somebody else could turn out to be you, Mr. Loomis." *Or me.* Nick retrieved the threatening note from his coat pocket and spread it open on the desk. Taylor peered at the scrap of paper, his eyebrows tucking tight as he tried to read what was written on it. "You leave this for me last night, Mr. Loomis? Maybe you don't like that we've been asking questions about you. You and Eckart."

His eyes widened. "I wouldn't ever threaten an officer of the law!"

"Then maybe it was one of your friends who left it for me," he said. "Or the person you're protecting."

"I don't know anything about that note, Detective."

"What about Eckart's apartment?" Nick asked. "Was it you who turned it upside down yesterday or maybe the day before? What were you looking for?"

"It wasn't me! Honest!"

"Mr. Loomis, I'm just finding it hard to believe you," Nick said, returning the note to his pocket. He stood. "But it strikes me that the best way to encourage you to talk is to allow you to spend some time in one of our holding cells."

"What? You're arresting me?" he asked. "You don't have any proof I'm guilty!"

"Try not lying to the police next time if you want us to trust you." Nick nodded at Taylor, and his assistant took the man's arm, knocking Loomis's derby out of his grip.

"You're all dirty," Loomis shouted as Taylor dragged him away. "All you cops are dirty!"

• • •

"How might I help you, miss?" Celia asked the young woman occupying the cane-seated chair in her examining room. She'd hoped that the ring of the doorbell meant her scheduled patient had arrived early, allowing Celia to begin her search for Judith Whelan sooner than planned, but Addie had informed her that someone else was waiting.

"Oh, Mrs. Davies. Good morning." She smiled thinly at Celia. Hiding her teeth, perhaps. Her hands were folded at the waist of her check blue-gray dress, its pattern faded from repeated washings. The gown appeared to have been altered to fit her small, slim form. A pair of sturdy low-heeled leather boots, their toes scuffed, peeked from beneath the hem. All that was missing was a cap covering her light brown hair, because Celia was positive she was a servant.

Celia returned her greeting and closed the door to afford them privacy. "Now, what can I do for you? Please describe your symptoms, if you will." Aside from being thin, she did not appear unwell, and her voice had been strong.

"I'm not here because I'm sick, ma'am." The young woman got to her feet. Unlike so many others, she'd apparently never suffered from smallpox, for the light coming through the window fell on her cheeks and revealed their enviable smoothness. "I'm . . . you are the lady detective, aren't you? I've heard all about you. Cook reads the newspapers and follows your adventures."

Gad. Not again. "Adventures?" Not how Celia might describe them.

"Oh, yes." She nodded. "She tells us about them. I don't have time to read the papers, but I do know all about you."

This was the penalty for her embroilment in Nicholas's cases—unwanted notoriety, which had been dogging her for months. "If you are in need of someone to conduct an investigation, miss, I suggest you contact the police."

"But you *are* the lady detective Mrs. Davies, right?" she asked, scanning the room for evidence of Celia's investigative work. However, all there was to observe was a large glass-fronted cabinet containing medical supplies, a heavy walnut desk topped with stacks of patient logs and the box holding her stethoscope, and a bench used as an examining table.

"I am a nurse who operates a free clinic for women, and I have a patient scheduled to arrive in fifteen minutes," she replied tersely.

"Sorry, ma'am. I really don't mean to be taking up your time."

Celia exhaled a sigh. "No, I should be apologizing for my tone. But if you are here simply to satisfy your curiosity—"

"I'm not! I'm not. Not completely, that is," she said, sitting down again. "I wanted to meet you because you were at the house asking about any friends of Meg Greaves's, and I was curious why."

"You work at the Chases' house out near the Mission."

"I used to be the housemaid there, but now I work at their California Street house," she said, smiling proudly. "I was out at their old place yesterday, though, when you came by."

So much for fooling anyone with her tale about being Meg Greaves's concerned relative, recently arrived from Pennsylvania. "How did you know who I was?"

"I didn't. Not exactly," she replied. "When I asked Mrs. Victor about your visit, all she said was that you were some nosy relative asking questions about Meg and her former friends. But that didn't sound right. Not all these years later. And Mrs. Victor doesn't remember ever receiving any correspondence for Meg from you. So I made a guess. I mean, who else might it be except a detective? You do look like the woman I saw yesterday at the house, and you just admitted that you're her, so my guess was correct."

Gad.

Celia drew her desk chair over to the young woman and sat. "Very clever of you, Miss . . ."

"You can just call me Eileen," she said, smiling. "I wasn't sure where you lived, of course, so I asked the gardener where Mrs. Davies the lady detective lived, and he found you in the city directory—there's only one Mrs. Davies listed—and that's how I got to this house."

"Were you a friend of Meg's?"

"I was," she said. "But I don't get why anybody would care to ask about her anymore. It's been so long."

"Mrs. Victor told me there was no longer anyone around who'd known Meg." Had there been a reason to lie beyond simply wishing to be rid of Celia as quickly as possible?

"It was just me, ma'am. Meg kept to herself," she replied. "I did like her, though. She was so pretty and smart and funny. She loved music and would sneak into the house when the youngest Miss Chase was practicing the piano."

Of which the Chases possessed two in their new house on California Street. "Was she not supposed to be inside the house? You said 'sneak into.'"

"The folks renting rooms in the outbuilding beyond the garden aren't supposed to, ma'am." She puckered her brow. "I wonder what they're going to do, where they'll go, since I've heard that the people renting the house right now mean to move them out."

"It is fortunate for you, then, that the Chases transferred you to their California Street house."

"Yes, ma'am," she agreed. "I'm really grateful to them for taking me on and keeping me with them."

"I take it you enjoy working for the Chases," Celia said, closely watching the young woman. She was nervously picking at her nails, which were chipped. "I have heard Mr. Chase has a terrible temper, which might make your situation difficult."

Eileen considered that for a moment. Wondering, perhaps, what she dared to acknowledge.

"He is an important businessman," she said, as though the statement supplied a sufficient excuse for his temperament.

"What about Meg? Was she happy to work for him?" Celia asked. "She was employed at the auction house, I gather."

"I think she was happy."

"But you are not certain."

"All she'd say was that she found the work interesting," she said. "She liked being around all the fancy goods Mr. Chase sells there. One time, he had a whole supply of Chinese porcelain on offer. Another time, they were auctioning a bunch of silk fabric in all the colors of a rainbow, according to Meg. I would've like to have seen that."

Her voice trailed off as she contemplated shimmering, colorful silk.

"If Miss Greaves enjoyed her position at the auction house, why did she abruptly abandon her position?" Celia asked. "I was told that she had done so."

"I . . . well, ma'am, maybe it had something to do with a man who came to visit shortly before she moved away from the Chases'," she said. "She got all anxious afterwards. Started to act jumpy. Would startle when folks spoke to her, like she was so deep in her thoughts it was a shock to be drawn out."

Jumpy. The same word the clerk had used to describe her state of mind. "Was this man's name Sy Eckart, by any chance?"

"Her beau? It wasn't him, Mrs. Davies."

"You knew Mr. Eckart?"

"Oh, no. I never met him, but I knew about him."

"Then how are you certain the man visiting was not Mr. Eckart?" Celia asked.

"Because I heard her tell the boy who used to help with Mr. Chase's horses it wasn't him," she said, proving that her ability to be observant extended to more than noticing the arrival of a nosy woman in widow's weeds. "He was teasing her about the fellow coming to visit, asked if he was her sweetheart, and she got angry. Terrible angry."

"Did you see this man? What did he look like?"

"I only caught a glimpse from one of the upstairs windows, so I didn't see his face," she said. "But he was a policeman. I could tell that from his uniform."

"A policeman?" The fellow could not have been Nicholas; he had yet to return from the war. "Perhaps the man was her uncle. He was a detective for the police force before he died."

Although, from Celia's experience, the detectives never wore a uniform like Mr. Taylor or the other officers did.

"Oh? He might've been her uncle?" Her brow creased again. "I wonder why she didn't just tell the stable boy who he was, then. Rather than get so angry."

"Mrs. Victor did not tell me about this man's visit with Meg."

"She mustn't have noticed," she said.

Or the woman had not wanted Celia to know, for some reason.

"But then Meg was gone. Moved out," Eileen was saying. "Mrs. Victor didn't know to where. I tried to find out, but Meg hadn't told anybody. Like she wanted it to be a secret."

What were you fleeing from, Meg Greaves? "You must have been worried about her, after she'd left so abruptly."

"I should've been, shouldn't I, Mrs. Davies? Given what did happen." She lowered her head for a moment and sighed. "It wasn't until a month or so later that I heard she'd taken her own life. How terrible, to get so low as to do that."

"Did anyone come looking for her *after* she had moved out?" Celia asked.

"Not that I recollect, Mrs. Davies," she said.

"What about Mr. Eckart?"

Eileen shook her head. "Him neither."

"Curious, then, that he recently visited the Chases' house on

California Street," she said.

Eileen rolled her lips between her teeth. "I was at the market when he came by, but I sure did hear about it. How upset he was about not being able to speak with Mr. Chase," she said. "And then to learn that he's been found shot dead, his body floating in the bay . . . It's awful, Mrs. Davies."

"Eileen, I am reluctant to mention this, but I have heard a rumor involving Mr. Chase," Celia said, proceeding carefully. "A rumor that makes me question if he could be responsible for Mr. Eckart's death."

Her eyes went wide. "Mr. Chase? Oh, dear," she said, neither confirming nor denying the rumor.

Celia heard the chime of the entry hall clock; her patient was due any minute. She got to her feet. "Thank you for coming, Eileen. You have been most helpful."

"But there's more, ma'am," she said. "This might be what that policeman wanted with Meg."

She untied her net purse and withdrew an item of jewelry from inside. She examined it for a moment before holding it out to Celia. A gold brooch lay on her palm. The item was made with garnets of an unusual shade, a red that bordered on a rich amber, the stones forming a flower. It was an exquisitely beautiful piece.

"What is this?" Celia asked. Some form of payment? Eileen had not asked her to do any investigating, though.

"I found it. In Meg's room after she'd cleared out. She'd taken all of her clothing and whatnot, but the brooch was hidden under her bed." She reluctantly handed it over, her gaze lingering on the warm red of the jewels. "I shouldn't have kept it, I know. But it's so pretty."

Celia turned the brooch over in her hand. "A piece of jewelry she may have inherited, perhaps?" Nicholas had never indicated that his family had the sort of money that lent itself to purchasing lovely gemstones, though. They'd been farmers and not particularly successful ones. But Meg would likely not leave behind a precious heirloom, no matter how hasty her departure.

"I hate to say this, but I got to wondering if she'd taken it from Mr. Chase's auction house, ma'am."

Celia regarded the young woman. "That is a serious accusation, Eileen."

"I know. I know. I'm sorry, but I can't help thinking that," she said.

"I've also been wondering if it's a fake."

"Why would you think that, Eileen?"

"Just something I heard. About Mr. Chase's business."

Intriguing. "You suspect Mr. Chase of selling counterfeit jewels?" If his auction house was indeed where Meg had obtained the item from.

"I'm not sure what to think, Mrs. Davies," she answered. "That's why I came to you."

The "lady detective."

"Was the brooch all you found?" Celia asked, closing her fingers around it. "No letters, for example, which you or someone else at the house sent on to her family?"

"Letters? What sort of letters?"

"Personal letters," Celia replied. "I gather by your question, though, that you did not know of them."

"No, ma'am. I didn't. You're not going to tell the police I kept the brooch, are you?" Eileen asked, a worried hitch in her voice. "I mean, I didn't know what to do with it after I found it. I wasn't sure I should try to return it to Meg's family, not that I knew how to find them, and then I got scared the cops would think I'd stolen it. And I didn't want to snitch on Meg. And I didn't want Mr. Chase to find out. So I kept it. And forgot about it until yesterday."

"Unfortunately, I do have to inform the police," she said. "But I trust in your innocence and I have faith they will as well. Once I have explained the situation."

"If you're sure."

"I am." Celia tucked the brooch into her skirt pocket. "Thank you, Eileen, for bringing the brooch to me. But I now have a favor to ask of you. I need you to keep quiet about this conversation. Can you do that?"

"Of course I can, Mrs. Davies," she replied eagerly, perhaps excited by the opportunity to assist in her investigation.

"There is one more thing," Celia said. "Mrs. Chase is holding a benefit tonight. I am planning to attend but would prefer the Chases not become aware of my interest in Meg."

"Are you sure that's wise, ma'am? Attending her party tonight?" she asked nervously. "She might not take kindly to you being there, asking her guests about Meg. If that's what you intend to do."

"I shall attempt to be as discreet as possible, Eileen."

Eileen got to her feet and accompanied Celia to the examining room door. "And you're not planning on telling Mrs. Chase that I gave you the brooch, are you?"

"If I discover a reason to mention it to her, I shall not tell her who I obtained it from."

"Sorry. I just don't think she'd believe me if I told her where I'd found it."

Just then, the bell rang. Addie's footsteps echoed in the front hall as she hurried to answer it. The patient she'd been expecting had arrived.

"If you learn anything else . . ." *find anything else* . . . "do not hesitate to contact me, Eileen." Celia opened the clinic door to find Owen standing on the other side.

"Mrs. Davies, ma'am." He glanced at Eileen and blushed. "I . . . um . . . hello. My name's Owen Cassidy," he said to her.

Well, now.

Eileen smiled, slipped past him and out the front door Addie held open.

Owen stared after her. "Who's that, ma'am?"

"Someone who knew Meg Greaves, Owen, and brought me this. Which Meg apparently once had in her possession." Celia showed him the brooch.

He whistled admiringly. "That had to have been expensive. Could Mr. Greaves's sister have been able to afford it?"

"Unless the gemstones are of paste, no, I'd imagine not."

"Do you want me to find out if it's real, ma'am?"

"Thank you for the offer, Owen, but I presume Mr. Greaves will wish to make that assessment." She returned the brooch to her pocket. "If you are wanting breakfast, Owen, Addie should be able to cook you an egg and there are fried potatoes." His landlady never seemed to feed him enough.

He hesitated before answering; he was always hungry, after all, even if he had been adequately fed. Celia's brother had been the same at Owen's age.

"That's okay, ma'am. I just thought I'd stop by before I headed to the warehouse for the day. To see if you needed me to do anything for our investigation."

"I *could* use your assistance, Owen," she said. "We need to locate a woman named Judith Whelan."

Owen grinned. "I'm good at finding people."

"Yes, you are." Which meant Celia could prioritize delivering a brooch.

℘ CHAPTER 10 ℧

"Mr. Loomis is all settled in, sir," Taylor said, closing the door to dampen the ruckus a pickpocket was causing as one of the officers dragged him through the station toward the lockup. "And kicking up a storm."

"When he gets tired of kicking, maybe he'll talk."

Taylor leaned over the desk to study the notes Nick was examining. "Is the handwriting the same, Mr. Greaves. Sir?"

"Doesn't appear to be. See here? The *n*'s are not the same," he pointed out, comparing the *n* in *next* with the *n* in *learn* on the prior note he'd received. "The way the *ou* is written out is different between the two messages, as well. And in general, the handwriting is clumsy, like the person wasn't taught proper penmanship." Or that was what he was supposed to believe.

"Who all knows you're looking into Mr. Eckart's murder, Mr. Greaves?"

He returned the notes to the drawer, setting them alongside Meg's letters. "Everybody in San Francisco, Taylor. My name was in the newspaper accounts about the investigation into his death."

"Oh. Right," he said. "Bet Mrs. Jewett wasn't happy about that note."

"Good thing I didn't tell her."

Knuckles rapped on the door, a rhythmic set of taps he'd come to recognize. It opened before Taylor could respond, and Celia stepped inside.

"Good, you are here." She smiled at Taylor. "Mr. Taylor, it is nice to see you. It has been a few days."

A few days? Was he neglecting his ladylove, Miss Ferguson?

His assistant blushed and shot Nick a look. "It's been busy around here, ma'am."

"Yes. The case concerning Mr. Sylvanus Eckart," she said, taking the chair in front of Nick's desk, her black skirts cascading around her. She meant to stay for a while, apparently. Until she extracted the details of the case from him, which she usually succeeded at doing.

"Yes, ma'am."

"Any updates since yesterday, if I might ask?" she asked Nick.

"The man who identified Eckart's body, Mr. Loomis, has been forced to backtrack on claiming he'd spotted Raymond—Raymond

Fuller—with Eckart the day he was shot. The waiters at Bauman's deny his story," he replied. "I'd wager Loomis knows who killed his friend but is too scared to give us the name. I've had him put in one of our holding cells. Maybe time spent with the rats will encourage him to talk."

"The company of the rats might be uncomfortable, Nicholas, but Mr. Loomis may discover that he is safer inside your jail than out on the street," she said. "Perhaps the rats will *not* encourage him to talk."

Out of the corner of his eye, Nick noticed Taylor purse his lips as he considered that she might be right.

"Also," Nick continued, "according to Eckart's landlord, Eckart had returned to San Francisco from Oregon because somebody had given him a reason to think he could 'fix an old problem.'"

"Revenge, then. But revenge for what, exactly?" Celia asked, her glance taking in Taylor and Nick. "What of Mr. Fuller? Have you been able to interrogate him?"

"Another individual who's gone missing," he said. "Skipped out on his job at one of the sawmills as well as the room he'd been renting."

"How discouraging."

To say the least.

"And Mr. Greaves got another warning note last night, pinned to the front door of Mrs. Jewett's," Taylor helpfully added.

Nick would've preferred that he hadn't been so helpful, based on the alarmed look on Celia's face.

"Another message warning you, Nicholas?" she asked. "What did it say?"

"The usual sort of thing."

"That's it? That is all you mean to tell me?"

Yes. "While you're in my office, I suppose I should ask what you've uncovered," Nick said. "Because I'm sure you haven't been sitting around waiting for a report from me. Despite having agreed yesterday to go home and let me do the investigating."

"Mr. Greaves, there truly is no need to scowl at me."

"There is *always* a need to scowl at you."

Taylor snickered.

"Firstly, I have discovered the full name of Meg's friend Judith," she replied. "One of Mr. Chase's clerks remembered her and her name. She is apparently rather handsome."

"Well, let's be grateful for good looks," said Nick. "But do you trust him? Nobody at the auction house gave *me* the name of a friend." Just like nobody at the Chases' place had told him about Sy Eckart's agitated visit.

"The fellow who informed me was not at work the day you stopped by to ask questions."

His rotten luck.

"Her name is Judith Whelan," she continued, and Taylor reached for his notebook to record it. "She is not listed in the most recent city directory, but Addie fortunately held on to the prior one that was published. I found an address for Miss Whelan in that. Outdated but a place to begin. I copied it down for you, Mr. Taylor."

She handed Nick's assistant a folded piece of paper.

"On Green?" Taylor asked.

Nick felt a pang. He'd no idea, when he was younger, how much memories could physically hurt. "Uncle Asa used to rent a house on that street. When Meg lived with him."

Celia's gaze was gentle. Sympathetic. She'd lost her brother during the war in the Crimea; she understood some of his grief. But her brother had died nobly and Meg . . . *had not.*

"Was a place of work listed for Miss Whelan?" Nick asked, collecting himself. He'd save reflections and recriminations for later, when he was alone at home.

"Yes. She worked for a sewing machine distributor as a saleswoman," she said. "The shop is not far from Mr. Chase's auction house, which likely accounts for why she so frequently met your sister there in order for them to walk home together at the end of the day."

A close friend of Meg's, somebody she'd written about to Sy Eckart but never to Nick. Or maybe she had, in one of the letters she'd tried to send to him on the battlefield. The army was so often on the move, though, and letters didn't always arrive.

"Isn't it possible Miss Whelan got married, and that's why you can't find her any longer, Mrs. Davies?" Taylor asked.

"That could be the situation indeed, Mr. Taylor," she replied. "Or she moved away. Either of which makes our discovering her a trifle more difficult."

"Thank you, Celia."

"There is more, Nicholas. One of the servants who works for the

Chases, a young woman named Eileen, was friends with Meg when she briefly roomed at their house near the Mission. She observed my visit to the house and decided to stop by my clinic to talk to me about your sister," she said. "And before you complain about witnesses speaking to me and not to you, I believe that the housekeeper had not informed anyone of your visit last week."

He folded his arms. "I mean, why would she?" he asked sarcastically.

Celia ignored his petulance. "Eileen spotted me and managed to deduce who I was," she said. "Which does not make me happy, I should tell you."

"And what did she have to say about Meg?"

"She told me about a policeman who'd come by to see her. After his visit, Meg became rather agitated," she said. "The clerk at the auction house also described her as being 'jumpy' around the same time. She moved out shortly thereafter. Not long before she passed away."

"A policeman? My uncle, you mean."

"The fellow wore a uniform, according to Eileen," she said. "Did your uncle ever wear a police uniform?"

Taylor furrowed his brow. "He wouldn't have, would he, sir?"

"No, he didn't."

"That is what I thought. Also, there is this." Celia reached inside her small, embroidered purse. She set the item she retrieved on his desk.

"A garnet brooch?" He picked it up, the copper-red jewels glinting back the late morning light coming through the window behind him. They glowed like a fire had been lit in the depths of the stones. "Where'd this come from?"

"According to Eileen, she found it underneath the bed in the room Meg had occupied at the Chases'," she said. "It is not a family heirloom, is it? The color is very clear and of an unusual shade. Quite valuable, from what I know of garnets. If it is real."

"A family heirloom?" He wanted to laugh. When had they ever been able to afford jewels? Half the time, they could barely afford the rent they'd owed on the place in Sacramento. "The best piece of jewelry my mother ever owned was a pin set with a bit of coral. Pretty enough, but nothing this nice."

"Which does make me curious about how Meg obtained the item."

"Eileen is probably lying about finding the brooch because she stole it, feels guilty, wants to get rid of it but needs to pin the blame on somebody," Nick said. "So she chose my dead sister. You don't really believe she's been innocently holding on to it all this time as a memorial to Meg, do you?"

Celia exhaled quietly and tugged on the ribbons of her purse to close it. "She said she did not know how to return it to your family and then became frightened that the police would accuse her of stealing it—which you just did—so she hid the brooch away and forgot about it."

"Right." Nick tossed the brooch to his assistant, who fumbled and dropped his notebook in order to catch it.

"Eileen has also considered the possibility that Meg took it from Mr. Chase's auction house."

"She wants us to believe Meg stole it from Chase?" he asked, irritation rising.

"I am merely relaying what she told me, Nicholas," she replied stiffly. "In the end, the brooch might not be worth much. Eileen has heard a whisper of gossip that Mr. Chase is offering counterfeit jewels. Unbeknownst to his customers. It may be fake, if the auction house is where the item has indeed come from."

Taylor peered at the brooch. "Should I have a jeweler look at it, sir?"

"Yes, Taylor," he answered. "Also, find out if anybody's worked on a jewelry store theft in the past couple of years, and if a garnet brooch was among the items taken. We might need to arrest Eileen for stealing it."

"Nicholas, she'd not have come to me with the brooch if she had stolen it."

"So, rather than think some stranger is a thief, you'd prefer that I think my *sister* was one. Is that it?"

"I did not intend to—"

"Meg was everything that was good, Celia. Everything," he snapped.

"Sir?" Taylor asked, concerned.

Frowning, she gathered her shawl around her shoulders and stood. "I do not doubt that, Mr. Greaves," she said flatly. "But I remain mystified how she obtained the brooch and what it means that she had done. Furthermore, all I ask is that you please use my information wisely and not make me regret my decision to tell you." She turned to

Taylor. "I will give your regards to Addie, Mr. Taylor, and do know that you are welcome to dinner any evening."

"Thank you, ma'am."

She inclined her head and gave Nick the briefest of looks. "Good day to you both."

And with that, she swept out of the office.

• • •

"We only sell the best sewing machines made, ma'am." The sales-woman, whose smile had not left her face the entire time Celia had been inside the shop, beamed reassuringly. By the end of the day, her cheeks must ache from the permanent expression.

"I have every confidence that is true."

The young woman took Celia's elbow, a trifle forward of her to do so, and began to guide her through the narrow shop. A selection of sewing machines were lined up against the walls, and the room smelled faintly of lubricating oil and the curious aroma of metal. Another saleswoman was demonstrating a machine to a matron, who bent over her shoulder in rapt attention. The repetitive mechanical clack of the arm driving the needle—not as loud as Celia had anticipated—might be almost pleasant if not for her headache. She'd allowed Nicholas's outburst to annoy and distress her. *What had I been expecting? What in heaven's name had I been expecting?* That Nicholas might accept with equanimity the least suggestion that his beloved sister had been a criminal? Ridiculously naive of her.

His outburst had precisely demonstrated, however, what Mrs. Jewett had been worried about—that Nicholas could not remain clearheaded when it came to Meg. Could not calmly consider what Eileen's discovery of the brooch meant. Whether the jewelry was in any way relevant to Meg's behavior in the weeks before her passing or to the present-day murder of her beau, Sylvanus Eckart. Instead, he preferred to rebuke her.

"Ma'am?" the woman, whose trustworthy face and manner had likely been the characteristics that had obtained her the job, along with her skill at maintaining an unwavering smile, peered at Celia. Her smile was in danger of slipping. "Are you feeling unwell?"

"Oh. I apologize for my woolgathering," she replied. "What were you telling me?"

"I was saying that Wheeler and Wilson are the only sewing machine manufacturers to win a gold medal at the Grand Paris Exposition last year, you know."

Celia did know; she'd read the claims, and the counterclaims by other sewing machine sales agents, in the newspaper. "Which is why I have come to your business."

"Of course."

They stopped in front of the latest model, and the saleswoman swept her hand through the air over it. "Isn't it lovely?"

The small iron machine, no larger than a breadbox, had silver-plated fittings and was attached to a polished rosewood table that perched atop scrolling iron legs. Two treadles, shaped like the soles of a pair of shoes, were fitted at the bottom and connected to a wheel that would drive the sewing arm when pressed. The table itself had a wood cover that contained small drawers for supplies and would fold over the sewing machine when it was not in use, turning it into a piece of furniture.

The saleswoman slid over a chair for Celia to occupy. "If you'd like to take a seat, I can show you how it works."

Celia obliged and sat down, despite having no intention to purchase a sewing machine today. Although Addie had been hinting that she'd like to own one. How they would ever afford such an instrument had not, however, been part of her hints.

"It's quite simple to thread, once you know the trick," she said. "First, the spool goes on the pin at the back here. Then the thread goes through this guide and round the tension wheel and then into the next guide on the arm here, do you see?"

"Yes, yes I do," she said, though she was hardly paying attention. Her mind kept returning to Nicholas's outburst and her reaction—startled, disappointed—to his anger. Despite her assurances to Eileen, she could not rely upon him to calmly and properly investigate. *Truth be told, how calmly and properly can I?*

"Then the thread goes through the guide above the needle, then the needle itself, of course, and lastly through the hole in the glass foot," she explained, her fingers limber as she easily maneuvered the thread. "See? Simple. And on the side here is where the bobbin is located."

"Ah," Celia replied. "I do not believe I can afford this model, however."

A model that cost, according to a discreet tag at the back, an eye-watering one hundred and thirty-five dollars. Addie would be shocked to learn the amount, which was more than two months' rent on a decent house. Six months' rent on a four-room tenement in a cramped part of the city. Not that anyone living in a tenement would contemplate purchasing a sewing machine when a simple needle could be made to suffice.

"We have many different options, ma'am, including ones without the case cabinet that aren't as expensive," the woman said, her tone becoming increasingly urgent and encouraging. She did not wish to lose a potential sale. "Or you could always purchase a basic machine that sits on a plain table for under sixty dollars."

Celia ran her hand down her shawl, her gloved fingers arriving at the barely detectible lump of stitch-work where Addie had repaired a hole; even sixty dollars was far too dear a price when Celia had delayed buying any new clothes.

Smiling apologetically, she stood. "I shall have to consider the purchase for a while longer," she said. "Perhaps if I am more frugal with my expenditures, I shall eventually be able to afford such a lovely item. In the meantime, perhaps you can give me your card?"

The young woman fished in her skirt pockets and pulled out a simple card, her name printed in cheap ink.

"Thank you." Celia placed the card in her reticule. "Do you happen to be new here? Another saleswoman assisted me previously. Her name was Judith. Judith Whelan."

"Oh, Judith. A very confident and smart sort of person."

"Indeed so, which is why I recall her," Celia said. "So knowledgeable and congenial, also. Quite friendly, in fact. She used to tell me stories about a friend of hers named Meg. How close they were before the poor young woman died. Has she ever told you about her? She apparently met a tragic end."

"A tragic end? That's downright sad, ma'am, but I don't recollect any stories about her friend."

Drat. "Is Judith still employed here?"

"Oh, no. Not for some time," the young woman replied. "She up and quit one day a few weeks ago. No explanation."

Rather like Mr. Fuller had done. "In trouble with the law?"

"The law? Judith?" She laughed, then sobered when she realized that Celia had been serious. "Well, I don't know about that, ma'am."

"Afraid for her safety, perhaps?"

"I . . . uh . . ." The girl became alarmed. "Ma'am, what are you asking?"

"Forgive my excessive curiosity, but did she ever talk to you about a friend of hers who'd moved to Oregon. A Mr. Eckart?" she asked. "She used to tell me about him as well. Perhaps he could help me locate her. In order to ensure that she is quite all right. I fear I shall not sleep for fretting over her, given your news concerning her abrupt departure."

"She did, ma'am," she said, giving no indication that she read the newspapers and was aware of his untimely death. Thankfully. "She said he was going to be returning to San Francisco. Told me that not too long ago. Well, before she quit, that is."

"I expect she was looking forward to their reunion, as they were good friends."

"Looking forward, ma'am? That's not how it seemed to me. Oh." She pressed her fingers to her open mouth. "Oh, dear. Her safety."

Indeed. And how fascinating to learn.

So fascinating that the news had, for a moment, completely taken her mind off how concerned she was about Nicholas.

• • •

"You still wading through those letters, Greaves?" Briggs swiped doughnut crumbs off his checked vest and onto the floor, where they'd become ant feed.

"I thought you had an assault and battery case to present evidence on this afternoon, Briggs," said Nick, flipping over the letter of Meg's he'd finished and moving on to the next one in the pile atop his desk.

"Maybe you should ask Mrs. Davies to have a crack at them. She might get somewhere," he said, flicking away the last crumb. "Oh, wait. You two have had a shouting match and might not be on speaking terms anymore. Did I hear that right?"

Nick sucked in a hot breath. "You looking for a fight, Briggs?" Nick could take him, easily. Briggs was large but he wasn't quick.

"Attacking a fellow detective who was merely enquiring after an investigation?" Briggs tutted. "Your temper is getting the better of you, Greaves."

Nick got to his feet. "We can go out to the alley, if you'd like. Or we can have it out in here. Push the desks out of the way."

"I'd love a chance to complain to the captain about your antagonistic behavior, Greaves, but I'm needed at court. Evidence and all." Smirking, Briggs grabbed his hat off his desk and clomped out of the office.

Don't let him get to you, Greaves. Don't.

Uncle Asa would have been disappointed in Nick. Letting a man like Briggs get under his skin like a ragged splinter, irritating and prickling. Forgetting how to laugh off his annoying comments and snide remarks. But he'd been in a foul mood since Celia had walked out of the office like she had no plans to return, the angry swish of her skirts sucking the energy and air from the room, and all his short-tempered bad habits had rushed back to fill the void.

Nick retook his chair and grabbed the letter he'd been reading. He wasn't going to find an answer in Meg's letters as to who'd sent him a lovely little threat, he knew that by now, so he figured it was more useful to hunt for any mention of the brooch. So far, he hadn't found a single reference to any jewelry, either.

He stacked the letter atop the turned-over pile. But Meg wouldn't directly bring up the brooch, would she? Too incriminating to specifically write about in a letter, if she had taken it from Chase's auction house.

"Which she did *not* do," Nick muttered.

What if instead, say, an acquaintance of hers had snatched the brooch, Meg had somehow gotten ahold of it, but then was stuck trying to figure out what to do with it without getting the person into trouble? That might explain the visit by the policeman and why she'd been jumpy afterward. Might also explain why she hadn't gone to Uncle Asa with the information, even though she should have.

Nick scrubbed his fingers through his hair and lazily reviewed the nearest letter. *Damn. Have I been missing the obvious?*

Nick held the letter up to the window light.

I think you're right about what's going on, but what should I do now? I wish you were here to help, like I always do. I could ask Judith for advice, but I don't want to concern her.

What was Sy Eckart supposedly right about? Could've been anything, frankly. Didn't necessarily mean she'd found that a mutual acquaintance was a thief. But maybe there was more, hidden inside her letters. Nick rifled through them again, concentrating on the notes she'd written nearer to the time of her death.

Funny how you think you know folks but you really don't. Nick pulled out a letter dated a week later, searched the sentences he'd read multiple times. *I went for a stroll and saw all manner of sights.* He examined the next letter then the next one. Halted on a comment she'd made to a concerned beau thousands of miles away. *Try not to worry about me.* Casually tucked among other comments about the weather and that there'd been a small earthquake, but no damage done. He'd tended to skip over the sentence when he reread that particular letter because, to him, it indicated Meg's unhappiness and that she'd planned for a while to kill herself.

What did any of it have to do with a garnet brooch hidden away in a room she'd rented from the Chases, though?

Knuckles rapped on the door and Mullahey strode into the office, a box tucked under his arm. "Got a minute, Mr. Greaves?"

He pushed aside the letters. "You're finally finished with Eckart's place."

"Been through it with a fine-tooth comb, Mr. Greaves. There wasn't much and certainly not any evidence of who it was who'd killed him," he said. "The room was turned over."

"Taylor told me." What had the individual been searching for? A brooch, four years later? Stacks of letters? "You brought me something, though. Based on that box you're carrying."

"His belongings," he said. "Aside from his clothing, which I was thinking you'd not be wanting piled up in your office."

"Correct."

Nick cleared a space on his desk, and the officer dumped the contents of the box onto it. A comb, a box of matches, a bone toothpick, a small scissors and a pocketknife with an ivory handle. An IOU for two dollars to a man whose name Nick couldn't make out. A bill from an oyster shop. "The usual items a man might own, Mr. Greaves. Apart from a coin purse or money clip, which he probably had on him when he died."

Along with a miniature of Meg and a strand of hair secured within a locket. "Thank you. I'll look through it."

"There was this, too, Mr. Greaves." He retrieved a scrap of paper from his coat pocket. "I found it in his bed, stuck between the mattress and the headboard. Like Mr. Eckart had been reading it before he fell asleep. Don't know why the fellow who searched the room before us did not find it."

"Luckily for us, I suppose."

The bit of paper was a torn-off portion of a letter. *Damn.* The handwriting was Meg's, no denying. Why had Eckart kept this one, though? Or part of one, since much of it was missing.

"'He's found out I know,'" Nick read aloud. He flipped over the paper, searched both sides, but Meg hadn't said more about who "he" was. Not on this scrap. So why keep the note at all? "That's it?"

"That would be it, Mr. Greaves."

Nick folded the note, ran his thumbnail along the crease his sister had formed years earlier, and set it down. *He's found out I know.* And then she was dead.

☙ CHAPTER 11 ❧

"Thanks for agreeing to speak with me," Nick said to the fellow who'd rented Sy Eckart his upstairs set of rooms. And the lower set to Loomis, presently enjoying the musty confines of the police lockup. A definite downgrade from this place, located in a quieter, cleaner neighborhood than Nick had anticipated. No noisy clanging from the wharves. No stink from manufactories. Maybe the pleasantness of the area was the reason Loomis had owed Eckart money. More expensive than near the warehouses or in Tar Flats.

"Not a problem, Detective, but your officers have already questioned me," he said. He shot a look up at a curtain flapping through the second-floor window somebody had left open. "And torn my best apartment to bits."

"It was like that when my men arrived, so don't blame the police."

The fellow frowned, adding creases to his weather-worn face, and folded his arms. "What is it you want, Detective?"

"Did you observe the individual who might've been responsible for tearing your best apartment to bits after Mr. Eckart died?" Loomis wanted them to believe he wasn't that individual.

"One of your men already asked me that, and like I told him, I didn't. I live four doors down," the landlord said by way of explanation, indicating the clapboard house with a jerk of his head. "Plus, I don't make it a habit to keep track of everybody's comings and goings."

"You have two other renters in this building, correct?"

"Your officer told me Mr. Loomis is in jail," he said. "My other renter has been away this past week."

Convenient. For the renter, not for Nick. "I've heard that Mr. Loomis owed Mr. Eckart money. What do you know about that?"

"I wouldn't be surprised if he did, Detective. He likes to gamble."

"Might he have killed Mr. Eckart over those debts?"

"Like I also said to your officer, I can't imagine Loomis summoning the gumption to kill anybody. I know he's had run-ins with the law before, but murder?" He shook his head. "No."

Nick tapped the pencil he'd brought with him against the folded scrap of paper he'd also thought to bring. Not that he'd made use of either yet. "Any thoughts on who might've wanted Mr. Eckart dead?"

The man sighed, tired of repeating himself. "He'd only been renting from me for a couple of weeks, Detective. I didn't know him well enough to have compiled a list of his friends or enemies."

"My apologies for asking you questions my men likely already asked. I just want to hear your answers myself," Nick said. "So, did you notice anything strange about Mr. Eckart's behavior in the days before he died? Acting scared, maybe. Anxious."

"I did. When I saw him Tuesday or Wednesday last week. Shouted a greeting. Startled him so badly, I thought he'd jump right out of his skin," he replied. "I've been thinking about it, and I wonder if his reaction had anything to do with that fellow who came around looking for him. Knocked at my house. Annoyingly."

Nick readied his pencil. "Do you have a name? A description?"

"Called himself Raymond Fuller."

Fuller. "An average-sized fellow missing several fingers on his right hand."

"Missing fingers?" Confusion puckered his forehead. "He wasn't missing any fingers, Detective. Not the man I spoke with."

• • •

"It was the worst attack I've had, Mrs. Davies." The woman gazed woefully at her foot, the swelling of the big toe significantly reduced from her description of how bad it had been—*big as a plum and red as a cherry*—but it remained inflamed around the joints. "It felt as though I'd dipped my toe in scalding water. Awful pain for days. Days!"

"Have you decreased your consumption of red meat, as I suggested?" Celia rarely saw a female patient with gout, being a disorder that most commonly afflicted males, but this woman had a history of the condition.

She eased herself off of Celia's examining table, gingerly testing her swollen toe before putting her weight on her feet. "I have been trying to cut down, Mrs. Davies, but it's not easy. My husband is very fond of a good piece of beef. I hate to deny him."

"For your health." Celia smiled at her and went to her desk to write out a prescription.

"Cold water baths do help, like you told me they would," she said, steadying herself against the examining table while she drew on her stockings. "I prefer them to your recommendation of a warm water bath with saleratus dissolved in it."

"Whichever works best." Prescription finished, she handed it to the woman. "Any apothecary or druggist should be able to provide you the ingredients."

Celia's patient read the piece of paper. "Colchicum root to mix with peppermint water as a drink."

"It should be effective."

The woman tucked it away. "My husband thinks I should just buy myself a bauble to feel better," she said. "Have you ever noticed how pretty jewels can lift a lady's spirits, Mrs. Davies?"

No, thought Celia.

"There are stores where you can get beautiful jewelry for cheap, you know," she continued as Celia escorted her to the front door. "But how many rings or fancy pins can a woman own?"

Celia smiled at her. "Less red meat," she instructed, showing her out.

"I'll try, Mrs. Davies. Good day," she said as she limped down the steps to the street.

Sighing, Celia rubbed an ache in her lower back and closed the door.

"Ma'am, are you all right?" asked Addie, who'd stepped into the entryway from the parlor, a feather duster in her hand.

"What do you mean?"

"You've nae been yourself this afternoon."

Celia returned to her examining room, Addie following. "I am tired, that is all."

"Is it?"

"No, that's not all. Nicholas and I had a disagreement at the police station." Celia sat at her desk, flipped open her notebook, and stared at the blank page. She hated to fight. Had always hated to fight. When she was young, quarrels with her brother would leave her in tears for hours. Arguments with Patrick had been no better, although she'd learned to never cry in front of him.

"More than a disagreement, aye, ma'am?"

Celia looked over at Addie. "Eileen, the young woman who stopped in this morning, brought me an item she claimed she'd found in a room Meg Greaves had once rented. A brooch," Celia explained. "She also suggested that Meg may have taken it from Mr. Chase's auction house when Meg worked for him. I gave the brooch to Nicholas, along with Eileen's story. He became rather angry, Addie."

"Mr. Greaves loved his sister. 'Tis only natural he would want to defend her character," she said. "Besides, he is hurting, ma'am. He feels guilty he was not here for his wee sister when she needed him. Give him time."

Time heals all wounds. Did it?

Celia turned back to her notebook. "He has received a threatening note, Addie." He'd not wanted to tell her about it any more than he'd wanted to tell her about receiving his sister's letters.

"Dinna you *fash*, ma'am. Mr. Taylor will keep him safe."

"Mr. Taylor cannot be with Nicholas every hour of every day, unfortunately."

She inked her pen and dashed off a summary of her patient's visit. "I would like dinner early, if that is possible," she said, closed her notebook, and wiped the pen nib clean. "I have an event to attend with Jane tonight. At the Chases'."

"The Chases'?"

"Yes." She got to her feet. "And you may remove that apprehensive look from your face, Addie. Mrs. Chase is hosting a charitable evening to benefit a new organization, the Society for the Prevention of Cruelty to Animals. There have been articles in the newspaper about them. It shall be a harmless evening in support of an excellent cause, so do not worry. I shall be fine."

Addie scowled. "Aye. I've heard *that* before."

• • •

"Are you a friend of hers, too?" the landlady asked, making it sound like Owen had better not answer in the affirmative. She balled her fists at her wide hips. Or maybe her hips weren't wide and it was just her rust-colored skirt, the material shiny in spots from wear, that was wide. Ladies' dresses could be just that confusing. "Well? Is that why you're asking after her?"

"So Miss Whelan *did* used to live here," Owen said.

The woman rolled her eyes. "Of course she did. You found her name in the directory with this address, didn't you?"

Put that way, his had been a dumb question. "Where does she live now, do you know?"

"I don't."

The woman switched from fisting her hips to folding her arms. She had a scar along one muscled forearm—which he could see because her sleeves were rolled up to her elbows—which made her look sorta menacing. Although Owen was starting to wonder if there were any landladies in San Francisco who weren't at least somewhat menacing; toughness helped keep the lodgers in line.

"It's awful important that I find her, ma'am," he said. "I'm helping an acquaintance of hers locate her. They're worried about her."

She seemed to like being called ma'am, because the stiffness in her torso softened a bit. He always called women "ma'am" or "miss," though, because that was just the polite thing to do. More folks needed to try being polite. World might be a better place if they did.

"Well, Judith Whelan moved out almost a month ago. Cleared out in a hurry, too," she said. "Don't know why. Didn't ask why."

"A hurry? Like she was scared of somebody, maybe?"

The woman squinted at him. "What do you know about her?"

"Nothing," he said. And her former landlady wasn't exactly adding to his supply of knowledge. "Did she give you any idea where she was headed?"

"Like I already told you, no."

Shoot. "I was really hoping I could find her."

He hadn't meant to sound pitiful, but he must have, because her unfriendly manner eased.

"I'm sorry I can't help you, and you're not the first person to come looking for Judith Whelan recently."

Maybe Mrs. Davies had been by already today. Which would've been mighty quick of her. Or maybe Mr. Taylor or Mr. Greaves had stopped by. *Shoot. What am I doing here if they've already been?*

"Oh?"

"Yep," she said. "Last week, in fact. She claimed she was a friend, too."

Not Mrs. Davies or the others. And he hadn't claimed he was a friend of Miss Whelan's. Had he? "Did she give you her name?"

"No, she didn't." She gave a look implying how suspicious that was. "She was a pretty thing, if you like cold and haughty. Sharp jaw, reddish hair. She gave me the creeps, though, and I was happy to see the back side of her."

• • •

"I doubt Eileen will have informed Mrs. Chase that I was the woman asking questions about Meg Greaves, Jane," Celia said, gathering her skirts in her hands to climb the wood steps up to the veranda, which spanned the lefthand side of the house. The gasoliers and lanterns in the ground-floor rooms had already been lit, even though the western horizon still glowed golden. They gleamed like beacon lights signaling the splendors within. "She was quite alarmed, in fact, by the prospect of my attendance this evening. Even though I assured her that I'd say nothing to her employer about the brooch."

"If she *has* told Marian Chase that you were that woman, we won't be here for very long," Jane said, tidying the crumpled folds of her mauve gown until her skirt lay smoothly atop her crinoline.

"I suppose we shall find out directly."

And then what?

While Jane finished fussing with her attire, Celia examined her surroundings. The exterior had been decorated with elaborately carved porch supports and cornices. Bay windows—two facing the street, and two on the left side of the building—were fitted with arched frames. The wood trim had been painted a rich brown to offset the soft cream of the house itself, a pleasing effect that drew the eye and would make the residence difficult to ignore. Which would be the effect the Chases had intended.

"I'm glad you're with me, because I haven't been up to attending one of these events on my own. And I've been itching to get a peek at the place for months," said Jane, coming to Celia's side, her outfit tidied. "Frank has refused to drive me past in order to satisfy my curiosity, though, claiming it would be gauche of us. Although who would ever notice? It's not as though we know anybody who lives out this far."

"Not even if the trip might convince you to purchase a new house on a sought-after hill?"

"I love our home and have no desire to move. Even in the middle of refurbishments." She gestured toward a wing that spread out from the right side of the main building. The addition unfortunately made the entire structure asymmetric. "Although I would like a chance to see inside the conservatory. I wouldn't mind having one of those."

Overhead gas lamps lit the plants—palms and miniature orange trees and ferns—growing inside the structure. Through the multiple windows, she could make out a marble fountain splashing water among all the greenery. *How very sophisticated.* If Celia ever suggested to Barbara that they append a conservatory to their house, Addie would resign in protest rather than agree to clean the overwhelming quantity of glass.

"How much money is there to be made as the proprietor of an auction house, Jane?" Clearly, more than Celia had ever conceived.

"Maybe we'll discover that half of the house is unfinished inside, Celia."

"But they *are* in possession of two pianos, Mrs. Hutchinson," Celia teasingly replied. "How could that possibly be?"

"By the way, none of my acquaintances have heard any gossip about Mr. Chase being a criminal of any sort, Celia, so perhaps owning an auction house *is* profitable," Jane said. "No rumors of him being responsible for somebody's death, either. Although there was a lot of gossiping when Miss Greaves died, apparently. He wasn't blamed, however."

"Thank you for asking around, Jane."

"I do wish I could've learned more."

"*Any* information is useful information."

Celia peered through the nearest window, where the French lace curtains had been drawn aside and the bottom sash lifted to allow the spring breeze to waft through the parlor beyond. The room was thronged with women in the latest fashions, silks in lush shades of blue and purple and green, trimmed in satin and velvet and the occasional row of tassels. Brilliant colors arising from the recent discovery of aniline dyes. Celia glanced at her own black bodice and skirts. She'd be a drab crow among glossy songbirds.

"Ready?" Jane asked. "Because if anybody noticed our arrival, they have to be wondering what we've been doing out here on the porch."

"Admiring the architecture, as the Chases intend for us to do."

"Oh, should we need to make a rapid escape, Celia, I'm ready to run for the tilbury with you. I wore my sensible slippers tonight." Jane winked and hiked the hem of her dress to display a pair of low-heeled black leather shoes.

"Admirable preparedness, Mrs. Hutchinson." The livery stable where they'd left her horse and carriage was a block distant, however.

An appreciable dash in corsets and hooped skirts. "Although I doubt we shall be required to flee, Jane. Even if Mrs. Chase has learned that it was Celia Davies, and not some woman named Mrs. Walford, who was at her former residence making enquiries. I anticipate nothing more serious than a stern demand to leave. Embarrassing but not dangerous."

"You don't know these women, Celia. Could be very dangerous," she said, chuckling. "Before I ring, how can I help you this evening? I'm not sure, though, that any of the guests in attendance tonight will admit to Mr. Chase being a criminal. Not while they're inside his house."

Guilt tweaked Celia's conscience, but not enough to stop her from instructing Jane on what to do.

"Discover if anyone present heard about the scene Mr. Eckart caused the other week, and if they are willing to share what precisely was said," Celia replied quietly. "Or why Mr. Eckart might have been so keen to speak with Mr. Chase in the first place."

"I'll see what I can find out," Jane said and twisted the brass doorbell crank.

A servant had apparently been waiting in the vestibule, possibly overhearing their conversation, for the door opened promptly.

The young woman's eyes went wide. "You *did* come."

"Yes, Eileen, I did," Celia said quietly, glancing past her in search of anyone who might overhear. "And try not to look so alarmed. We do not want Mrs. Chase becoming suspicious. And this is my friend, Mrs. Hutchinson, who has an invitation."

Eileen remembered herself enough to nod an acknowledgment. "It's just that . . . Mrs. Victor was here earlier, helping the staff set up the parlor to Mrs. Chase's liking," she managed to say. "I overheard her telling Mrs. Chase that a woman had come to the Mission house asking questions about Meg."

Not surprising, but unfortunate.

"Do we need to run, Celia?" Jane whispered.

I wish I knew. "Did she mention my name?"

"Not that I heard. I can't be sure, though," she said. "But she left. A half hour or more ago. So you don't have to worry about her being here."

"Then show us in, Eileen," Celia said. "People will become curious about why we have been standing on the threshold for the past few minutes, and the last thing we presently need is curiosity."

"Oh. Of course."

She scurried into the parquet-floored hallway, which stretched the depth of the house to another outside door at the rear. The evening air had been cool, but inside the space was warm and smelled of newness—the scent of recently sawn planks, paint and wallpaper paste, the wool of freshly lain Turkey carpeting, an example of which climbed the massive oak staircase that rose along the right-hand side of the hall. An aroma quite unlike the mansions and manor homes Celia had, on occasion, visited with her aunt and uncle back in Hertfordshire. Those buildings had smelled of damp from leaks that had sprung in the roofs, the must of ancient furnishings, the pleasing sweetness of old, creaking wood. Celia preferred the must and the damp, but that was nostalgia tugging.

"Let me take your wraps," Eileen said, collecting their capes and draping them over her arm.

The parlor doors had been pushed open, and the sound of the dozen or more chatting women inside the room hummed. None of the occupants appeared to have noted Celia and Jane's arrival or that they had been stalled in the vestibule by a flustered servant wishing they—or at least Celia—would turn around and leave.

"The musicians are setting up in the library, where some of the other ladies have already gathered," Eileen said. "Mrs. Chase is there, as well. Mr. Chase is in his billiard room."

Escaping the glossy, chatty songbirds. A missed opportunity to meet and assess the fellow, though. Perhaps he would make an appearance later.

They hadn't taken two steps when a tall woman in a copper-colored silk gown separated from the gaggle within the parlor and swept over to greet them, her fingers extended. Her bearing radiated an assertive congeniality, much like that of a politician attempting to convince you to support him. Or her cause, in this situation.

"Ah, Mrs. Hutchinson. I am so pleased you finally accepted one of my invitations and decided to attend tonight," she said. "I see you've brought a friend."

"This is Celia Davies, Mrs. Chase," Jane said, smiling warmly, because Jane never smiled in any other fashion. "Celia, this is Marian Chase."

"Welcome, Mrs. Davies." She affixed a smile to her face that would not be described as warm, but it did pass muster. "I have heard of you."

"It seems everyone has, Mrs. Chase."

"Yes. Haven't they."

Mrs. Chase had even features that were handsome but not showily pretty. She was younger than Celia had anticipated she might be, given that she had four daughters, three of whom were married—no older than forty-five or -six years of age, she would guess; she must have wed young—and owned the most lustrous dark hair. It had been braided and coiled around her head to form a crown, and was ornamented with a thin strand of pearls. It was not the pearls that drew Celia's attention, however. It was the brooch pinned at the neck of her gown, where the Valencienne lace collar dipped above her sternum.

A brooch made from the most lovely garnet stones, their depths glowing the color of coals smoldering on a hearth. A shade much like amber.

❦ CHAPTER 12 ❦

"I had a jeweler examine the brooch, sir," Taylor said. "The garnets are colored glass. Really good fakes, he told me."

Nick's assistant lurked in the doorway of the detectives' office.

"You can step into the office, Taylor. I'm not going to bite. Honest." He needed to apologize to Celia for his outburst, and he probably also needed to apologize to his assistant.

"Yes, sir," he replied, inching forward a foot. He unbuttoned his coat and retrieved the piece of jewelry from an inner pocket. "Said that if it had been real, the garnets would be a rare type, given their color and all. Would make the brooch more valuable than one with regular garnets."

Taylor set it on the desk. In the light of the overhead gas lamp, the stones—glass stones—took on an even warmer shade. Where *had* it come from? The fact that it was a fake was significant, however.

"Thank you, Taylor. Good work," he added.

"Why do you think your sister would have a piece of jewelry made with glass stones, sir?" he asked. "And go to the bother to hide it?"

"Maybe there's a hint at an answer here, Taylor." Nick turned to the torn scrap of note Mullahey had found.

"A couple of hours ago, Mullahey brought me this after going through Eckart's room more thoroughly. It's a portion of one of my sister's letters, which had gotten wedged between the bed's mattress and the headboard," he said, sliding the piece of paper across the desk toward Taylor. "It's my sister's handwriting. For some reason Eckart had thought the note worth holding on to. Even after all this time since she'd passed away. Even though the man's identity isn't indicated."

Taylor bent down to read. "'He's found out I know.'"

She hadn't lived long after she'd written those words.

"After reading that, some of what my sister wrote in her letters might actually explain what was happening in the weeks before she died. I've just been slow to figure it all out," Nick said. "But from what I can make out, it seems that she'd stumbled onto something, Taylor. Maybe this brooch and its fake garnets is a clue as to what she'd discovered."

Taylor straightened. "You know, sir, I've been thinking about what

Mrs. Davies told us. That one of the Chases' servants noticed an officer speaking with Miss Greaves. I can't recall any of the fellows mentioning that they'd ever met your sister, though," he said. "And there aren't any records that she'd been questioned. I looked."

"O'Neal had met her." He'd admitted as much without Nick even asking. "What I don't get is why my uncle Asa never mentioned that a policeman had gone to talk to Meg. He had to have known."

"There's a lot of officers in San Francisco, sir. Maybe he didn't know."

"If there'd been any indication that Meg had learned of a scheme to sell counterfeit jewels, or had been involved herself and been questioned about it, Asa would've heard." Nick opened the top drawer in his desk and set Meg's letters and the brooch inside. Nestled them alongside the locket Eckart had been carrying when he'd been killed, and which held the miniature of a young, vibrant woman who'd taken secrets to her grave. "So we have to ask ourselves who the man was."

"Could he have been Raymond Fuller, sir? Pretending to be a cop."

Nick locked the drawer. "Interestingly, Eckart's landlord told me about a man looking for Eckart a few days before he was killed," he said. "The fellow claimed he was Fuller, but he wasn't. Didn't match the description we have. No missing fingers."

"Not wanting folks to know his real identity." Taylor whistled. "Who was he, then? Mr. Loomis?"

"Or maybe Archibald Chase, responding to Eckart's attempts to contact him?" Nick asked. "We need to get him in here. He has a few questions to answer." Including questions about a rumor he was hawking counterfeit jewelry.

"Yes, sir." Taylor peered at him and cleared his throat. He was about to say something he feared Nick wouldn't like.

"Umm, sir. Mr. Greaves, sir. If your sister sent a message to Mr. Eckart telling him about a fellow who'd 'found out' she knew, might that suggest she didn't kill herself?" he asked. "I mean, maybe that fellow killed her because of what she'd learned about him. His criminal activities."

Not until Taylor spoke the words aloud did Nick accept that he'd been considering the possibility all along. Maybe even since the day Uncle Asa had first informed Nick about her death. The strangeness of it, her body found in a dingy hotel room, her hair dyed red and a false name given to the landlady. Meg had gone to great lengths to hide and stay hidden. Her efforts making it difficult for anybody who'd read the report of a woman found dead to identify her. His stomach clenched and nausea rose. Murdered.

"You're not mad at me for suggesting that, are you, sir?" Taylor asked tentatively, the length of time Nick had taken to answer worrying.

"No, Taylor. I'm not mad at you," he said. "Because I think you're right."

Murdered. Sweetest Meg, murdered.

• • •

"Hello, I am Deborah Hunter. I didn't realize you were acquainted with Marian."

The woman held out her hand, convivially taking Celia's as she introduced herself. She was lovely in an unusual, almost exotic way—strong yet even features, large pale eyes, smooth skin a shade warmer than porcelain. Prior to accosting Celia, she'd been locked in conversation with Mrs. Chase, both of them standing off to one side of the parlor. Between comments to Mrs. Chase, she'd surveyed the room as though monitoring it for enemies. Or prey, like a hawk on the hunt. Eventually, she'd concluded that Celia was the prey of interest and cornered her between the parlor fireplace and a large armchair.

"I am pleased to meet you," Celia replied, slipping her fingers out of Mrs. Hunter's firm grip. "I am—"

"The famous Mrs. Davies," she interrupted. "Yes, I know who you are. I would've expected Marian to tell me that she was acquainted with you, though."

"We are not," Celia replied, alert to the possibility that Mrs. Hunter's friendly overtures masked other intentions. "My friend, Mrs. Hutchinson, is."

She indicated where Jane stood speaking with a young woman who could be the double of Mrs. Chase in her youth. Likely one of her daughters. The youngest, unmarried one, perhaps.

"Ah," she said. "Have you accompanied your friend because you support the cause of the Society for the Prevention of Cruelty to Animals, or are you here to conduct an investigation?"

She had wasted scant time on the friendly overtures. "Why might you imagine I'd be investigating the Chases, Mrs. Hunter?"

"I heard about the fellow trying to speak with Archibald a couple of weeks ago, upset over something or another. That he was found dead the other morning," she answered.

"You knew they were the same man?"

"Marian mentioned it," she replied offhandedly.

Did she, now.

"I presume the police have decided the two events are related," Deborah Hunter said.

"Have they questioned Mr. Chase about the matter?" Celia asked.

She sipped from her glass of red wine before responding. "Why should they when they have sent you?"

"The police have not requested that I question him, Mrs. Hunter," she said in all honesty. "I am here merely to support a worthy cause." *Not in all honesty.*

The woman's restrained smirk lasted only long enough to be noticed before it vanished. "Certainly," she said. "Although I understand that the fellow was a ship's crewman. A rough crowd, from what my husband and those who work in the shipping business tell me. The sort of men who wouldn't hesitate to kill one of their own over a slight."

Celia considered her. "You have developed an explanation for a stranger's murder. Why is that, Mrs. Hunter?"

"When a friend's name is dragged into the conversation surrounding that murder, I feel the need to."

Who has done the dragging? Not me. Not Nicholas. Not the newspapers, so far as she was aware. "Mr. Chase was previously embroiled in terrible gossip involving the death of a young woman in his employ, was he not?"

"Then you appreciate my desire to defend his good name."

"I do."

"Pleased to have made your acquaintance, Mrs. Davies." She nodded her head and glided off, as smoothly as a punt poled down a stream, her destination the adjacent library and Marian Chase.

Jane strolled over. "What did Deborah Hunter want, Celia?" she asked, masking her words with a broad smile.

"To inform me that Mr. Chase could not be responsible for Mr. Eckart's death, I believe," she replied quietly. "Who was that you were speaking with?"

"The youngest Chase daughter," Jane said. "She was willing to tell me about the commotion Mr. Eckart caused, how dreadful it was. She didn't hear much, however, aside from him shouting 'he has to help me.' Whatever he meant by that."

"'Help me . . .' Intriguing," Celia mused. "Well done, and now I have another task for you. We need to discover from Marian Chase if she ever owned a duplicate of that brooch she is wearing."

Jane slid a discreet sideways glance in the direction of Mrs. Chase. "It is unusual, isn't it? The color of those stones. Really pretty."

Celia looked over as well. Mrs. Hunter was no longer with Mrs. Chase, who was overseeing the preparations of the string quartet in the library. "Very pretty, Jane."

"But why do you want to know about a duplicate?" Jane asked, pretending to be admiring the various landscapes and portraits suspended from the picture rail as she slowly moved her attention back to Celia's face. She is enjoying herself, thought Celia. Frank would not be pleased in the least, were he here to witness his wife's behavior.

"Because her brooch is identical to the one found in Meg's rented room," she replied, collecting a full wineglass from a passing servant and using it to hide her mouth. "And no, Miss Greaves was not wealthy enough to have purchased jewelry that Mrs. Chase might also own."

"How did Miss Greaves obtain it, then?"

"Take my advice, Jane, and do not ever suggest to Nicholas that his sister might have been a thief, for he will turn quite red-faced and shout at you."

"Oh, no, Celia." Jane paused to smile at a woman ambling past them and into the library. She slowed to examine Celia—*observe the lady detective!*—before continuing on her way. "Did you two have a fight?"

"A minor disagreement, but that is neither here nor there, Jane," she said. "My primary concern is determining if Mrs. Chase will admit to a duplicate of that brooch existing."

"She might not be aware of a duplicate."

"True, but I remain interested in her response."

"While I am asking questions about the brooch, what do you mean to do?"

"I intend to discover all I can about Mrs. Chase by a thorough examination of her possessions."

Jane subtly shook her head. "You'll definitely get tossed out on your ear if somebody finds you nosing around in her bedroom, Celia."

"Then I'd best be quick."

Still shaking her head, Jane set down her wineglass. "I'll go see what I can discover."

Celia waited for a number of beats, ensuring that Jane had fully engaged Mrs. Chase's attention, before wandering out of the parlor and into the hall. She glanced over her shoulder to ensure that no one had marked her departure. *All clear.* She set the glass she was carrying on the étagère out in the hallway, hoisted her skirts, and ran up the stairs. Now, which of the rooms would belong to Mr. and Mrs. Chase? Or, if they slept separately, Mrs. Chase's? The largest chambers were often found at the front of the house.

Listening for any footsteps that might indicate someone had followed her and hearing none, she hurried down the hall. The Chases apparently trusted their guests, because the first door handle she tried turned. It was a small bedchamber, though, meant perhaps for a servant or a young child. She grinned to herself when she discovered it was empty of any furniture. She would have to tell Jane.

She was luckier with the next room, a spacious chamber at least fifteen feet on each side with three large windows to bring in sunlight. It was not empty of furniture. Instead, the chamber was decorated in pale pinks and creams and yellows. A room for Mrs. Chase and Mrs. Chase alone, was Celia's guess. A rosewood four-poster filled the space between two of the windows, and a dressing table covered in crystal perfume jars and pots of hair and skin preparations sat alongside. A delicate glass oil lamp had helpfully been left burning on the table, not requiring Celia to hunt around for matches to light it, as she'd had to do on prior occasions of "nosing around."

"Thank you," she whispered to the unknown servant who'd been considerate—or lax—and crossed to the dressing table.

She took a seat on the thickly padded chair and inspected the contents arrayed on the surface of the table. The items were mostly bottles of perfume or preparations to smooth and soften a lady's skin. Glycerin balm. Rimmel's Lotion, a product Celia had not encountered since leaving England. Cold cream soap. A preparation labeled Chevalier's Life for the Hair. Perhaps Mrs. Chase's thick brown mane was not all it seemed on first inspection. A variety of floral-scented toilet waters. The usual collection of combs and pins and silver-backed brushes. A porcelain bowl, about the size of a teacup saucer and covered in brightly colored painted images of Chinese people in their gardens, sat to one side. Mrs. Chase likely used it to store her rings when she was not wearing them, and it was empty at the moment. The rest of her jewelry must be locked away somewhere else. Celia could not resist picking up the bowl to examine it. It weighed no more than the canary a former neighbor of hers had owned, which would perch on Celia's finger, a bright spot of yellow. The bowl was as lovely as that bird had been, and far more exquisite than the typical imports sold in the Chinese shops Celia occasionally passed on her way to and from home.

The walnut bracket clock on a shelf off to her right chimed. *Gad.* She'd been dawdling and needed to resume searching before she *was* found out.

Setting down the bowl, she tested the drawers of the dressing table. The Chases might trust their guests to not wander about inside bedchambers and pilfer belongings, but they clearly did not trust their servants, because the drawers were fastened tight. Celia rattled them again for good measure but none of them yielded. "Bloody . . ."

Next, then, the wardrobes. Their doors did yield, opening to reveal carefully folded items of clothing, stacked on the shelves and wrapped in brown paper scented with lavender to repel insects. An embroidered purple silk shawl was stored in one of the drawers, stockings and handkerchiefs in another. The contents of the next wardrobe were no different, aside from a lacquered pasteboard box tucked behind a lace mantilla cape hanging from a peg.

Celia pulled out the box and set it atop the bed. Inside, she found a stash of receipts. The name of the business was printed at the top of each one. They all appeared to have come from Mr. Chase's auction house and were made out to a variety of individuals. Why, though, would Mrs. Chase be holding on to receipts from her husband's business and keeping them hidden away in her wardrobe?

"Mrs. Davies?"

She spun to face the owner of the voice. "Oh, Eileen. You startled me. I did not hear you approach." *What a poor detective you make, Celia Davies. Anyone could sneak up on you.*

"What are you . . ." Eileen squinted at the open pasteboard box and the also guiltily open wardrobe. She glanced behind her into the hallway then stepped closer. "What are you doing inside Mrs. Chase's room, looking through her things?"

Celia restored the box to its place inside the wardrobe and shut the door. "Were you sent to look for me?" Perhaps by Mrs. Chase on the advice of her hawk-like friend, Mrs. Hunter, noting her absence.

"Mrs. Hutchinson was wondering where you'd gone to," she said, kneading her hands together at her waist as though she could squeeze her anxiety out through her fingers. "I said I'd go look for you while she took a stroll through the conservatory."

Jane, finding an opportunity to satisfy her curiosity.

"Well, you have found me, Eileen," Celia replied. "It is best we not descend the stairs together, however. We do not want to appear to be acquainted. So tell Mrs. Hutchinson I shall be down presently."

"But the entertainment is about to begin and the ladies are taking their seats," she said. "They're sure to realize you're missing. You need to come downstairs quick."

"I will. Thank you."

Eileen scurried off, and Celia surveyed the room to ensure she'd not left behind any evidence of her presence. Smoothing the dimple in the white Marseille counterpane left by the pasteboard box, she counted to ten then proceeded out of the chamber. Uncertain what of significance she had discovered, Celia frowned as she quietly shut the door behind her and slowly made her way down the hallway to the stairs. The receipts were odd, though. What might Nicholas make of them? If they were still speaking, which she was far from certain they were.

She reached the bottom of the staircase, pleased that no one was out in the entry hall or near the parlor doors to notice she'd been upstairs. Settling an innocent expression on her face, she was making the turn into the parlor when a bloodcurdling scream echoed through the dining room from the direction of the conservatory.

Mrs. Chase's guests—and a few of her servants—came running, shoving Celia aside. They rapidly clogged the doorway to the conservatory, drawn to the scream without considering that they should perhaps run the other direction. Celia's attempt to push through the crowd failed, forcing her to stand on her toes and peek through the gaps between the ladies' elaborate hairdos. At some point, someone had lowered the conservatory's gas flames, adding to the general confusion. Celia could just make out Eileen bent over someone lying in the central gravel path of the conservatory.

"Excuse me, please," Celia said, spitting out a feather that had previously drooped from the coiffure of the woman ahead of her. "The victim needs my assistance. I am a nurse."

At last, several of the guests breached the doorway and burst into the conservatory, dragging Celia with them like a stick bobbing on a current.

"It's terrible!" a woman shouted. "She's been assaulted by an intruder! Get help!"

"It's not Mrs. Chase, is it?" another woman, dressed in a gaudy cyan-blue check, asked, craning her neck with morbid curiosity.

"Please, let me through," Celia begged. The babbling and gasping was too loud, echoing off the glass, for anyone to hear her, though. "Ladies, it could be unsafe. The person who attacked our friend might still be in the conservatory or on the grounds!"

The clamor of a dozen women's voices abruptly ceased. Those nearest to Celia turned to gape at her, her words sinking in. The women changed course and started thronging back out of the greenhouse.

"And contact the police," Celia called after them.

She rushed over to Eileen and the woman sprawled on the ground, her body unmoving. She was dressed in the loveliest mauve, her skirts spilled across the gravel and the dirt.

Dearest Lord, no. No! "Jane!"

"Oh, Mrs. Davies!" Eileen, pale as chalk, straightened. "She was attacked by some man! I saw him! He ran that way!" She pointed at the conservatory's rear door.

Celia sank to her knees at her friend's side and gently turned Jane onto her back.

"Jane? Jane?" *I should never have had her ask questions. Draw attention to herself. Frank will never forgive me for this. I will never forgive me.*

She groaned and peeled open her eyes. "Celia? What . . ."

Thank God. "At least you're alive," she breathed. "Do not move, Jane. I will be right back."

Celia got to her feet and sprinted over to the rear door of the conservatory, threw it open as well as the one beyond that led outside. She peered into the night. There was no movement out in the darkness. No sound but the whisper of the wind rustling leaves, the whinny of a horse. The thud of her pounding heart.

• • •

Owen turned the corner onto Mr. Greaves's street. He'd been to Mrs. Davies's house, where Addie had told him she'd gone with Mrs. Hutchinson to a party at the Chases' place. Which sounded a bit like a pair of Daniels marching into the lion's den, only without the part where God might save them.

He had to tell somebody what he'd learned about Judith Whelan, though. He just wished he hadn't had to wait until after he'd finished up at Mr. McCann's warehouse and it had turned dark and the fog spilling over the western hills made everything seem menacing. He wasn't all that comfortable with darkness anymore. Uneasy, even though Mr. Greaves's neighborhood was pretty safe—Owen had passed a patrolling cop not a block ago, in fact—and Owen had spent his first months in San Francisco living in trash-strewn alleyways alongside rats. He should be hardened against evening sounds and shadows. But he wasn't.

He trotted up the road, unnerved by how few folks were around, doors and windows locked against the night, even at the butcher's. The only resident appeared to be a stray dog that had been following him for a while. He'd had to shoo it off several times already, but Owen could hear it padding behind him again. *Durned pest.*

He was almost at Mrs. Jewett's place. Was that Mr. Greaves up ahead, climbing the steps to his landlady's?

"Mr. Greaves!" Owen called out.

He hesitated, looking Owen's direction. *Wait.* That wasn't Mr. Greaves. Didn't move like him and wasn't tall enough, neither. Either. Owen didn't like what he was up to, though. Moving stealthily. Not good.

Owen started running toward him. "Hey, you! Wait there!"

Just then, a man wearing a long duster coat bolted from between two houses across the street and raised his arm. The barrel of a pistol glinted in the streetlight, followed by the crack of gunfire. Dropping the other fellow to the ground.

✂ CHAPTER 13 ℛ

"This is all my fault, Jane," Celia said, cursing her crinoline and the stiffness of her corset as she leaned over her friend.

"It's not," Jane groaned. "It's mine."

"That man," Eileen said, her voice quavering. "He hit her."

A man who had succeeded in vanishing into the night.

Celia unbuttoned her gloves and stripped them off. "As you have said, Eileen." She snaked her fingers through the coils of Jane's hair to feel for lumps on her head, finding swelling on the back. Her fingers came back bloodied. "You have quite a bump, Jane."

"Yes. Oh . . . ah, yes . . ." She attempted to sit up. "I . . . what . . ."

"Jane, lie back down. Do not move." Celia lowered her back onto the ground. Behind them, near the doorway that linked the conservatory to the dining room, a group of Mrs. Chase's guests murmured together.

"My head hurts. And I feel ill. Oh." She grimaced and pressed a hand to her waist.

"Mrs. Davies." Marian Chase appeared at her side. She towered above Celia, finding no need to squat in the gravel path and sully the skirts of her copper silk gown. "Your friend. Is she all right?"

"I came into the conservatory to tell Mrs. Hutchinson that the entertainment was about to begin and found her lying there, Mrs. Chase," Eileen explained. "I saw a fellow running off through the door to the back porch. Mrs. Davies went outside to look for him, but he got away."

Mrs. Chase eyed Eileen as though suspecting her of tippling the wine that had been served that evening. "Some man?"

"I don't know who he was, Mrs. Chase," her servant answered.

"Do you remember anything, Jane? Anything at all?" Celia asked.

"Umm . . . I came in here to admire the azaleas." She pinched her brows together as she tried to recall. "Then—"

"Marian, what is going on out here?" a man shouted. Mr. Chase had finally made his appearance, which had the effect of not only interrupting Jane but silencing the murmuring women.

"One of my guests has had an accident, Archibald," Marian Chase replied. "Nothing to worry about."

Compared to his elegant and lovely wife, he had an unremarkable appearance, being of average height and width, with gray flecking his brown hair. His equally average face was decorated with a wisp of chin hair that the Americans referred to as a goatee. Despite all his averageness and the fact that he was down to his shirtsleeves—an informal display that likely enabled him to better manipulate a billiard cue—Archibald Chase exuded confidence, wearing it like an expensive cologne. A man used to having his own way.

"Mrs. Hutchinson was hit on the head by an intruder, Mr. Chase," Eileen said, daring to dispute her mistress. "I saw the fellow running out the back door there after he'd attacked her."

"An intruder? That door is always locked except when the gardener is here, girl. What an idiotic statement," he scoffed, his strong voice clipped with an East Coast accent. Eileen turned red and retreated a few steps. "The woman tripped and fell and hit her head. That's all." He glanced around at the assembled women. "That is all."

"Mr. Chase," Celia said, "I apologize for contradicting you, but the doors were not locked. I know because I went outside to search for the fellow."

Archibald Chase scowled. "And who are you?"

"Mrs. Celia Davies," she answered. "A nurse. I accompanied Mrs. Hutchinson this evening."

He exchanged glances with his wife. "I believe I have read about you, Mrs. Davies. In the newspaper."

Indeed. "Furthermore, Mrs. Hutchinson was lying on the ground facedown, and there is a sizable bleeding lump on the back of her head." For reference, Celia gestured to the spot on her own skull. "If she had tripped and fallen, there would be a bump on her forehead or temple. As most people fall forward, not backward."

"You believe some fellow broke into my house and attacked your friend."

"I am positive she was hit on the head, Mr. Chase," she stated. "And it would have been easy enough for an outsider to gain entry, as the doors providing access to the conservatory were both unlocked."

"Which sounds to me like an accusation that a member of my household let this person in, Mrs. Davies."

"I suppose it does."

The younger version of Mrs. Chase separated from the gaggle of women collected near the doorway and crept over to Mr. Chase. "Papa, several of the ladies are asking if you want the police sent for."

"No one has yet?" Celia asked.

"The police? Why would I want the police sent for?"

His wife scowled. "Don't worry, Archibald."

Worry? About what specifically?

"Mrs. Davies said to send for the police because of the intruder . . ." Eileen's voice trailed off, realizing she'd only anger Mr. Chase further if she continued.

"If you do not, Mr. Chase, I shall contact them myself," Celia said. Bluffing because she had no intention of leaving Jane, who required her assistance, in order to do so. "We need to locate the man who attacked Mrs. Hutchinson before he gets too far away."

"This is preposterous," Mr. Chase spat.

"I'll go," one of the servants offered, dashing off.

"I apologize for all the fuss, Mr. Chase, Mrs. Chase," Jane said, struggling to sit up without waiting for Celia's approval. "Maybe if I can get a warm drink, I'll feel better enough to leave."

The prospect lifted Mr. Chase's sour expression. "Marian, see that she's given something and promptly escorted to whatever conveyance she traveled here in," he said and marched off.

"Jane, you should not be attempting to go home in your carriage any time soon. The jarring would be harmful to your concussion." Which Celia expected she had suffered.

"Frank will come and fetch me anyway, if I don't return when I'm expected. So we may as well plan to leave, Celia," she replied. "But first I really could use some tea."

"Carefully, Jane." Celia helped her to her feet.

"Eileen, show them into the kitchen," Mrs. Chase ordered.

The women who'd congregated in the conservatory parted like the Red Sea in order to permit Celia and Jane to pass, several of them trampling the ferns edging the path in the process.

"The kitchen is right through here," said Eileen, pushing through a door in the dining room. Their arrival startled the cook, who'd been slicing a tea cake into tiny portions to hand around. A large Stewart cook stove was pumping out heat, making sweat bead on her broad forehead. "This lady is unwell and needs tea, Cook."

"What was all the screaming about, Eileen?" the woman asked.

"I'll tell you later."

Jane, who'd been probing her head and had located the lump,

smiled at the cook then at Celia. The fingertips of her fine silk glove came back bloodied. "Oh, dear. I am a mess. I'm dizzy and need to sit down. So sorry. I feel like I want to cry, Celia. What is the matter with me?"

"You have a concussion. It's normal. Trust me."

Eileen thoughtfully shut the connecting door behind Mrs. Chase, keeping the guests from following them into the kitchen. She pulled out a chair at the large oak table for Jane.

"Cook, get some tea and a bite of cake for Mrs. Hutchinson," Mrs. Chase instructed the woman. "I'll see to my guests and the musicians. The evening's event will have to be canceled. The ladies are too upset."

With a departing glare at Jane and Celia, she stomped from the kitchen.

Eileen also departed, the din of raised voices cut short by the closing of the hall door, leaving Celia and Jane in the hands of a confused cook. Who placed a kettle on the stove and, thankfully, did not ask Celia any questions, because she had absolutely no answers.

Yet.

• • •

"Cassidy, what in he— heck are you doing here?" Nick stood over the kid, on his knees at the bottom of Mrs. Jewett's front steps. A man's bloodied body lay at his side. "Don't tell me you've shot somebody outside my house."

"Not me. Some fellow in a duster coat. He jumped out from over there." He pointed to a gap between two houses across the street. His hand was shaking; it should be. "And shot this here fellow, then ran off down the road," he said. "For a minute I thought he was you, Mr. Greaves."

Nick crouched next to the fellow, his body half on and half off the steps. He felt for a pulse. There wasn't one. There wouldn't be, given the amount of blood leaking onto the steps from the bullet's exit wound. It had passed through his upper back and out the base of his neck.

"Do you know who he is, Mr. Greaves?" Owen asked.

"Don't recognize him."

The front door flung open and Mrs. Jewett thundered onto the porch. "What in heaven's name is going on out here? I thought I heard—"

132

"Gunfire."

"Gunfire?" His landlady shrieked. "Is that a . . . is that a dead man on my walkway, Mr. Greaves?"

The shades in the front window of the neighbor's house clattered upward. The owner and his wife bent down to peer through the glass.

"Afraid so, Mrs. Jewett," he said. The fellow's clothes were rumpled and dirty, as if he'd been sleeping rough. An ugly cuss, his greasy brown hair was unkempt. He stank like he'd been sleeping rough, too. "Guess the warning note wasn't enough."

If he hadn't stopped at Harris's to ask him to review Meg's autopsy report, he would've arrived home earlier. It might've been him shot, like Cassidy had feared, and not this man.

Mrs. Jewett gaped at him. "What do you mean, 'guess the warning note wasn't enough'?"

"Cassidy, go inside with Mrs. Jewett."

"Don't you need me out here, Mr. Greaves?" he asked. "To guard the body while you get somebody to alert the coroner?"

He had a point.

Mrs. Jewett tightened her evening wrapper around her chest and stepped to the edge of the porch. She gasped. "It's him, Mr. Greaves!"

"Who?"

"The fellow who brought your sister's letters."

"You sure?"

He didn't need her to move into the light from the nearby streetlamp to see she was scowling. "Of course I'm sure!"

Nick rolled the dead man over and examined his right hand. His first three fingers had been severed.

Well, now they knew where Raymond Fuller was.

• • •

Celia closely watched Jane as she drank her tea. She was grateful to observe that her color had improved and she did not appear particularly unsteady.

"How am I, nurse?" Jane asked. She smiled and set the teacup and saucer aside. "Please tell me you're not going to suggest that I have my head shaved so that it can be blistered. Or that a lengthy course of bleeding is required."

Thank goodness she is well enough to tease. "Nowadays, the standard treatment for a concussion is a bland diet and rest for several days until fully recovered, Jane, so fear not. Your lovely hair is safe."

"Good. I can tell you I'm going to enjoy the rest part. Especially if it means that Frank will need to send the carpenters away for a few days," she said. Eileen had brought Jane her cape, and she wrapped it tightly around her shoulders. "Frank will be annoyed with me, though."

"No, Jane, he shall be annoyed with *me*." Furious, actually. Her friend had lost her baby not two months ago; she was not fully recovered from the experience.

"It was my idea to bring you along, Celia. You didn't cause this to happen," she said. "I'll tell him I tripped and fell and hit my head."

"As if he might believe you would be so clumsy. Besides, I doubt we could keep him from learning that the police have become involved." Although she'd not heard a peep indicating that the maid who had volunteered to run to the nearest police and fire signal box had returned. Perhaps she'd been prevented from summoning them, after all. "And it was my idea for you to go around and ask questions of the guests and Mrs. Chase."

"Oh, yes. The brooch." Jane clutched the edge of her cape. "When I admired it and asked where I might obtain a similar one, Marian told me that it was unique."

Celia looked around for the cook, who'd been occupied in returning the silverware and china dishes to the pantry. Which was where she was presently located. "Either an intentional lie or, as you suggested earlier, she is unaware of the duplicate."

"Why lie to me, though?"

"Because you are a friend of mine." Celia leaned closer to Jane. "Tell me what happened in the conservatory. Do you remember?"

"I recall going out to have a look at the azaleas." She furrowed her brow. "I was bending over to examine them when I heard a rustling behind me. I turned and, right then, something struck the back of my head." She peered at Celia. "That's all I remember. And now I have a headache and desperately want to lie down."

"Eileen mentioned the man running out through the rear conservatory door," she said. "Did you notice him?"

"I didn't. You didn't see anybody outside, did you?"

"No one at all. He must have been very fast on his feet, to have gotten away so quickly," she said. "And as I told Mr. Chase, the door to the conservatory was not locked. I did not require a key to exit the building."

"If one of the servants had forgotten and left the doors unsecured, they'll never admit it," Jane said. "They all seem to be frightened out of their wits by Mr. Chase."

Just then, the cook exited the pantry and crossed the room to retrieve another stack of china plates she'd washed and dried.

"I am curious about something," Celia said to the woman.

The cook looked around, as though attempting to find the object of Celia's comment. Perhaps she rarely was addressed except to be reprimanded. "Yes, ma'am?"

"Mr. Chase informed me that the door to the conservatory is always locked. Is that correct?"

"That one and the one to the outside are always locked after dark, ma'am," she replied, squinting uncertainly over why Celia wanted to know. "If I need to go out, I have to unlock it."

"The rear door is secured even when there is a party in progress?" Celia asked, noticing Jane reaching up to remove one of her earrings. What *was* she up to?

"It's not like we were expecting a large delivery of foodstuffs or drink for Mrs. Chase's event tonight."

No, as a solitary cake cut into the slimmest of slices and a tray of biscuits appeared to be all the food on offer for the twenty or so guests. "Strangely, I found both of the doors unlocked not a half hour ago."

The cook's eyes widened. "You did? That's not right."

"Who might have unlocked them?"

"I have no idea. That's not right," she repeated. "Mr. Chase will be upset to hear that."

He already was. "Not one of the servants or Mrs. Chase, perhaps?"

"Not one of us, that's for sure. We don't want to get fired, now do we?"

Frightened out of their wits. "Are the keys readily accessible?"

Hands full, the cook gestured with her elbow. "They hang on the hooks by the rear door."

"Would that door there take me out to the porch?" Celia asked, indicating a closed door at the far end of the kitchen.

The cook nodded and disappeared into the pantry again.

"Oh, Celia, could you do me a favor? Could you go back into the conservatory for me?" Jane asked, loud enough for the cook to hear. "I seem to have lost one of my earrings, and this is my favorite pair."

"Jane, you are very clever," Celia mouthed to her friend. She must be recovering rapidly to have concocted the pretense.

"Hurry," she whispered and tossed the purportedly lost earring to Celia.

Pocketing it, Celia entered the enclosed porch attached to both the conservatory and the kitchen. The room was stacked with empty pots and gardening tools, serving as a sort of potting shed. She located the rack of hooks the cook had referred to. All of the keys were in place. The intruder had not taken a key then run off with it.

Celia scoured the floor of the potting shed for evidence that anyone had come through the room from the outside during the benefit. There had been spotty rain the past few days and Celia anticipated finding a trail of muddy prints. But she couldn't find any. So, had Jane's assailant *not* come from outside, or was it simply too dark to properly see? A lantern would be helpful, but then she'd have to explain why she needed one when the light was adequate for simply passing through the room.

Out in the conservatory, the gas lights remained dimmed. *Blast.* Hunting for any clues was nearly impossible. Could the Chases not afford their gas bill? Or were they intentionally making it difficult for her to collect evidence? Not that there appeared to be any evidence waiting to be collected.

What had the intruder been doing inside the conservatory? Celia wondered. She doubted the fellow had been lying in wait for Jane or another guest to come along to knock on the head and cause a commotion. Had he been planning on a rendezvous with someone? Plotting to thieve one of Mrs. Chase's plants? Her collection of roses and azaleas was quite lovely but not particularly valuable. Also, why choose the evening of a charitable event, when the house was full of people? The guests, however, had been preoccupied with their conversations or with listening to the string quartet. Aside from Jane, admiring the contents of the glass-enclosed garden, and Celia, nosing around upstairs. And Mr. Chase, hiding away in his billiard room. The entertainment would have kept everyone engaged for a good hour. Perhaps it was *not* such a bad time to . . .

"To do whatever it was he intended," Celia said aloud.

The next question to answer was what had happened to the implement the man had used to strike Jane. He'd not have taken it with him, would he? She searched through the azaleas that had caught Jane's interest. What size would it have been? Not too large, she presumed, and light enough to swing at head height.

She shoved aside a nearby stand of ferns.

"Voilà!" she breathed. A discarded edging spade, its length and weight perfect for swinging. Thank goodness a trowel with a sharp tip had not been within reach.

The spade had recently been put to use for its intended purpose; mud caked its blade. She ran a finger over the dirt. Not fully dried. Had the intruder been using it to dig out here? Celia glanced around her, looking for signs the soil had been disturbed.

"Is that you out there, Mrs. Davies?" a servant called through the doorway between the conservatory and the dining room.

Celia set down the spade and straightened. "It is. My friend lost her earring when she fell and I have been searching for it. Luckily, I found it!" She pulled the earring from her skirt pocket to show to the young woman.

"All the other guests have gone home," she said. "I went to the kitchen to ask if you needed a cab hired, ma'am, but I saw you weren't in there with your friend."

"I shall be driving Mrs. Hutchinson home. Thank you."

The girl did not move. Wanting to ensure that Celia departed the conservatory, undoubtedly.

"It is best that I return to the kitchen the way I came," she said. "My shoes are a trifle dirty."

"Yes, ma'am."

Celia exited the conservatory, stepping through the rear door at the same time the servant extinguished the gas, plunging the space behind her into darkness. Fortunately for the intruder, there had been lights lit in the conservatory, or else he would have stumbled around in the pitch black, knocking into pots and plantings. So fortunate for him.

• • •

"First a parcel of your sister's letters four years after her death, then an investigation into the murder of some sailor, followed by a threatening note you didn't tell me about, and now we've got a dead man on our doorstep," Mrs. Jewett muttered, depositing a heated mug of milk in front of Owen, who sat at the dining room table. "What next, Mr. Greaves?"

"Something even worse," offered Owen.

"Precisely," she responded.

The beat cop had finally shown up to take charge of Fuller's body, and Dr. Letterman had been notified. Mrs. Jewett had sacrificed one of her lap rugs to toss over the corpse. She'd never want that returned.

"Did you notice anybody outside earlier tonight?" Nick asked her.

"No, Mr. Greaves," she said. "I was in the kitchen for the past hour finishing my dinner and then doing some mending by the stove. It's too damp and cold tonight to sit in the parlor."

"It's okay. You don't have to justify why you didn't spot the fellow. What about you?" he asked Owen. "Did you get more than just a glimpse of the fellow in the duster coat?"

"That was all, Mr. Greaves. Was awful startled to see him point a gun and fire it," he said. "And there wasn't anybody else around, except for the cop the next block over. And the dog that was following me. Spooky how quiet it is around here."

That officer hadn't noticed the man; Nick had asked him.

"Mr. Greaves, I've been sitting here wondering if it was Mr. Fuller who that fellow meant to shoot," Owen said. "I mean, this isn't his house. It's your house."

"Oh dear. Oh dear, oh dear, oh dear," Mrs. Jewett mumbled over and over again. "This'll be the death of me, Mr. Greaves. The absolute death."

"When I'm not here, Mrs. Jewett, you should let Riley out of my room and into the house to roam around. Just as a precaution."

"Riley? A guard dog?" She rolled her eyes. "That dog of yours would lick folks to death before ever thinking of biting them."

"But those folks don't know that, and that's what I'm counting on," he said. "Unless you'd like me to leave my gun with you."

"And have me shoot myself with it?" she asked. "No, thank you, Mr. Greaves. You keep it to protect yourself."

It appeared he might need it for just that reason.

His landlady rested a motherly gaze on Owen. "And what are we to do with you tonight, young man?"

"I can go home after I drink this. I'll be fine," he replied, not sounding at all convincing.

Nick sighed. "If Mrs. Jewett doesn't mind, you'll be staying here tonight, Cassidy."

"I don't mind at all," she said. "I'll tidy up the spare bedroom."

Owen's grateful smile would've melted anybody's heart. *Great.* They might never pry him out of the house after this.

⌘ CHAPTER 14 ⌘

"Who do you think it was, Mr. Greaves?" Owen, an excessive number of pillows propping him up on the bed, tucked the quilt Mrs. Jewett had also supplied under his chin. Like a little kid. Meg used to do that, too, her blue counterpane tight against the contours of her face. "Who shot Mr. Fuller?"

"Too early to even guess. All I know is it wasn't Loomis," Nick replied, leaning back in the cane-bottom chair set next to the bed and stretching out his legs. Riley, given the freedom to roam the house, came into the bedroom. He wagged his tail as he sniffed the hand Owen dangled for the dog, then plopped down at Nick's feet. "Maybe the fellow pretending to be Fuller who was looking for Eckart. Has to know them both."

"Hmmm," Owen said thoughtfully.

"You're lucky you didn't get shot too, Cassidy."

"I wasn't anywhere close, Mr. Greaves, and the fellow looked in a hurry to vamoose," he said. "But do you think Mr. Fuller might still be alive if I hadn't called out? I mean, I might've distracted him, making him an easier target. Feel sorta bad about that."

"It's not your fault." He hoped the kid believed him. Guilt over something you couldn't have prevented had a way of carving a hole in your insides and turning them black. His old wound took to aching, the image of Jack Hutchinson taking a bullet meant for Nick playing over and over in his head, the shock on Jack's face as he fell . . .

"Why were you looking for me tonight, Cassidy?" he asked.

"I wanted to tell you that I stopped by Miss Whelan's former lodgings," he said. "I went to Mrs. Davies's house first to talk to her, but she's at the Chases' place with Mrs. Hutchinson. A party, I guess."

Taylor had been too busy with Eckart and the brooch to get over to Miss Whelan's old place yet.

"The landlady told me a woman with reddish hair had come by last week looking for Miss Whelan, too," Owen said. "The landlady didn't like the look of her, and even though she claimed to be a friend of Miss Whelan's, she'd never been by before."

"I take it this supposed friend didn't leave a name."

"Nope, she didn't," he said. "The landlady also told me that Miss

140

Whelan cleared out of her rented room almost a month ago. In so much of a hurry that it seemed mighty suspicious."

"A month ago?" Fuller had made himself scarce around that same time.

"Around then."

Two hasty departures coincident with when Sy Eckart had returned to San Francisco, meaning to "fix an old problem," according to his former landlord. Was Fuller the problem he'd wanted to fix? Or was Judith Whelan? Or had *she* been afraid of the hornet's nest Sy Eckart's vengeful return had been about to stir up?

And was the red-haired woman part of that hornet's nest?

• • •

"I'm sorry about what happened tonight, Mrs. Hutchinson," said Eileen, offering a hand to Jane as she climbed into the Hutchinsons' tilbury.

"I'll be all right, Eileen," Jane reassured her.

"I do wish I'd had a better look at the intruder."

So do I, thought Celia, tucking the wool carriage rug around Jane's legs. Her friend relaxed back against the leather squabs with a shaky sigh.

"Did you find out if that brooch was fake, ma'am?" Eileen asked.

"I've not heard yet," Celia replied. "Try not to worry too much about it, Eileen."

"All right." Eileen glanced over at the house, the lamps that had blazed so brightly inside being extinguished one by one. "It's all been so peculiar lately. That fellow wanting to speak with Mr. Chase, then getting himself killed. An intruder tonight . . ." She stopped and chewed her bottom lip.

"There have been additional 'peculiar' events beyond tonight's, Eileen?" Celia asked.

"Other folks have come around to speak with Mr. Chase," she said. "Unsavory folks."

"Here? Not at the auction house?"

"I shouldn't say any more."

"Eileen!" Mrs. Hunter called from the veranda. "Mrs. Chase needs you."

"I've got to go, ma'am," she said and scurried off.

Celia watched her depart, then climbed onto the driver's side of the bench.

"How curious," Jane said. "Somebody else who wants you to assume that Mr. Chase consorts with criminals."

"Despite the utter lack of gossip to that effect," Celia said, taking up the reins and urging the horse into a steady walk. She'd ask it to go faster, but, for Jane's sake, she wanted to prevent too much jarring and swaying of the carriage. Plus, she was not the most accomplished driver. Wrecking Frank's precious tilbury would not improve the evening.

"My acquaintances might simply not know, or be willing to talk about something like that," Jane said, trying to get comfortable in the corner of the cushioned seat. "What do you think of him, based on what you observed tonight?"

"The minute or two I interacted with Mr. Chase did not provide the best impression. But a criminal?" Celia shrugged.

"I'm familiar with most of the women who attended tonight," Jane said. "I have to say I can't imagine any of them willingly associating with the Chases if they thought they were lawbreakers."

"Perhaps Mr. Chase has been clever enough to conceal his activities," Celia suggested. "Activities that may explain why he insisted that the police not be sent for." They never had shown up.

"If we ever had an intruder, Frank would be frantic to have the police hunt down the man."

"Unless he did not want the police to apprehend the person."

"What about the possibility that Mr. Chase was my assailant?" Jane asked. "Not likely, I guess, since he was in the billiard room the entire evening."

"Up to the point where he finally put in an appearance to see about the commotion inside the conservatory," Celia said, slowing to turn onto the road leading to the Hutchinsons' house. Thankfully, both the hour and a sudden downburst was reducing the amount of traffic. So, aside from a broken-down wagon left in the street, it appeared she'd not have to contend with many carriages or carts or pedestrians out late and wandering across the street.

"Which means we don't actually know where he was all night. Maybe Mr. Chase had been expecting one of his 'unsavory' friends for a meeting out in the conservatory," she proposed. "He exited the house, entered the conservatory from the back, found me there, knocked me on the head, then returned the way he came without being seen. After all, the cook didn't appear to be particularly attentive, and the door between the kitchen and the potting room was shut."

"Eileen would have recognized him."

"True." Jane massaged her temples. "Maybe there's an innocent explanation, Celia. Maybe the fellow had snuck into the conservatory, hoping for a romantic interlude with one of the ladies present, and I startled him."

"Startled him into smacking you on the head. A not-so-innocent act." Celia steered to avoid a cat trotting across the road, the animal likely intent upon inspecting the contents of the brick sewer at the intersection.

"Or maybe it was a disgruntled employee looking to disrupt the evening and upset the Chases."

"A possibility. But whoever he was, it was reckless of him to assume he wouldn't be caught," Celia said. "He'd have to have known when the musicians were playing in order to take advantage of the diversion they provided."

"An article about the benefit was in the newspapers, Celia," Jane pointed out. "With some details about the quartet scheduled to play."

"So all of San Francisco was aware of the particulars of Mrs. Chase's event," she said. "However, the intruder still required knowledge of the layout of the house and for the doors to be unlocked."

"It's obvious from the street where the conservatory is in relation to the rest of the house," Jane said. "And if the intruder was a good picklock, they might not have had too much trouble with the doors."

"Are you certain you were knocked unconscious, Jane? Because my brain appears to be more befuddled than yours," Celia said. "By the way, I found the tool the fellow used to hit you. A short-handled edging spade."

"An edging spade? No wonder my head hurts."

"It was tossed into the ferns. Not a likely location for the gardener to have left it, and especially not with mud remaining on the blade."

"Somebody was digging around in the conservatory," Jane said. "This is all too strange, Celia. What were they doing?"

"Also, is what happened tonight in any way related to the murder of Sylvanus Eckart?"

"It will all come together, Celia. I have faith in you." Jane drew in a breath. "Oh, no. Frank is waiting for us."

Her house's front porch had come into view. Along with Frank, standing on the top step, his arms folded. Celia slowed the carriage and reined in at the curb. She climbed down in order to assist Jane.

Jane unwrapped the rug from around her legs. "Don't come with me, Celia. Drive yourself home. I'll send somebody to fetch the carriage from the livery stable near you tomorrow."

"Jane, where have you been?" Frank shouted, charging along the path toward the carriage. He ran to the side of the tilbury to help Jane descend to the street. "Celia, what are you doing with her and why are you driving?"

"I had a little accident at the Chases', Frank. Nothing to worry about," Jane replied.

"An accident?" His gaze went straight to Celia's face. He always blamed her when there'd been trouble. *Rightly so.* "In your condition?"

"Just a small bump on the head," Jane said. "Celia thought it best to drive me home, though."

"Your dress. It's covered in dirt. And is that blood on your glove?" he asked. "What did you get her involved with, Celia?"

"Not now, Frank," Jane said. Hetty had heard their arrival and come outside to take Jane's arm. "I can tell you what happened tomorrow. Right now, I want to go to bed. I'll send somebody to fetch the carriage, Celia. Good night."

Hetty guided Jane up the path and into the house.

"No more, Celia." Frank marched over to her. "How could you, of all people, be so reckless with her? You know what she's been through. You need to leave my wife out of your affairs from now on. Am I clear?"

For once, Celia was thankful for a wide, belling skirt. It prevented him from trodding on her toes. "I would never want her injured, Frank. Never."

"Funny, though, that whenever she goes off with you, one or the other of you manages to *get* injured," he said, his breath clouding in the damp air. "You're not welcome to contact her any longer, Celia. Got it? Never again."

Celia held her tongue and watched as he stomped off, grabbed the lantern left behind on the porch, and stormed into the house, slamming the door behind him.

A sound nearly as chilling as Eileen's scream had been.

• • •

"Did that woman inform you about a supposed intruder inside my house last night, Detective Greaves? Even though I'd expressly told her and everyone else that it was unnecessary to notify the police, as there was no such person." Archibald Chase had refused to take the chair Taylor had offered, preferring to stand and glower at Nick. He took a moment to also glower at Taylor, who stared back blankly. "Hm? Is that what this is about, Detective? I was accosted on my way into my auction house this morning—a ridiculous inconvenience when I have cataloguing of newly received items to oversee before today's auction—and dragged to the station by your man here because some silly, confused woman claimed she'd been assaulted in my conservatory by an intruder?"

Well. This is an interesting turn.

"Please tell me about this intrusion and the assault, Mr. Chase," Nick said. "When did this take place?"

His thick brows jerked together. "Weren't you given the details?"

Not yet. "I always like to hear the story from everybody involved."

"It happened at my wife's charitable affair last evening. Supporting the Society for the Prevention of Cruelty to Animals." He made a dismissive noise implying he wasn't completely certain of the worthiness of the cause. "But there was no assault, and there was no intruder."

"Then why did the woman, the purported victim, claim there had been?"

"She was out in my conservatory, tripped and fell and struck her head, and became confused. That's all," he said. "And I don't care what her friend had to say about the location of the bump indicating she was struck from behind."

Out of the corner of his eye, Nick noticed Taylor glance up from his note-taking and shoot him a look. "Did the name of the victim's friend happen to be Mrs. Davies?" She'd been at his house last night.

"I don't know what she was doing there last night, Detective. My wife did not invite her."

No, Celia probably invited herself. "And who was the woman who may or may not have been assaulted?" Nick asked, already certain of Chase's response.

"Mrs. Hutchinson is her name, I believe."

Frank must be thrilled. "Did anyone else see the supposed intruder?"

"One of my servants claimed she did. Said she'd spotted a man sprinting from the conservatory, saw Mrs. Hutchinson unconscious on the ground, screamed, and brought everyone in the house running. The girl can be fanciful, though." Chase glanced over at Taylor, scribbling notes. "Detective, didn't that woman tell you all this already?"

"Can you get into the conservatory from the outside without anybody in the house noticing?" Nick asked.

"The potting shed behind the conservatory connects to the kitchen and also lets out onto the yard," he said. "That Mrs. Davies woman claimed the doors were unlocked, but I don't see how that's possible."

"Why? Are the keys secured in some way or another?"

"There was *no* intruder, Detective, which is why I did not send for the police last night," he replied defensively. "Although someone informed you, since your officer dragged me here."

"This intruder—or non-intruder—is not why I had you brought here, Mr. Chase," Nick said. "I wanted to talk to you. About Sylvanus Eckart."

Chase drew back, suddenly wary. "Who?"

"Maybe you should sit down, Mr. Chase. You might be more comfortable."

Surprisingly, he did. Maybe he'd finally tired of standing and glaring.

"I've been informed that Mr. Eckart came to your house a couple of weeks ago, demanding to see you."

"Oh, that fellow. Marian mentioned him," he said. "I've never met the man and I don't know why he came to my house to harass my family. He tried to speak with me at the auction house, as well. Turned away both times."

"What specifically did he want? Did Mrs. Chase tell you?"

"According to Marian, he was shouting some nonsense about my needing to help him," he said. "A grifter, no doubt. Looking for money."

"Did he mention Meg Greaves, by any chance?"

Comprehension lit his eyes. His thick eyebrows moved again, descending as he peered at Nick. "Meg. Of course. You're related."

"That's Miss Greaves to you, Mr. Chase," Nick replied testily. "And she was my sister."

"My apologies, Detective." Chase raised his hands to push back on Nick's anger. "I don't see why his attempts to contact me would have anything to do with Miss Greaves, though."

"We suspect she and Sylvanus Eckart had been romantically involved."

"Is that meant to be an explanation for what he wanted with me, Detective?"

Chase's responses were coming quickly enough to be honest ones. Or he was an accomplished liar.

"I hear that some folks blamed you for her death," Nick said.

Chase blanched. "I was not in any way responsible, and I will speak to your captain about such accusations if they persist."

Folks were always wanting to complain to Captain Eagan about Nick. "Had Eckart ever tried to contact you before? Back when Meg died, for instance."

This time, he didn't respond straightaway. "No."

"Are you sure about that, Mr. Chase?"

Taylor flipped to a new page in his notebook, the sound unnerving Chase, who frowned. "Yes. I'm sure, Detective."

"What sort of work did Meg do for you?"

"She helped in the auction house when we had items that ladies might be interested in. Fabrics or shoes or the occasional kitchen goods. Small lots that we hadn't sold to stores," he answered. "Our female customers are sometimes more comfortable dealing with other women, you see."

"What about jewelry? Do you handle that sometimes, too?"

"We do."

Nick retrieved the brooch from his desk drawer, set it on his desk, the colored-glass garnets glowing amber. "Was this a piece your auction house ever handled?"

Chase examined the brooch. "I'm not certain, Detective. I don't inspect every article we're asked to auction." He set the piece of jewelry down again. "We get thousands of items over the course of a year. I can't be expected to remember them all."

"So, you don't recognize it."

"No." One corner of Chase's right eye twitched.

"Do you ever handle paste jewelry at your auction house, Mr. Chase?" Nick asked.

"Never. We carry only the finest of items."

"Ah," Nick said, returning the brooch to his desk drawer. "Where were you last Friday evening, Mr. Chase?"

"What do you mean?"

"Where were you?" Nick rifled through papers on his desk and located the coroner's autopsy results on Sy Eckart. "After dinner."

Dr. Letterman hadn't been able to be more precise about when Eckart had been shot than to estimate sometime Friday evening. Which left a whole lot of hours to consider.

"Wait . . ." he sputtered. "Your men didn't drag me here just to ask about Sy Eckart wanting to talk to me, did they? What is this about?"

"Please answer my question, Mr. Chase."

"I was . . . well, I went out to eat with my wife. Valcin's. Nice place."

"I've been. It is nice."

Chase looked amazed that Nick might've eaten at a restaurant he frequented.

Nick glanced over at Taylor, who nodded and wrote down the specifics. "Afterwards?"

"We went home. Straight home," he replied, clearing his throat. "Marian will vouch for me. As will our housemaid."

"And you didn't go back out again."

"No. I played some billiards and retired to bed."

"What about last night?"

"I've already told you about the benefit my wife hosted last evening."

"You stayed for it?" Nick asked. "Good for you, Mr. Chase. I know plenty of men who absent themselves whenever their wives have women friends over."

"I was at home," he stated. "As I expect Mrs. Davies can tell you. She works for the police, doesn't she?"

He would *not* respond to that. "What about all the others? Did they stay for the entire evening?"

His forehead creased. "Who do you mean? My wife? Her friends?"

Nick inclined his head.

"As far as I know, they all stayed until the commotion about an intruder sent them home," he said. "Marian had planned entertainment. I doubt anyone would have left before then. Why?"

"Have you ever heard of a man named Raymond Fuller?" he asked.

"No," Chase said. "Who is he?"

Nick pushed back his chair and stood. "Thank you, Mr. Chase. You're free to go."

Chase, startled by the abrupt dismissal, took a moment before getting to his feet and exiting the office.

"What do you think, sir?" Taylor asked.

"I don't trust Chase, Taylor. For someone who supposedly didn't know Eckart, he is familiar with the man's nickname. And I'd lay odds he's lying about not recognizing that brooch. About his whereabouts last Friday. Maybe even last night," he said, locking his desk. "Get Mullahey over to the Chases' house. Have him search for any evidence of an intruder. And while he's there, have him ask the staff if they're positive Chase stayed home after returning from his fine dinner at Valcin's. Also, see if anybody can confirm that Chase never left his house last night. Not likely he's the one who killed Fuller, but I want all the i's dotted."

"Yes, sir," said Taylor, tucking his notebook into his inner coat pocket and heading for the door.

"Oh, and get Mullahey to find out if Chase happens to own a .31."

"The caliber of the weapon used on Mr. Eckart."

"Exactly," he said.

"I heard that Dr. Letterman has concluded that Mr. Fuller was shot with a .44, Mr. Greaves."

Taylor. Always hearing news about the new coroner's findings before Nick did. "Then have Mullahey look for one of those, too."

• • •

"Mr. Hutchinson will forgive you, ma'am, ne'er you worry. Mrs. Hutchinson will force him to." Addie offered her most soothing smile and set the plate of broiled ham and warmed potatoes in front of Celia. "Besides, she might've gone and gotten hurt even if you'd nae been at Mrs. Chase's with her. You didna tell her to rootle around in the conservatory. Her husband canna blame you."

"You may believe that. I may even believe that. But you did not see Frank's face last night, Addie," Celia replied. "He will *never* not blame me for Jane's injuries."

"What's happened?" Barbara asked, strolling into the dining room.

"I'll fetch your breakfast, Miss Barbara."

Barbara poured herself a cup of coffee from the pot on the sideboard and sat down opposite Celia. "You were back awfully late last night, Cousin. Was the entertainment at Mrs. Chase's charitable event especially diverting?" she asked. "Or did something happen to Mrs. Hutchinson that you're to blame for and that's why you were late?"

Celia exhaled. She could never keep anything from her cousin. When Barbara was not listening in at the register in her bedchamber floor, she was lurking around corners.

"She suffered an injury to her head that required me to drive her home," Celia replied, cutting her ham into pieces with feigned nonchalance.

"Somebody at the party hit her?"

"Jane wanted to have a look at Marian Chase's azaleas. There was an intruder in the conservatory," she said. "It seems he did not welcome Jane's presence."

"Did she see who it was?" her cousin asked and thanked Addie for her plate of food.

"No. He hit her from behind. With an edging spade."

"Poor dear," Addie tutted sympathetically.

"Why would anybody attack Mrs. Hutchinson inside Mrs. Chase's conservatory, though?" Barbara asked, tucking into the potatoes.

"Shall we consider the possibilities?" Celia set down her knife and fork and ticked off the options with her fingers. "The individual was a daring, reckless thief caught in the act of breaking into the home. Without leaving any obvious evidence of a break-in."

"And with dozens of people present," Barbara pointed out, waving the potatoes she'd stabbed with her fork.

"Jane interrupted a planned liaison with an individual who did not wish to be identified," Celia next suggested. "Either romantic or otherwise illicit."

"Or maybe somebody didn't like that Mrs. Hutchinson had been asking questions," Barbara said. "Because I'm sure you asked her to, Cousin. You always do."

"I have considered that possibility, Barbara," she replied. "And feel terribly guilty about it."

"There are those who believe Mr. Chase is responsible for someone's death, ma'am," Addie reminded her. "Perhaps he planned to lure his most recent victim into the conservatory last night in order to murder them—which may be why he didna want the police brought—but encountered Mrs. Hutchinson instead."

"Eileen would have recognized Mr. Chase, though."

"Well, there has to be an explanation, Cousin," Barbara said, skewering some ham. "We just haven't thought of it yet."

We? Celia smiled at the slip and resumed eating her breakfast. She needed the sustenance; she had a long day ahead.

• • •

"Thanks for coming into the station this morning, Harris," Nick said.

"Better in the morning than later today, Greaves. I have patient appointments starting in an hour," he said, closing the detectives' office door and settling onto the chair in front of Nick's desk. "I heard that you sent our coroner another body last night."

"Fuller. The man who brought me my sister's letters." For all that Harris wasn't supposed to be involved in the coroner's office any longer, he sure managed to hear news from the place quickly. Just like Taylor. He was grateful to them both. "My landlady identified his body. He was shot right outside my lodgings. Cassidy was there when it happened."

"Did he see the gunman?"

"Not enough to get a description beyond the coat he was wearing," Nick replied. "Taylor told me that Letterman has findings from the man's autopsy already." He expected Harris would have more details on that, too.

"He's completed the initial postmortem," he said. "Mr. Fuller was shot with a .44. The bullet managed to sever his left carotid artery. No chance of recovering from that. Pretty quick death."

"It's not the same caliber weapon as was used on Eckart."

"Folks can own two different guns, Greaves."

A reality that often made Nick's job more difficult. "Nothing else?"

Harris shook his head.

"What about Meg's autopsy report?" Nick asked. "Did you have a chance to read it?"

"I did," he replied. "I'm lucky Dr. Letterman let me have a look. He doesn't like people in his business."

"And here you've been telling me, ever since he took over your old office, how great he is."

"He is a good coroner. I'll leave it at that."

"What did you find?"

Harris considered Nick, a sympathetic expression on his face. This was going to be a difficult topic, and he wasn't keen to launch into it. Nick wasn't keen, either, but he had to know. *Time to learn the truth . . . Yes. It was.*

"Nick, I'm not sure what you're hoping I'll say."

"You're going tell me whether or not my sister was murdered, Harris," he replied. "That's what I want you to say."

"After all these years, will it make a difference?" Harris asked. "Will it? She'll still be gone and nothing can bring her back."

"I'm aware of that, Harris, but I've got to know," he said. "What did you find?"

"You're certain?"

Harris would only hesitate because the news was going to be bad.

"Go ahead," Nick said, steeling himself against the pain of the answer.

"I can't be positive, but my reading of my predecessor's report is that your sister may have been dosed with something stronger than laudanum, some corrosive substance that could have poisoned her," he said. "Might've been mixed in with the laudanum. There were signs of inflammation in her throat, which laudanum alone would not cause."

"Forced on her?"

"Nothing noted in the autopsy report that indicated a struggle, Greaves. I'm sorry to say," he answered. "The coroner decided not to do a thorough autopsy. Nobody seemed interested in her, Nick, so he only completed a cursory evaluation."

He was shaking, trembling deep inside. Impossible to ever steel himself when it came to Meg's death. Impossible.

"Asa didn't recognize the description of her that had been put in the newspapers, Harris. He didn't come to collect her body for days."

Leaving the police and the coroner to conclude she was a streetwalker. Not worth the effort it would take to do a proper investigation.

"I know, Nick. I'm sorry."

"You're telling me, though, that she was murdered. That it wasn't suicide." Taylor's hunch had been correct.

How would he tell Ellie? What would he tell her? Nick pinched his eyes closed, seeing in the darkness the image of the daguerreotype he'd been sent. His two sisters and him together, the love they held for each other obvious despite the stiffness of their poses. They had been so happy then, all the pain of their lives still ahead. He wished he'd known to savor that happiness more. To not have presumed there'd be more happy days to celebrate together. His twin sister would be distraught. Or maybe the news would offer some relief. Ellie might prefer to think that Meg hadn't resorted to taking her own life, but instead had become the victim of another's murderous intentions. All Nick knew was that *he* didn't feel relieved; he still felt responsible.

A deep, empty chill spread. Somewhere out in the world walked the person who'd killed Meg. Sweet, funny Meg. When Nick found him— not *if* he found him, but *when* he found him—he'd see him strung up.

"I'm telling you that it is possible she was murdered, Nick, not that it's definite," Harris said, keeping his tone even and his demeanor calm. Unlike Nick, whose agitation itched along his skin. "And I can't condemn my predecessor's decision to rule her death a suicide. The other tenants of the hotel told him that she'd been overwrought in the days before her death. And a friend informed him that she'd been dosing herself with laudanum. I might've presumed suicide, as well. There wasn't enough evidence to decide otherwise."

"You wouldn't have presumed that, Harris," Nick said.

"Wouldn't I?" he asked. "I wish I could be as positive."

Nick exhaled and scrubbed his fingers through his hair. "Is there more?"

"Yes, Greaves," he said. "A laudanum bottle was never found in her room. Additionally, a witness reported seeing a woman with her that evening, but they never located that woman. A lost opportunity to learn more."

"She must have been the poisoner and took the laudanum bottle with her, Harris."

"Even if you find her, Greaves, how are you going to prove she's responsible? Prove even that Meg had been killed?" he asked. "It's been a long time."

"I'm not going to let it go."

"I'm not suggesting that you should. I'm just suggesting that it's going to be hard," he said. "Possibly even pointless."

Nick leaned forward. "Something has recently changed, Harris," he said, tapping the fingers of his right hand on his desk to emphasize his words. "Spurred folks into action. Encouraged Eckart to come back to San Francisco after a lengthy absence, looking for revenge. Eager to speak to Chase, the fellow who'd employed my sister, who'd also provided her a place to live after she'd left Asa's house. The arrival of Meg's letters, delivered to me by a man who ended up shot dead on my doorstep last night. A friend, mentioned in those letters, suddenly scared enough to go into hiding. A mysterious woman recently attempting to locate that friend. Last night, while Fuller was getting gunned down outside my house, an intruder breaks into Chase's house and attacks Jane Hutchinson. Why now? Why all this now?"

"How can you be sure that any of this is related to your sister's death, Greaves?" Harris asked. "Can you honestly say that it is?"

"I can't be sure," he admitted. "But what I *can* say is that I'm going to get an answer, one way or the other. I promise you I will, Harris. I promise."

❦ CHAPTER 15 ❧

"Mr. Greaves. 'Tis you," Addie said, answering the knock on the front door. To Celia, seated at her desk, her housekeeper sounded startled. Frankly, Celia was startled, too.

"Is Mrs. Davies home?" he asked.

"She is in her examining room."

Celia closed her notebook and got to her feet. Had he come to apologize? Should *she* apologize? She had a great deal of apologizing to do lately, it seemed.

"Mrs. Davies," he said, striding into view. He removed his hat and took to running its brim through his fingers.

Not "Celia." Likely as leery of her frame of mind as she was of his.

"Mr. Greaves," she replied. Out in the hallway, Addie passed by and shook her head. Indeed. What a quandary. "Have you come because you have discovered who killed Mr. Eckart?"

"Not since I saw you yesterday," he said stiffly and stared at her. For a length of time that caused her to fidget.

Celia closed the clinic door behind him. "Nicholas, this is ridiculous. Inasmuch as I can, I apologize for what I said about—"

"All that doesn't matter now," he said. "It looks possible that Meg was murdered, Celia. Harris has reviewed the autopsy report . . . I don't know why, but it looks like my sister was killed."

"Oh, Nicholas. I am sorry. So very sorry." She rested her hand on his arm, the one with the old wound. She'd prefer to embrace him, hold him close, but he might resist and she'd not force the gesture. "Would you care for something to drink? Tea or something stronger?"

"No." He dropped onto the corner chair, his hat dangling from one hand, using the other to swipe back his hair. "Much as I'd like a whiskey, if I start drinking now, I might never stop."

"Tell me what Dr. Harris learned," she said and dragged over her desk chair.

"She'd reportedly been using laudanum, but there were burns in her throat that indicated she'd consumed something caustic."

"She still may have used a caustic substance to take her life, Nicholas." A horrible, painful way to kill oneself, but it was done; she had read of cases.

"There's more. They never found the laudanum bottle. Never were

155

able to locate and question a woman seen with Meg that evening, either," he said. "She must've taken the bottle with her because she'd poisoned Meg with the contents."

"But why?"

"Mullahey discovered a torn scrap of one of Meg's letters in Eckart's room. It said 'he's found out I know.' The motive, maybe, for wanting to kill her. She'd learned something she wasn't meant to."

"That letter implicated a 'he,' though. Not a female."

"Maybe the unidentified woman with Meg the night she died is in cahoots with him." A muscle in his jaw flexed. "I'll kill him, Celia. Kill the both of them if I have to. I swear I will."

"Oh, Nicholas." She reached for his free hand and closed her fingers around it. He did not pull away. They sat like that, the two of them quiet, until the heat of his words dissipated. She released her hold with a soft smile.

"Have you learned anything else?"

"Learned anything? No. But the man who delivered Meg's other letters was shot outside my house last night, Celia," he said. "Cassidy saw it happen."

Gad. "Is he all right?"

"He's fine. He spent the night in Mrs. Jewett's spare room, getting pampered," he said. "No idea who the gunman was, though. A man wearing a duster coat was the only description Cassidy had for him."

A common clothing item in San Francisco. "Between you and Owen, I do not know who to worry more about."

"Maybe you should worry about yourself," he said, frowning. "What exactly happened last night at Mrs. Chase's charity benefit?"

"You've heard."

"I brought Mr. Chase in this morning for questioning," he said. "Without my prodding, he started shouting about the event and the intruder his servant spotted."

"The *supposed* intruder, according to him," she said.

"How is Mrs. Hutchinson, by the way? Chase mentioned her injury."

"She was well enough last evening, but I intend to stop at her house this morning, presuming I can avoid encountering Frank," she answered. "He was not happy with me in the least."

"For once, I can't blame him." He peered at her. "*Was* there an intruder?"

"Someone struck Jane from behind. With an edging spade, no less," she said. "Eileen spotted the individual—"

"Eileen? The servant who brought you that brooch? Interesting it was her."

Put that way, it was. "She could not describe the fellow, however. In her defense, someone had turned down the gas. It was rather dark out there."

"I've sent Mullahey over to the Chases' to look around," he said. "Chase didn't recognize the brooch, Celia. Maybe he didn't want to admit recognizing it because the garnets aren't real."

"They are not real?"

"No."

Well, then. "Have you considered that their being artificial is the reason Meg had the brooch? She'd found proof her employer was selling fake gemstones. Perhaps that is what the police officer wanted with your sister."

"There aren't any records that a police officer ever went to question my sister, Celia," Nicholas said. "And it's only a crime if those gemstones were labeled as being genuine. Chase maintains, however, that he never offers paste jewels."

"Mrs. Chase was wearing an identical brooch last night, Nicholas. I cannot say if those garnets were real or fake, however," she said. "Furthermore, she is a connoisseur of imported Chinese goods and keeps a stash of receipts from her husband's auction house secreted away in her bedchamber wardrobe."

"Not that you were in her room investigating." He released a sigh and ran his fingers through his hair again. A dark strand rebelliously flopped across his forehead. "Could Chase have left the house last night and made it over to mine in order to shoot Fuller, all without being noticed?"

"I saw Mr. Chase only briefly last night. When he came out into the conservatory because of all the shouting," she replied. "He was supposedly in his billiard room all the rest of the time."

"What about the other guests?"

"I am confident Mrs. Chase was in the house all evening, along with nearly all of her guests. The only one I lost track of was Deborah Hunter. She is a close friend of Marian Chase's. I gather her husband is a business associate of Mr. Chase's. I encountered Mr. Hunter at the auction house the other day, in fact," she said. "I spoke with Mrs. Hunter before I went upstairs to investigate but did not notice her the rest of the evening until when Jane and I were departing."

"Is she the type of female who might wield a weapon? A heavy gun. A .44."

"I'd not put it past her," she said. "She insisted on expressing her opinion to me as to who may have killed Mr. Eckart, which I find odd. Maintained that she was defending Mr. Chase from scurrilous gossip by proposing that one of Mr. Eckart's rough friends is the villain."

His hat brim made a lazy circle through his fingers. "I'll see what I can find out about her."

"Nicholas," she said quietly. "Was Mr. Fuller the intended victim or were you?"

"Cassidy asked the same question, Celia. And I don't know why anybody would expect to find Raymond Fuller at my lodgings," he replied. "Unless they'd been following him."

"Jane did learn something interesting, before she was attacked," she said. "Apparently, when Mr. Eckart showed up at the Chases' home, he shouted 'he has to help me.' With what, though?"

"Chase told me something similar." Nicholas's brow furrowed. "I don't know what Eckart meant, and Chase was no help, either. He wanted me to believe he'd never met the guy."

"Where does all this leave us?"

"On the hunt for Fuller's killer, in addition to Eckart's. Debating if I have enough evidence to keep Loomis in jail for killing Eckart, even though he had a motive—he owed Eckart money—and his alibi for Friday evening has fallen apart. Confirming Chase's alibis for last Friday and last night," he said. "And trying to locate Judith Whelan, because Meg's letters make me think she knows who killed my sister. Cassidy spoke to her former landlady. Right around the same time Sy Eckart returned to San Francisco, she packed up her things and fled her rented room."

"She also abruptly left her position at the sewing machine shop where she used to be employed," she told him. "Afraid of Mr. Eckart?"

"Or of his plans to get revenge for Meg's death," he said. "We're not the only ones searching for Miss Whelan, Celia. A woman with red hair was looking for her recently. She didn't leave a name."

"We have to find Miss Whelan, Nicholas. She could be in serious danger," she said. "She cannot have vanished into thin air."

"Into thin air?" he asked, frowning. "Or someplace more solid?"

• • •

Shoot, thought Owen. Mr. Greaves mightn't have been disappointed that he hadn't found Judith Whelan, but *he* sure was. *What can I do, though?* Knock at the door of every boardinghouse in the city, asking if she was living there? It was clear she didn't want folks to know her whereabouts. Especially that red-haired woman who'd been looking for her, too.

He turned the corner and picked up his pace. He was late—again— to work. They had a delivery of velvet curtains and tapestry carpets due off a steamer that morning. But Mrs. Jewett could cook a breakfast near as good as Addie's and he'd had a second helping, even though he shouldn't have. Which had made him late. He could just imagine what Mr. McCann was going to say about his tardiness.

"You're fired, Cassidy!" Owen said aloud, mimicking his boss's tight, high voice.

The neck of a broken jug littered the sidewalk and Owen kicked it, sending it skittering into the gutter. Nobody ever appreciated the work he was doing for the police. How important it was.

If it's so danged important, Cassidy, why aren't they paying you?

"Shoot."

He hurried past a lumber wagon and a group of sailors, the lot of them staggering up the road like they'd forgotten how to walk on a surface that wasn't swaying. Up ahead was Mr. McCann's wagon. The driver slouched on the seat and was reading a newspaper. How he could concentrate with all the dockside clamor, a mess of ferry whistles and stevedores' shouts and lines slapping against masts and wheels rattling over cobbles, Owen could never figure. The fact that the driver was sitting there reading, though, might mean that Owen was in luck and the boat had been late docking. Or maybe Mr. McCann was off trying to hire another hand to load his cargo onto the bed, because he'd given up on Owen ever turning up.

Owen paused at the corner as a wagon stacked high with barrels slowly rumbled by, its cargo threatening to break its lashings and topple onto the ground. Beyond the end of the road, out in the bay, a steamer chugged black smoke into the sky. A three-masted sailing ship was tucking into the nearest dock, the crew busy furling the sails and passengers gathering along the railings. He idly wondered if he'd spot that pretty woman with the large eyes, like he had the past two days. If she had red hair instead of black, he'd get to thinking *she* might be the person hunting for Judith Whelan.

The wagon traveled past the intersection and, just as Owen made to cross, he caught sight of a woman. Not the one he'd been noticing but one he'd seen at Mrs. Davies's place only yesterday morning. Eileen, wasn't it? She was hurrying along, her head down. For a second he was afraid she was going to collide with some crates that had been stacked next to a gangplank, or maybe trip over the ropes somebody had left coiled near one of the bollards.

What in heck was she doing here, though? Wasn't she one of the Chases' servants? This wasn't someplace she should be. Was it? Heck, he never could figure out what servants were or weren't supposed to be doing. It wasn't like he hung around any, aside from Addie and the girl who helped with the laundry at his boardinghouse.

A man stepped through the open door of a nearby warehouse. Eileen caught sight of him and dashed over. Was that Mr. Brodie she was talking to? The customs official who liked to yell at Owen almost as much as Mr. McCann did? What would she want with him? He wasn't much older than her, though, and sorta handsome, he supposed. Maybe they were sweethearts. Although why was she acting like she didn't want to be spotted with him, her shoulders hunched and trying to duck into the shadows cast by the building?

Whistling casually—"Camptown Races" always came to mind, for some reason—he began to stroll their direction. Eileen wouldn't remember meeting him at Mrs. Davies's place. Heck, she'd hardly noticed him gawking at her in the hallway. Whatever they were saying to each other looked to be mighty urgent, though.

He'd gotten within fifty feet of them when he heard his boss shouting his name.

Shoot.

"Cassidy! What in blazes are you doing?" he yelled. "Get over here right now if you want to keep your job!"

Mr. Brodie heard the shouting and looked Owen's way. Owen tried to change direction, go back toward Mr. McCann's wagon, but for some reason his feet didn't want to work. Eileen, catching sight of Owen too, scurried around the side of the building. The customs officer measured him with a glance, raising goose pimples on Owen's arms, before returning to the inside of the warehouse.

Shoot. This was plain not good. Not good at all.

. . .

Celia hopped down from the Hutchinsons' tilbury and surveyed their house. She might be able to persuade Hetty to let her inside in order to visit with Jane, but could she persuade Frank?

"Impossible," she muttered.

Screw your courage to the sticking-place, Celia. As Mr. Shakespeare would say.

Squaring her shoulders, she tied off the carriage horse and climbed the short rise of steps. *Please let Frank be downtown at his office. Please let—*

The door swung open. "Mrs. Davies?" Hetty asked, blinking at her in surprise. She carried a whicker beater and a rolled-up rug, intent upon a bit of housework only to find Celia on the doorstep.

"Ah, Hetty. Is Mr. Hutchinson in?"

"No, but he told me—"

"Yes. I was expecting him to order you to turn me away. But I must see Jane. I cannot rest until I am reassured that she is recovering. Surely you understand, Hetty, and might take some pity on me." She threw in that comment when it appeared that Hetty might be wavering in her obedience to Frank's orders. "I shall only be a few minutes. I do not wish to overtire Jane by visiting too long."

"He'll fire me if I let you in, ma'am."

"If he *discovers* that you've let me in, Hetty," she countered. "I promise you I shall not inform him and neither will your mistress."

Hetty opened the door all the way and deposited the rug and beater out on the veranda. "Only a few minutes, ma'am. I'll be keeping track of the time." She nodded toward the tall mahogany case clock ticking away next to the staircase.

Celia stepped inside. "Is Jane upstairs?"

"She's resting in the parlor, Mrs. Davies."

The doors were open. Inside the room, all was hush and darkness, the curtains pulled tight to block out all but the narrowest sliver of sunlight. Jane, seated on the sofa with a floral-patterned wool lap robe tossed over her legs, was waiting for Celia with a smile.

"I thought I heard you," she said. "You returned the tilbury."

"I did." Celia sat next to her. "I was on my way to Mr. Chase's auction house to attempt to learn more about those brooches and thought I would stop in to see how you are feeling."

"Better. Still a bit dizzy and queasy at times, but my headache has lessened." She reached for Celia's gloved hand and squeezed. "Frank was furious with you last night. All that kept him from endlessly shouting at me was my headache. Maybe I shouldn't tell him it's better."

"Perhaps not, Jane," Celia replied, smiling.

"I've been sitting here, Celia, racking my brains all morning, trying to figure out who my assailant might've been," she said. "I keep returning to it being one of those 'unsavory folks' Eileen mentioned Archibald Chase consorting with. Whoever they are."

"Officer Mullahey is over at the Chases' house right now," she said. "Confirming Mr. Chase's alibis for the night of Mr. Eckart's murder, along with the murder of a Mr. Fuller, shot outside Nicholas's house last night."

"Oh, my!" Jane exclaimed.

"Indeed."

Celia quickly relayed what she'd learned from Nicholas that morning, including that Meg Greaves may not have died by her own hand.

"You are thinking that her death is linked to the death of her sweetheart, Mr. Eckart, and the killing—possibly unintentional—of Mr. Fuller. Aren't you, Celia?"

"I am."

"Does Mr. Greaves have any suspects?" she asked.

"He has a man in custody, a fellow who owed Mr. Eckart money, but he obviously was not the person who shot Mr. Fuller."

"And we can eliminate anybody in attendance at Marian's party last night."

"Can we conclude that?" Celia asked. "I return to Archibald Chase, scarce most of the evening and absent when we finally departed."

"Maybe so, but it certainly wasn't any of the guests or Marian herself. I can't imagine a one of them hurriedly leaving the benefit in order to rush over to Mrs. Jewett's house, revolver in hand, to commit a murder, Celia." Jane sat up to fluff the cushion at her back, then reclined again. "Maybe it was somebody else entirely. Somebody we're unaware of."

"Mr. Chase's 'unsavory' friends?"

"Well, why not?"

Whoever they were.

The melodic chime of the Hutchinsons' doorbell sounded in the hallway, followed shortly by Hetty sliding open the parlor doors. "It's a Mrs. Hunter, ma'am. Should I tell her you're resting?" she asked in a low voice.

Jane looked over at Celia. "I wonder what she wants."

"Shall we find out?"

Hetty made a strangled noise in her throat; there would be trouble for her, indeed, if Frank learned that she'd allowed a parade of visitors to troop into their hushed parlor to disturb his wife.

"Show her in, Hetty," Jane said.

Deborah Hunter, dressed in an ice-blue gown that complemented her eyes, a straw hat decorated with silk flowers perched atop her curls, swept into the parlor with a broad smile.

"Mrs. Davies. I'm surprised to find you here," she said. "But you are a nurse, aren't you? So it makes perfect sense you'd want to attend to your friend."

"Mrs. Hunter."

Her unfaltering smile turned on Jane. "I hope you'll pardon the intrusion, Mrs. Hutchinson, but I was in the area and thought I'd see how you are doing."

Deborah Hunter had gone to the bother of discovering where Jane lived?

"Please have a seat, Mrs. Hunter," Jane replied. "Hetty, bring us all some tea."

Hetty reluctantly went off to fetch tea.

"How *are* you doing, Mrs. Hutchinson?" Of the two armchairs situated across from the settee, Deborah Hunter chose the one farthest from Celia. Despite the distance, the aroma of jasmine eau de toilette—likely French—that surrounded her like an expensive and fragrant cloud drifted over. "You sustained quite an injury last night."

"But not caused by a blow from an intruder, according to Mr. Chase," Celia said.

"Archibald doesn't want to imagine his sanctuary could possibly be breached, Mrs. Davies," she responded. "I had to remind him that they're not living out on the fringe of town any longer and that, sadly, there are criminals in the city. Marian was very upset by the whole incident, as you might expect."

"I wonder, did you happen to notice a stranger on the grounds last evening? I did not see you in the conservatory after Jane was attacked," Celia said. "Perhaps you were in a different part of the house, one that may have afforded a better view of an intruder out in the yard, for instance."

The parlor doors slid open again, and Deborah Hunter waited until Hetty had set down the tea service and departed before answering.

"I was in the kitchen, relaying instructions to the cook from Marian, who was so busy," she said and accepted a cup of tea from Jane.

"During the attack upon Jane?" Celia asked.

"How can I say? I didn't hear any of the uproar. The kitchen is very secluded."

"Celia and I both noticed that. Didn't we, Celia? Marian's cook kindly brewed me a cup of tea after I was knocked unconscious," Jane said. "But Celia and I didn't see you in there."

Bravo, Jane.

"You must have missed me by mere seconds," Mrs. Hunter replied smoothly. "Then I was in the library consoling Marian, after we'd shooed off the musicians."

"Ah." Celia would have to confirm her tale.

"I may have noticed someone in the conservatory, however," she continued, calmly stirring milk into her tea. She was cool-headed, thought Celia, and not easily flustered. Admirable qualities. "When I arrived earlier in the evening. Before any of the other guests had shown up."

"The gardener, perhaps," Celia suggested.

"Him? Couldn't have been him," she said. "He broke his arm last week. Fell off a ladder while he was trimming the ivy Marian had him plant last year. Hasn't been at the house since."

His absence providing a perfect opportunity for someone to leave the doors unlocked, at any time during the day, since he'd not be conducting his regular task of ensuring they were secured.

"The intruder was already in the conservatory?" Jane asked, somewhat alarmed.

Lurking, perhaps, behind the stand of compact date palms in the corner. If Deborah Hunter's story was to be believed. "Did you inform the Chases that you'd seen this person, Mrs. Hunter?"

"I didn't connect the indistinct movement I'd noticed to a report of an intruder until this morning," she said. "Did you see the person's face, Mrs. Hutchinson? Could you describe them?"

"No, I didn't," Jane said. "I didn't see him at all."

"Not even a reflection in the glass?"

Jane's gaze lost focus for the briefest moment. "Not even that," she said. "Silly of me to be so blind, but I was completely absorbed in admiring Marian's azaleas. That'll teach me to be more cautious, won't it?"

"What a pity." Mrs. Hunter clucked her tongue against her teeth. "I suppose we'll never learn who the individual was."

"Do you have any ideas, Mrs. Hunter?"

"As to why anybody would break into the Chases' conservatory?" She shrugged. "Not because there's anything valuable stored out there. It's awfully damp and warm. The atmosphere would rot or tarnish most items."

"What the individual was after might not be stored in the conservatory but elsewhere in the house, Mrs. Hunter," Celia said, their conversation giving her the idea. "The conservatory does link to the dining room, by which someone might access the upstairs if they were cautious enough to not be observed."

The woman considered Celia. "Were you trained to be a detective, Mrs. Davies, or did you come by your vocation naturally?" she asked without a hint of derision. Which did not mean that she did not *feel* disdainful, merely that she was capable of concealing her intentions.

"My vocation is to be a nurse, Mrs. Hunter. I did not seek to get involved in police investigations."

"But you are such a natural at it."

"What *do* you make of the intruder last night, Mrs. Hunter?" Celia asked, refusing to be drawn into a discussion of her detecting skills.

"I believe you have already supplied a reason, Mrs. Davies. A local criminal attempting to access the house and thieve valuables," she said. "Or maybe the fellow meant to burst into the library where we'd all be gathered and rob us. But he got no farther than encountering Mrs. Hutchinson."

"A concussion is a small price to pay, if that's the case, Mrs. Hunter," replied Jane, looking pale and tired. They'd overstayed their welcome. But Celia was not yet finished.

"No disagreeable individual with whom Mr. Chase has had the misfortune to become acquainted, perhaps?" Celia asked.

"No one who knows Archibald would even think to make such a suggestion, Mrs. Davies."

"Perhaps the person was a disgruntled employee seeking to disrupt the evening and upset the Chases," she said.

Deborah Hunter rolled her eyes. "Why would Mr. Chase have a disgruntled employee? He treats everybody at the auction house fairly."

"I find it perplexing, then, that I have been warned to never confront him with questions," Celia said. "I gather he has a quick temper."

"What man doesn't?"

Celia could think of quite a number. "I cannot stop thinking about the story connecting him to the death of a woman who used to work for him, Mrs. Hunter."

"Well, you should, Mrs. Davies," she said, steadily swallowing the tea she'd been sipping then lowering her cup to its saucer, her hand not revealing any tremor. "You should know better than to believe rumors about wealthy men, Mrs. Davies. The usual targets of such nonsense."

"I have found gossip often contains a kernel of truth."

"Not this gossip, Mrs. Davies. As I told you last evening when you brought it up."

"Were you and your husband friends of the Chases' at the time her death occurred?" Celia asked. "Four years ago, I believe it was."

"We were, which is how I know that you should not trust this particular tittle-tattle, Mrs. Davies, and cease hunting for a kernel of truth that doesn't exist."

"The story must have caused Mrs. Chase a great deal of grief," Celia said in a sympathetic tone.

"It did. She came to stay with us in Santa Clara to calm her nerves."

"I thought you lived in San Francisco at the time."

"We rented a home for a brief period," she said. "Our main residence was in Santa Clara. Although we have sold it now and rent the Chases' house out by the Mission."

So *they* were the residents there. And where might Marian Chase escape to *now* to calm her nerves? The Mission house might not be far enough. "I see."

Mrs. Hunter got to her feet. "I'm sorry my visit has to be so brief, Mrs. Hutchinson, but I must go. I'm glad to find you looking well. Mrs. Davies. Good day to you both."

She swept from the parlor, leaving behind the aroma of jasmine. And an uneasy feeling in Celia's chest.

"What was that all about, Celia?" Jane asked. "Because I got the impression her visit didn't have much to do with an interest in my health."

"My guess, Jane, is that Deborah Hunter needed to know if you could identify the intruder last night," she replied. But why? "You hesitated when she asked if you'd seen the fellow's reflection in the conservatory's glass windows. Did you?"

"I may have," she said. "Some movement, nothing more. However, when Mrs. Hunter questioned me, I remembered hitting the person when I fell. I struck them on their arm. Sharply."

"If only I could say whose arms were worth examining for bruises, I would proceed immediately," Celia said. "How frustrating this all is, Jane. I wish I knew more about Mrs. Hunter and the reason behind her interest in the identity of an intruder."

"There is somebody who might be able to tell you more about her, Celia," she said. "But you won't be happy to speak with her."

"Why not? Who is she?"

Jane drew in a breath, released it again. "Lena Douglass."

Gad. A woman Celia had hoped to never have to interact with again.

✂ CHAPTER 16 ❧

The showroom of Mr. Chase's auction house bustled with activity. The trunks and crates that had lined the walls on Celia's last visit had been cleared away and replaced by tables displaying the articles on offer that day—small goods, fabric, clothing in tidy stacks. Workers were busy arranging the items while a handful of customers, women like herself, mostly, strolled among the tables, making notes in the catalogs they carried. Likely of the articles they were most interested in.

Among the workers stood a man she remembered from the prior time she'd been here.

She walked over to him with a broad smile. "Mr. Hunter. How wonderful to see you again."

"Have we met before?" he asked, his handsome features shifting with displeasure. He did not appreciate a strange woman accosting him, it seemed. Or perhaps she was not as much a stranger as Celia imagined, and his reason for frowning at her had an entirely different cause.

"I encountered you just the other day, outside this very establishment," she said. "I am Mrs. Celia Davies."

His features shifted yet again, ultimately arriving at carefully blank as the proper outward emotion to display. "Oh, yes."

"I met your wife last night at Mrs. Chase's charity benefit," she said. "I am sorry that you were not in attendance as well, so that I could have had a chance to meet you then."

"I was otherwise engaged last evening, Mrs. Davies. Regrettably."

And where had you been? At Mrs. Jewett's house, shooting Mr. Fuller? "Ah, well, you are a very busy man, of course."

"Yes, I am. And because I am, I must bid you a good day, Mrs. Davies." He tipped his hat and strode away, brushing off the clerk he'd been speaking with, who pursued him as far as the pavement outside.

How curious.

One of the other clerks noticed Celia and hurried over.

"The auction does not begin until two this afternoon, ma'am," he informed her politely. He shot a glance in the direction of the front door and the now departed Mr. Hunter, briefly frowning, before continuing. "However, you are free to examine the items of interest until that time."

"Thank you," she said, thankful that the clerk she'd spoken with the other day was nowhere to be seen. "I am specifically interested in jewelry. Do you have any available today?"

"Why, yes. We have a nice collection of necklaces, brooches, and earrings on offer."

Her ears perked at the mention of brooches. She scanned the contents of the tables. "That sounds perfect. Where might I find them?"

"Over here, ma'am."

He led her to a table nearer the window, where the light would better show off the sheen of gold, the glimmer of gemstones. Another clerk, diligently guarding the boxes containing the jewelry, stood behind the table, his sharp eyes observing her approach.

Celia leaned over the various cases. "This is quite a fine selection," she said to him. "Mrs. Chase was correct when she suggested that I come here today."

"Yes," was all he replied.

"I suppose, though, that she herself never has to attend an auction. She must obtain her lovely jewels directly through her husband."

"She attends sometimes."

"Then maybe I shall see her here today. And possibly Mrs. Hunter as well," Celia added.

"Mrs. Hunter is often here," he said, growing more loquacious. "She or her husband frequently consigns items to be auctioned. Mr. Hunter only just left, in fact."

"I met Mrs. Hunter last evening for the first time, you know. But she did not share with me the association that she and her husband have with this establishment."

"A long-standing association," he said. "Goes beyond consigning goods. She's even occasionally brought young women here to work. Young women she helps."

"Was Meg Greaves one of those young ladies?" And would that not be quite curious if she had been?

His expression went as carefully blank as Mr. Hunter's. "Don't know her."

"Nonetheless, the women must be very grateful to Mrs. Hunter for the assistance she provides in finding employment."

He set his jaw and did not answer.

Celia made a cursory examination of the remaining jewelry boxes, finishing her ruse of interested customer, when an item in the final box caught her eye.

She bent low over it, the stays of her corset jabbing. "I have seen another brooch very much like this one," she said to the clerk, who was doing his best to avoid speaking to her. "Mrs. Chase has a nearly identical brooch, except with garnets instead of topazes."

He grunted to indicate he'd heard her but made no comment one way or the other. He did not need to confirm what her eyes told her, though. If only she could comprehend the meaning.

"I do hate to ask, but these stones are real, are they not?"

He turned very red in the face. "We never deal in paste or other fakery, ma'am."

"Never?"

He went even redder, which made her worry for his heart. "If you seek to question the quality of the items available in Mr. Chase's auction house, ma'am, then I suggest you leave and take your business elsewhere."

Which she did, but not for the reason the clerk assumed. Her conversation with Lena Douglass about Deborah Hunter was overdue. A woman who may have an unanticipated connection to Meg Greaves.

• • •

"Do you want me to put a message in the newspapers asking Miss Whelan to contact us?" Taylor stood just inside the doorway to the detectives' office. "Mr. Greaves. Sir."

"If she didn't come forward two weeks ago when we asked for information from folks who'd known Meg, why would she now?" Nick turned away from staring out the window. The day was heavy with clouds, and the view was depressing anyway.

"Yes, sir," his assistant said, sounding about as depressed as Nick felt. "Bothers me, though, that she never contacted you after your sister died. Unless she didn't want to upset you by reminding you of her death."

"We'd have to find her to understand her reasons." *Into thin air.* If they'd lost Miss Whelan, Nick likely had no chance of finding Meg's killer.

One of the officers trotted into the office, handed Taylor a message, and trotted back out. It used to annoy Nick that the men were more comfortable with his assistant than with him, but if it meant he learned what was going on, then a little bit of discomfort was worth it.

Taylor hastily read the slip of paper. "The coroner's done with Mr. Fuller's autopsy. No other wounds aside from what was caused by the slug, so that was what killed him. Stomach was empty. Probably weak and hungry." He looked up at Nick. "That's it, sir."

"Why do you think he was headed to my house, Taylor?"

"Maybe he was coming to kill you, Mr. Greaves," he said. "You did get that warning note."

"He didn't have a weapon on him. I searched," Nick said. "He wasn't looking to kill me, and I'm starting to think he didn't shoot Eckart, either."

"The officer who has the beat in your neighborhood has been hunting for the cartridge, in case there's anything useful to learn from it, but he hasn't found any in the area Owen reported seeing the shooter," he said. "Maybe the fellow left it in the revolver chamber."

Behind Taylor, Mullahey strode through the station, headed for the detectives' office. He was back from his visit to the Chases' house.

"Nothing, Mr. Greaves," he said after greeting Taylor. "If you'd be wanting my opinion, I'd say the Chases made sure the gravel in the conservatory has been tidied since last night. Hiding any evidence that someone had mucked it by dragging dirt in on their shoes."

"Did any of the servants see or hear an intruder last night? Besides Eileen."

Mullahey retrieved a slim, small notebook—when had he taken to using one like Taylor?—from inside his coat. "Not a one. Claimed all they noticed was the shouting and the screaming of Mrs. Chase's guests," he said. "And Mr. Chase was in his billiard room all evening, according to the same folks."

Would they lie to protect their employer? Maybe. "What about his alibi for the night Eckart was killed?"

"He returned home from dinner with Mrs. Chase around seven. Did some work in the library followed by an evening nightcap—he's fond of port, I was told—and then he went up to bed. Around ten or so."

"The servants can confirm that he was in the library the whole time?"

"They said he was," Mullahey replied. "But I did some looking on my own, and there's a passageway next to the library that goes from the front of the house to a porch at the back. The library has a door onto that passageway."

"He could've snuck out without being noticed," Taylor said.

Mullahey nodded. "The Chases have a stable at the back of their property, but they don't keep a boy full-time to take care of their horse," he said. "So I had no one to question about whether Mr. Chase had taken the animal out that evening."

Or if anybody else had, either. "What about a weapon? Find one in the house?"

"A .52 caliber Sharps carbine, Mr. Greaves. In a cabinet in his walnut-paneled billiard room," Mullahey said.

Not a .31 or a .44. Maybe Chase was innocent. Or he'd hidden the other weapons. "Thanks, Mullahey. Good work."

"I've something more, Mr. Greaves. One of the lads has received a report of gunfire on Friday evening, Mr. Greaves," he said, returning his notebook to his inner coat pocket. "Down by the Central wharf. Two shots fired, to be precise. The officer who covers that area has been told to hold the witness for you, Mr. Greaves."

"That's only a couple streets south of where Mr. Eckart's body was found off Washington Street wharf, sir."

"It's been almost a week. What took the witness so long to make a report?" Nick got to his feet and grabbed his hat off his desk. "Mullahey, discover what you can about the Hunters. Don't know his first name. Wife is Deborah."

"Aye, Mr. Greaves."

"Taylor, come with me to the wharf. Let's find out what this witness has to say."

• • •

Celia stared for a long time at Lena Douglass's brass doorbell, reluctant to ring. She'd never forgiven the woman for the dismissive way she had once treated Barbara, despite her position as the chairwoman over the Ladies' Society of Christian Aid. A gathering of women whose raison d'être was, purportedly, to help the downtrodden females of San Francisco forge paths to new and better lives. A charity that had seemed purpose-built to assist many of the patients who visited Celia's medical clinic. She'd learned otherwise, however, for the women of the Ladies' Society of Christian Aid were singularly disinterested in aiding the Chinese girls Celia had been working with at the time.

Yet, here you are, Celia. Seeking information from a woman who had no more fondness for Celia than Celia had for her. Reluctant to ring that woman's doorbell. *In delay there lies no plenty.* Perhaps this situation was not precisely what Shakespeare had had in mind, but the words would serve.

She twisted the bell's turn knob. Mrs. Douglass's servant was efficient and answered the summons quickly.

"Is Mrs. Douglass at home?" Celia asked. "I am Mrs. Davies. She knows me. I would like to speak with her about an urgent matter concerning a mutual acquaintance."

The young woman showed her into the entrance vestibule. "I'll see if Mrs. Douglass is available, ma'am."

She disappeared into one of the rooms off the hallway, returning moments later. "She'll be happy to speak with you in the morning room, ma'am."

Happy? Doubtful, but she'd not quibble.

Celia followed the servant into what turned out to be a small dining room with a view over a narrow side garden. A sudden beam of sunlight slanted through the tall bay windows, illuminating the blues and golds of the cushioned chairs and the Brussels carpet, glinting off the gilt-edge china displayed on a narrow sideboard before clouds once again obscured it.

Her graying hair scraped into a chignon at the nape of her neck, Lena Douglass looked up from the newspaper she was reading at the mahogany table. The remnants of an early midday meal were pushed to one side. Her servant rushed to clear the table and make room for Celia.

"Coffee, ma'am?" the girl offered.

Celia shook her head and took a seat. "How have you been, Mrs. Douglass? It has been some time."

She folded the newspaper and set it down. "Well enough, Mrs. Davies. What is this urgent matter concerning a friend that you wish to speak to me about?"

"I am here about Deborah Hunter." Lena would undoubtedly inform the woman that Celia had been asking questions. She'd have to proceed with caution. "I am seeking supporters for a new clinic I am considering opening, and was wondering if she might be a candidate worth pursuing."

"*That* is your urgent matter?"

"I anticipated you'd not agree to see me if I did not express some urgency."

"I probably wouldn't have and should toss you out immediately," she said. Curiosity, though, prevailed and she didn't toss Celia out. "Maybe you can explain why you're asking me rather than approaching Deborah directly, Mrs. Davies."

"I wanted your opinion, which I value, on her respectability and trustworthiness. You are acquainted with her through the Society, are you not?" According to Jane, they were, which was why Jane had sent Celia to this woman's morning room. "I had only the briefest conversation with Mrs. Hunter last evening—at Mrs. Chase's benefit—but was struck by her strength of character."

Lena Douglass's gaze narrowed, wrinkles fanning out from the edges of her eyes. "I have heard about the intruder who attacked Mrs. Hutchinson."

Gossip winging its way to Lena Douglass with the efficiency of a carrier pigeon. "It was quite terrible," she said. "Mrs. Hunter visited Jane this morning, very concerned about her injury. It was kind of her."

"Deborah is a kind woman." Spoken without any warmth or conviction.

"I have heard from others that she helps find employment for needy women in this city."

"Yes, she does. In fact, she regularly brings females to the attention of the Society," she said. "Deborah and two or three others are brave enough to approach the unfortunate women of our city and encourage them to let us help them follow a more productive, Christian life."

"Was a young woman named Meg one of those unfortunates whom she assisted, Mrs. Douglass?"

"You really need to talk to Deborah about this, Mrs. Davies."

"So you will not help me? I expect you know the answer," Celia said. "I do not ask about Meg frivolously, Lena. This matter is very serious. And urgent."

She pressed her lips together for a few seconds before answering. "I don't recollect that name."

"What about someone named Judith?"

A spark of recognition lit her eyes. "Possibly," she said. "We allocate our funds to various women based on their needs, and I believe a woman named Judith was on that list not long ago."

"I need to speak with her. About Meg, in fact. They were friends," she said. "Do you know how I might contact her?"

"I keep the ledger of all the females who solicit our support here," she said without moving to fetch the book.

"Might I see it, Mrs. Douglass?" Celia asked. "Lena, please. Judith could be in trouble."

She drew back, leery of the mere mention of Judith Whelan's potential problems. "What sort of trouble?"

"I am not free to explain. But if I locate her quickly, I might be able to save the Society from any . . . unwelcome repercussions."

The opportunity to protect her precious Society from scandal persuaded Lena to act. She rang for her servant and instructed her to retrieve the ledger. The young woman shortly returned and handed over the leather-bound book.

Lena contemplated Celia before giving it to her. "I always review the entries before taking the names of the most deserving to the other members. As I said, I recall a young woman named Judith approaching us a few weeks ago," she said. "There was a notation stating that she'd contacted us once before. She was seeking assistance to remove herself from an abusive relationship, is what she told us. That may have been her motive the first time, as well."

Celia flipped to the ledger's most recent entries and inspected the names. There was Judith, listed as Judith W., from a date in mid-February. The timing worked for when she might have needed money, after having abruptly departed her job at the sewing machine shop. Celia withdrew a scrap of paper from her reticule and scribbled down the recorded address. It was different from Miss Whelan's city directory entry and more likely accurate.

"Who all has access to this book, Mrs. Douglass?"

"Only the chairwoman, which is me," she answered. "Of course, portions of the information contained within the lists are held by various members for the purposes of contacting the women if necessary. But I take the responsibility to compile and maintain this primary ledger."

"Is this date written here the date when Judith previously had approached the Society for assistance?" A December date in 1863. When had Meg Greaves died? In the spring of 1864, if Celia remembered correctly.

Lena peered at the entry. "Yes. That's what that date signifies."

Celia flipped to the prior pages in the book. The ledger fortunately went back to 1863. She found December's entries and Judith's name. Another name caught her eye, inscribed about two weeks later. Margaret G. *Meg*.

"I see that the Society did indeed assist my friend Meg. In December of 1863, according to this entry."

"I was not responsible for recording the ladies' information at that time," she said. "That is why I did not recognize her name when you mentioned it, Mrs. Davies. Marian was in charge then."

Gad. "Marian Chase?"

The other woman nodded.

"Thank you, Mrs. Douglass." She closed the ledger and got to her feet. "Thank you so much."

• • •

Owen loaded crates onto Mr. McCann's wagon faster than he ever had, working at a pace so feverish that the driver took to staring at him like he was all possessed. But he had to finish up and tell Mrs. Davies about Eileen and Mr. Brodie as quick as possible. Maybe she could figure out why Eileen was talking with the customs officer. After all, their conversation had been mighty suspicious. Mighty suspicious.

He did regret letting Mr. Brodie spot him. Worse than letting that happen was Owen's certainty that for the past hour somebody had been watching him. He'd feel their eyes on him almost as surely as if they were standing behind him, breathing down his neck. But every time he turned to look, he never caught sight of anybody. But, still . . .

"Shoot," he muttered.

"Cassidy, you sure you're okay?" the driver asked, drawing the tarpaulin over the load. "You're acting awful strange."

"Um, I'm sure I'm okay." Owen tied off the tarpaulin on his end. "Are we done here?"

The driver squinted at him. "You planning on running off right now? Because there's another shipment due in an hour, and I don't think Mr. McCann will take kindly to you being absent again."

"An hour? I'll be back." *If whoever's been watching me doesn't stop me.*

He'd have to be careful and not get followed, though, because he didn't want the person to trail him to Mrs. Davies's house.

Owen tucked his hands into his pants pockets and strolled away from the Market Street wharf. He had a bit of a walk to get to Mrs. Davies's house on Vallejo. Down Sacramento to Kearny then up a few blocks. Maybe he should run. Or would that make it more obvious that he was onto the fact that the fellow was after him? *Maybe you're letting your imagination run wild, Cassidy.* But, after having Mr. Fuller shot dead right in front of him last night—shoot, there'd been a lot of blood; more than Owen had ever seen in his life—it was only natural to be jumpy. He risked a glance behind him as he turned the corner, choosing to head up Front instead. He didn't see anybody. Or at least, he didn't think he saw anybody. Was that a fellow hiding behind those barrels over there? He wouldn't try anything, would he? In the middle of the day, in a busy part of town? All sorts of folks were hanging around.

Although how many of them would help a kid like him if he shouted? Would that thick-muscled stevedore there? Nope. Or that black-haired fellow, who looked to be from South America? Nope. The Chinese laborer with his long queue swinging, looking just as desperate as Owen was to move quickly and get away from the rough crowd that spent their time around the wharves, wouldn't either.

He increased his pace, dodging carts and workers and pedestrians. Maybe he should've stopped at the nearest police telegraph box, but he wasn't sure exactly where it was. Maybe he *should* run.

Owen dashed across the street. A porter hauling parcels lurched out of his way, shouting after him in German or some other language. Traffic on the road was heavy, and Owen stopped and started, trying to find a way through the tangle of wagons and horses, loads left in the street, barrels getting rolled down ramps.

"Hey!" a man behind him yelled. "Stop, kid!"

Shoot! Owen sprinted up a narrow road. He caught his toe on a broken cobble and fell, scraping his hands and knees. He hopped up, brushing grit off his bleeding hands as he ran. *Is he still following me?*

Owen darted toward the cross street. Headed right for the gap between two buckboards parked at the curb. He had to get away. He *had* to. Owen lunged through the gap. Not noticing the speeding carriage bearing down on him.

• • •

"A small fellow, you say?" Nick asked the witness, who was attempting to hide in the doorway of his lodging house. Maybe he didn't like being seen with cops.

"Small and short. Like a Mexican kid. Or maybe a Chinese fellow," he said. "When I heard the gunshots, I looked out the window and saw him running down the street. Hear gunshots every so often, of course, being where I live and all." He paused to spit a gob of chewing tobacco onto the plank sidewalk, barely missing Nick's foot. "But it's not so routine that I didn't decide to have a look-see."

"Any more description than that? Which direction did he run, for instance?" Taylor asked, his pencil poised above his notebook.

"Away from the wharf. Disappeared down that cross street there." The fellow gestured up the road toward a lane that angled between a saloon and a ship chandler's. "It was nighttime, though, Officer. Hard to see more than a shadow, frankly."

"Why did you wait so long to inform the police?" Nick asked.

"I was in Oakland the past few days, Detective. I'm a jobber, and I had a shipment of goods to inspect before they got sent on to the merchants I supply," he said. "Only heard about the dead fellow at the Washington Street wharf when I got back. Put two and two together . . ."

Nick had a mathematician on his hands. "Did you happen to know the dead man? He was a ship's carpenter. Name of Eckart."

"Nope," he said.

"Hear any rumors as to what might've happened? Who might be responsible?"

He licked his chapped lips. "I heard Archibald Chase's name come up."

Ah, Mr. Chase. "As the killer?"

"Just talk, Detective."

Not very useful talk. "Why would anybody link his name to the murder of a ship's carpenter? An upstanding businessman like Mr. Chase."

His witness laughed so hard he started choking. "Chase, upstanding?" he asked once he recovered. He glanced up and down the street before slinking back into the meager cover the doorway provided. "Also heard he bribes customs officials to look the other way."

"Import tax evasion?" Otherwise known as smuggling.

"Helps a person get rich, doesn't it? If you're in the business of selling imported goods."

"If you've heard, the harbor police have to have heard, too," Taylor pointed out. "And the customs officials."

"You'd think," the man agreed.

"Which of them should have heard but are acting like they haven't?" Nick asked.

"I'm not naming names, Detective. I'm only standing here because I know when it's smart to look the other way." He sobered. "And don't tell anybody I told you. Don't want to end up like that dead guy."

The sound of distant shouting interrupted Nick's interrogation. A pair of boys ran down the street in the direction of the commotion, chased by a mangy dog yapping at the top of its lungs.

"What in tarnation?" Nick's witness asked.

"Taylor," Nick said.

"I'll be right behind you, sir."

Nick jogged after the boys. People were collecting at a nearby intersection, where it looked like there'd been an accident. A buggy driver, his carriage perched cockeyed on the sidewalk, was trying to calm his rearing horse. Squealing kids darted in and out of the crowd, adding to the uproar. A man driving a gig bellowed for someone to explain why the road was blocked.

One of the onlookers spotted Taylor. "Hey, Officer! Come quick!" he called out. "This here driver was speeding through the streets and nearly ran over a kid!"

"Let me through," Nick ordered.

A kid slumped on the ground in the middle of the crowd. An Irish kid. Owen Cassidy. *Of course.*

"Damn it, Cassidy," Nick swore.

"Sorry, Mr. Greaves." He scrambled to his feet. His clothing was torn in spots and bloodied. "Sorry."

"It's his fault my buggy is damaged, Officer," its owner protested. "Look at the right front wheel. It's ruined! He needs to pay."

Owen? Pay for repairs? "What happened?"

"He ran out from between those two buckboards so quick I didn't have a chance to stop. Lucky I didn't get thrown."

"You were tearing down the road like you were loco," a fellow accused. A couple of the assembled gawkers murmured in agreement.

"The kid's lucky he's not dead!" one of the buckboard owners yelled. The other one was nowhere to be seen, along with his wagon.

"Shoot, Mr. Greaves. I've torn my jacket and pants to shreds."

"I'll pay to replace them," Nick said.

"You will?" Owen asked, his face brightening.

"What about paying for repairs to my buggy?" the owner asked.

"Yes, Cassidy. Just stop getting yourself into fixes, all right?" he asked. "And what in hell were you doing, running out into the street?"

"Didn't mean to, Mr. Greaves, but there was a fellow chasing me."

"Anybody see the man?" Nick asked the crowd.

"I might've, Officer," a woman wearing a sea-green shawl said. "He ran down the street thataway."

"Taylor, try to get more details from these very helpful people."

Nick turned and sprinted down the street that the woman had indicated.

"Hey! What about the damage to my carriage?" the buggy owner shouted after him.

Nick examined every shadowed doorway, checked behind every stack of barrels and crates. Maybe the fellow had found an unlocked door and bolted inside. Nick couldn't inspect every building, though. He halted at the next intersection. Nobody was running down the road like they didn't want to be caught. In fact, nothing unusual was going on at all. The man had gotten away.

Damn.

CHAPTER 17

The Chases' California Street house was considerably more quiet than it had been last evening. It nearly looked deserted. Perhaps the staff was tiptoeing around, afraid to disturb an upset Mrs. Chase. Or perhaps they huddled in corners to whisper about the attack on Jane and who the perpetrator could have been. The quiet was beneficial. It meant that no one was outside to monitor Celia while she searched the grounds for any clues left behind by an intruder.

After one more glance around, she skirted the right side of the house. A pair of fruit trees—one pear, one apple, the flower buds on the pear beginning to show—stood sentinel over a patch of expertly trimmed ivy and a trellised stand of grape vines. In the daylight, they'd be noticeable from the conservatory. Fortunately, no one was inside to observe her creeping about. Unfortunately, there was no evidence that anyone had passed this way recently. Perhaps the intruder had been light on their feet and not left an imprint in the soft dirt like she was doing.

"Ma'am?" asked the cook. She stood on the rear porch, the door to the potting room hanging open behind her. "What are you doing out there, ma'am?"

"I was admiring the Chases' grape vines," she said, smiling. "And the ivy is so tastefully planted around the house. I did not have the opportunity, obviously, last night to inspect them."

She squinted at Celia. "You're the woman who helped the lady with the head injury, right?"

"That indeed was me."

The woman pursed her lips. "You've come back to inspect the garden? At this hour? The sun is going to set soon."

"Gardens are an interest of mine, no matter the hour."

The cook reached for the door, signaling she intended to return to her work in the kitchen. "Are you done admiring the grape vines and the ivy? I'm busy with dinner."

"Ah, yes, I am," Celia replied. "Might I ask if Mrs. Chase is in?"

"Well, yes. She is."

"Good. Very good," Celia replied. "Oh, before I visit with her, can I ask you a question? This might seem quite odd, of course, but I was wondering if Mrs. Hunter came into the kitchen last evening, during the benefit, to speak with you?"

She looked at Celia as though she might have suffered a head injury along with Jane. "Mrs. Hunter? Talk to me in the kitchen?"

"I shall take that as a no," Celia said. "Rather than troop through the kitchen, I will go around to the front and ring the bell there. Inform one of the other servants to answer, if you will."

Celia marched off in the direction of the veranda. A housemaid—not Eileen—was waiting for her. Celia cleaned the soles of her half boots and followed the maid into the parlor. Marian Chase sat on the sofa, an afternoon newspaper folded on the seat next to her. The room was cozier than it had been last evening for the benefit, the furniture no longer pushed out of the way but arranged so that guests could comfortably converse while admiring the art and the Chases' collection of Oriental porcelains.

"Mrs. Davies," said Marian Chase. "Was I expecting you? It's rather late in the day for a visit."

"I hope I am not disturbing you," she said, taking the chair the woman indicated. A rosewood easy chair upholstered in the same golden-yellow ribbed silk as the sofa.

"I've already been disturbed by the police today. Hunting around in our possessions. Inspecting my husband's Sharps rifle and upsetting Archibald in the process. Questioning the staff about my husband's whereabouts last Friday evening, when we were at dinner and here in the house afterward, as all of them can attest. Ridiculous," she huffed. "So if you're here to search for clues on your own, you're too late."

"I was at Mrs. Hutchinson's—she is recovering well from her concussion, by the way—when Mrs. Hunter stopped in," she said. "She told us you were quite upset last evening."

"Wouldn't you be if some stranger broke into your home and terrorized you?"

"You are convinced it was a stranger?" Celia asked, shifting her weight to get more comfortable, as she kept sinking into the overstuffed cushions of the chair.

She looked disturbed by the question. "No friends or staff of mine would ever conceal themselves in my conservatory and attack a guest."

"An enemy of your husband's, perhaps?" Or an unsavory friend.

"We have no enemies, Mrs. Davies," she stated. "Maybe you do, given your propensity for snooping around in matters best left to the police. But we don't."

"A businessman with no enemies? Mr. Chase would be the first of my acquaintance."

"He is an ethical man," she stated.

Were there those who claimed otherwise? Celia wondered. "At least you had a friend to stay with you and comfort you at such a distressing time."

An uncertain look crossed Mrs. Chase's face, then cleared. She'd not dispute Deborah Hunter's story.

"Your husband is certainly a successful businessman," Celia continued. "I happened by his auction house today—I've been wanting to procure a length of blue silk—and was impressed by the items up for auction. Which included a brooch nearly identical to the one you wore last night."

"Why the interest in my brooch, Mrs. Davies?" she asked stiffly. "Mrs. Hutchinson probed me with questions last evening, too."

"I am curious why multiples exist—one of which is a fake—yet you insist yours is unique."

"My husband's auction house would never sell paste jewelry. We are a business dealing only in quality items." Marian Chase's eyes narrowed. "It was *you* asking about Margaret Greaves at the auction house, wasn't it? And out at our old Mission house, too."

"You knew her through your work with the Ladies' Society of Christian Aid, did you not?"

Mrs. Chase had not instructed her servant to provide tea or coffee, so she had no cup to toy with while she decided upon a response.

"I did know Miss Greaves. Deborah brought Meg to the attention of the Society after she found herself on the streets," she said. "Archibald took her on at the auction house. She didn't last long."

"She left your husband's business, moved out of the room she'd been renting behind your house out by the Mission Woolen Mills, and died shortly thereafter."

Marian Chase appeared unmoved by Meg's fate. "She took her own life, Mrs. Davies. Reprehensible."

"I have heard rumors—"

"That you should ignore," she interrupted. "None of us were in any way involved in her death."

"What can you tell me about Judith Whelan? She and Meg were friends," she said. "Lena Douglass informed me that you likely interacted with her when she first approached the Society for help."

"I did," she answered curtly. "Why are you interested in Miss Whelan?"

Celia thought it wisest to not answer.

"You knew them all, did you not, Mrs. Chase?" she asked. "Meg. Judith. Sylvanus Eckart too, I would presume."

"That man who came here the other week, demanding to speak with Archibald?" she asked disdainfully. "I did *not* know him."

"And Mrs. Hunter knew them all, as well." Celia, tired of being rendered helpless from collapsing into the depths of the armchair, scooted to the edge of the cushion. "Through her work for the Society."

"What are you driving at, Mrs. Davies?"

I am stumbling in the dark, at the moment. "Did any of them ever confide in you, Mrs. Chase?" Divulge the secret that Meg may have been killed for?

"I do not know any of our ladies well enough for them to confide in me, Mrs. Davies. It is best to treat them with a certain level of detachment."

Rather than compassion and concern. "Might they confide in Deborah Hunter?"

Her lips puckered in a moue. "I have no idea."

"When Mr. Eckart came here looking for your husband, he was seeking help, I've been told."

"Clearly, you've been told a great deal," she replied. "Which leaves me curious why you are even questioning me."

"Because I am convinced that you know more than you are willing to admit, Marian," she said evenly. "What sort of 'help' was Mr. Eckart seeking?"

"He was going on about wanting some sort of 'proof' that my husband had," she said. "Proof? Of what? I have no idea."

Proof of who had killed Meg Greaves, perhaps. Proof he thought Mr. Chase was in possession of.

"I asked our gardener to toss him out," Marian was saying. "They got into an altercation and he ended up with a broken arm as thanks. And now I've no one to attend to my azaleas."

Celia leaned forward. "Marian, are you positive that you've not seen or heard anything that might indicate your husband is in trouble?" she asked. "I am concerned for your safety. Yours and your husband's. Last evening's intruder may have been attempting to deliver a warning."

"A warning?"

"A warning, Marian."

She hesitated. *Honestly, Marian.* Celia fought the urge to grab the woman by the shoulders and shake the truth out of her.

Marian groaned. "It has been so strange lately, Mrs. Davies. Not just what happened last night."

At last! "In what way?" she asked quietly.

"I shouldn't be telling you this, but I recently overheard a conversation between William . . . Mr. Hunter and my husband," she replied. "An odd conversation. About a fellow named Francis."

"Have you ever heard him mentioned before?"

"No," she said. "Mr. Hunter sounded angry about the man. Because he wanted a greater 'share of the business,' which upset my husband."

"A share of the auction business?"

"I don't know," she replied. "I asked Archibald about him, but he told me not to worry. That it was simply business talk among men and I wasn't to think about it. But I do think about it."

"Do you think he could have been last evening's intruder, Marian?"

Her gaze flickered. "I shouldn't have said anything. Archibald would be furious if he found out," she said. "So if you are finished, Mrs. Davies, I'd like to prepare for dinner before my husband returns."

Marian reached for the brass bell on the table at her side, readying to ring it to have Celia escorted out of the house.

"One more question, please, Mrs. Chase," Celia said, halting her. "And then I shall take my leave."

The other woman sighed, and set the bell on her lap, the clapper muffled against the thick folds of her emerald green shot silk skirt. "Go ahead."

"Mrs. Hunter believes she saw someone inside the conservatory when she arrived before the other guests. Did she tell you that?"

"No," she declared. Too quickly for Celia's taste.

"The edging spade I believe was used to strike Jane Hutchinson had mud upon the blade. Mud that had not fully dried." She'd forgotten to tell Nicholas about her discovery. "I have to conclude that someone—

possibly the intruder—had been using the spade to dig in your conservatory. Have you found evidence of digging?"

"I haven't. And no one had been admitted to the conservatory prior to Mrs. Hutchinson going in there. I don't know what Deborah saw." She rang the bell and stood. "I really must ask you to leave. Good day to you, Mrs. Davies."

Celia rose as well. Marian Chase strode over to the parlor doors and slid them open. She flung wide one arm to indicate that Celia was to leave, nearly trapping Celia's skirt as she slammed the parlor doors behind her.

Well. Celia drew in a breath and looked over at the conservatory, visible beyond the open dining room doors. She glanced around the hallway. Voices came from the direction of the kitchen, but none of the servants had responded to the ring of Marian's bell.

She looked over at the doorway onto the conservatory again. There was still enough light to see by. More than she'd had last night. Now to hope that the door was unlocked, because she was not the most skilled picklock.

Celia strolled across the dining room, her ears pricked. She tested the door handle. Unlocked. *Thank God.*

She hurried inside, quietly shutting the door behind her. She made her way down the central gravel path, scanning the area around the plantings, looking for any sign that someone had been digging in the conservatory.

A large display of ferns was arranged around the fountain, their dark green fronds graceful against the white marble. She'd paid them little attention last night, even though they were quite lovely. But something was amiss. Several of the potted ferns, a collection of maidenhair, had been set upon stands. However, the arrangement was disordered and asymmetrical, and not intentionally so.

Celia swept some of the fronds aside. There was a depression in the soil where a plant had been removed. She hunted around for a shovel and found one propped in the far corner. She dug down and found nothing. If an item had been buried in that spot, it was now gone. Along with any clue as to what that item had been.

Blast.

• • •

"Let's get you upstairs, Owen," Miss Walford said, recovered from her initial shock over encountering a wounded Owen in her entry hall. She perked her chin like her cousin might and indicated the steps leading to the bedrooms. "You can use our spare bedroom. It's my schoolroom at the moment, but you won't get in the way."

"Are you sure I need to stay, Miss Barbara?" he asked, sounding like he hoped she'd insist. "It's only some scrapes."

"Cousin Celia will insist you stay until she's positive you're not more severely wounded," she answered, making him smile. "At least for a short time. I'll bring up what I need to tend to your cuts."

"Thank you, Miss Walford," Nick said, watching them climb the stairs.

"Och, we should've gone and set up a wee cot in Mrs. Davies's clinic for the lad," Miss Ferguson said, wringing the life from the apron tied around her middle.

Owen wouldn't find much privacy in the middle of Celia's clinic. Although Miss Ferguson would probably prefer him to be closer at hand, so she could regularly pop in and check on him.

"Where is Celia, by the way?" Nick asked her.

"She went to visit Mrs. Hutchinson this morning."

"I know that," he said. "I'm wondering where else she went, Miss Ferguson. Because I don't need to tell you that it's not morning any longer. Not by a long shot."

She frowned. "She didna tell me."

Which meant Celia had gone investigating after her visit with Jane Hutchinson, and Miss Ferguson was no more happy about it than he was.

"I should fetch some fresh water for Miss Barbara, Mr. Greaves. She'll be wanting it for wee Owen's scrapes," she said and hurried off.

The front door opened. "Nicholas? I was not expecting to see you again today," Celia said, stepping inside.

"Where have you been?" he asked like an anxious mother hen. "It's almost dark outside."

"At Jane's, as I told you I intended to do," she answered. "Also at the Chases'. Before their house I visited the chairwoman of the Ladies' Society of Christian Aid. Somewhere in there I stopped for a bite to eat, I believe. And I briefly stopped in at Mr. Chase's auction house. A very busy day." She stepped around him, entering the house. "But you've not told me why you are here again today."

"Cassidy has been hurt. He's being tended to upstairs by Miss Walford."

"Injured?" She speedily peeled off her gloves and her bonnet. "You should have said so immediately."

She didn't stop to remove her half boots and pounded up the stairs. Nick climbed after her.

"How are you?" She took the chair at Owen's bedside that her cousin hastily vacated. Miss Walford had helped him out of his jacket and his brogans, which now sat in a neat pile atop a chair against the wall. "What did you injure?"

"Just some cuts and scrapes, ma'am," he replied, looking cozy among the bed's thick feather pillows.

Celia looked accusingly at Nick. "Not my fault," he said. "He had a near smashup with a carriage horse. Scraped himself up a bit."

"I'll go get bandaging and a solution of alum for his wounds," Miss Walford said, nodding at Nick as she exited the room.

"I was coming to see you, ma'am," Owen said. "To tell you I saw Eileen with Mr. Brodie. He's one of the customs officials down near the Market Street wharf, ma'am. Looked suspicious."

One of the Chases' servants talking with a customs official? Definitely suspicious.

"You are certain it was Eileen," Celia said, lifting his hands to examine the scratches on them.

"Pretty sure, ma'am."

"So far as I could tell, Eileen was not at the Chases' house when I went there this afternoon," she said. "The woman you saw very well could have been her."

"After I spotted them together, I headed this way." Owen winced as Celia's fingers probed a tender spot. "Somebody mighta followed me. I started running and ran into the street. Got hit."

"You appear to have dislocated your forefinger, Owen." Before he could register what she'd said, she yanked the joint into place.

"Ouch!" he yelped.

"I will have Barbara wrap that to hold it steady while the inflammation subsides."

"Yes, ma'am," he whimpered.

"Have you ever noticed Eileen with Mr. Brodie before, Owen?" She rolled up his pant legs to assess his scratches. Other than being filthy, they didn't look too bad, in Nick's opinion.

"Not sure. Didn't know her until the other day," he said. "Sorta disappointed she's not the black-haired woman. The one I always see hanging around the wharf. Getting off ships and whispering to folks. Don't trust her."

Inspection finished, Celia sat back. "Your cuts are mostly superficial, Owen, so you should heal well. However, the tendons of that finger may be swollen for some time. It would be best to rest your hand."

"But Mr. McCann is going to be mad if I don't come to work tomorrow," he protested. "If I don't get back there today!"

"Tomorrow, perhaps, but definitely not today," she said. "Besides, you'd be working in the dark by the time you got back."

Miss Walford returned with the bandaging and the alum.

Miss Ferguson scuttled into the room behind her, depositing an enamel basin filled with water onto the dressing table. "Och, lad. What are we to do with you?"

She didn't wait for an answer, rushing off again. Probably down to the kitchen, where a solution to everybody's problems might be found in a teapot or a recently baked batch of cookies.

Celia moved out of her cousin's way, allowing Miss Walford to tend to Owen's various wounds.

She joined Nick by the doorway, standing near enough that he could smell the lavender that scented her clothes, her hair.

"What should we do?" she asked.

"About Eileen and Brodie, you mean?"

"I wish I'd been aware of her relationship with Mr. Brodie and made enquiries while I was at the Chases'," she said, her voice low as she kept an eye on her cousin's ministrations.

"We don't know what it means that Cassidy saw them together, Celia," he said. "Could be nothing."

She scowled; she did *not* believe it was nothing.

"All of them are tangled up together, interwoven like hazel branches in a hedge. Meg, Judith, Sylvanus. Known by Mrs. Chase and Deborah Hunter through the Ladies' Society of Christian Aid. Eileen, who'd befriended your sister, entangled as well," she said. "Deborah Hunter has made it her mission to bring needy women to the attention of the Society. In December of 1863, they helped your sister *and* Miss Whelan."

It stung, deeply, that Meg had gone to them for help. Help that should've come from Asa, not the Chases or the Society. Should've come from Nick. But he'd been trudging across battlefields, fighting in a war that had cost him more than he'd ever imagined it could. Fighting far away when the battle he should have been engaged in had been so much closer to home.

He pulled her into the hall. "What does any of that have to do with Eileen?"

"I wish I could say. It's merely a muddled idea that I cannot wrestle into making sense." She anxiously rubbed her hand across her forehead. "But why suddenly remember a brooch she'd purportedly had in her possession for years? Suddenly decide to bring it to someone now? Why are there three nearly identical ones, though Marian Chase insists there's only one and also insists her husband's auction house would never sell fakes? Who is Francis, a man Mr. Hunter and Mr. Chase were worried about wanting a greater part of their business? What was the proof that Mr. Eckart believed Mr. Chase possessed? Where precisely *was* Mr. Chase all of last evening? Or Mr. Hunter, for that matter? Why was his wife intent upon discovering if Jane had had a view of the intruder's face? Was *she* the intruder, as her explanation for where she was during the attack on Jane might be a lie? Had Eileen recognized her, but is too frightened to tell anyone? What was buried beneath the ferns in the Chases' conservatory that has since been removed? I can tell you I barely escaped their house without my prying being observed, Nicholas. And, lastly, why was Eileen at the docks today, absent from her duties at the Chases' house, and speaking to a customs official?"

He wasn't ever going to remember what she'd just said. "All right, so we have a lot of questions to answer. We have all along."

"Here is another. What caliber is a Sharps rifle?"

The weapon Mullahey had found at the Chases'. "Not the caliber weapon used to shoot either Eckart or Fuller."

"I see. Oh, and another question. Did Meg ever mention Deborah Hunter in her letters to Mr. Eckart?" she asked. "I do not trust the woman."

"Meg never mentioned her at all."

"Blast," she muttered. "I did discover something very useful. I have learned where Miss Whelan is living. Around the time that Mr. Eckart returned to San Francisco, which coincides with when she quit her position, she sought help from the Society again. She provided them her current address, which they recorded in their ledger."

He held out his hand. "Do you have it written down? I'll go find her in the morning."

"That might be too late, Nicholas."

"Don't get that look on your face like you mean to tear over there yourself," he warned. "Give me the address. I'll go tonight."

She gave it to him. *Damn. Damn and damn.* "There's no point in anybody heading there in a rush, Celia."

She stared at him in disbelief. "But we have to locate Miss Whelan. Meg was very likely murdered, Mr. Eckart is dead, as is Mr. Fuller," she said. "Someone is attempting to silence all those who knew what Meg had learned. Miss Whelan could very well be next."

"Celia, I know she's in danger, and I'm worried about her, too," he said. "But the real reason that there's no point in rushing off to that address is because it's not the address of a house. It's a store, and it won't be open at this hour."

She peered at him. "How do you know that?"

He drew in a long breath, blew it out again. This was going to hurt. But which of them would it hurt more?

"Because it's a wig store, Celia," he said. "And Mina Cascarino works there."

✍ CHAPTER 18 ꙮ

Celia paced the length of the dining room. She'd sat at the table, gotten up, sat once more, gotten up again to walk loops through the first-floor rooms, and still could not settle her restive mind. Nicholas had promised to have Mr. Taylor question Eileen as soon as possible, perhaps this evening, hoping that a visit by a police officer would encourage her to speak honestly. Celia doubted that his efforts would bear fruit, however. He'd also promised that he would go to the wig shop first thing in the morning. Where the exquisitely lovely Mina Cascarino worked, thought Celia jealously.

"Honestly, Celia," she muttered.

"Ma'am?" Addie asked from the doorway between the kitchen and the dining room. "You'll wear a hole into the rug with your treading back and forth. You should calm yourself by making your notes on this case, like you always do."

"How can I sit here and compose notes when Miss Whelan's life could be at risk? Two of her acquaintances have been shot. She is likely next." Or Nicholas, if the person who'd nailed a warning message to Mrs. Jewett's front doorframe followed through on their threat. Perhaps last night they had tried. "And there is Owen, who has witnessed a shooting and been chased through the streets near the Market Street wharf."

Addie cocked an eyebrow. "And what do you mean to do about these troubles this evening? Run off into the night and land yourself in danger?" she asked. "Isna it enough that wee Owen is hurt and Mrs. Hutchinson has been injured? You're so keen to join them? Besides, Mr. Greaves promised to make enquiries. He will. You know he will."

She sighed. "Bring some tea, Addie. Let us sit and think together." *And in the morning I will run off and land myself in danger.*

While Addie heated a kettle, Celia gathered her usual items—pencil, notepad, block of India rubber for erasing—and laid them out on the dining room table. She pulled out a chair, one facing the parlor. *To prevent Barbara from sneaking up without warning.* Although her cousin was occupied with fussing over Owen; she could hear them talking together in the spare bedchamber, their voices a low, distant hum.

Addie returned with the tea things and set them down. "You're needing to discover who killed Miss Greaves's beau."

"Mr. Eckart, along with another man last night."

"Have you nae settled on someone, though?" she asked, taking the chair across from Celia.

"Truthfully, no. But let us begin with Deborah Hunter."

She wrote her name at the top of the paper. *Deborah Hunter.*

"This is what I know about her, Addie. A woman with a forceful personality, she'd met Meg through the Ladies' Society of Christian Aid and encouraged the Chases to take her on at the auction house. She may have provided help to Judith Whelan, the friend of Miss Greaves's we are trying to locate, as well," Celia said as she made notes. "She and her husband are friends of the Chases'. Or, rather, her husband is a business associate of Mr. Chase's, and a rather handsome man, I might add."

"Does handsomeness make a man guilty, ma'am?" Addie asked.

"Certainly not. Just a pointless observation," Celia said. "To finish, the Hunters currently rent the Chases' Mission area house. Not long ago, they moved from Santa Clara back to San Francisco."

Addie poured out the water for their tea. "Why might Mrs. Hunter wish to kill Mr. Eckart?"

"I am at a loss as to what her motive would be. I cannot even be certain she'd ever met him," Celia said. "However, I am unaware of her alibi for the evening of his death. Also, she was quick to implicate one of Mr. Eckart's shipmates as his likely murderer. She claimed she did so to protect Mr. Chase from unwarranted suspicion."

"Weel, then."

"Precisely," Celia agreed. "As far as Mr. Fuller's murder is concerned, she attended Marian Chase's benefit last evening. However, she was curiously absent when the entire household, including Mr. Chase, gathered in the conservatory to witness the uproar caused by the assault on Jane. Her claim that she was in the kitchen with the cook is untrue. Although I did notice her on the veranda when Jane and I left."

"Was her husband at the benefit, ma'am? Canna think he is not somehow involved, if we're to suspect his wife."

"He was not, Addie. So let us return to him."

Mr. Hunter.

"I encountered him at the auction house again today. He informed me that he was unable to attend Mrs. Chase's benefit because he was otherwise occupied," Celia said. "He did not elaborate on precisely what had occupied him, though."

"He was occupied in killing Mr. Fuller?"

"It would be amateurish of me to assume that simply because he was not in attendance means that he is responsible. None of the ladies had their husbands with them. We cannot suspect them all," she said. "Furthermore, I am unaware of any motive for him to want to kill Mr. Eckart or Mr. Fuller. Perhaps I should simply erase his name from my list." She didn't, though.

Addie stirred sugar into her tea. "Should we suspect Mr. Chase in any of these crimes, ma'am?"

"Let us turn to him next."

She sipped her tea and jotted down his name. *Archibald Chase.*

"A former neighbor of his accused him of being involved in someone's death. Mr. Eckart's? Or Meg's?" *Or both?* "Others, including his wife, have acknowledged the rumor but denied the truth of it. Does that mean he *has* killed someone, though?"

"Where there's smoke, there's fire, ma'am."

"Mr. Eckart had attempted to meet with Mr. Chase two weeks ago. Wanting his help. Seeking 'proof.' Possibly information about who killed Meg Greaves, but I cannot be certain."

"Does that mean Mr. Eckart did not believe Mr. Chase was her killer? God rest her soul."

"He may have been wrong to believe that but learned of his error too late to save himself," Celia said. "Mr. Chase is known to be ill-tempered. Mr. Mullahey did not find a weapon in his house matching the caliber of the one used to shoot Mr. Eckart, however." Or the one used on Mr. Fuller, either.

"He has hidden it."

Beneath his wife's display of ferns, perhaps? "Somewhat unfortunately for us, he also appears to have an alibi for the evening of Mr. Eckart's murder."

"What about Mrs. Chase?"

"She has the same alibi as her husband does. A night out dining followed by a quiet evening at home. Servants willing to attest to that fact," Celia told her. "She did inform me of a man named Francis who wants a greater part of the business along with her husband and Mr. Hunter. She made the fellow sound rather alarming. Eileen also told me about 'unsavory' people Mr. Chase has been entertaining at the house."

"Hmph," Addie grumbled.

Indeed. "Meg Greaves wrote to Mr. Eckart about a man who'd 'found out' that she knew. Knew about a crime, is what Nicholas and I have concluded," Celia said. "Was the mysterious Francis that man?"

Addie squinted at Celia's notes. "Did you write his name down?"

"I shall." Which she did. Followed by a large question mark.

"What about Miss Greaves's friend? The one who has disappeared?" Addie asked. "Should we consider her?"

"Miss Whelan?"

Celia must have sounded skeptical, because Addie scowled. "A friend can murder someone just as readily as an enemy, ma'am. Love turns to hate. Husbands murder wives. Children murder parents."

Parents murdered children. Siblings murdered siblings. The list could go on. "Yes."

Judith Whelan.

"She is afraid for her life, clearly," Celia said. "She hastily moved out of her lodgings and quit her job at the sewing machine shop around the time that Mr. Eckart returned to San Francisco."

Addie refreshed her cup of tea. "She killed Miss Greaves, Mr. Eckart learned of her guilt and came looking for her, but she killed him in self-defense."

"It is my understanding that he was shot in the back." Which, in Celia's mind, negated self-defense.

"*He* killed Miss Greaves, Miss Whelan knew, and she killed him when he returned to San Francisco," Addie suggested. "She has gone into hiding because she doesna want to be accused of the crime. 'Tis the answer, ma'am." She punctuated her statement with a brisk nod.

"Or Mr. Eckart's murderer is someone else entirely and who also presents a danger to her. An individual who may have come to believe that they had gotten away with a crime." Until Sylvanus Eckart reappeared.

Addie nodded sagely. "Who else is there to consider?"

"Excluding last night's victim, Mr. Fuller—whose actions suggest to me that he was a witness who knew too much—I will now turn to the fellow presently in jail."

Mr. Loomis.

"He was acquainted with Mr. Eckart and had implicated Mr.

Raymond Fuller in his murder," Celia said. "Mr. Fuller was the man who'd delivered Meg's letters to Nicholas. He may have been intending to deliver more letters to Nicholas last night."

"Och."

"Mr. Loomis owed Mr. Eckart money, which does give him a motive," she said. "His alibi was weak enough for Nicholas to justify jailing him. He could not have shot Mr. Fuller, obviously."

"So do we eliminate him, ma'am?"

"There could be two different people involved, Addie," she said. "Let us turn to Mr. Brodie, customs official."

Mr. Brodie.

"To be frank, I know nothing about him, Addie," she said, considering his name. "Other than what his occupation is and that Owen spotted him whispering with Eileen."

Addie's forehead creased. "Wasna Mr. Eckart a sailor, ma'am?"

"A ship's carpenter."

"He may have been acquainted with Mr. Brodie, then," her housekeeper said. "Met him because of Mr. Brodie's work, or at one of the saloons the sailors and dockworkers go to."

"So we have established a possible relationship between the two men but have no idea of a motive," she said. "I have to next consider the young woman visiting him at the docks when she should have been tending to her chores at the Chases' house."

Eileen.

"She'd befriended Meg when she lived at the Chases' Mission area house, Addie," she said. "She knew of Mr. Eckart but had never met him, which leaves me wondering what motive *she* would have to kill him."

"Because he knew she'd killed Miss Greaves."

"It would be very bold of her to speak with me about Meg, if that was the case. And to bring me that brooch she'd found," Celia said, writing notes as quickly as she could. She should get tips from Mr. Taylor someday. "Furthermore, Meg's message to Mr. Eckart suggested a very different reason to have wanted her dead. Her discovery of a criminal activity led by a man. By the way, Mrs. Chase has a copy of that brooch. Plus, there was another one, very similar, being sold this morning at Mr. Chase's auction house."

"Is someone fencing jewelry at the auction house?" Addie asked.

"'Fencing,' Addie?"

"You know, ma'am. To knowingly sell stolen items to profit off them."

"I did not realize you were aware of such activities," Celia said, smiling at her housekeeper. Her romance with Mr. Taylor was turning her into a proper detective. "Thank you."

Addie blushed. "Och, ma'am."

"Perhaps this is more to the point—the brooch Eileen brought me is fashioned of colored glass instead of real garnets and not worth much, in fact."

"Perhaps the auction house is offering goods that are not real."

"Which the staff and Mrs. Chase vehemently deny," Celia said. "I wonder if Meg Greaves had discovered this was going on, though, and that Mr. Chase was the man who'd learned that she knew about his illegal activities." Or Mr. Hunter, his close business associate.

Addie forcefully set down her teacup, which rattled against the saucer. "He *is* the murderer, ma'am," she stated. "Both of poor Miss Greaves and Mr. Eckart."

"He could not have been the man who shot Mr. Fuller last evening, though. He was at the house during the benefit." She frowned. "Conveniently hidden away in his billiard room."

"Verra convenient."

Celia examined what she'd written about Archibald Chase.

"Why did Meg not go to her uncle to inform him about what she'd discovered, Addie?" she asked. "If she'd become aware of a crime, she should have told him." Nicholas's beloved Uncle Asa.

"She'd not had the chance to?"

"Or she'd been afraid to," Celia added sourly. "A police officer—not her uncle—had visited Meg shortly before she died. However, according to Nicholas, there were no records of police interest in his sister. So who was he?"

Mysterious police officer.

"Detective O'Neal knew her, though," Celia added. "He'd worked for Nicholas's uncle, been a friend to him as well. Meg had lived with her uncle while Nicholas was off fighting. Until she'd abruptly gone to the Society and begged for assistance."

"She fled from the relative who should've protected her."

Celia could think of many reason why she'd done so, none of them savory. But Asa Greaves was long dead and not responsible for Sylvanus Eckart's death or Mr. Fuller's. Mr. O'Neal, however, was very much alive.

She erased "mysterious police officer" and inscribed Mr. O'Neal's name instead. What was his first name? she wondered. Francis, perhaps? A common enough name for an Irishman. Was it the Christian name of a murderer, though?

• • •

"Now lie still and rest, laddie." Addie smoothed the coverlet spread atop him, the morning light soft on her face. Aside from some aches and the sting of the dressing Miss Barbara had used on his cuts, Owen felt fine—well, his finger did hurt a lot, too—but he enjoyed when she fussed over him, so he didn't protest. "I'll go fetch you some eggs and potatoes. How does that sound?"

"That sounds perfect," he said, smiling.

Satisfied, she left. Barbara passed her in the hallway. She stormed into the bedroom and flopped onto the chair next to the bed, set so she could face him.

"She's gone to the police station this morning."

He didn't have to ask who Barbara meant; she meant Mrs. Davies. "What for?"

"She said something to Addie last night about Detective O'Neal, so I guess she wants to talk to him." She gave a wicked smile. "I was listening in."

"Oh." But why did she want to talk to him? This wasn't his case.

"After that, she's headed to the wig store where Mina works to find Miss Whelan. Apparently, she gave the store's address to the Society, claiming that was where she lived."

Owen shifted to better look at her, the movement sending a jolt of pain through his knee. It did hurt too, from banging it against a broken cobble sticking up in the street. Plus, if he was honest with himself, all his scrapes burned like the dickens. *Dang.*

He gave his knee a rub. "Might that be risky? Her going there?"

A furrow creased Miss Barbara's smooth forehead. "She should be okay. It's just a store to buy hairpieces."

She didn't sound certain. He wasn't certain either. But it was morning time. Bad stuff didn't happen in the morning. Usually.

"Anybody looking into what's going on between Eileen and Mr. Brodie?" he asked.

"Mr. Taylor was told to interrogate Eileen," she said. "I haven't heard what he found out, though."

"I never have liked Mr. Brodie. Don't think it's good if she's mixed up with him."

He struggled to sit up, banging his injured forefinger in the process. Barbara leaned across him to help. Her hands on his torso were firm and warm through the undershirt he had on. The press of her fingers gave him sensations he wasn't comfortable with. Not where Miss Barbara was concerned.

Finished wrestling Owen into a seated position, she sat back. "Do you think Mr. Brodie is a criminal?"

"Mr. Brodie?" He might not care for the fellow, who was always yelling at the porters and stuff down by the wharf, but that didn't mean Owen had ever suspected him of being a crook. The idea did take his mind off of how Miss Barbara's touch had felt, though. "Dunno. Should I?"

"Why not? Haven't you read about what goes on at the wharves? Import duty avoidance," she said matter-of-factly. Owen could read, but his landlady didn't exactly supply newspapers at his lodging house and he surely couldn't afford to buy any himself. "Businessmen—like Mr. Chase, who owns an auction house and also imports merchandise to sell on consignment for his clients—occasionally sneak goods into the city without paying the taxes they owe. Which can be as high as twenty-five percent, mind you. Sometimes they pretend the crate of fabric is all cotton material, not telling anybody about the rolls of silk stashed underneath. Or they use false-bottom barrels to hide smaller items. Or they claim the Canadian whiskey actually came from a distillery in California."

"I didn't realize you knew so much about this sort of thing, Miss Barbara," he said admiringly. *Shoot.* She was smarter than him. Just like Miss Grace. Now he had a whole other feeling. Like he couldn't hope to measure up. Which made him miserable. "But what's a person like Mr. Chase trying to avoid paying taxes got to do with Mr. Brodie?"

"It's his job to make sure folks pay the duties on those imports," she said, tucking a loose strand of her glossy black hair into the coil knotted at the base of her neck. Her hair was really pretty. "What, though, if he's happy to accept a portion of the profits to look the other way?"

"If that's true, the harbor officers should arrest him."

"Maybe he's really good at hiding his illegal activities and the police don't realize what Mr. Brodie is up to," Barbara said. "Or maybe *they* are being bribed to look the other way, too."

Owen thought hard about the harbor police being crooked along with the customs officials, even though trying to think made his brain hurt. "Still don't get why Eileen was whispering to Mr. Brodie so furtively."

"Maybe she'd heard the police are after him, so she wanted to warn him."

"But I don't think the police are suspicious of Mr. Brodie. If they are, Mr. Greaves doesn't seem to know about it."

"Good point." She wore a pink-and-white cameo of a woman pinned at her collar, and she stroked it as she thought. "Mr. Eckart worked as a ship's carpenter, according to what Cousin Celia was saying to Addie last night. I wonder if he'd found out about criminal activities at the wharves."

"He might've known folks involved in illegally sneaking goods into the city."

"Mr. Eckart might've even been involved himself," she said. "Or he'd told Miss Greaves about those folks, and that's why she was killed and he ran off."

"Why did he come back to San Francisco, though? He had to realize he was in danger."

"Maybe he was afraid for their friend, Miss Whelan. Maybe somebody recently threatened her, and Mr. Eckart wanted to protect her." She scrunched up her nose. "Does that make sense?"

"Mrs. Davies is in trouble then, Miss Barbara, if she's trying to find Miss Whelan. She's playing with fire," he said. "I've gotta help her. Help me get out of bed." He tried to swing his legs over the edge and winced. Dang, but his knee hurt. What good was he, if all he could do was hobble?

"You can't go anywhere, Owen Cassidy. You're too banged up," she said, moving his legs back, making him feel all those uncomfortable feelings again.

"Then what do we do?"

Miss Barbara's dark eyes took on an ominous shine and she jumped to her feet. "I can go."

What? "You can what?"

"Go help my cousin."

"You can't go out and do that, Miss Barbara. Not you. Not by yourself."

She scowled. "You mean because I'm half Chinese?"

Yes. That was absolutely what he meant. She'd been attacked before, simply because she'd been walking where some people thought the Chinese shouldn't be. Which was a large part of the city, in those same folks' estimation. "It's plumb not safe. You'll get hurt."

"We'll see," she said and dashed from the room.

Shoot.

• • •

"A young woman named Eileen, who works for the Chases, was seen with you yesterday, Mr. Brodie." Nick leaned his hips against the edge of his desk and folded his arms. Brodie, seated in the usual chair Nick put folks in, wore a flat expression on his face. A face that plenty of women might describe as handsome, with his square jaw outlined by a neatly trimmed beard. Maybe even Eileen thought so. "What did she want?"

"You brought me into the station to ask me questions about one of the Chases' servants, Detective?"

"You're not going to deny that she spoke with you yesterday, are you?" he asked. "Because my witness is reliable."

"No, I'm not going to deny knowing Eileen."

"What did she want to speak so urgently with you about?"

"She wanted to know where I was Wednesday evening."

The night of Mrs. Chase's benefit. Off to Nick's right, Taylor cocked an eyebrow but kept on jotting notes. "Why?"

He sighed, a man annoyed by the requests of females. "She'd wanted to meet. I went to a play at the Metropolitan, instead."

Charming. "And you have friends who can testify to that?"

"I do," he said firmly.

"How do you and Eileen know each other?" Nick asked.

"I'm acquainted with Archibald Chase and have been a guest as his house on occasion."

A customs official and an auction house owner. What a cozy arrangement.

"Where you struck up a friendly conversation with one of his housemaids," Nick said. "Or maybe more than just a friendly conversation."

Brodie frowned and didn't reply.

"Mr. Taylor, what was the reason Eileen gave you for speaking with Mr. Brodie?" Nick asked.

He flipped to the prior page in his notebook. "She claimed that Mr. Brodie is the brother of a friend of hers, sir, who has been sickly lately. Eileen went to ask him if she was feeling better."

"That's pretty interesting, don't you think, Mr. Brodie?" Nick asked. "The reason she gave my assistant. Doesn't sound like your explanation."

"She'd lose her job if she admitted to being smitten with me," he replied smugly.

"So that was it? You missed a rendezvous with her on Wednesday evening and she was chastising you."

"That's it, Detective."

Nick considered him. He wasn't sweating like a lot of the people he interviewed. Folks who didn't sweat when interrogated bothered Nick. Even innocent people sweated.

"I have a question about your friend Mr. Chase," he said. "Has he ever been suspected of engaging in selling smuggled goods?"

Brodie shot a look at Taylor before answering. What was he hoping to see? "No."

"And he has never bribed you to look the other way while he brought in imported goods without paying a fair import duty."

"No," he replied more firmly.

Well, it wasn't like a customs official would readily answer in the affirmative. "And what about a man named Sylvanus Eckart. Ever met him?" Nick asked.

"No, but I was there when they pulled Eckart's body out of the water off the Washington Street wharf."

He looked genuinely bothered, even though he must've seen other bodies collected from the water before. Sadly, dead men floating in the bay was not an uncommon occurrence.

"Thank you, Mr. Brodie," Nick said, pushing away from his desk. "You can go."

He didn't have to be invited twice and casually strolled from the office. A bit of an act, in Nick's opinion.

"What's it mean, sir?"

"Obviously, one of the two of them is lying to us about Wednesday night." Nick grabbed his hat off his desk and strode out of the office. Taylor scrambled to follow him. "Brodie's explanation is logical but I don't completely trust it. Or him."

"Do you want me to go over to the Chases' and question Eileen again?"

"No, I want you to get down to the wharf. Try to learn more about the rumors that Chase might be involved in smuggling goods that he later sells in his auction house," he said, climbing the steps that led out onto the alley. "And find Mullahey and have him bring the Hunters into the station for questioning."

"All right, sir. Mr. Greaves."

"Any news about the person chasing Cassidy yesterday?" Nick asked.

"A man who operates a boot and shoe store nearby thought he saw the fellow," he said. "He had on a gray coat like what we wear. What I wear, that is, sir."

"Not a long duster coat." Were they dealing with two different people, or did their murderer own two coats just like he owned two different guns? Sadly, Brodie hadn't been wearing either a gray coat or a duster.

"Because of the coat, the store owner thought a cop was chasing Owen. He figured Owen had stolen something," Taylor said, politely tipping his hat at a demurely dressed young woman, a cascade of blonde curls peeking out beneath her flower-trimmed straw bonnet, passing on the sidewalk. Her answering smile was too knowing for her to be as demure as she wanted to appear. "Didn't want to get involved and didn't pay too much attention, unfortunately."

"Unfortunately." Couldn't blame the fellow, though. "I'm off to discover why Judith Whelan gave the address of a wig store as the place for the Ladies' Society of Christian Aid to contact her."

"Miss Mina's wig store?" his assistant guessed.

He must be made of glass, as easy as it was for Taylor to see through him. "Believe me, I don't like the coincidence, Taylor. But Mina knew Fuller; she gave me his name. And Fuller knew Eckart, who knew Judith Whelan."

"So Miss Mina had met Eckart?"

"I don't know," he said. "I'd bet anything either Fuller or Eckart introduced Miss Whelan to Mina, though. It's the most logical explanation for why she chose that particular store to use as her address. I just need to get Mina to admit it and help me find her."

. . .

One of the officers, seated at a desk in the police station, looked up as Celia strode through the room, bound for the detectives' office. "You've just missed him, ma'am."

She definitely stopped in the station far too often. "Mr. Greaves?"

"Yes, ma'am."

He must have gone to the wig shop, as promised. "Ah. Well, I am not here to speak with him," she said. "I was wondering if Detective O'Neal was in."

The officer studied her. "You want to see Detective O'Neal."

Would the entire police force now be gossiping that she'd abandoned Nicholas and taken up with Detective O'Neal?

She lifted her chin. "Yes, I would. Is he in the office?"

"Yes, he is, ma'am," he said with a sly smile.

The door was open and she went inside. Mr. O'Neal was at his desk, scribbling notes.

"Mrs. Davies," he said, hearing her enter. "You have just missed—"

"I have been informed already. Mr. Greaves is not here," she said. "However, it is you I would like to talk to."

Eyeing her inquisitively, he wiped the nib of his pen and set it down. "How might I help?" he asked, politely getting to his feet.

He did have a lovely, soft Irish accent, but she'd not made the trip to the station to admire the sound of his voice.

She took Mr. Taylor's chair, and Mr. O'Neal resumed sitting. "I want to ask you about Meg Greaves."

His demeanor shifted, became wary. This was delicate territory for her, as treacherous to traverse as a skim of ice upon a pond.

"I barely knew her, Mrs. Davies. You would be better to speak with her brother about her."

"I would, if Mr. Greaves had been in San Francisco in the months before she died. But he was not," she said. "You, however, were."

"For a brief time before I moved to Chicago," he said. "I've heard that Dr. Harris thinks she could have been murdered. He shouldn't be making that claim without having examined the body himself."

How had he heard? She doubted that Nicholas had shared the information with him.

"I trust that Dr. Harris would not question the manner of her death without careful consideration, Detective O'Neal," she said. "But I am not here to debate his conjecture, either. I am here to inquire if *you* were the policeman who'd visited Miss Greaves at Archibald Chase's house out near the Mission. Not long before she died."

He narrowed his gaze. "What is it exactly that you are wanting to know, Mrs. Davies?"

"Meg Greaves may have discovered that Mr. Chase was selling counterfeit jewelry at his auction house," she said flatly, watching for his reaction. Noticing none beyond a normal curiosity which anyone might have.

"Do you have proof?"

Only if the brooch Eileen gave her, which was now in Nicholas's possession, could be proven to have come from Mr. Chase's auction house. Marian Chase owning an identical one was not proof, but certainly was incriminating.

"Do you know if Miss Greaves contacted the police about any such concerns, Detective O'Neal?" she asked.

"Not that I am aware, Mrs. Davies."

"Why might she have not done so, Detective?"

"Probably because she did not actually discover that Mr. Chase was selling counterfeit jewelry, Mrs. Davies."

She stepped out onto the ice. Would it hold? Or would it crack beneath her weight and plunge her into the freezing depths? "Or she was afraid that one of the members of the police force might not be happy if she made her discovery known."

"That is a terrible accusation, ma'am."

"It is, Detective O'Neal. But it might explain why she'd moved away from the security of Asa Greaves's house. Why a police officer had visited her before her death without any record that he'd done so. Why she'd become so frightened after that visit that she dyed her hair to conceal her identity and went into hiding. Why Sylvanus Eckart returned to San Francisco after four years, telling his landlord that he may finally have the opportunity to 'right an old wrong,' as he put it. Only to end up shot in the back," she said. "Now, another of his acquaintances has been murdered and a friend has also decided to hide."

"Greaves *is* working on this case, is he not?" he asked, amused.

She was *not* amused by his reaction. "Did Meg ever tell you what she'd discovered, Mr. O'Neal?"

"No."

"Was she afraid of *you*, Mr. O'Neal?" she asked, her pulse thrumming in her head.

"Mrs. Davies, I have no need to tell you that that was an unwise question," he answered. "Because if I were the fellow she was afraid of, then I'm a very dangerous man to be accusing of murder."

Why had she come here? Had she honestly expected that she would get answers out of a police detective?

She got to her feet. "Thank you for your time, Mr. O'Neal."

"Take care, Mrs. Davies." He retrieved his pen, inked it, and returned to his writing.

She paused at the door. "Oh, Francis . . ."

He looked up. "Aye?"

Indeed. "Nothing. I . . . nothing. Thank you again."

✂ CHAPTER 19 ✄

A balding fellow carrying a cardboard box was striding out of Atwood Bros. Wig and Toupee Makers as Nick arrived. He cast a glance at Nick's head—plenty of hair—pulled a face and stalked off. There weren't any other customers in the store, but Mina was inside, returning toupees to their stands.

The bell jingled as the door shut behind him. It took her a few minutes to realize that he was standing just inside the entrance.

She looked over and scowled. "What do you want now, Nick?" She finished tidying the display. "I gave you all the information I could find about Raymond Fuller."

"Did you see in the papers, Mina? He was shot outside my house two nights ago," he said bluntly. "Not sure his killer wanted to shoot him or shoot me. Either way, he's dead."

"Oh. That's awful," she said. "Is Mrs. Jewett okay?"

Typical that she'd kept herself from asking if *he* was okay. "She startles easily, but she's recovering from the scare."

Another of the employees parted the curtain at the rear doorway and poked her head through the gap. "Do you need any assistance, Mina?" She looked pointedly at Nick.

"No. Thanks." She waited for the curtain to swish into place before turning back to Nick. "So what is it you want? Not to tell me about Raymond Fuller."

"You should've told me you knew Sy Eckart, Mina."

"I didn't. Honest, Nick, I didn't."

"How about Judith Whelan?"

She folded her arms. "I don't know who you're talking about."

He crossed the room to where she stood. "Yes, you do, Mina," he said quietly, not sure who all might be listening on the other side of the curtain. "You're not a good liar."

Her dark eyes glittered. "Not as good as you."

That hurt.

"She gave this address to the Ladies' Society of Christian Aid as the place to contact her," he said. "Why?"

"I have no idea."

Dragging answers out of her was going to take longer than he had time for. "Let's go outside and talk. I don't want eavesdroppers."

She hesitated.

"Please, Mina. Fuller's dead. This is urgent."

She sighed and followed him out onto the sidewalk. "All right, Nick. I do know Judith Whelan."

"How did you two meet?"

"Through Raymond. He said he had a female friend who needed help. I can't say why he approached me. Maybe because I treated him well. Doubt most folks did." Her gaze drifted. Maybe she was reflecting on how pitiful Raymond Fuller had been. "I also can't say what possessed me to agree to help. Judith didn't want much, though. Just to use the store as a place for the Society to bring money to her. Not that they ever provided enough," she added bitterly. "And I wasn't to ever tell anybody where she lived."

"This scheme was risky, Mina. Both for you and for Judith," he said. "She couldn't guarantee that one of the other folks working here wouldn't get curious about the deliveries from the Society and start poking around."

"Mr. Atwood never bothers with people who aren't paying customers," she said. "And I explained to the other woman who works here that I was receiving payments from my sister's deadbeat of a husband, because she didn't want him to know where she lived."

She was clever; he'd never doubted that. "Has a redheaded woman come looking for Judith here?"

"A woman showed up a week or so ago. She didn't give her name." She paused as an aproned clerk from a nearby store rushed past them on the sidewalk. "She asked specifically for Judith. She wasn't the young woman who's been making the deliveries from the Society, though, and I was suspicious. I told her that Miss Whelan had moved on and I didn't know where to."

"Has she?"

"What? You mean you can't be sure, after all, if I'm telling the truth or not?"

"Mina, I need to find her before the person who killed Sy Eckart, and who probably also shot Raymond Fuller, does," he said. "Could be the person who killed Meg, too. Forced poison on her."

"Killed Meg?" A look of shock crossed her face, and she leaned nearer to him. "Oh, God, Nick. I'm sorry."

She meant it. She'd known how much Nick had loved his little sister. How badly her death had scarred him. Continued to scar him.

"Dr. Harris isn't certain she was murdered, but I'm certain, Mina," he said. "I need to find Miss Whelan. I need to protect her from what's out there."

"You're going to protect her?" She scoffed and stepped back. "She's perfectly safe where she is as long as you stay away from her. That's usually how that works, Nick. It's always safer when you stay away."

"You have to tell me," he insisted.

"No, I don't, Nick."

"Then warn her about the danger she's in."

"She's already scared."

He gripped her arm. "I can help, Mina. I can."

She glared at his hand until he released his hold. "She won't trust you."

"Why?" What had Celia mentioned? Something about a policeman visiting Meg not long before she died, sending her on the run . . . "Miss Whelan is afraid of the police, isn't she?"

Mina didn't say yes. She also didn't say no.

He pulled out his money clip and shoved the dollars he had into her hands. "Tell her she needs to move and now, Mina. But first, get her to tell you who killed Meg."

She tucked the money into her pocket. "She won't tell me, Nick. She won't put me in danger."

He couldn't demand that Mina risk her life. Not for him.

"Take care, Mina." He nodded to her, and she went back inside the store.

Reseating his hat, he turned on his heel. Just as two children—well, one wasn't a child—came hurtling up the sidewalk.

"Mr. Greaves! Is my cousin here?" the one who wasn't a child asked. She had a bad foot and the run had cost her; she limped the last few steps. "Is she all right?"

"What are you doing here, Miss Walford?" Nick looked over at the boy who'd accompanied her. "Angelo, take her back home."

He gave Nick a sober look. "We are here to save Signora Davies."

Great. A scrawny kid and a teenaged girl. Young woman, he corrected. "She's not here. What made you think she would be?"

"Because she told Addie that she wanted to find . . ." Miss Walford glanced around them. Just the usual crowd on the streets, too busy with their own business to pay attention to anybody else's. For once. "Miss Whelan," she whispered.

"I told her I'd take care of it." Not that Celia ever listened to him. "Besides, she's not here either, and you're not going to find out where she lives. I already tried."

"I know," Angelo piped up. "I can show you."

Dammit, Mina, you forgot about keeping secrets from your little brother.

"You can *tell* me, Angelo Cascarino. You are *not* going to show me. You are going home with Miss Walford right now," he ordered. "Immediately, because we're attracting attention."

With a jerk of his head, he indicated a crew of workers. They'd been painting a nearby building but had become more interested in staring at them. Or, to be precise, at Miss Walford. They weren't friendly stares, and if she stood around much longer, their attention might turn from foul looks to insults or worse.

"And you, Miss Walford, need to return home before Miss Ferguson discovers you've come chasing after your cousin and are wandering around downtown."

She glowered. "I expect that she's already wrung the truth out of Owen. What time I get back won't make much difference now."

"I appreciate that you both want to help, but you can't. It's not safe. Go home."

Shoulders sagging, Miss Walford exhaled. "Come on, Angelo. Tell Mr. Greaves how to find Miss Whelan and then let's head back."

"Sì, Signorina Barbara," he said woefully, told Nick what he knew, and loped after her.

• • •

"Ah, Mr. Taylor." Celia had not gotten far when she'd noticed Mr. Taylor striding up the road toward the police station. He dashed across the street to join her. "Have you been to the Chases' to question Eileen?"

He politely tipped his policeman's cap. "I went last night, ma'am," he said. "She gave me a story about Mr. Brodie being the brother of a friend of hers. That she'd gone down to the wharf to ask how her friend was doing, because she'd been sickly."

"Oh. Perhaps, then, I am wrong about her."

"Don't think so, ma'am," he said. "Mr. Brodie was in this morning telling us that she came to see him in order to chastise him about missing a liaison Wednesday night." Mr. Taylor lifted his eyebrows knowingly.

"The night of Mrs. Chase's benefit."

"Yes, ma'am."

"Why might she have planned a rendezvous with Mr. Brodie that night? When she knew she would be busy." Neither story that they had been given appeared truthful.

"I plan to head back over to the Chases' house to confront her, once I've left a message for Mr. Greaves. It seems that what we've heard about smugglers and the customs officials might be true."

"Oh?"

"That one or two officials *are* being paid to ignore what's going on," he explained. "Mr. Brodie's name came up."

"How interesting," she said. And very incriminating, as well. "Has Mr. Greaves had an opportunity to visit the wig shop and locate Miss Whelan yet?"

"I haven't heard, ma'am. Been down at the wharf," he said, sounding apologetic.

"Of course, Mr. Taylor. I am getting ahead of myself; Mr. Greaves only left the station fifteen or so minutes ago." She considered him. "I have another question for you that might seem odd. Do you trust Mr. O'Neal?"

He gave her a quizzical look. "He's a good police detective, as far as I can tell, ma'am. Mr. Greaves's uncle trusted him."

"So I have been told," she said. "Have you ever had any suspicion that he might be closely acquainted with Mr. Chase? Or with Mr. Hunter, who regularly consigns items to be sold at Mr. Chase's auction house?"

He narrowed his gaze. "He's never mentioned either of them to me or Mr. Greaves."

"His first name is Francis, I believe."

"Yes, it is, Mrs. Davies."

"Curiously, Mrs. Chase overheard a conversation between Mr. Chase and Mr. Hunter where they were discussing a fellow named Francis," she said. "Mr. Hunter informed her husband that Francis wanted a larger 'share of the business.' Mr. Chase became upset, according to her, about this request. When she questioned him about the conversation, he did not want to explain."

Mr. Taylor retrieved his notebook to jot down what she was telling him.

"Now, Mr. Taylor, how might we interpret that conversation?"

"Are we sure he meant Mr. O'Neal?" he asked.

"We cannot be positive—there are many men named Francis in San Francisco—but that is why I asked if you thought he could be trusted."

He frowned. "A witness saw a fellow in a gray coat chasing Owen yesterday. He thought the man was a cop," he said. "And the weapon used to shoot Mr. Fuller was a .44. Almost all the detectives carry that caliber revolver. Old Army pistols."

A shiver danced along her spine. "As I was afraid."

"I'll tell Mr. Greaves as soon as I can, ma'am, but I don't know where we go from here. I've never had to deal with something like this before."

"We proceed with great caution, Mr. Taylor," she replied.

• • •

"I was told I could find Miss Whelan here," Nick said to the woman who'd answered his knock. The directions Angelo supplied—he must've followed Mina to the place at some point in order to know where to send Nick—had taken him up the street, around the corner, and over to a small white house made conspicuous by how clean and tidy it was compared to its surroundings. "By Mina Cascarino."

Mina wouldn't appreciate him blaming her, but he needed the woman to trust him. Especially after learning that Miss Whelan was leery of the police. Her aversion went a long way toward explaining why she'd never contacted Nick after Meg's death.

The woman considered him through the pince-nez clipped to the bridge of her nose. She was short and silver-haired, her pale orange dress old-fashioned and trimmed in an excess of lace. She had the air of a frail, doddering elderly female. But her eyes . . . there was no frailness in their depths.

"Mina Cascarino told you that you could find Miss Whelan here?" she asked.

"Miss Cascarino and I have been acquainted a long time, ma'am," Nick said, sliding the brim of his hat through his fingers.

Her eyes scanned him. She hadn't decided how best to get rid of him yet. "Does that mean you are also acquainted with Miss Whelan?"

"Miss Whelan knew my sister well. I've been told they were good friends, before Meg died."

"Explain to me why Miss Cascarino would've told you—lengthy acquaintance aside—where to find Miss Whelan?" she asked, not bothering to mask her skepticism.

"All right, she didn't. She admitted that Miss Whelan is in hiding but didn't want me to know where. She kept Judith's secret," he said. "Unfortunately, her little brother *did* know and directed me here. To you."

She examined him through her pince-nez glasses. "I see. Well, thank you for your honesty, Mr. . . . ?"

He wasn't going to be completely honest with her, and it made him feel guilty. But not guilty enough to change his answer. "Mr. Taylor."

"Mr. Taylor," she repeated. "You should come inside, Mr. Taylor. We can speak more freely there."

Nick stepped inside. She scanned the street before shutting the door with a firm click. He followed her into a room just off the entry hall. It was stuffed full of furnishings and bric-a-brac, a glut of floral chintz and striped silk cushions and fringed pillows. Where guests sat was a definite question. She answered it by tossing a pillow off the sofa and taking a seat, forcing him to do the same with the nearest chair.

The woman settled in among the cushions and considered him, a polite smile on her thin lips. "I'd offer you some tea, but I expect you are not staying long." Expressed as a statement of fact. The more time he spent here, the more Nick liked her.

"That's all right, ma'am."

"Do tell me who you are," she said. "And I don't mean for you to repeat your name."

"I'm somebody who's been searching for anyone who can explain why a packet of my deceased sister's letters were delivered to me recently. Miss Whelan was mentioned in them," he said. "My sister had originally sent those letters to a man who was murdered last Friday. Delivered to me by another man who was shot dead outside my house two days ago."

"Ah. I did read about him. About both of them," she said.

"Does Miss Whelan know about their deaths?" He glanced up at the ceiling overhead. "Is she here in the house?"

"The answer to both your questions is no," she replied. "I should clarify. She is aware of Mr. Eckart's death, but not of the man who was killed two days ago."

He leaned forward. "Has she said much about Mr. Eckart's death?" he asked. "About who she thinks might be responsible?"

She considered him so long that he took to wondering if she'd fallen asleep with her eyes open.

"Why might she say anything to me about who may have killed him?" she asked coolly.

"Because she trusts you."

"But it appears she must not trust *you*, the brother of her dear friend whom she has not elected to contact," she retorted.

Clearly. "Was she afraid of Mr. Eckart or of Mr. Eckart's killer?"

"The latter, I believe."

Well, that was something. Just not enough. "Ma'am, you and I both know she is in danger," he said. "I have to find the man who killed Mr. Eckart and Mr. Fuller. Before they get to her."

"How do I know that person is not *you*?"

He lifted his eyebrows. "I suppose you don't, ma'am."

"No, I do not," she said. "You comprehend my dilemma, Mr. Taylor. Or should I call you Mr. Greaves, since I am aware of who your sister was?"

Not doddering in the least.

"Listen, I've got to find the killer and soon," he said urgently. "I believe Miss Whelan knows who he is. She's never going to be safe, ma'am. If I found her here, others will too. Don't let it end tragically."

At last, she released a lengthy sigh. "Well, you have convinced me."

"I'm glad to hear that."

She got to her feet and so did Nick. "Judith is staying in the annex. The best way to access it is to go outside and around the house to the rear yard. Rather than walk through the kitchen. You'll see the room my husband added to the house. His private little office, which he used when he was still alive." Her lips curled with a soft, sentimental smile. "It has an outside door. Just knock."

"Thank you, ma'am."

"Leave the outside door open and don't take long," she added. "I'll be watching from the dining room to be sure you don't overstay your welcome."

Nick exited the house, taking a flagstone path that led around the side and into the backyard. A narrow room had been tacked onto the rear of the building, extending from what was probably the kitchen. As promised, it had an exterior door. The blue curtains in the single window overlooking the garden were closed, and there wasn't any smoke rising from the stovepipe sticking up through the shingled roof. Maybe Miss Whelan wasn't inside. Maybe he'd been led on a wild-goose chase by a protective, shrewd elderly woman with a pince-nez.

Here goes nothing.

He climbed the rotting steps and knocked. The door hadn't been latched and it squeaked open. Inside, the room was gloomy. All he could see was what the rectangle of light afforded by the open door provided, and that wasn't much. A rag rug on the wood floor. The footboard of a bed.

He eased his gun out of its holster. "Miss Whelan? Are you in here?" He listened for breathing, for the rustle of clothing or the scuff of feet across the floor. On the street outside the main house, a cart rattled past, disrupting the quiet. He took another step forward. "Miss Whelan?"

The movement from behind the door was quick. Too quick for him to react. All he could do was try not to jostle the gun being held to his head.

"Hand me your pistol. Hand it to me," she demanded, adding insistence to her words by jabbing the gun's muzzle into Nick's temple. It wasn't every day that a woman held him at gunpoint. He'd be more amused by the situation if he weren't so concerned that she might actually shoot him.

Nick carefully released the hammer of his Colt and gave her the gun. She deposited the weapon on a table at her back.

"Okay, you've got ten seconds to tell me who you are and what you want before I pull this trigger," the woman holding the revolver said. "And I *will* pull this trigger. I know how to fire a gun and am confident the police will understand my need to defend myself from a man barging into my room." The cartridge cylinder clicked as she cocked the hammer. "Ten seconds. Starting now."

℘ CHAPTER 20 ☇

"Do you know who shot Raymond Fuller, Miss Whelan?" Nick started with.

She couldn't conceal her sudden intake of breath; she was standing too close to him.

"What do you mean, who shot him?" she asked. "Who are you?"

More than ten seconds had passed and he still had his head. That was good, at least.

"I'm Nick Greaves. Meg's brother."

"A damned cop." She released a further string of curse words Nick usually only heard around the station and certainly not coming from a woman. "I should shoot *you* right now. You and the person who told you how to find me."

"Please put the gun down, Miss Whelan," he said. "It's making it hard to talk with you, having that thing pointed at my head."

"I don't want to talk with you, Mr. Greaves. I thought you'd figured that out."

His eyes were adjusting to the darkness. He could make out the rest of the bed, a threadbare quilt tossed over it. A straight-back chair where the husband of the owner of the house might've sat when he'd used this room. A drop-leaf table with a handful of mismatched chairs around it. A stack of books collecting dust in the corner.

"I think you do want to talk with me, Miss Whelan." A bead of sweat worked its way down his neck. It tickled. "About who might've shot Fuller and Eckart. About Meg."

She jabbed the muzzle into his temple. "I do not want to talk to *you* about Meg."

"I've been given evidence that suggests she was murdered, Miss Whelan."

"That's not what the coroner concluded."

"He was wrong, wasn't he? And you suspected. You and Sy."

"But not you. Why is that?"

"I didn't have any reason to suspect Meg had been murdered."

"You didn't suspect because you didn't want to, Mr. Greaves," she accused. "Sy paid Raymond to deliver her letters to you, hoping you'd finally act in case he failed to get his revenge. I told him it was stupid to expect a cop to do anything about it. I was right. You haven't done anything."

"The letters I received, the photograph, didn't tell me enough in order *to* suspect, Miss Whelan." Another bead of sweat joined the first one. It wasn't a hot day by any means. "It wasn't until one of my officers found a scrap of one of Meg's notes, which Sy had misplaced, that I even got a hint. A note indicating that she'd stumbled upon something dangerous."

"Raymond was supposed to get all of her letters to you. All the ones she'd written to Sy," she said, sounding confused.

His plan was likely thwarted by whoever had ransacked Eckart's rented room.

"They weren't on him when he was shot dead outside my lodgings." But maybe he'd still wanted to tell Nick about their contents, risking his life by coming out of hiding. "Lower your gun, Miss Whelan. Killing me won't help you get revenge on the man who killed my sister. Won't help either of us. And I sure in hell would like to get revenge on him."

She withdrew the muzzle from his temple, but didn't lower the gun. He slowly exhaled, releasing some of his tension; it was too early to completely relax, though.

"Why should I believe you?" she asked. "How do I know you're not here to kill me?"

"I'm not, Miss Whelan," he said quietly. "I'm here to learn the truth."

Up went the gun again. *Damn.* He should've brought Taylor.

"The truth? A cop wants the truth about what led to Meg's death? That's funny."

A cop. "Who is he, Miss Whelan? The cop you hate so much?"

"Miss Whelan?" a woman out in the yard called, halting any answer Miss Whelan might've given. "Mr. Greaves? Are you there?"

Miss Whelan shifted so she could see through the gap left by the open door. Light fell on her face, lit the scowl she turned on Nick. "Who is that?"

"Her name is Celia Davies," he said, relief washing over him. For one of the few times since he'd known her, he was grateful she was nosing around where he'd told her not to. "And I don't think you intend to kill us both."

Celia marched up the steps to the room. "Ah, there you are. And you, Miss Whelan, should probably put down your gun."

• • •

Her heart slammed against her ribs so fiercely that Celia was certain both Nicholas and Miss Whelan could hear the pounding. Possibly the neighbor, hanging laundry on a line strung in the adjacent yard, could hear as well.

Celia had taken Miss Whelan by surprise, and the woman was upset that she'd done so. Her glare distorted her otherwise attractive features. It was not her handsome appearance that concerned Celia, however. It was the pocket revolver she pointed at Nicholas's head.

"You really shouldn't have come here, Celia," he said, his face—what she could see of it, as he was reluctant to fully turn her direction with a weapon pointed at him—shiny with sweat. It was unlike him to be so unnerved; Miss Whelan had gotten the better of his composure.

"On the contrary, Nicholas, it looks to me as though I most definitely needed to come here."

"What do you want?" Miss Whelan asked.

"The same thing that he wants, Miss Whelan," she replied, forcing her voice to not tremble. She did not know how much longer she could maintain her pretense of calmness. Especially in view of Nicholas's current condition. "To find a killer and stop them from killing again."

"How did you ever find us, Celia?" Nicholas asked.

"A boy noticed you with a dark-haired Italian boy and a young Chinese woman." She would have to speak with Barbara when she returned home. And she could just guess who the Italian boy accompanying her was. "He followed you, Mr. Greaves, and decided, in exchange for a nickel, to divulge your location to me when I stopped in at the wig and toupee shop. Mina had not breathed a word, you shall be glad to hear, Miss Whelan."

He cursed under his breath. *Indeed.* It had been very sloppy to have not noticed that he'd been followed. By a scruffy boy, no less.

"I should also inform you, Miss Whelan, that before coming here, I sent a message to Mr. Greaves's police assistant that I was heading to this house," Celia said. Not that she had actually done so. "If you shoot us both, you will surely hang for the crime."

"I don't care," she said flatly. "And I expect you're lying."

"She's not going to believe anything we say, Celia." Perspiration trickled down Nicholas's face. He could not wipe it away without risking an injurious response from Miss Whelan. "I'm pretty sure she thinks a cop killed Meg."

"Mr. O'Neal, perhaps," Celia proposed. "Francis O'Neal. Is that who you suspect, Miss Whelan?"

Nicholas risked a glance her direction. "Why would she suspect him?"

"For one reason, a man named Francis is a close associate of Mr. Hunter and Mr. Chase, according to Mrs. Chase. And that association upsets her. Likely because she suspects it is of an illegal nature," she explained. "Mr. O'Neal's Christian name is Francis."

"Sy hated O'Neal, Mrs. Davies. For what he'd done."

Nicholas went so still he could have turned to stone. "O'Neal," he breathed.

"You must have been frightened to learn of his return to San Francisco, Judith," Celia said, using her most soothing voice. In the past, she'd quieted soldiers, made delirious by their festering wounds and screaming for their mothers, whom they would never again see alive. She should be able to calm Miss Whelan, whose hand quivered as it held the gun. "The man who may have murdered your friend."

"Meg was an innocent," she said.

"And her brother is a good man," Celia responded. "A good police officer who has suffered from the death of his sister. He wants justice, even if a fellow detective is the man responsible."

"*Especially* if a fellow detective is the man responsible," Nicholas spat.

"However, we cannot obtain any justice without your help, Judith," Celia continued. "Without you sharing what you know about what happened. You will run forever until he finds you."

Judith Whelan retreated a step, slowly releasing the pistol's hammer as she lowered the gun.

"Thank you, Miss Whelan." Nicholas grabbed one of the chairs tucked against the oak drop-leaf table and collapsed onto it. "I appreciate you trusting me."

"I don't trust you, Mr. Greaves," she said. "I trust *her*. And I'd prefer that you not pick up your gun just yet." She hooked his Colt with her weapon's muzzle and slid it out of his reach.

"Might we all sit, Miss Whelan?" Celia suggested. Her knees were knocking. "That way we can be more comfortable as we talk. I do find standing about in a corset and crinoline tiresome when I am attempting to have a conversation with a witness."

She bristled at Celia's choice of word. "I haven't witnessed anything."

Nicholas shook his head. "Celia."

"Well, I intend to sit." Which she promptly did. "Because you have a story to tell us, Miss Whelan, and I presume it may take some time."

Judith Whelan eyed her. "Who exactly are you?"

"Celia Davies. A nurse who operates a free clinic for women."

"And who also happens to poke her nose into police business on a regular basis," Nicholas added. "Miss Whelan, I'd like you to start by telling us what was in those letters Raymond never delivered to me."

"Information, Mr. Greaves," she said, remaining standing. "About Mr. O'Neal. And about your uncle."

• • •

Nick felt like someone had stabbed a shard of ice into his heart. "What about my uncle? What did Asa have to do with Meg's death?"

Celia reached for his hand, resting at his side, and squeezed. Her fingers were cool and comforting. He needed to keep his anger under control. He couldn't afford to have Judith Whelan go silent because he'd been combative.

Nick returned Celia's squeeze and she let go. "What exactly was that information, Miss Whelan?" he asked more calmly. "What was it I needed to know? The truth I needed to know?"

Judith Whelan drew in a breath and glanced at the gun in her hand, seemingly disgusted by finding it there still. She set the weapon on top of the shelf at her back. Not too far out of reach, if the need arose to use it.

"It all started when Meg was living with her uncle. Your uncle, Mr. Greaves. He had friends that often came around to visit. To share a drink in the evening, play cards, other such things. Most of them were policeman, she told me. They spoke about work. All typical," she said. "Until a conversation about smugglers slipping goods into the city under the noses of the revenue men came up one evening. That it had to be true that the revenue men were being paid to look the other way. Your uncle laughed, Mr. Greaves. Said he could use a nice source of cash like that. He passed his comment off as a joke. Meg began to believe he meant it, though."

"Asa did like to joke." He didn't want to accept what she was saying. Didn't want to imagine that Asa had been corrupted by the promise of cash.

"At some point, I gather, Mr. O'Neal became involved. When?" Celia asked.

"Not long after that evening. He was at the house one night without the others. Just him and Mr. Greaves. And Meg, listening in from another room. She was too curious for her own good. I told her that," she said bitterly. "They took to discussing the smugglers and counterfeiters Mr. O'Neal regularly investigated."

"The brooches, Nicholas," Celia said as an aside to him. "The fake one."

Judith Whelan shot her a look and frowned. "According to Meg, they began to talk about how a regular police officer might profit. And your uncle, Mr. Greaves, sounded very interested in learning how *he* might profit."

Nick clenched his teeth and noticed Celia watching him. He'd told her about Asa, his admired uncle, more times than he could count. A man the exact opposite of his brother, Nick's father. Ready with a laugh, where Nick's father had always been too proudly serious. Happy to spend an evening in the nearest tavern or theater, where his father had coldly abstained from frivolous entertainment. Full of life, unlike his father, shriveled by his harsh fault-finding and disapproving nature.

"Tell me you're not lying, Miss Whelan," he demanded.

"I swear I'm not lying, Mr. Greaves."

Maybe Nick finally understood why his mother had disliked Asa so much. Why she'd always tried to warn Nick away from following in the worthless—her words, not Nick's—Asa Greaves's footsteps. He'd been as bad as she'd claimed. Maybe worse.

Damn, Asa. I believed every word you ever spoke. Followed every bit of advice like it was some sort of police commandment engraved on stone tablets.

And Nick had left Meg in Asa's care while he was away fighting. Exposing her to dangerous men she should've been able to trust. Possibly his worst mistake in a long list of mistakes.

"O'Neal is investigating a smuggling case right now, Miss Whelan,"

Nick said. *You're next.* Maybe he'd tried to warn Nick off with that note. He might've had the stomach to kill an innocent young woman and her sweetheart, a man who knew he'd killed Meg, but not to kill a fellow cop without giving him a chance to save himself. But Nick hadn't listened, and Raymond Fuller was dead. He'd kill O'Neal. Damn, but he would. "What about the names of the revenue men being paid to overlook what was going on?"

"Meg never mentioned any other names to me," the other woman said. "She probably told Sy, though."

And now Sylvanus Eckart was dead, too.

"Why all these years later, Miss Whelan?" Celia asked.

"Sy wanted to expose O'Neal straight away, make him pay for what he'd done, but O'Neal fled San Francisco right after Meg died," she said. "Sy gave up after that. He couldn't stand staying here any longer, either. He saw your sister's face everywhere, Mr. Greaves. He thought heading north to Oregon would help him forget."

Sy Eckart had died wearing a locket holding Meg's picture and a strand of her soft hair. He hadn't tried to forget her. Not really. Hadn't tried to forget a woman whose laughter could warm a person's soul on a cold day.

"But Mr. Eckart came back," Celia pointed out.

"He got news that Detective O'Neal had returned and that proof, solid proof, had finally been found that he was responsible for Meg's murder."

"His return luring Mr. Eckart back in hopes of exacting revenge at last," Celia said. "Forcing you into hiding, Miss Whelan."

"I was frightened that Sy might not succeed in carrying out his plan. I would be the next target."

"But O'Neal got to him first." Shooting Eckart with a .31 instead of his police revolver might've been a clever attempt to divert attention. But he got careless with Fuller and used his .44.

"Why did Mr. Eckart think that Archibald Chase might have been able to help him?" Celia asked her. "Was he the individual who'd offered to provide proof, no longer wanting to take part in illegal activities, perhaps?"

Miss Whelan shifted on her feet, probably regretting that she'd decided to remain standing. She looked more tired now than she had when she'd been shoving a gun into his head. He doubted she'd had a decent night's sleep in weeks. After today, he wouldn't be sleeping for months. Maybe years.

"He must've believed Chase knew something useful about O'Neal and the smuggling," Miss Whelan said. "Sy might not have been content to deal with O'Neal alone and be done with it. He wanted to expose all of them, if there were more guilty individuals to drag into the light."

"Mrs. Chase does own an appreciable collection of Chinese porcelains and silks and French perfumes," Celia said. "Perhaps Mr. Chase only recently discovered the provenance of the goods passing through his business. Many of which have been provided by the Hunters, I believe."

He couldn't sit here any longer and discuss Chinese porcelains and Archibald Chase. He had to get to O'Neal. He had to finish what Sy Eckart had never managed to do.

Nick got to his feet, startling Miss Whelan, who grabbed her gun. "Miss Whelan, I think we've established that I'm not interested in killing you, so you can put your revolver down."

She lowered the gun to her side but didn't set it down.

"I promise you, Detective O'Neal is going to pay for my sister's death and the deaths of your friends," he said. It was too late to confront Asa. Too late to understand his exact role in it all.

"I can't help you any more than I have, Detective," she said. "I expect they're going to come for me soon, anyway."

"I'll send one of my men, Officer Mullahey, here to guard you until this is all over."

"Can you trust Mr. Mullahey, Mr. Greaves?" She clearly didn't think he should.

"If I have to start doubting all of the men I work with, Miss Whelan, then there's no point in my ever doing police work."

"In that case, you may want to begin considering another occupation, Mr. Greaves."

Celia stood. "Nicholas, let her come with me. To my house. Send Officer Mullahey there."

Was she out of her mind to suggest that? "It's not safe enough there, Celia."

"It is safer than leaving Miss Whelan here alone until he arrives," she said. "I would stay with her, but I fear that, since you and I were able to locate Miss Whelan, others will be able to as well."

She didn't say O'Neal's name, but she meant him.

He considered them both, one with her shoulders set and her chin up, her pale eyes confident in what needed to happen. The other stern, mistrusting, watching him like a bristling cat on alert, questioning if she needed to run or pounce. "Don't make me regret this, Celia."

"I do not intend that to be the outcome."

No. She never did. "I'll get you a cab."

· · ·

Celia looked over at the woman seated alongside her, quiet since they'd left the room Judith Whelan had been hiding in. The elderly woman who'd provided her sanctuary had watched them depart, her shoulders sagging with worry. *I had attempted to convince Nicholas that I could keep Judith safe. Am I wrong, though?*

"I'm not going to jump out of this carriage and run off, Mrs. Davies, if that's why you keep staring at me," she said.

"I keep staring at you because I am concerned that I'll not succeed in ensuring that you stay safe, Miss Whelan." *That all of us stay safe.* She was risking Barbara and Addie, too. Along with Owen, if he was still snuggled away in the spare room's bed. "I also have a niggling question I would like resolved, if you can help me."

The young woman lifted her eyebrows. "What is your niggling question?"

"I have learned that it was Mrs. Hunter who brought Meg to the attention of Mrs. Chase, who then saw that Meg was given a job at her husband's business."

Judith had been rubbing her thumb over her opposite hand in a soothing manner. The movement stilled at Celia's mention of Mrs. Hunter. "Yes."

"Further, I learned that she also helped you receive support from the Ladies' Society of Christian Aid," Celia continued softly. "What precisely did she do for you?"

"She also found me a job."

"The one at the sewing machine shop?" Celia asked. "How very kind of her."

"I suppose." She didn't sound grateful.

"It seems to me, though, that you did not want her nor anyone else from the Society to know exactly where you were living," Celia said. "Are you afraid of the women?"

"Are you one of them?" she asked, reaching for support as the cab turned the corner, rocking heavily. They would be at Vallejo shortly and have to disembark to climb the remainder of the way to Celia's house.

"No. They mistreated my half-Chinese cousin," she stated. "But I would still like to know the answer, Miss Whelan. Are you afraid of the women?"

"Why would I be?" she asked.

The cab stopped and the driver called out that they had arrived at the corner. His small horse could not manage the steep road from here. They climbed down, Celia paying the fare and Miss Whelan collecting the carpetbag holding her few possessions.

"I have met Mrs. Hunter," Celia said, striding up the road, Miss Whelan keeping pace alongside. "I found her to be a very intriguing woman with a strong character."

"Are you asking if I'm afraid of her specifically?"

I do not know, am I? Perhaps she was.

"She is not someone I would wish to cross, Miss Whelan," Celia replied. "That is my assessment of Deborah Hunter."

"No, she's not." She let out a heavy sigh. "She tried to recruit me."

Celia glanced over at her. "Recruit you to do what?"

"To sew concealed pockets in petticoats, Mrs. Davies."

"Petticoats she then purchased, I presume?" Celia asked, her brain spitting out thoughts faster than she could collect them.

"Yes."

"For the purposes of concealing small items, perhaps," she said. "Such as, oh, French perfume bottles?"

"Jewelry, too. Patek Philippe watches. Diamond rings and scarf pins. Expensive things like that," she said. "I refused."

They stopped at the bottom of the steps leading up to the house. Next door, Angelo was leaning over the porch railing, his eyes tracking them. Inside the house, Cascarino children shouted noisily. Otherwise, it was a quiet Friday afternoon.

"Is she a smuggler, Miss Whelan?" A question that was hazardous for her to answer. She'd not handed Deborah Hunter over to the police, which might make her an accomplice. Unless she had insufficient evidence aside from a request to sew concealed pockets in petticoats. No more proof than Celia presently had. "Along with her husband, perhaps? And Mr. Chase's involvement is that of selling their goods at his auction house for a tidy profit. A profit undercut by the money paid to Mr. O'Neal and Mr. Brodie to look the other way, I suspect."

"You have all the answers, don't you, Mrs. Davies?"

The way she asked set Celia's teeth on edge. "Not by a long chalk, Miss Whelan."

She climbed the rest of the way, crossed the porch, and opened the door. "Addie, I am back. Along with Miss Whelan."

Eileen stood in the entrance to Celia's clinic room. "Mrs. Davies, I hope you don't mind my waiting—" She gasped, her gaze fixed on the woman who'd entered the house behind Celia. "Why have you brought *her* here? She's . . . she's a killer!"

⚡ CHAPTER 21 ⚡

"Where is O'Neal?" Nick shouted, pounding down the steps into the station. An officer, seated at one of the desks, jumped up from his chair in alarm. "Where is he?"

He'd been composed when he'd left the house where Miss Whelan was staying, thinking that he had a plan and he would execute it and everything would work out. But the closer he got to the station house, the more furious he became. O'Neal. Friends with all the other officers. Joining in on their jokes. Acting like he respected Nick. Pleased to have taken the job that should have been given to Taylor. In cahoots with Chase. Maybe Captain Eagan was in on the racket, as well. Both of them, crooked.

The booking sergeant stepped out from behind his desk and into Nick's path. "What is wrong with you, Greaves?"

Nick stormed across the room. "Stay out of my way, Sergeant. I'm going to kill him."

O'Neal had heard him shouting and was on his feet in the center of the detectives' office. "Now, what have I done to upset you, Mr. Greaves?"

Nick slammed the door, rattling the glass inset. He strode over to O'Neal. Got so close he could see a faint scar next to O'Neal's left eye. Get a whiff of the shaving soap he liked to use. Bazin's, by the smell of it. "You killed my sister. Admit it."

His left eyelid twitched, causing the scar to become more obvious. "Who told you that?"

Nick grabbed his coat lapels and shook him. "Admit it!"

O'Neal's gaze flicked over Nick's fisted hands, his knuckles turning white. "Let go of me, Nick."

"I ought to kill you. She was innocent and you are filth."

"Nick. Let. Go."

The door opened behind them. "You okay, O'Neal?"

He shot the man a look over Nick's shoulder. It wasn't easy; Nick was taller than him by several inches. "Shut the door, Sergeant." It closed again.

How nice. The officers took orders from O'Neal. How nice.

"I did not kill your sister, Greaves," he said calmly. "Let go of me

227

and we can discuss this like two civilized men."

His eyes were the same color as Owen's. Maybe that was why Nick decided to make an attempt to be a civilized man. He couldn't fathom any other reason.

Nick released the lapels of O'Neal's coat, shoving him backward as he let go. To the man's credit, he didn't stumble. Barely moved, in fact. "I'm civilized. I don't know about you."

O'Neal straightened his coat lapels. "Who told you I killed your sister?"

"Eckart thought that you had. Raymond Fuller and Judith Whelan did as well." He might've been swayed by the color of O'Neal's eyes to stop choking him with his coat collar, but Nick's trust didn't extend to revealing that he'd met Miss Whelan, knew where she was hiding. "Is that why you shot Eckart and Fuller? Because they knew you'd killed Meg? She'd discovered that you and my uncle were accepting bribes to overlook the work of smugglers and counterfeiters, jeopardizing your careers, and she had to be silenced."

O'Neal exhaled. "Not me, Greaves. Asa."

"Asa didn't shoot Eckart in the back, O'Neal. Didn't murder Fuller outside my lodgings."

"No, but he *was* accepting bribes," he said. "It hurt to learn that, Nick. I admired your uncle. I believe you did, too." All stated as if he was talking about a stranger and not a man he professed to have admired.

"Why should I trust that you weren't a part of the scheme? You didn't report him," Nick pointed out. "Instead, you skipped town as fast as you could. Like you were guilty."

"I didn't report him because I needed more proof."

Proof. He was beginning to hate that word.

"Did Asa kill Meg, O'Neal?" Nick was shaking so hard he was afraid he might bite his tongue. "Did he?"

"Asa?" he scoffed. "Meg *had* found out about the bribes, but he didn't kill her as a result. He wasn't that much of an animal. He didn't kill her and neither did I."

Nick took a few steps back, needing space. Maybe O'Neal was telling the truth. If he'd killed Meg, it would be easy to deflect the blame by accusing Asa. But he wasn't doing that. Unless O'Neal was playing him for a complete fool. Which was always possible.

"Say for a minute that I believe your story," he said. "Who do you suspect killed my sister?"

O'Neal's shoulders, which had been hunched in preparation for a fight, relaxed.

"Possibly the individual in charge of the smuggling gang," he said. "But I'm not finished with my investigation."

"Tell me his name and that of the others involved," Nick said, keeping an eye on O'Neal's hands. He wanted to be ready in case he reached for his gun. Although shooting Nick in the detectives' office might force O'Neal to have to answer some difficult questions. Even Eagan, who didn't particularly care for Nick, wouldn't like one of his men shot inside the station by another of his men. "And the names better be names of people I already suspect."

"Bill Hunter. Archibald Chase," he said, names Nick had been expecting. "Francis Brodie."

So was Francis O'Neal *not* the Francis Mrs. Chase was worried about? Brodie made more sense, though. Given his job. *Damn.*

"Go on," Nick said.

"I suspect that Brodie killed Eckart," O'Neal said. "I don't have enough evidence, though. That's what I've been looking for. I almost had it when that Irish kid stumbled upon Brodie with one of the Chases' servants and caused a ruckus."

Nick eyed him. "You were the cop chasing that kid? But you don't wear a gray uniform coat."

O'Neal waved off his observation. "I also think Brodie killed Fuller."

"Different weapons were used."

"I heard, but it's not impossible, right?" he asked. "He has got to be searching for Miss Whelan now. The last one to put under the sod."

"She's in a safe place."

"You've seen her? Because if you found her, Greaves, he's going to find her, too." He grabbed his coat off the back of his chair. "We better get to her before Brodie does."

Nick didn't move. He was being stupid, probably, but he didn't move an inch.

O'Neal hurried toward the office door, threw it open, stopping only to look over his shoulder at Nick. "Are you coming, Greaves?"

"Why in hell should I trust you, O'Neal?"

"Do you have any choice?"

• • •

"You're accusing me, Eileen?" Judith Whelan charged across the entry hall and grabbed Eileen's left arm. She cringed in pain. Was Miss Whelan that strong? "It was you! You shot Sy in the back. I saw you."

"Why does your arm hurt so badly, Eileen?" Celia asked. She walked over and peeled back Eileen's sleeve. Enough to reveal an ugly purple bruise discoloring her skin.

"There was no intruder," Celia said angrily. "*You* struck Jane. Why?"

"I didn't, ma'am," she protested, twisting her arm to get Judith to release it. "That wasn't how it was at all."

"She's lying, Mrs. Davies. That's what she does," Judith said. "Admit it, Eileen O'Neal. Admit that you were part of the plot to pass off counterfeit jewels as real. To help smuggle goods into the city. You and your brother."

Bloody . . .

"You are Detective O'Neal's sister?" Celia asked.

Eileen retrieved a pocket revolver, a .31 caliber weapon, from a deep pocket of her skirt and pointed it at them. "That brooch was fake, wasn't it? That's all I came here to learn. Was it?"

"If that is all you want, then you need not aim a gun at us, Eileen," Celia said, mustering as much composure as she could. How many women had guns in their possession? If only Judith had not packed hers away in the carpetbag she'd set by the front door. "Put the revolver down."

"The brooch! Just tell me, Mrs. Davies." Eileen brandished the weapon, which shook in her hand. "Were the garnets fakes?"

"Yes, they were fakes, Eileen," she said, wondering where Addie and the others had gotten to. Praying they were cautiously staying away.

"She lied to me."

"Eileen, you are an idiot," said Judith. "Of course she lied."

"You did not find that brooch in Meg Greaves's room, did you, Eileen?" Celia asked, as puzzled as if she'd happened upon a theatrical performance without benefit of a playbill or having watched the entire first act.

Eileen, ashen-faced, moved into the entry hall. "Stand over there." She gestured for them to step over to the staircase.

She shifted her own position until she stood in front of the open outside door, but not near enough so that anyone out on the street might spot her and perhaps rush her. There were so few people out there on the street to notice a young woman holding a gun, anyway.

"Eileen, do not compound your difficulties by shooting us. This is not the sort of person you are."

"Yes, she is, Mrs. Davies," said Judith, her gaze fixed on the gun. "She was happy to shoot Sy in the back. Sy had gone to confront her brother, but she shot him. Didn't even blink an eye."

"Judith, if you witnessed the crime, why did you not tell Mr. Greaves?"

"He's my brother, Judith. What was I supposed to do?" Eileen interrupted.

Not kill a man, thought Celia.

"I should've told you what she'd done straightaway, Mrs. Davies," said Miss Whelan, her voice full of apology. "All I wanted, though, was to escape. I made plans to leave town in a couple of days. Bought the tickets. If I'd told Mr. Greaves what I knew, though, I would've had to stay to testify. Testify and probably not be believed. No one else saw her shoot him. Why would a jury listen to me?"

Eileen moved again, this time exposing her back to the parlor door, which was partly open. Obscuring anyone who might be hiding behind it. Dare Celia hope someone was hiding behind it?

"My brother only wanted to help your friend, Judith." Eileen was trembling, making the hand holding the gun unsteady. How easily she could accidentally pull the trigger. "He wanted Mr. Eckart to know that he wasn't responsible for killing Meg, even though all of you blamed him. That whoever had told Mr. Eckart he was responsible had been lying."

"Who did murder her then, Eileen?" Celia asked, her ears perked for the least sound indicating someone was moving through the parlor. But she could hear nothing over the thrum of blood in her head.

"I don't know."

"You're lying now too, aren't you, Eileen? Continuing to protect your brother." Judith was furious. Rightfully so; she'd lost two friends. But her anger risked agitating Eileen into shooting. "Admit he did it. Admit that he killed Meg."

"He didn't! She told me he didn't! She swore to me!"

"'She,' Eileen?" Celia asked.

"Shut up. Stop asking questions." She waved her revolver at them. "I'm going to shoot you both. I am!"

"Deborah Hunter," Judith guessed. "That's who you mean! Oh my Lord. Of course. She killed Meg! It *was* her I saw that night."

Dearest God in heaven.

"No." Eileen shook her head. "You know her, Judith. She'd never have hurt Meg."

"Deborah Hunter killed Meg because she'd not only discovered your brother's crimes but hers, as well. Is that not so, Eileen?" Celia asked quietly.

"No, no, she wouldn't!" she maintained, sobbing. "She wouldn't!"

"You trusted the wrong person, Eileen." Judith, Meg . . . they were not the only women Deborah Hunter had helped. And how grateful Eileen had been for the position with the Chases, dear friends of the Hunters.

"I never did!"

Right then, a ferocious roar echoed in the hallway, and a body hurtled through the opening in the parlor doors. The person collided with Eileen, ramming her against the staircase, the gun skittering out of her grip.

• • •

The front door to the house shared by Celia and Miss Walford and Miss Ferguson stood open. It shouldn't be like that. The only explanation was that somebody had forced their way in. *Damn.*

Nick took the stairs from the street two at a time.

"Greaves, be careful!" O'Neal hissed, climbing behind him. "He'll have a gun."

"Good thing I do too, O'Neal."

Nick unholstered his Colt and eased back the hammer. Next door, Angelo, who'd been watching the arrival of two police officers with keen interest, yelped at the sight of a weapon and ran inside his house. *I'd like to run too, kid.* But not if Celia and all the others were in danger. He couldn't run. And he wouldn't freeze like he had in the woods of the Wilderness. Unable to move while a friend was shot dead in front of him, the shock and confusion on Jack's face as fresh in Nick's memory as when he'd first witnessed it.

He drew in a breath and crept forward. His heart pounded, slamming in his chest so hard it hurt, as he tried to recall which of the boards on the porch creaked. Not that one. Maybe this one, he told himself as he moved across the span of planks. The sound of people shouting came through the open door. Maybe nobody would notice if he stepped wrong.

He reached the doorway and peered around the corner of the doorframe, O'Neal pausing just behind him. He had his gun out, too. *Here's hoping I'm not wrong about him and he's going to use it to shoot me in the back.* Like Eckart.

"Get off me!" a woman screeched.

"Stop it!" a familiar voice responded. "Ouch!"

Nick inched forward. Just then, Miss Walford ran into the entry hall with a length of drapery cord in her hands. "Use this to tie her up, Cousin."

Celia came into view. She stood over a woman lying on the floor at the foot of the staircase. She struggled under the weight of Owen, seated on her back. Celia must have noticed Nick's shadow, because she looked over. "Ah, Nicholas, you are here. Good. Help me with Eileen, if you will."

Eileen?

Nick gestured for O'Neal to lower his gun. He reset the hammer on his Colt and reholstered it. "You're going to explain what's going on, right, Celia?" he asked, crouching next to the woman and taking the length of cord from Miss Walford. He grabbed Eileen's flailing arms and bound her wrists with the braided roping. "Thank you, Cassidy, Miss Walford, for your assistance."

"You're welcome, Mr. Greaves," Owen replied, his skinny chest puffing with pride. "I knocked her down. She didn't even hear me coming!"

"Get off me!" Eileen cried, kicking her legs and catching Owen's knee.

"Ouch! That hurt!"

"Mr. O'Neal." Judith Whelan, standing off to one side, was staring at him like she was facing down a rattlesnake.

Nick looked over. O'Neal hadn't lowered his gun. Instead, he had it up, aimed at Nick.

"What in hell are you doing?" Nick asked, getting to his feet. *Damn.*

That'd be the last time he trusted somebody because they had green eyes like Owen Cassidy's.

"Mr. O'Neal is coming to the aid of his sister, Eileen, who happens to be Mr. Eckart's killer, Nicholas," Celia said, clutching Miss Whelan's hand. "Miss Whelan witnessed it."

"She's O'Neal's sister?" Nick asked, pointing at the woman hogtied on the ground.

She twisted to look up at her brother. Her forehead was bleeding; she must've hit it when she fell. "Francis, help me! You've got to untie me!"

"Don't reach for your gun, Greaves," he said, the only one of them in the hallway sounding calm. "I don't want to upset Mrs. Davies."

Owen scrambled away from them and toward Miss Walford, who he pulled down next to him. They crouched against the wall between the staircase and the parlor doors, their eyes wide and unblinking.

"Move aside, Greaves." O'Neal pushed Nick and bent to release the knots binding his sister's wrists without taking his eyes off the others. Or off Nick, making it blasted impossible to retrieve his own weapon.

Freed, Eileen scurried out of the way.

"It really wasn't Asa accepting bribes, what is it, O'Neal?" Nick asked. "It was *you* accepting bribes to ignore the smugglers working the docks, the counterfeiters selling colored-glass jewels and other fakery. Lining your pockets, and bold enough to inform me that you were investigating a smuggling case. Daring me to question your activities."

"It wasn't bold to inform you, Greaves. Everybody at the station knows I handle smuggling cases." O'Neal tossed away the length of drapery cord. "The captain is impressed with my ability to get arrests."

"How does Eagan feel about you killing my sister?" Nick asked, cold hatred spreading. "Because she'd found out that you're a criminal."

"I believe Mr. O'Neal is not the individual responsible for poisoning Meg, Nicholas. Mrs. Hunter is," Celia said. "With your encouragement, perhaps, Mr. O'Neal."

O'Neal backed through the hallway toward the front door. "Eileen, let's go."

"I'm sorry about Meg," she said to Nick.

"I'll find you, O'Neal," Nick threatened. "I will hunt you down."

"Eileen, now!" He grabbed his sister's hand and turned.

Straight into the raised pistol held by J. E. Taylor.

∅ CHAPTER 22 ☡

Nicholas pulled his weapon so quickly, Celia did not even have time to register that he'd reached for it.

"Hand me your gun, O'Neal," he said, aiming his revolver at the back of the other man's head.

Eileen skittered away from her brother and the others. "Don't shoot him. Don't anybody shoot him."

"It's okay, Eileen. Mr. Greaves is honorable," Mr. O'Neal said derisively.

He released the hammer and handed his weapon to Mr. Taylor, who secured the revolver inside his coat. Celia finally let herself breathe.

Nicholas slammed O'Neal against the doorframe. Eileen yelped and backed into Celia's clinic room.

"I ought to put a bullet hole in you, O'Neal." Nicholas pulled him up close. "For your part in what happened to my sister."

"Mr. Greaves. Sir." Mr. Taylor rested a quelling hand on Nicholas's shoulder.

He retreated.

Mr. Taylor dragged out the handcuffs he kept inside his coat and attempted to secure them around Mr. O'Neal's wrists. The fellow was not cooperating. "That was a close one, sir."

"Taylor, let me help you." Nicholas grabbed the handcuffs and slapped them around Mr. O'Neal's wrists.

"Is all the fuss over?" Addie asked, bustling through the front door.

"Near enough, Addie. Is everyone else all right?" Celia asked, scanning them for evidence of any injuries.

Owen was nursing the aching shoulder he'd thrust into Eileen's back. Another injury to add to the ones he already had. "I'll be fine," he said, hugging Barbara—who did not resist—to his side.

"Och, come now, you two. Let us be away from here." Addie motioned for Owen to get up and help a crying Barbara to her feet. "Miss, will you be coming into the dining room, as well?" she asked Judith.

"Yes, thank you."

"Lean on me, Miss Walford," Owen said to Barbara as they all obediently followed Addie.

"Damn, Taylor, but what *are* you doing here?" Nicholas asked, an elbow jabbed into Mr. O'Neal's back.

"Went to the Chases', sir. To talk to Eileen. But they told me she'd come here to Mrs. Davies's, so I headed this way," he replied, retrieving Nicholas's hat, which had fallen off at some point. "There's a cab down at the corner. We can use that to take Mr. O'Neal to the station house."

"We'll need to take his sister, too. Eileen O'Neal. She murdered Sy Eckart, Taylor."

Mr. Taylor's eyes widened. "You did hear right, Addie."

"Aye, of course I did," she said. "I was in the kitchen and heard all the commotion going on, ma'am. So I snuck around the back and went out to the street, looking for help. Saw Jer . . . saw Mr. Taylor coming along just in time."

"Thankfully," Celia replied. But how near they had all come to disaster. "I believe Miss O'Neal is hiding in my examining room, Mr. Taylor."

Owen reappeared in the parlor doorway, appearing recovered from the excitement. Proving his resilience. "Is there anything I can do to help, Mr. Greaves?"

He looked ready to say no, but changed his mind. "Tell the cab on the corner to wait for me and Mr. Taylor."

"Yes, Mr. Greaves!" He jogged off.

"Sir! She's gone!" Mr. Taylor shouted from inside the examining room. "Out the window!"

Mr. O'Neal chuckled.

Nicholas cursed and slammed him into the doorframe again. "Shut up."

Celia rushed over to see for herself. The street-facing window was thrown fully open and the curtain flapped in an afternoon breeze. "She has likely gone to warn Mrs. Hunter, Nicholas."

"The Hunters are probably at the police station with Officer Mullahey right now, ma'am," Mr. Taylor said. "I gave him your message to bring them in, sir."

"Then unless Eileen is headed to the police station, Celia, she won't find Deborah Hunter in order to warn her." He scowled. "Let's go, Taylor. I can't wait to see what the other men are going to make of the sight of Mr. O'Neal in handcuffs. Can't wait to come face-to-face with the Hunters, either."

"Yes, sir."

He handed Mr. O'Neal off to Mr. Taylor, pausing on the threshold to look back over his shoulder at Celia.

"I'm going to kill Deborah Hunter, Celia, and I don't care that she's a woman," he said angrily. "She poisoned Meg, left her to die in that room—"

"Nicholas. You cannot bring Meg back by exacting revenge on Deborah Hunter." Celia took hold of his arms, feeling the muscles corded tight beneath his coat and the sleeves of his shirt. Searched his eyes for the person she loved, buried deep beneath the anguish. "Let the law take its course. She will be punished, but not at your hands. Please, Nicholas. Choose an outcome that will let you live with yourself. That is what Meg would want."

He raised his hand to sweep a fingertip across her cheek, letting it linger on her skin. Then he slipped out of her grasp and thundered down the steps, racing to catch Mr. Taylor up. Racing to have his revenge.

• • •

"I'm sorry about shooting Mr. Eckart, Mr. Greaves. I'm sorry," Eileen said, her sobs making her hiccup. Taylor handed her a handkerchief to wipe her face.

"He was far more sorry, Miss O'Neal," Nick replied, unswayed by her tears.

Mullahey and another officer had cornered Eileen at the Chases' former house out by the Mission, the same day Nick and Taylor had hauled her brother into the station and booked him into one of the cells. The cell Loomis—whose only crime had been lying to protect himself from being accused of shooting Eckart—had vacated. The sight of O'Neal in handcuffs had caused an uproar in the station. The officers' reactions, however, hadn't been as satisfying as Nick had hoped. Hadn't felt good at all.

He'd marched right back out of the station that day. Took a couple more days to return, spending much of the intervening forty-eight hours wallowing in blame and misery. He'd prefer to continue wallowing in his room, a bottle of whiskey at his elbow, Riley's mournful eyes watching him. But by this morning, Mrs. Jewett had decided it was time for Nick to get back to work, her chosen method of persuasion an endless round of pestering. She believed in the benefits of honest work to the same degree that Addie Ferguson believed in the wonders of tea.

"Tell us why you shot him, Miss O'Neal," Nick said, leaning against his desk with his arms crossed. He needed her answer for the record; he already knew why she had.

"Mr. Eckart wanted to kill my brother. Because he believed that Francis had murdered your sister, Detective. They all believed it," she said, sniffling heavily. "But they were wrong."

"You were aware they planned to meet, though, came upon them arguing, and shot Mr. Eckart in the back."

"I suppose I shouldn't have told Francis that Mr. Eckart was back in San Francisco and had turned up at the Chases', angry as all get-out. Maybe then Francis wouldn't have been hunting for him." She pinched her eyes closed, which squeezed more tears onto her cheeks. She sopped them up with the already damp cotton handkerchief. "Making me have to protect him."

Hunting was a regrettably accurate word for her to have used.

"When Mr. Eckart finally encountered your brother, Miss O'Neal, did he have a gun?" Nick asked. "Miss Whelan, who'd accompanied Mr. Eckart and witnessed you shooting him, doesn't think he was carrying one."

Eileen didn't reply. Which meant he hadn't been.

"Had Meg told you her concerns about your brother?" Nick asked. *He's found out I know* . . . Judith Whelan had tried to warn his sister to be careful, but Meg had insisted on learning the full truth. The truth had cost her—cost him—too much. "Were you the one who informed him that Meg suspected him of helping smugglers get away with their crimes in exchange for a fee?"

She balled Taylor's handkerchief in her fist. "I'm sorry."

Damn. She had.

Nick waited as Taylor flipped to a new page in his notebook before continuing.

"After what she'd discovered, Meg had to be silenced. Brutally silenced," he said, his arm aching. "Not by your brother, though, but by the individual at the center of it all. Somebody who'd come to your aid, Miss O'Neal, at a desperate time for you. Deborah Hunter."

He'd avoided facing the woman, letting Taylor question Mrs. Hunter himself. If Nick had been left alone in a room with her, he doubted he could've stopped himself from causing her damage. Maybe even killing her, like he'd threatened to do. He'd wrestled down his impulse, though, because Celia had been right. Meg would never have wanted him to avenge her murder in that way. And he never would've been able to live with himself if he had.

"I still can't believe it, Detective," Eileen said. "It must've been an accident. Or Judith is lying about having seen her."

Deborah Hunter had prepared an explanation for why Judith had noticed her outside the hotel where Meg had died, saying she'd gone there solely to check on Meg. And that, if only she'd been aware of suspicions surrounding Meg's death, she would've given a statement to the police to that effect.

"I wouldn't be alive if it weren't for Deborah, Detective Greaves," Eileen was saying. "You don't understand how difficult it was for me after Francis left and went to Chicago. So difficult."

"My sister *would* be alive if it weren't for her, Miss O'Neal."

She sobbed more loudly than before. Taylor didn't offer her a fresh handkerchief. Maybe he didn't have any more to give. Or maybe he'd used up all his sympathy.

"I suppose that when Mrs. Hunter invited you to help her move jewelry and other small items between her and a jeweler she'd befriended, you thought nothing of it. Thought it completely innocent," Nick said. "Wouldn't dream of questioning the woman you felt so indebted to."

Judith Whelan had provided some of the specifics of Mrs. Hunter's scheme. Nick and Taylor had guessed the rest.

"I had no idea it might be a crime, Detective."

"Then why bring that brooch you claimed you'd found in Meg's rented room—but actually hadn't—to Mrs. Davies? Wondering if it contained real garnets or fakes, if you had no idea?" he asked. "I'll answer for you. You did suspect Mrs. Hunter. You suspected that she was asking you to carry items to a jeweler to be copied and then auctioned as authentic, and you had the proof in your possession. Mrs. Hunter's crimes had gone beyond smuggling, hadn't they, Miss O'Neal? And you were up to your neck in it."

Her tears became a torrent.

Nick pushed away from the desk; he'd had enough of Miss O'Neal and her crying. "Taylor, finish up here. I'm going for a walk."

• • •

"You've got a visitor, Detective," one of the station officers said to Nick when he returned from his walk, which had been more of an enraged march around the square than a refreshing, head-clearing stroll.

His visitor turned out to be Harris. He'd have preferred it to be Celia. But, as usual, it was his fault that he hadn't seen her. He'd stormed away from her house like a vengeful madman.

"You've found your killer, Greaves," Harris said to him, twisting around to watch as Nick strode through the office.

"It's killers, Harris. More than one," Nick said, dropping his hat onto his desk and settling onto his chair. Which squeaked. Some things never changed, which he was glad for. "O'Neal's sister Eileen shot Eckart. Trying to protect her brother from Eckart, she insists."

"Because of Meg," the former coroner said.

"Yes, Harris. Because of Meg."

Harris was watching him closely, like Taylor tended to do. Nick stood to avoid the scrutiny and turned to look out the window. The dreariness outside wasn't able to compare to the dreariness inside. He envied the passing pedestrians, looking like they were just going about their business for the day. Looking like they weren't weighed down by remorse.

"Eckart and Judith Whelan—and Raymond Fuller—believed that O'Neal had killed Meg. It's looking like he wasn't her murderer, though. He had, however, been stupid enough to talk openly to my uncle Asa about his getting paid to overlook smuggling down at the docks. Which got Meg to asking too many questions. She always had liked to ask questions, Harris. Used to annoy my father to beat all. But she was a Greaves. There was no stopping her," Nick said, appreciating that the former coroner knew how to listen. That made him a good doctor and an even better friend. "Unfortunately, she got so curious that she discovered what was going on."

"I read that you arrested the Hunters," he said. "I've met them. At a charity ball."

"Did they look like criminals, Harris?"

"Not in particular," he said.

He should have Harris tell that to Briggs. That not everyone's forehead or curve of their skull could be used to distinguish between the villains and the virtuous.

"Mrs. Hunter had a position with the Ladies' Society for Christian Aid that involved selecting needy women for the Society to assist," Nick said, tracking a pair of boys racing across the dusty ground of Portsmouth Square. "She helped Meg, she helped Miss Whelan, she even helped Eileen O'Neal find her position with the Chases. But what she really wanted from her women was to have them smuggle small, expensive foreign goods off boats and into Mr. Chase's auction house, where they would be sold without having had to pay import duties."

"The Society would be the perfect way to meet women who might be persuaded into a life of crime," Harris said, somewhat admiringly.

At least they hadn't been persuaded to work in a brothel like other equally needy women had, trapped by their poverty.

"Brodie suspected but he was bought off. O'Neal was in on it. And my uncle . . ." Nick paused, an upwelling of emotion catching in his throat. *One day I'll forgive you, Asa.* At the moment, Nick couldn't imagine that ever happening, though. "I'm not sure, frankly, how much my uncle knew or wanted to know. I'm also not sure that Archibald Chase was ever aware of what was taking place in his auction facility. He might've trusted his good friend Bill Hunter to deliver him goods that were exactly what Hunter claimed them to be."

"It'll be hard for Chase to claim ignorance, Greaves."

"He's been trying to." According to Taylor, who'd been managing most of the interviews in Nick's absence. Maybe he'd get that promotion to detective that he'd been wanting and deserving for months. A job O'Neal had taken instead.

"Smuggled goods weren't the only items he's been selling in that auction house, Harris," Nick continued. "Deborah Hunter got greedy and concocted a counterfeiting scheme that involved selecting certain items of jewelry from Chase's catalog, having a copy made, which was then auctioned as being the genuine item, while the original piece was sold at an auction house Hunter operates in Sacramento."

Nick heard Harris's heels scrape across the floor as he shifted in the chair and stretched out his legs. "Chase has been selling fakes?"

"And claiming he didn't know. Eckart was naive to go to Chase's house and attempt to get him to help pin a crime on any of these people. The fellow would never risk his reputation by cooperating. His wife suspected, though, but she didn't want to believe it." Nick got bored with watching hackney-coach drivers, their carriages parked at the curb across the street, argue with customers about fares and turned away from the window. "We might've taken a long time figuring this out, if Eileen O'Neal hadn't brought Mrs. Davies a brooch."

Harris didn't grin like he usually did when Nick mentioned Celia. This case wasn't like the others he and Nick had worked on together. It was deeply, achingly personal.

"She told Celia that my sister had taken it from Chase's auction house," Nick said. "In reality, the brooch was of far more recent vintage. She brought the brooch to Celia hoping to confirm whether or not it was a fake. Got the idea of saying she'd found it in Meg's old room after learning that Celia had come to the Chases' Mission house, asking about my sister. Eileen couldn't ask the cops for help or take the brooch to a jeweler without being questioned. If it turned out to be a fake—which it was, made with colored-glass garnets—she wanted out of Mrs. Hunter's criminal enterprise. Was going to beg to get out."

On his way back to the station after his circuits around the square, Nick had run into Taylor, who'd filled him in on what else Miss O'Neal had decided to confess.

"Both Detective O'Neal and his sister were involved. That's incredible, Greaves."

Nick could think of other words to describe the situation.

"Eileen was the link between the counterfeiter and Deborah Hunter, shuttling items back and forth," Nick said. "Sometimes Eileen took the copied jewelry to the Chases' old house out by the Mission. Other times, the goods changed hands at the Chases' new house, whenever Deborah Hunter visited. Such as Wednesday night at a benefit Mrs. Chase was holding for a new charity. Where Marian Chase wore the original of that brooch, arousing Celia's curiosity."

"Miss O'Neal foolishly gave Mrs. Davies the evidence that revealed her involvement." Harris whistled.

"She mustn't have appreciated just how skilled a 'lady detective' Celia is."

"So who killed Mr. Fuller?"

"Now that *was* O'Neal. His alibi for Wednesday night is as full of holes as a coal sieve. We didn't find a duster coat like the shooter was wearing but, of course, he owns a .44. One of the chambers still had the spent cartridge he hadn't removed after shooting Fuller," he said. "Furthermore, a friend of Fuller's came forward yesterday. Fuller was the one who'd encouraged Eckart to come back to San Francisco. He'd become convinced that Chase had evidence of O'Neal's involvement in Meg's death. But he soon got scared that O'Neal was on to him."

"I never would've suspected Detective O'Neal, Greaves."

"He was counting on that," Nick said. "Deborah Hunter isn't just a smuggler, Harris. She likely was with Meg the day she died. Judith Whelan spotted her leaving the hotel that night. She was worried and tried to get into Meg's room, but the door was locked and nobody responded when she pounded on it."

"The tainted laudanum had made her insensible."

If Miss Whelan had been able to get inside, would Meg still be alive? "What I can't figure out is if Meg carelessly let Deborah Hunter into her hotel room that night, or if Deborah Hunter found another way to get that poisoned laudanum into the room."

Harris made a sympathetic noise in his throat.

"We found fragments of Meg's letters to Sy Eckart burned on Mrs. Hunter's parlor grate." Mullahey had salvaged enough of the fragments for Nick to identify Meg's handwriting. "She got ahold of them somehow—somebody had broken into his room after he'd died—wanting to destroy what Meg had revealed in those letters."

"The names of everyone involved," Harris suggested.

"Maybe. But you know what's really frustrating, Harris? We actually don't have enough blasted evidence to link her to Meg's murder. Being seen outside the hotel that night is not enough to prove that she poisoned my sister. Finding fragments of burned letters isn't, either," he said. "Maybe she isn't responsible. Maybe we'll never know for certain."

"I'm sorry, Nick."

"You really don't need to be."

He cocked his head to one side as he looked at him. "What now? After the trials are concluded."

"Are you asking me about my work, or about something else?"

"What do you think?"

Nick exhaled and grabbed his hat off his desk. "You and Mrs.

Jewett are two of a kind, you know that?"

"She's a good woman, Nick. I'd marry her if I were you."

Harris wasn't talking about Mrs. Jewett.

"Give my best to your wife," he said and stomped from the room.

❧ CHAPTER 23 ❧

"It's Mr. Greaves, ma'am," Addie whispered in Celia's ear. "I've left him in the hall. Didna think you'd want me to bring him into the parlor."

Celia had presumed that the sound of the front doorbell meant that another of Mrs. Reynolds's students had arrived for the exhibition of their educational attainments. For the past half hour, the young ladies, attired in their finest dresses, had been filing into the parlor where Celia had offered to hold the event.

"Thank you, Addie. See if any of the girls or their parents require anything." She stepped into the hall, where Nicholas stood, running his hat brim through his fingers.

"Nicholas, I was not expecting you today." Or, perhaps, any day soon.

"I wasn't planning on coming here, but Harris convinced me to."

Dr. Harris's urging was the only reason Nicholas stood in the entry hall, looking uncomfortable? She was not certain whether she should thank the doctor the next time she saw him or not.

Nicholas looked over at the parlor. "What exactly is going on?"

"Mrs. Reynolds, Barbara's tutor, has scheduled an exhibition of her students' talents," she said. "I offered our parlor for the purposes of displaying them."

Addie had gathered straight-backed chairs from every room in the house to accommodate the guests of the handful of young women, a hodgepodge of wicker-seated pine and carved walnut and even the rosewood chair that had belonged to Uncle Walford and presently resided in Barbara's bedchamber. The hum of nervous and excited voices filled the room.

"Can we go into your clinic to talk, where it might be quieter?" Nicholas asked, going from running the brim of his hat through his fingers to crushing it. Being forced—*be more generous, Celia*—being encouraged to visit might not be the only cause of his unrest. Perhaps the presence of so many females and their guests chattering away made him ill at ease, too.

"Certainly." She led the way inside the room. She left the door open, though; she'd not want Mrs. Reynolds to observe her closeting herself away with a man who was not her husband and draw scandalous conclusions.

"I have read that Deborah Hunter and her husband have been jailed," she said, opening the conversation, as he seemed prepared to stand in the middle of her examining room until he'd finished strangling his hat brim.

"I didn't try to kill her, Celia," he said, gazing at her. How brown his eyes could be in the soft afternoon light. "Thank you for stopping me from doing something I'd regret. That I'd be ashamed of."

"You would have stopped yourself, Nicholas," she said. "You did not require my entreaties in order to conduct yourself like the man who you truly are. The man you always have been—a decent and just one."

"Thank you for believing in me."

She placed her hand on his forearm. "I have always believed in you, Nicholas." Despite her momentary doubts.

"I don't know why."

Out of the corner of her eye, she noticed Mrs. Reynolds cross the parlor and glance their direction. Nicholas stepped back from Celia, smiling. She loved his smiles. They were too few.

"As I was saying, I see that the Hunters have been jailed on charges of smuggling," Celia said, resuming their discussion of the case. "But not Mr. Brodie or either of the Chases."

"Brodie has assisted us with the investigation into the smuggling accusations against the Hunters, so he's been granted bail and some measure of leniency. As for the Chases, they appear to be innocent," he replied. "Or really good at hiding their knowledge of what was going on at the auction house."

She would assume the latter more likely. "How much has Eileen confessed?"

"A lot. She's the reason the Hunters have been indicted, in addition to Brodie's testimony," he said. "Miss O'Neal has also admitted there was no intruder the night of the benefit. That she'd knocked out Mrs. Hutchinson to stop her from finding the box of jewelry—two pairs of emerald earrings, one a copy made of colored glass—that she'd hastily buried under Mrs. Chase's display of ferns."

"Jane's interest in azaleas had brought her too close to the items Eileen had concealed. But why bury them in the conservatory in the first place?" Celia asked. However, it had become a good location to hide contraband or counterfeited goods, given the temporary absence of the Chases' gardener. Who would notice a patch of disturbed soil?

"When you showed up that night, she got scared you'd catch her handing the box to Mrs. Hunter, which had been the plan," he said. "She panicked and looked for somewhere to hide it."

"I told her I would be there," she said. "Although she did encourage me to not come."

"I suppose she didn't believe you actually would show up."

"It appears that all the stories written about me, Nicholas, fall short in indicating how determined I am."

"Reporters don't know you as well as I do, Celia," he said with another smile.

No, they did not. Thankfully.

"So Eileen invented a story about an intruder, going so far as to unlock the conservatory doors, in order to hide her guilt. Obviously, she dug the box back up before I had a chance to examine the area around the fountain," she said. "But what about the policeman and Meg? Had she also invented that tale?"

"Yes," he answered. "And if you're wondering where that brooch she brought you came from, she picked it up from the jeweler who's been counterfeiting stones for Mrs. Hunter. Miss O'Neal kindly provided his name to Taylor and we found the records the man has kept of the transactions."

"Do you believe Eileen comprehended what she was involved in, Nicholas?" she asked.

"To ask you if the garnets might be fake was the giveaway, Celia. She'd figured it out."

"What about Deborah Hunter's role in the death of your sister?" There had been no mention in the newspaper of her being indicted for that crime.

"I can't get her, Celia. I can't get her for that, despite what we've learned from Miss Whelan. Not enough proof," he replied, his voice tightening with frustration.

"And Mr. Fuller?"

"O'Neal," he said. "But all he's admitted to is pinning that warning on Mrs. Jewett's doorframe. A weak attempt to get me to stop investigating. Not a crime, in and of itself, since the words could be passed off as an honest effort to warn me I was in danger."

"And I had become rather convinced that Mrs. Hunter was responsible for Mr. Fuller's death," Celia said. "She became scarce the night of the benefit and provided me a false alibi of her whereabouts."

"Maybe she was hunting around, trying to locate where Eileen had hidden that box of emerald earrings," he said. "I expect I'll discover that she is an excellent customer at one of the city's wig stores, by the way. She's got to be the red-haired woman who'd been searching for Judith. And Cassidy has identified her as the woman he's noticed down at the docks. One day with black hair, another, a blonde. Smuggled goods concealed in pockets sewn into her petticoat."

A clever deceit, but then Deborah Hunter was a clever woman.

"I do continue to wonder why people believe that Mr. Chase was involved in someone's suspicious death, Nicholas," Celia said. "Why so much insistence on telling me that he has a terrible temper and should not be questioned?"

Nicholas frowned at her. "Celia, don't get any ideas about going back out there to poke around and find out the answers, do you understand?"

"But are you not curious, Detective Greaves?"

"Not at the moment, Mrs. Davies."

Addie hurried across the entry hall, stopping at the doorway to the clinic. "Ma'am, they are ready to begin."

"Thank you, Addie. I will be in shortly," she said. "So, Nicholas, despite some unanswered questions, can we call this case closed?" Could they? Or would he continue to brood over his sister's death, wearing himself down with self-recrimination?

"I'm ready to call it closed."

"Then, would you care to partake of an exhibition of educational attainment, Mr. Greaves? Barbara would appreciate your attendance, I am certain," Celia said. "She plans to display her skills at translating French, as well as at reciting a small poem that she has memorized."

He inclined his head. "Why not?"

They found chairs at the back of the parlor and settled in. The room hushed in anticipation as the first student rose and took her spot at the front of the room.

Nicholas leaned close to Celia. "Miss Walford matters that much to you, doesn't she? *This* much to you." He indicated the people collected in the parlor, Barbara sitting nervously off to one side, the refreshments waiting to be served in the dining room, the stern-looking Mrs. Reynolds watching her charges and their guests with an eagle eye.

"Barbara is like a daughter to me, Nicholas, even though I am not old enough to be her mother," she whispered. "And Owen is nearly like a little brother. And Addie . . . what would I do without Addie? Barbara matters. They all matter."

"Miss Ferguson's probably going to marry Taylor pretty soon, you know."

"I do know, but I will hold on to her, to all of them as long as I can," she said, searching his face for understanding. "Life is short, and love is too precious to let go of when you find it."

"You always amaze me, Celia Davies."

Her cheeks heated under the warmth of his gaze. "I do?" She had been complimented on her eyes, her loveliness, but never on her ability to amaze. "Why, thank you, Mr. Greaves."

Mrs. Reynolds was staring. She cleared her throat, quieting them like two naughty school children. They grinned just as foolishly as children and reached for the other's hand. Intertwining their fingers, drawing strength and comfort.

Holding on.

AUTHOR'S NOTE

In 1868, San Francisco was the largest port on the West Coast. Millions of dollars of domestic and foreign products streamed into the city. Particularly desirable foreign items, such as tobacco (Cuban cigars were very popular), liquor (whiskeys and brandies) and opium, were heavily taxed. Unscrupulous people were tempted to find ways around the import duties, and these goods were the ones most commonly smuggled past the harbor police. Various methods were employed, such as the use of false-bottom crates or by mislabeling the origin of the goods. Or by other means. A true story inspired me to create Deborah Hunter's tactics. In March, 1870, a steerage passenger disembarking from a European steamer in New York City was stopped by the harbor officer and found to have sixty-one watches concealed in pockets in his undershirt. Not the lightest of loads!

Being the largest port—and a beneficiary of the gold rush—San Francisco was booming in the 1860s, and its wealthier residents were not immune to the burgeoning Victorian passion for excess. This included greenhouses and their displays of exotic tropical plants. It was a grand age of travel, and collecting items from faraway places was supposedly the mark of a person of wealth and taste. A scan of property for sale at this time reveals large homes equipped with not only conservatories but billiard rooms as well. People did like to flaunt their riches, and my fictitious Chases would be rare but not alone in the lavishness of their house.

The increasing availability of domestic technology in the later nineteenth century meant families were offered the latest in everything from stoves to spring mattresses to newfangled sewing machines. Wheeler and Wilson was considered the premier brand at the time that Celia is examining one, and their products were quite expensive as a result. An advertisement listed prices ranging from fifty-five dollars, around the average monthly wage of a common laborer, to the most expensive at one hundred ninety-five dollars. This works out to a cost of about thirty-five hundred in today's dollars! A prohibitive expense, as Celia points out, for many people. Fortunately, as more sewing machines began to be produced by other companies, the prices went down. By the 1880s, you could purchase a small, simple machine for only two or three dollars.

The female occupants of the city were also not immune to the fashion for wigs. Most women did not have enough hair to produce the popular hairstyles of the period, which favored masses of elaborate curls. An April, 1867, newspaper article about the hair trade stated that nearly one million dollars' worth of hair was annually imported from Europe and Russia (and taxed at forty percent—I wonder if folks smuggled in hair?). German hair was considered the best for wig-making, apparently because of its length and texture. But wigs could be as costly as sewing machines, and women of lesser means might make do with hairpieces constructed from hair they'd gleaned from their own brushes.

As ever, I extend my continued thanks to the people at Beyond the Page Publishing, who do such fabulous work. Also, my thanks to you, my faithful readers, who continue to support Celia and Nick and their adventures. You have my endless gratitude.

About the Author

Nancy Herriman left an engineering career to take up the pen and has never looked back. She is the author of the Mysteries of Old San Francisco, the Bess Ellyott Mysteries, and several stand-alone novels. A winner of the Daphne du Maurier Award, when she's not writing, she enjoys singing, gabbing about writing, and eating dark chocolate. After two decades in Arizona, she now lives in her home state of Ohio with her family.

Made in United States
Troutdale, OR
05/26/2024

20128415R00159